Silver & Gold

Silver & Gold
Edited by Amanda Jean

Published by Less Than Three Press LLC

Edited by Amanda Jean
Cover designed by Natasha Snow

First Edition October 2015
After the Dust Copyright © 2015 by Eleanor Kos
Coffee Boy Copyright © 2015 by Austin Chant
One Last Leap Copyright © 2015 by Helena Maeve
A Corgi Named Kilowatt Copyright © 2015 by C.C. Bridges
The Memory of You Copyright © 2015 by Erica Barnes
Runner Copyright © 2015 by Sam Schooler
Printed in the United States of America

Digital ISBN 9781620046166
Print ISBN 9781620046173

Thank yous are owed to the trio of awesome ladies at LT3, to Sam Schooler, and to the glorious cast of characters I call my friends. You're all saints.

And to my late mother: Thank you for the unsolicited career advice you gave me when I was 15. Funny thing—it turns out you were right.

AMANDA JEAN

Table of Contents

After the Dust
ELEANOR KOS

Zev looked around his brother's apartment. Bare walls, clean swept floor. A picture of the two of them was stuck to the fridge with a magnet from the local pizza place.

The rabbi shifted his weight and cleared his throat but didn't speak. He was a small, round man, younger than Zev felt a rabbi should be.

"Where did it happen?" Zev asked.

"On the way to work," the rabbi said. "An accident on the beltway. They didn't tell you this?"

"I was on a flight back from Afghanistan. He was supposed to meet me at the airport."

He'd gone outside to wait in the cold, annoyed when he didn't see Beni's battered blue Toyota. And then he'd turned his phone back on and listened to the voicemail.

The rabbi put a hand on his shoulder, but Zev stepped away. He didn't know this man. He didn't know anyone in Beni's life anymore.

"Will you sit shiva for him? There are people who would sit with you."

"I don't want to be with strangers."

"They weren't strangers to him."

"They are to me," Zev said shortly. He breathed in, breathed out, watched dust particles in a wash of sunlight from the window. The sun was weak here compared to the Afghan hills. It left him homesick for the simplicity of combat.

"If you stay here," the rabbi said carefully, "they will come to you. At least to visit. To speak of him."

Zev nodded. He supposed he couldn't stop them.

"Your family?"

"Our parents died when we were in high school. Distant relatives in Israel. In Safed. I don't have an address." He'd have to find them. Somehow. He rubbed his hands over his face, palms catching on stubble, more than usually aware of the deep lines the last few years had carved into his skin.

"If you give me names, I can try to find them."

Zev turned to him, with his struggling beard and serious face and eyes that never strayed from Zev's, no matter how many times Zev looked away from him, no matter how uncomfortable the conversation became. Beni must've liked him.

"Thank you," he said stiffly. He wrote down the names in a notebook that the rabbi produced from his shirt pocket. A few minutes later, he was alone.

He looked through Beni's kitchen cabinets and found them well stocked. The fridge held lettuce and cabbage, carrots and radishes and homemade chicken soup. Beni had always been the cook in the family. He'd taken over with no discussion when their parents died, dinner waiting when Zev came home from his second of two after-school jobs.

Zev took the bowl of chicken soup out and set it on the counter. He imagined Beni chopping onion and carrots and garlic. He saw himself eating bowl after bowl until the last thing Beni would ever cook was gone. He put it back in the fridge.

The funeral was crowded with strangers. Zev eased away from the grave as soon as he could and pretended not to hear the rabbi's invitation to attend Maariv that night. His interest in religion had died with his parents. Now, losing Beni the same way he'd lost them, even to the same stretch of road, belief stirred again, but only in the form of a grudge.

People came, and people went. Most of them brought food. Not many of them stayed for more than a few minutes. Zev supposed he was being inhospitable, but when he tried to find words of gratitude or welcome, speech deserted him entirely.

He slept on the foldout couch and dreamed of sunshine and heat and the smell of smoke.

On the fifth day, it started to snow. Zev watched it fall until the room grew dark. Snow changed to sleet that pecked the window with icy splats. Streetlights shattered through each slushy drop until the window looked like it had been pelted with soft-edged stars.

The buzzer for the building door rang. It rang twice more, long and insistent, before Zev managed to pull himself off the couch. He pushed the intercom button.

"Yeah, what?"

A pause. "Is this Benjamin?"

The voice was young and a little shaky. Zev closed his eyes and banged his forehead against the wall. He pressed the red button to unlock the door. He hadn't had to tell anyone yet. Everyone had already known. The words just weren't there, and they were still MIA by the time he heard a knock on the door.

The kid shifted from foot to foot in the doorway. His skinny frame was dwarfed by the pack on his back, Army green, second- or third-hand, covered in patches and scribbles done in permanent marker. He had a thin face, spiked purple hair, and wary eyes behind tortoiseshell glasses.

"You're not Benjamin," he said and started to back away.

"I'm his brother."

"Yeah? What's your name?"

"Zev."

The kid considered him, one hand on the banister, ready to run. "I guess you do kind of look like him."

"You think so?"

"Sort of? Not as hot."

Zev raised his eyebrows at that, and the kid lifted his chin, like he was waiting for Zev to make a comment, anger loaded and ready to go. The motion brought his jaw out of shadow and revealed the purple bruise there.

"What's your name?" Zev said.

"Julian." He looked away. "He wouldn't have mentioned me. I mean, maybe. Probably not."

"You better come in," Zev said.

"I can come back when he's here."

Zev still couldn't find a good way to say it. Maybe there wasn't one. The last few years of breathing dust and flies as one op after another went south hadn't left him with much tact. "He's not coming back. He's dead."

Julian jerked his glasses off and started polishing them feverishly on his grubby T-shirt. Zev could see his throat work, his hands unsteady as he shoved his glasses back on his face.

"Okay," he said. "I mean—I mean, shit, I'm sorry. I'm sorry for your loss. I'll go."

Zev stepped away from the door. "Get in here."

"I didn't even know him," Julian said, but his voice cracked on the last word.

"Is that why you look like you're gonna bawl?"

"Shut up. I am not." Julian ran his hands back through his hair, which made it stand up even more.

"Just come in. You've got nowhere else to go, right? You're not going back out in *that*."

"I could have places to go," Julian said.

"Yeah, right. You want to come in and get warm, or do you want to go die of hypothermia and terminal pride?"

Julian slid in past him and dumped his backpack by the couch. He looked around at the room like he'd never seen it before. Zev wondered where his brother—bookworm, chess fanatic, and law librarian—could've met this kid. It'd have to wait.

"Go take a shower and get warmed up. Do you have clean clothes in that bag?"

Julian looked at it. "Not really."

"Laundry room in the basement. You can do it later. Here." He dug out a pair of sweat pants and a T-shirt from his own things and tossed them over.

Julian clutched them to his chest for a second and then gave him an oddly sweet smile. "Guess you really are his brother."

He vanished into the bathroom. Zev heard the door lock and sat heavily on the couch. Beni was the one prone to taking in strays, not him. Zev had invited him in without knowing the first thing about him. He glanced at Julian's bag, customary suspicion kicking in.

He opened the top flap. Half-empty water bottle, mostly frozen. He'd been out in the cold a while. Wondering what to do, where to go. Zev dug deeper. He found a pair of underwear, a filthy T-shirt, a paperback copy of *Treasure Island*. He stopped there. He recognized the cover, faded in a specific pattern, the top corner torn. He opened the book and saw Beni's name written in careful cursive.

He was still holding the book when Julian stepped out of the tiny bathroom in a cloud of steam.

Swimming in Zev's clothes, he looked even younger and thinner than the he had before he showered. He stopped scrubbing his hair with a towel and froze when he saw Zev. "Hey! You can't just go through my stuff!"

Zev held up the book. "Where did you get this?"

"Where do you think?"

"Did he give it to you, or did you steal it?"

"What the hell kind of question is that? He gave it to me!"

Zev stood up. Julian was taller than he was by about four inches, but he'd learned a long time ago that he didn't need a height advantage to intimidate. "Our father gave him this," Zev said.

Julian snatched the book and took a step back. Zev followed, until Julian was up against the opposite wall, eyes very wide, clutching the book with pale, spidery fingers.

"He gave it to me, okay? We met in the park at the chess tables. We played a couple times and we talked and—You're hurting me. That hurts."

His hand was wrapped around Zev's wrist. Zev, at some point, had taken hold of the front of his shirt. His knuckles were digging into the bones of Julian's chest. He let go, but he couldn't make himself back up. He felt heat and dust flay the back of his neck.

Julian stared at him with wide, frightened eyes, swallowed hard, and then kneed him in the crotch. Zev doubled over in silent agony.

"He gave it to me!" Julian yelled. "I said I liked to read and he said I'd like this one and he gave it to me, okay? Because he was a nice guy, and not everyone's a sadistic bully. Some people—" He was across the room, stuffing the book into his bag and hoisting it onto his shoulder. "Some people are okay," he said, but he didn't sound like he believed it. And then he was out the door.

Zev ran after him. A film of blood coated the world in red and put him back in a state of operational readiness he'd left less than a week before.

He hit the cold air of the sidewalk. Freezing slush whipped the side of his face. Cars rushed past, headlights and taillights both blinding, too many people on the street. Any one of them could have a concealed weapon.

The familiarity of the feeling let him start to take control of it. He leaned against the side of the building and took slow breaths. He'd dealt with this before. He'd make the call in the morning, get back on deployment as soon as possible. When his chest felt looser and he thought he could unlock the door without his hands shaking too bad, he straightened up.

Julian was watching him from a few feet away. He had his arms wrapped around himself, weight shifting, ready to run again.

Zev took off his coat slowly and tossed it at him. "At least take that."

"I don't want it."

"What do you want?"

"I heard you can die from getting kicked in the balls too hard," he said in a rush. "You're not gonna die, right?"

"I'm not going to die." He dug his nails hard into his palms. "I'm sorry. I don't sleep, and—" And every time he came home, it got worse. "I get angry. About stupid shit."

"It's not stupid. He's—He was your brother. It's not stupid."

"It was stupid to think you took it."

"Well, yeah. Who the hell steals a beat up old paperback with the cover coming off?" Julian picked up the coat and held it against him, hands tucked into its warmth.

"Not much of a gift when you put it that way."

"I liked it." Julian edged closer. "You want it back?"

Zev shook his head. It was exactly Beni's brand of impulsive kindness. He should've seen that from the start. "Keep it."

"It's really cold," Julian said.

"You can come back in if you want."

They walked up together.

Julian perched on the arm of the couch. "He said you were in Afghanistan."

"I was on my way home the day he died."

"It sucks that you didn't get to see him again. I'm sorry."

The simple honesty caught Zev off guard and loosened the knot in his chest he'd been breathing around since he got back. "Yeah. It does. You hungry?"

Julian nodded.

Zev took two bowls of chicken soup out of the freezer where he'd stashed it and heated them up. "Beni made this," he said, after they'd taken a few bites.

Julian stared at him, spoon halfway to his mouth.

Zev smiled a little. "Don't stop now. It'll get cold."

"You're not a little uncomfortable eating a dead man's soup?"

Zev took another bite and sucked a noodle off the spoon. "I was uncomfortable eating it alone," he said. "Felt too much like a last meal."

"Is it PTSD or something?"

Zev's hand tightened on the spoon. "Is what PTSD?"

"The reason you're an asshole."

Zev snorted, nearly aspirated a chunk of carrot, and coughed for a few seconds. "What makes you think it's not natural?"

"He asked me about my family, and I said there wasn't anyone I could call. That's when he gave me his card. He said I could call him if I was ever in trouble or didn't have anywhere to go. He said everyone should have a backup plan."

Zev stayed quiet. He'd told Beni that about a hundred times. *Don't just jump in, have a backup plan, have backup for your backup.*

Julian tipped the bowl to get the last spoonful of broth. "I asked him what his backup plan was, and he said it was you. That if he was ever in trouble, he'd call you and you'd fix it."

"I can't fix everything," Zev said. He hadn't cried for Beni, not when they told him and not at the funeral and not after. He felt tears sting his eyes now, and his throat locked up so tight it hurt.

"I'll go do laundry," Julian said. He slipped out of the apartment and left him alone.

Zev didn't really cry even then. His eyes ached, and he shoved the heels of his hands against them, more to force out the tears than the hold them back. No good. His eyes stayed wet and raw, but there was no overflow. All his grief and anger huddled in the pit of his stomach and wouldn't be coaxed out.

He collected their bowls and washed them, dried them, put them away. Out the window, the sleet outside had faded back to feathery flakes that stuck to every surface. It obscured street signs and clung to the hats and coats of passing pedestrians, a pale shroud over the city.

Zev unfolded the couch. It was for guests, and Julian was a guest. It would look weird to take it himself as he had every night prior to this. It would look like he couldn't handle sleeping in his brother's bed. He changed the sheets, both on the foldout and in the bedroom.

When Julian came back, he had the bag with his laundry slung over one shoulder and a loaf of challah under his arm like a football. "Uh, a lady downstairs gave me this? She wanted to give me oranges too, but I didn't have any more hands. French toast in the morning?"

Zev had to smile a little. "You know how to make French toast?"

"Doesn't everyone? It's like grilled cheese. You can make grilled cheese, right?"

"Nope."

"He did all the cooking?"

"Yeah."

"And then you joined the Navy and went away?"

"Had to pay for college somehow. The jobs I was working back then wouldn't cut it."

"You don't think he would've rather you stayed home with him and got a loan or something?" Julian asked.

"You really don't know when to shut up, do you?"

"Never did."

Zev jerked his head toward the couch. "You can sleep there. I'm calling it a night."

"Isn't it weird to sleep in his bed?"

Zev closed his eyes for a second. "Yeah. It's fucking weird. I was sleeping on the couch up to now."

"So sleep on the couch. It's big enough. Or I can sleep on the floor if you want. It's better than the bus station."

"Forget it."

"He told you, didn't he?"

Zev stopped in the doorway of the bedroom and looked back. Julian looked like a pissed-off cat, hunched up and defensive, glowering at him from underneath thin blond eyebrows. "Told me what?"

"I told him I was hooking. Just for a while. It was like maybe a dozen times. Doesn't mean I wanna do it with you."

"He didn't say a word about you."

Julian crossed his arms over his chest. "Then it's because I'm gay. You're not hot, you know. I don't like military assholes who slam me against walls anyway. It's against my whole aesthetic."

"I know I'm not. I've been told." Zev looked between Julian, who for all his insults and posturing seemed desperate not to be left alone, and Beni's bed, all smooth with the top sheet folded down over the comforter just the way he'd liked it. "Fine. You want to sleep with me so bad, we'll sleep. I snore and I kick and I don't want to hear any complaints, got me?"

"Fine."

"Good."

They brushed their teeth. Julian mumbled something about using a dead man's spare toothbrush, and Zev cuffed the back of his head, made sure to keep it gentle, made damn sure not to let his hand linger. He closed the door to the bedroom.

They got into bed, and Zev switched out the lights. He lay in the dark and listened to Julian breathe and to the barely audible puffs of wind that drove the snow against the window.

"Did you ever kill anyone?" Julian said.

Zev blinked up at the ceiling, just visible in a strip of light from the street outside. "You have less tact than anyone I've ever met. And spec ops guys aren't known for their tact."

"People should just say stuff. I wanted to know, so I asked. You can tell me to fuck off if you want. There's no reason to be polite when I'm not."

"What are you doing here, kid? Did one of your tricks go bad on you?"

"Fuck off," Julian said immediately.

Zev smiled. "Same to you."

~~*

A hammering on the door roused Zev from a deeper sleep than he'd had for months. He shot out of bed, heart pumping, adrenaline running through him. His sidearm wasn't where it should have been. The room was too cold, the angle of the sun wrong, everything wrong.

More pounding. A smooth floor under his feet. No dust, no grit. He let out a breath and went to answer the door.

TJ and Felipe stood outside the door and launched into "The Twelve Days of Christmas" as soon as he opened it. TJ held out a collection tin in the form of an empty beer can he'd clearly found on the street. It still had snow clinging to it.

He dragged them inside so they wouldn't wake the neighbors. "Christmas was two weeks ago, it's six in the morning, and you're both assholes," he said. "What are you doing here?"

"I told you we should've gone with the dreidel song," Felipe said. "We were just in town, man, just passing through."

Zev looked at both of them, and their faces went solemn and still and hard. There was a certain look spec ops guys got when they talked about loss, and this was it. Zev knew why they'd come. He hadn't thought the news would've made it to Norfolk yet.

"We heard about your brother," TJ said.

"I'm dealing with it," Zev said.

"We know." Felipe gripped his shoulder and shook it. "But you know, we're here."

"Uh," TJ said. His eyes had focused on the fold out couch over Zev's shoulder.

Zev had a clear and certain premonition that he was going to hate everyone in the room in about five minutes. At least the bedroom door was closed, so hopefully they'd assume he'd slept in there.

"Julian," he called, and stuck two fingers between his lips to whistle.

Julian sat straight up, all flailing limbs and epic purple bedhead. It made Zev smile despite himself. Julian fumbled for his glasses, shoved them on his face, and squinted across the room at TJ and Felipe. "What the hell," he said. "I want a cigarette so bad, why did I ever quit. Fuck."

TJ laughed. "What the hell is this, Z?"

"Julian—TJ, Felipe." Zev made introductory gestures. He saw TJ gearing up for some kind of comment, saw Julian open his mouth as well, and cut them both off. "He was Beni's friend."

That shut everyone up, at least for the moment. Julian pulled on his jeans from the day before, now clean, though he was still swamped in Zev's T-shirt. He approached the kitchen cautiously and edged around TJ and Felipe toward the challah.

"So French toast for everyone?" he said.

Zev folded the couch back up into a couch and flopped down onto it while TJ and Julian argued about cinnamon. Felipe sat on the coffee table.

"We're not just here about your brother," he said.

"Are we shipping out again?" Zev tried not to sound eager, tried not to let his disappointment show when Felipe shook his head.

"You're up for a commendation," he said. "That thing last year. With Tom."

"I don't want it."

Felipe just looked at him. He took an envelope out of his jacket pocket and tapped it against Zev's knee before handing it over. "They want to give you the Navy Cross, Z."

"They could give it to you or Buck or Andy. They could give it to anyone who was there. I don't want a medal for doing my job."

"You think the rest of us do?"

"They should give it to Tom."

Felipe was quiet for a second. "You want Tina to have to accept it? We barely got her through the funeral."

Zev bent over and rubbed his face hard with both hands. He opened the envelope. The letter inside said nothing unexpected until he got to the end. "Closed ceremony?" he said.

"They're worried about reprisals if the names of the people involved in the mission become known."

"Who's making this fucking French toast, you or me?" Julian demanded, loud, poking a finger into TJ's chest. "I say you cut it thin, you cut it thin."

Felipe gave Zev a speculative look. With Beni and Tom both gone, he was the only person on Earth who knew Zev liked guys just as well as women, if not more.

"Don't start," Zev said. "He's just Beni's friend. He didn't have anywhere else to go."

"How old is he?"

"I don't know, and it doesn't matter, because *it doesn't matter*. Okay?"

Felipe held up his hands. "Okay, man. You say it doesn't matter, it doesn't matter." He twisted around to direct his next words toward the kitchen. "Hey, kid, you want to come out with us tonight? You old enough to drink?"

"I've got ID," Julian said, which definitely meant *no*.

Zev put his face in his hands and left it there, premonition now a reality. Felipe rubbed his knuckles hard against his scalp. Zev punched him in the shoulder without raising his head.

"Go back to Norfolk," Zev said.

"Negative, no can do. I am your friend and I am a great guy, and therefore we will pay for all the drinks. Even his," he said, with a nod to Julian. "He'll probably slide under the table after two beers anyway."

~~*

Julian did not slide under the table after two beers.

Zev had pulled him aside after TJ and Felipe took off, boxed him in against the wall, and not let him slide away until he confessed to being "almost twenty-one" which turned out to mean barely twenty. Zev let it go. His ID looked real, and, at the time, he'd thought Felipe was right—two beers and he'd be down for the count.

TJ had taken them to a shithole on Third Avenue, a place called Silverado, with walls painted black, faux-Wild West decor, actual sawdust on the floor, and the worst jukebox selection in the history of humanity. Felipe had started them off with boilermakers and a toast to Beni, and it had gone downhill from there.

Now, Zev watched Julian climb up onto the bar and dance to some pop song about fast cars and designer jeans and getting your own way no matter what. TJ was filming it on his phone.

"He looks like a Muppet," Felipe said.

"With some of his strings cut," Zev agreed.

Long, jerky limbs moved to the beat, or sometimes just after it. Purple spikes bounced as he nodded his head, lost his balance, and braced a hand on the ceiling. Zev was a little impressed he was managing even that much after four shots and hardly any dinner.

"Don't put that on YouTube," he told TJ.

"Why not? My fans would love this."

"You don't have fans."

"Fuck you, I have like fifty subscribers."

"You put up videos of you brushing your teeth," Felipe said. "How do you have fifty subs?"

"Didn't you see me making vodka bacon? I am a fucking genius."

Julian's arms windmilled in the air after a particularly violent interpretation of the chorus. Zev shoved his way through the crowd just in time to catch him as he fell, nearly body checking one man into the bar as Julian toppled over.

"What the hell, asshole?" The guy grabbed his shoulder.

Zev knocked his arm away hard and took a step forward before Julian lurched sideways and Zev had to catch him again.

One of the guy's friends pulled him back with a nod to Zev's table, where TJ was already on his feet.

The guy scowled and rubbed his arm, but turned away. "Whatever. Fuck you, man."

"I might barf," Julian said.

"Wait till we're outside."

"But there's sawdust. Isn't that what it's for?"

Zev got an arm around his waist and guided him back to the table. "We're heading out. Say goodnight, Julian."

Julian waved vaguely.

"Night, Julia Child," TJ said.

Julian squinted at him. "No fucking cinnamon."

"You're so wrong there's no way to tell you how wrong you are."

"Go," Felipe said. "I can't listen to them anymore."

Zev dragged Julian out the door and waited and while he vomited into the gutter and groaned. He swayed afterward and looked around with eyes that might have been slightly less glassy than before.

"Better?" Zev asked.

"No, my mouth tastes like puke and I'm one step closer to sober. How is that better? That's not better."

"You'll have to sober up eventually."

"Says the guy who doesn't drink."

"I drink."

"So you just don't drink with me?" Julian crossed his arms, frowning, still swaying to the rhythm of his internal sea of vodka and cinnamon schnapps.

"Someone has to get us home."

He took Julian's arm and guided him down the street. Julian let him.

"Oh. I guess, yeah. Hey, do your friends hate me? Are they gonna strip me naked and tie me to a flag pole or something?"

"Would you like them to?"

"No? It's cold."

Zev snorted. "They don't hate you. TJ likes you. You're not scared of him."

"I'm not scared of anything."

"Must be nice."

Zev heard a few fast steps behind them. The muscles of his back tensed, but he didn't let himself turn. Even this late, even in this neighborhood, it was unlikely to be a threat, and he was tired of overreacting. The footsteps came closer. Julian wandered along beside him, still talking, completely unaware.

"Hey, asshole, turn around."

It was the guy from the bar. Zev sighed as he turned. Correction: the guy and his two friends. Fantastic.

"I apologize," Zev said, because that would, hopefully, be the fastest way out of this. "It was an accident. I was trying to keep my friend from cracking his head open. Can we all get on with our evening now?"

"You don't sound real sorry."

Zev kept his mouth shut. The only thing likely to come out of it was sarcasm. He shrugged and started walking away. With a little luck, Larry, Moe, and Curly would be too tired or too drunk to push it. He tried to remember the last time luck had been on his side.

More quick footsteps. He braced himself, but the guy grabbed Julian instead. Julian let out a squawk and struck out toward the guy's face. He landed glancing blow to his nose, and the guy retaliated with a solid punch to Julian's stomach. Julian went down with wide eyes and a surprised squeak as the blow drove the air out of him.

"You fucking little shit," the guy said, and pulled back his foot for a kick.

Zev swept his leg out from under him and slammed him down to the sidewalk. He could hear gunfire, could hear himself calling for a medic, but Tom was the medic, and Tom was already down. He saw his fist drive forward and expected the man's blood to land on rock and packed earth.

Hands on him. The man's friends. He felt his elbow impact against someone's ribs, his boot strike someone's side.

Julian was shouting at him. Police sirens. A crowd of people surrounded him, cut off his escape.

Zev blinked and feared he might end the night by puking in the gutter, too. He shut his eyes. The man underneath him wasn't moving. After a second, he made himself check for a pulse. With relief, he found it steady and strong.

He looked around. The crowd of people that had seemed so intimidating consisted of two bums and a little old lady, who looked over the scene, sniffed once, and kept walking. The police sirens were real, though, and they were getting closer.

"We should go," Julian said.

"You go. I'll give you my keys."

"Don't be stupid. I'm not leaving you here."

Zev sat down on the curb to wait for the police. He fully expected to be taken in and questioned, maybe charged. He'd bruised his knuckles on the man's face. He'd wanted to keep hitting him. He didn't really know why he'd stopped.

The officer took down his account and Julian's. The guy from the bar had regained a woozy sort of consciousness by then. His friends were long gone. The officer looked at Zev's out-of-date driver's license and then his military ID card. He thanked Zev for his service and told them to go home.

Zev watched the squad car drive away. "How many times did I hit him?" he asked.

"Three, maybe? You don't know?"

Zev shook his head.

"You were defending yourself. And me."

"With excessive force."

"It didn't look that excessive."

Zev rubbed at his knuckles. It had felt excessive. Worse, it'd felt uncontrollable.

Julian pulled at his sleeve. They started back toward Beni's apartment.

"Do you really have PTSD?" Julian asked.

"It's not a fucking disorder. I'm just tired of watching people die."

Julian didn't say anything else after that. When they got back, he cut slices of challah for them and made coffee and bread with butter and jam.

"You can eat right now?" Zev said.

"I'm probably going to barf again. I'd rather barf food."

They ate on the couch, hunched over their coffee.

"Did you really sleep with guys for money?" Zev asked.

"Yeah. It wasn't that bad. It paid a lot better than being a barista. People were nicer to me too."

"So why'd you stop?"

"Because I'm going to be president someday, and you can't be president if people find out you were a teenage hooker."

"President, huh?"

"Yeah. I'm gonna fix everything that's wrong."

"That's a lot of stuff."

"I know. And I can't start till I'm thirty-five."

"You've got a hard life, for sure."

"Shut up, asshole." Silence for a minute, and Julian turned toward him. He twisted his fingers into the fabric of Zev's sleeve and used the grip to pull them closer together until their bodies touched. "It's not so bad right now," he said.

Zev swallowed and looked away. "Glad to hear it."

Julian leaned closer still until he could rub his face along Zev's shoulder like a cat. Zev felt the brief smudge of warm lips against his throat. "No," Zev said. "This wouldn't even be a good idea if you were sober."

"All I have are bad ideas," Julian mumbled.

Zev's own poor choices marched briefly behind his eyes. "Bullshit. If I don't get to believe that, neither do you."

Julian rolled his head to one side to look up at him, blinking slowly. "Do you have a lot of bad ideas?"

"Everybody has some."

"Was letting me stay here one of them?"

Zev thought of the nights he'd spent listening to the hum of the fridge and wondering how so small a space could feel so empty. "No," he said. "I think that was a pretty good one."

Julian smiled at him, eyes closing. "That's nice. I'd like to be someone's good idea."

Zev looked at the fading bruise near his mouth and the shadows under his eyes. "Where are your parents?" he asked.

"Kicked me out when I told them I was gay. Boo hoo, me and a thousand other kids."

"Doesn't hurt any less because it happened to other people."

Julian squinted up at him. "That's what your brother said."

"It's what he used to tell me about our parents."

"He was pretty smart."

Grief rose in Zev's throat like bile. "Yeah. Pretty smart."

Julian's head tipped back against the couch and his eyes closed again. Zev took the coffee mug from him and set it aside. He got a bucket and a glass of water and put both nearby, rolled himself up in a blanket, and lay down on the floor. Headlights slid across the ceiling every few minutes like glow worms, but it was late, and the traffic was sparse. He closed his eyes.

He woke to the sound of Julian being violently sick into the bucket and sighed. It was still dark. He checked his watch. Just after three.

"You okay?" he said.

Julian only groaned in response. He was on the floor, holding onto the bucket with both hands. Zev took the opportunity to unfold the couch into a bed and get them both into it.

"Rinse and spit," he said, and handed him the water.

Julian obeyed and then fell back with his head on a pillow. "I was living with my boss," he said. "I worked at this coffee shop, and we got together and I didn't really have a place to stay, so I moved in with him."

"Didn't go well?"

"He hit me. So I hit him back. So he kicked me out and fired me, and then I slept in the bus station, but I didn't have much money and I couldn't get another job, and then after a few days I couldn't even buy food, and it just—it happened really fast. Everything was fine, and then it wasn't."

"Yeah. That's how it goes."

"I'm not really gonna be president. They're gonna kick me out of college when I can't pay, and I'll end up working at McDonald's when I'm fifty and I won't be able to fix anything."

"Don't worry about the money."

"What do you mean don't worry about the money? This is America. All we do is worry about the money."

"I mean, Beni wanted you to have someone. Back up. You've got someone. Don't worry about it."

Julian was quiet for a long time, pale face a blur in the dark. "You're crazy," he said.

"It's a job requirement. Brush your teeth and go back to sleep."

~~*

The next morning, Julian was gone. Zev conducted a brief, panicked search of the bedroom and bathroom, and then spotted his bag half wedged behind the couch. He let out a long breath, called himself ten kinds of idiot, and made coffee.

He should've been glad, he thought, mug cupped in his hands, staring out at a world of white. It was still early. Only a few cars had made tracks through the snow, not enough to turn it brown except at the very edges. He could see the plow edging closer and throwing up foamy powder as it lurched along. He should've been glad to find Julian gone, but he hadn't been.

Julian came through the door in a rush of cold air that had followed him up the stairs from the street. He pushed two take out cups into Zev's hands, dumped a grease-stained bag on the fold-out couch, and pulled something flat and rectangular out of the front of his pants.

"Can you play chess?" he said. He unfolded the board on the coffee table and started pulling chess pieces out of his pockets. Zev's pockets, actually, because he was wearing Zev's coat.

"Not well. Not like Beni."

"Great. I love winning."

Zev sniffed one of the cups. Hot chocolate. He took a sip and uncrumpled the top of the bag to look inside. Croissants, still warm.

"I took your wallet," Julian said. He tossed it back.

Zev looked through it, pulled out the cash, and held it out to him. Julian shook his head.

"You can't just walk around with no money."

"It is totally possible to walk around with no money. Lots of people do it."

"What if something happens?"

"What, like what if a money-eating lion gets loose and the only way I can save a small child is to divert it with a trail of tens?"

Zev just looked at him.

Julian sighed. "I'm not taking your money. You'll go all paternal and it'll be weird and gross and I don't want a sugar daddy."

"I'm not..." Zev blinked and rubbed his eyes and wished he'd gotten more sleep. "But you're okay with stealing my wallet?"

"That's just breakfast. It's not like you're giving me an allowance. Shut up and eat your croissants."

"Aye, aye, sir," Zev muttered.

He shut up and ate his croissants. They played chess. He lost, badly, but not as badly as he'd expected to. He frowned at Julian. "Don't go easy on me."

"I'm not."

"If you were playing with Beni, you're better than this."

"I'm better than this when I don't have a hangover the size of the former Soviet Union. You want to lose worse?"

"I'm used to it."

"I thought you'd get mad. A lot of people get mad when I beat them."

"That's on them, not on you. If they don't want to lose, they should practice. That's how life works. You don't win just by wanting it, and getting mad at the guy who beat you is like getting mad at winter 'cause you were too dumb to wear a coat."

Julian smiled at him, chin propped on his fist. "So I'm an unstoppable force of nature?"

Thankfully, Zev's phone rang just then. TJ. He answered. "How do you feel about going back?" TJ said.

"When?"

"Soon."

"How soon?"

A brief pause. "Three days, man. This is unofficial. I won't put your name in if it's too soon."

"I'll go."

"You sure?"

"I said I'd go."

"Yeah, okay. I'll call you."

Julian was staring at him when he hung up, as if he could divine the other half of the conversation through the power of intense eye contact with Zev's phone. "Go where?" he said.

"Probably Afghanistan."

"You don't even know?"

"Does it matter?"

"It should. Normal people want to know where they'll be going when they go somewhere."

"I'll find out before I leave."

"And give me an address or something so I can write you?" Julian asked.

"If you want."

"Would you want me to?"

Zev started setting up the board again. He should say no. He could see where this was heading. But he wanted it, and it'd been a long time since he'd wanted anything much at all. "Yeah," he said.

"Really?"

"Really."

"Because I'm a good idea and an unstoppable force of nature?"

"No, because you're going to be president someday, and I want to stay on your good side."

Julian smiled at him and then ducked his head to rub a hand over the back of his neck. "Okay. That's a good reason, too, I guess."

They played again. Zev lost again.

"Don't they teach chess in military strategy school?" Julian said.

"I went to BUD/S, not Westpoint."

"What's that?"

"Basic Underwater Demolition and SEAL training."

Julian's eyebrows rose, and his glasses slid slowly down his nose until they were in danger of falling off. "You're a SEAL?"

"I work with Naval Intelligence now. But yeah."

"Aren't you kind of short for that?"

Zev laughed. "Yeah. It was a pain in the ass. They separate you into boat crews by height. I got put on the Smurf boat. That's where I met Felipe."

"Why by height?"

"Because you spend a lot of time carrying it over your head, and you don't want one six-foot guy in a crew of shorties doing all the work."

"Is that where you met TJ too?"

"TJ's not Navy. Marine Recon. We've worked together. Tom—a friend introduced us."

"Tom?"

"A guy I knew. What do you want for lunch?"

Julian eyed him for a second and then seemed to let it go. "Subway."

"We've got homemade lasagna and you want Subway?"

"You asked. The stomach wants what it wants."

"Go get it, then. You can steal my wallet again if you want."

"I got breakfast. You and your SEAL training can go trudge through the snow this time."

He went. He thought about Tom as he walked. Tom had been from Georgia. The only guy who never complained about the heat. But then he never complained about the cold, either, or the flies, or the food. Zev remembered him best making his rounds in the evening, going from hut to hut, asking about small cuts and scrapes and blisters that people were too proud to report. Moleskin and blister cream, a dry smile and a flat, broad face.

Unfailingly kind, even when Zev had one too many beers their first night home and hit on him in the most awkward way possible.

He hadn't even known Tom was married. He never talked about home when they were away. Never showed anyone pictures of his kids, even though he'd had them with him all along. Zev had packed up his things after the ambush and found them, though by then he'd met the kids himself, and Tina, and found it impossible not to like her, despite everything.

Subway was nearly empty. He got two six-inch subs and chips and cookies and headed back. Cars had churned the snow to brown mush, and the plow had thrown up thick drifts at each intersection. He plunged straight through, more eager to get back than inclined to be careful of his boots. They'd seen worse.

He jogged up the stairs and unlocked the door just in time to see Julian shove the letter about his commendation back half under the couch where he'd left it. Zev looked at him.

"Is that why you wanted Subway?" he asked.

Julian crossed his arms over his chest. "So I'm nosy. You knew that already."

"You shouldn't read other people's mail." Zev picked up the letter and tossed it in the trash where it belonged.

Julian's eyes widened, but, for once, he didn't say a word. They set out the sandwiches at the kitchen table. Julian made it all the way through his and had put the cookies in the microwave to heat up before the words burst out of him like a dam breach: "But the Navy Cross! That's a big deal, isn't it? If even I've heard of it, it must be a big deal."

"It's a big deal."

"So why wouldn't you take it?"

"Because I don't deserve a medal for doing my job."

"Do you feel guilty about the people you killed?"

Zev paused with a chip halfway to his mouth, but he didn't feel the blinding anger he expected. In a lot of ways, Julian's complete lack of anything resembling tact was a relief. "Everyone I killed was trying to kill my friends. If I feel guilty about anything, it's the people I didn't kill."

The shot he should've taken, the one that might've allowed Tom to come home with them. The shot he hadn't fired because he'd been told to keep his head down and not betray his position until Buck gave the word.

The microwave beeped. Julian didn't move to get the cookies out. He just stood staring at Zev. "I thought you'd feel bad about it," he said quietly.

"I don't."

Julian got out the cookies and set them down on a paper plate in the center of the table. He picked his apart and ate it bit by bit in silence.

"You can stay here while I'm gone," Zev said. "Keep an eye on the place. I couldn't get it sold before I leave anyway."

Julian looked up at him, and not with the condemnation he'd expected. Nothing more than curiosity. "Will you tell me about it?" he said.

"What? What does it feel like to kill someone?" Zev tried not to sneer, but it was impossible to say the words with any kind of detachment, and the only possible emotion was contempt.

"No. Just what happened." He nodded toward the trash can that contained the letter. "That day. Or whenever. What do you do over there? You can't be in firefights the whole time."

Zev rescued the one remaining cookie fragment from Julian's searching fingers and stuck it in his mouth. He licked his fingers clean of chocolate.

"We were at Combat Outpost Hatchet. We collected intel. Our corpsman—Navy hospital corpsman, Navy's version of a medic. That was Tom. He was setting up a clinic in a village nearby. Him and the guy who was there before him, Army medic, they spent the better part of a year getting it going, getting people to trust us. When we left, I asked who was going to take it over after—after Tom. They didn't send anyone. They shut it down. The only useful thing we did over there, and they shut it down."

"He's dead, isn't he?" Julian said.

"Yeah, he's dead."

"He died during the thing they want to give you a medal for."

"Yes."

"So they want to give you the Navy Cross for getting your friend killed."

Zev waited for the anger to boil up inside him, but he only felt a weight on his heart, like a heavy stone pressing down. "That's about the size of it," he said.

Julian twisted off bits of the napkin and rolled them into pellets between his fingers. "I keep waiting for you to get mad at me for saying stuff like that."

"Nothing to be mad about. Just the truth."

"I'm sorry. I see why you don't want it."

He didn't, but at least he was trying. "Clean this mess up. I'm going to take a shower."

"What mess, it's like three crumbs!" Julian called after him, but Zev couldn't summon a smile.

He just wanted to get back where he belonged. Where there wasn't so much time to think.

~~*

He got his wish. TJ came through, and two days later Zev was on a Chinook transport from Kabul, the last member of a newly assembled spec ops team at FOB Harrier. The relief he was looking for didn't materialize. There was too much sitting around, too much waiting, too much nothing to do, so he found things to do.

He looked at the vehicles, checked the oil, checked the engines, got into a fight that almost came to blows with the Army guy whose territory he was poaching on. He got permission to line the interiors with ballistic blankets. He paced the perimeter of the camp. He failed to sleep.

Their corpsman was straight out of METC, a big, earnest guy called Rush with scarring across one cheek. He'd survived an attack on his transport, gone home to heal, and then retrained as a medic so he could come back and do it all over again. He wanted to open a clinic in the nearest village.

Zev couldn't listen to the discussion when he asked the CO for permission. He headed out into the dark to walk from fire to fire. Wind swirled dust through the flames, and sparks kicked up into the night. He put a hand in his pocket and felt the letter there. Julian had written him as promised. Eventually, he hovered near the outskirts of one fire to tear open the envelope. Red-orange light fell across a Subway napkin stained with chocolate. No message, just a scribbled notation: "e4".

It took Zev a second to place it, but he'd played chess with Beni by email back when he'd been with SEAL Team 2, before Beni had given up on teaching him anything beyond the basics. He'd said it was boring to win all the time. Julian didn't seem to mind. Zev smiled a little and tried to recall both the notations and a decent response to that opening move. Beni could do it in his head, but Zev had always needed a board. Not exactly standard equipment out on the frontier of nowhere.

He looked around the ground for possible chess pieces and saw nothing but stones and bits of rusted metal. That would do.

In the morning, he commandeered a piece of cardboard and a marker to make a board. The stones were black, and the metal was white. He wrote in the names of the pieces, P for pawn, Q for queen. He even managed to find more or less upright stones and metal bits for the kings and queens.

The whole thing would blow away in a stiff wind, so he stuck it in the corner of the command hut, next to the radio. Gawhar, their interpreter, gave it and him a look that said he hadn't expected to find anyone playing chess out here and that, if he had, it wouldn't have been Zev.

"Problem?" Zev said.

Gawhar shrugged one shoulder and went back to monitoring the radio, tuning from band to band, searching for intercepted communication. Zev stared at the board. He moved Julian's pawn into the e4 position and then his own to e5.

"He's playing the Ruy Lopez opening," Gawhar said. "I will bet you your next five desserts."

"How can you know that from one move?"

"It is a good opening against beginners. Very little uncertainty."

"So what's the next move if he is?"

"Knight to f3."

"Huh. Okay. You're on." Zev didn't like sweets that much anyway.

~~*

In retrospect, he should've seen that setting up in the command hut was asking for trouble. Gawhar basically lived in there, but all the guys were in and out all day long, and it was the only hut that had reliable electricity.

One night, about three weeks later, the wind screamed down the hills, scattered their fires, and drove everyone inside. Ten or twelve guys stuffed themselves into Command, which put it at least five over what it could reasonably hold.

Gawhar looked out of sorts, even while eating Zev's laughably tiny packaged vanilla pound cake. Zev passed him Julian's latest move, this one scribbled on a receipt for coffee, which was a bit cruel. None of them would see anything like decent coffee until they got home. The bishop to b5 just confirmed Gawhar's opinion on Julian's opening, and he nodded, frown easing.

"It's as I told you," he said.

"It's rude to say 'I told you so,' buddy."

"It is true to say I told you so," Gawhar said, with a small smile.

Rush and the camp's two Jasons came to look over Zev's shoulder. Big Jason was about Zev's height and build. Jason Heinz, known as Shrimp, towered over everyone else in the camp by a solid four inches. Some things in life one could always count on, and the nature of military humor was one of them.

"What's this?" Big Jason said.

"What's it look like, smart ass?"

"Who you playing with, the 'terp?"

"Guy at home. Gawhar just likes being right about things."

"I am often right, it's true," Gawhar said.

"Got anything else to be right about?" Rush said, with a nod to the radio.

He'd been waiting to get back out to a village in the next valley where he'd treated a little girl's broken arm, but the problem with revisiting patients was that the enemy knew they'd be coming back. Too often, they were waiting. The CO, Gus, had been waiting for intel on enemy activity and locations, but so far they'd had none.

"Maybe something," Gawhar said. "I would like to listen through the night."

"You ought to tell Gus," Shrimp said.

"Not yet. More than I enjoy being right, I dislike being wrong."

Rush nodded, fatalistic as they all were by this point, and bent over the chess board. He glanced at Zev. "What are you going to do next?"

Zev shrugged. He had time to think about it. The next mail bird wouldn't be in for another week.

"You should get something in front of your king," Big Jason said.

"You know chess?" Zev asked.

"I know if you lose the king, it's all over. So protect that fucker, like Secret Service around the president. That's just strategy."

"I don't think that's how it works," Rush said, but he didn't sound sure.

Gawhar muttered something in Dari that sounded like a prayer for strength.

"No, look," Shrimp said. "It's just like an ambush. The bishops move diagonal and the castles move straight, right?" He glanced at Zev and Gawhar for confirmation. Zev nodded. Gawhar ignored them, hands over his earphones, suddenly more attentive. "So you keep your king out of the kill zone and you're golden. It's just like in training."

"Get your commander," Gawhar said quietly.

They all stared for a second, and then Zev punched Big Jason's shoulder. "Go, he's with Major Stone by the vehicles."

Big Jason jogged out, hand clapped to his head to keep his hat on. Everyone else in the tent crowded around the radio so that Gus, when he arrived, had to shove his way through. He stubbed out his cigarette and stuck it behind his ear.

"What do you got?" he said.

~~*

The next morning, they gathered in the command hut again, this time for a mission briefing.

Gus leaned over the map, hair sticking up from the little sleep he'd had. "We'll do a circular route, up past Ak Goshteh and into the hills and then down around here, see what we can pick up in the way of intel. While we're doing that, Doc, this'd be a good time for you to head back to check on your girl. They'll be busy elsewhere, or they'll be busy with us."

Rush nodded and headed off to pack his bag. Gus looked at Zev. "You're with him, you and Shrimp and Gawhar, and two other guys for a second vehicle, your choice. See what you can pick up in the village while you're at it. If the radio chatter's for real, they must've heard something about it."

"Doc should be with you," Zev said. "You're more likely to run into trouble."

"We'll have the Army guys. They've got a medic." Gus grinned. "Not as good as Doc, obviously, but I guess he'll do. Who do you want?"

"Shawn and Sandoval."

"Go find them. Get geared up. We'll leave first, around sunset. Give us an hour's lead, then head out."

Zev slunk out of Command with worry gnawing at his stomach and an acid feeling in his throat. Before he went to find Shawn and Sandoval and Shrimp, he headed back to his bunk. Under the edge of the sleeping roll, he'd stuck the only actual letter he'd gotten from Julian since he deployed. It was written in blue marker on a white shoelace, both sides. He hadn't bothered to read it yet, more worried about the chess game, more worried about the possibility of a mission, more worried about anything that would keep his mind off what he'd do when he got back home.

He read it now.

I got a job!!! I sell people hotdogs and fries, it's awful. The bags of fries are so big it's like a mass of fries the size of your head and they're greasy and floppy and stuck together, between them and the hot dogs it's like a sad gross orgy in a paper bag. Still in school, going to be so in debt. Can we pretend I didn't tell you I was going to be president? I was really drunk. (I am though.) Taking some pre-law stuff and bio and Latin because your brother said I'd like it, HE WAS WRONG. I worry about you a lot. Please don't get killed. —J

Zev read it over again, and then once more, and then stuck it in a wadded ball in his pocket. He went to find his team.

That evening, he and Rush watched from the top of the wall as the convoy rolled down the dirt track toward Ak Goshteh. The wind was just as bad as the night before. It whipped their faces red and pulled at their clothes and shoved the lingering scent of wood smoke down their throats.

Zev climbed back down when the last vehicle disappeared. He looked at his little team. "Okay, guys, final checks. Doc, you need anything else in the way of supplies? The Rangers' CO said you could raid their med stash."

"I've got it, Z."

"Okay. You're with me and Gawhar. Sandoval, Shawn, and Shrimp, you're in the lead vehicle. I want everyone ready at the gate in thirty. Gawhar, you look like someone took a shit in your Cheerios. Why?"

Gawhar was silent for a moment and then spread his hands in frustration. "I should be with the other team. They are the more likely target. I spoke to your CO. He did not listen."

"They've got another 'terp. What's the problem?"

"Delawar has only been doing this for a short time. His languages are good, but one learns to listen for other things in these situations. Things that may mean more than spoken words."

Zev nodded slowly. He knew what Gawhar meant. The intonations, the word choice, the way people said things when they were under the particular sort of stress that combat situations produced. He'd heard it in his own guys, and he'd heard it over the radio, monitoring icomm on a mission in Argentina years ago.

"It's done now," he said. "We can't get them back. Get past it and get packed."

They rolled out through the gate at 18:00 with a sliver-thin moon hanging over the hills and the wind trying to beat the landscape into submission. Zev found himself counting and recounting the smoke grenades in the pouch at his belt and made himself stop. All of them were braced for something beyond the relentless wind, but they made it to the village without incident.

The village was a collection of small structures, more permanent than their own camp but less so than anything in Ak Goshteh, the nearest settlement of any size. It held about a dozen families at any given time, but only five or six seemed to be permanent residents. The families who stayed were ruled over by old men who seemed as wedded to the area as weathered rocks, men who had raised children and grandchildren and great-grandchildren there and would not move for anyone.

Three of these met them near the outskirts of the village. One of them gave Rush a nod and something that was almost a smile. It was his granddaughter, or maybe great-granddaughter, who Rush had treated for a broken arm. Zev relaxed a little. Presumably that meant the kid was doing okay.

Rush set up in the center of town with Gawhar at his side. He saw the girl again, who seemed happy enough and ran off to whisper with her friends after the examination. He saw various other people for minor complaints, and one man with an infected cut on his leg that had distended the skin of his calf and turned it nearly yellow. When Rush cut into it, there was more pus than Zev had ever wanted to see in his life. He looked out toward the dark edges of the village instead, keeping watch.

Rush packed up around midnight, which would give them plenty of time to get back to camp under cover of darkness, even at the slow crawl made necessary by the pitted, rocky dirt tracks that passed for roads. Gus had called on the sat phone to let him know everything was going as planned. Nothing logical explained the feeling in the pit of his stomach or his tendency to finger Julian's shoelace letter until the plastic bit at the end had cracked under the assault of his thumbnail.

"Eyes open on the way home," was all he said as they piled in and got back on the road.

The wind had quieted from a roar to a whisper. They shuttled through the night as if they were moving through an empty world.

"Atmospherics," Rush muttered.

Zev nodded. The sounds and the feel of a place could tell you more than any intel or icomm, no matter how good. Birdsong, or lack of it, the way people behaved. Rush was right. The quiet surrounding them had taken on a waiting quality.

"Everything is more quiet in the wake of the wind," Gawhar said, but he didn't sound convinced.

Zev radioed Shrimp in the vehicle ahead of them. "See anything?"

"Negative." A pause. Zev could see Sandoval's hand on Shrimp's shoulder and then a gesture. "Possible sighting. Check the ridge, twelve o'clock."

Zev got out his binoculars and caught one figure just disappearing over the edge. "Could be shepherds. Could be bandits."

"Or bad guys," Shrimp said.

They kept rolling. There was nothing else to do, no way off the road and no way to turn around with the hillside crumbling to their left and solid rock at their right. Around the corner, they'd hit a wadi where they could turn off if they needed to. Zev relayed their position and situation to Gus on the sat phone. The first team was already back at camp.

They rounded the corner. Zev saw the wadi to the right and debated the merits of turning around, going home by another route. As he did, a blast rocked the world, and the lead vehicle flew up nearly to a ninety-degree angle and crashed back down: an IED buried in the dirt.

Gunfire hit the road and the vehicles, and he was grateful for the ballistic blankets he'd installed. "Status," he yelled into the radio.

"Shrimp's hit, his leg," Sandoval said. "Shawn's unconscious." He sounded calm, and Zev could see him maneuvering to get into the driver's seat and out of the kill zone. A pause. "We're not going anywhere in this thing," he said.

The wadi would connect with another road at the bottom, assuming they could get past the boulders that had tumbled down it in the last major storm.

"Coming for you," Zev said briefly into the radio. "Cover fire," he said to Gawhar. "I'm going forward. Doc, get us air support. The lead vehicle's dead. They'll have to blow it if they don't want the Taliban stripping it for parts."

"I should go," Rush said. "We have casualties."

"And we will get them back to you, but that vehicle is a death trap right now. The best thing we can do for those men is get them out of there. You can treat them when we're on the move again."

Rush nodded, though he clearly didn't like it. He eyed the lead vehicle. "That's close for an air strike," he said.

"I plan not to be here when they join the party. Questions?"

There were none. Zev opened the door on the side protected by the rock wall. At the same time,

Gawhar started firing. Zev crouched and ran forward, expecting the hot sting of a bullet at any second. He made it to the lead vehicle, dust in his eyes and dry air scraping his throat.

"How bad?" he asked Sandoval.

"Bump on the head, broken leg. I'm not a doctor, but they're both still breathing, and Shrimp's whining like a bitch, so he's probably fine."

"Shut the fuck up," Shrimp muttered.

Together, they maneuvered Shrimp toward the far side of the vehicle and out the driver's side door. He balanced on his good leg, pale and sweating. Blood had soaked through his pants and painted them dark red from knee to ankle, but he was still upright.

"Hang on," Zev said. "We'll get you back to Doc." He lobbed a smoke grenade over the vehicle. As soon as the smoke had thickened enough to obscure their movement, they started out, low, as quickly as Shrimp could manage with one arm around Zev's shoulders. Behind them, Sandoval hoisted Shawn over his shoulders.

Halfway back, the mountainside above them exploded in fire, small boulders, and a drenching rain of grit, dust, and tiny rocks that pelted them like hail. Zev groped for his radio, couldn't find it, couldn't make his arm work right. He saw a blurred red image out of one eye and nothing at all out of the other. Something wet snaked down his cheek.

He gave up on the radio and yelled back to Rush and Gawhar. "RPGs! Move right now, down into the wadi! We'll get there, go!"

He couldn't tell if they'd heard him, couldn't tell if they'd listened if they had. Shrimp's body had gone limp, and Zev couldn't get him onto his shoulders with only one arm functional. He dragged him along as well as he could, afraid to check for a pulse.

"Sandoval, can you hear me?"

"I'm here, Z. Right behind you. I've got Shawn, just keep going."

His voice was strained with more than the stress of combat. Zev tried to look back, but his vision was so bad that all he could make out was one figure carrying another. They were both still back there, whatever their injuries. It would have to be enough.

The RPG blast had set the lead vehicle on fire. The smoke drifted around them, thick and choking, but it also covered their retreat. Zev felt his way down between two man-high boulders and into the wadi. With a surge of relief, he saw the other vehicle, now out of the kill zone, and Rush running toward them with the med kit bouncing on his shoulder. For a moment, with the light behind him and a fog spreading over what remained of Zev's vision, he looked just like Tom.

"I've got him," Rush said. "You can let go."

Zev unclenched his hands from Shrimp's tac vest, and the world slipped away with it.

The next thing he was aware of was being bounced along in the front seat. Except that when he pried his eyes—eye—open, the scenery out the window wasn't moving.

"Air strike," Gawhar said, next to him on the driver's side. "Quite close. You're back with us?"

"Think so. Did everyone make it?"

"Everyone is alive. If I still believed in any higher power, I might call it a miracle."

Zev peered at him. He wasn't sure if the red stain he saw on Gawhar's shoulder and neck was blood or just the bloody tinge of his own vision. "You okay?"

"Yes. I believe part of my ear is gone, but most of the blood is yours."

Zev reached a hand toward his face and lowered it again. "Is my other eye still there?" he asked.

"It's there. They're sending CASEVAC for you and Shawn and Shrimp. I suggest you rest until they arrive."

Zev didn't have a choice. He blinked his good eye, couldn't get it open again, and then he was out.

~~*

He woke up with rough cotton under his fingers and no sign of the gritty dust that crept into every bunk and piece of clothing in Afghanistan within two hours of arrival. When he got his left eye open, he could still see almost nothing, and panic made his heart scramble like a trapped thing in his chest until he saw the black sky and the streetlights outside the window. Nighttime. The only light came from the door to the hallway, which stood open a few inches.

When he touched his face, he felt one undamaged half and one mostly covered in bandages, including his right eye. He chose to take that as a good sign. At least there was something there to need bandaging. He could feel his eyelid trying to open, but it was either taped shut or stuck shut. He hurt, but in a distant way that he recognized as the effect of morphine.

A call button lay next to his hand. It was harder than he'd thought it would be to press it. His shoulder gave a sharp twinge, and his ribs ached. Even the tiniest shift of his head made him want to close his eyes and leave the world behind again, but he couldn't.

A nurse came shuffling in a minute later, a guy with short cropped hair and a kind smile. "I'm glad you're back with us," he said. "I know you must have questions, but can you please tell me your name—?"

Zev rattled off his name, rank, and serial number as fast as he could. He must've been hit on the head harder than he'd thought if they wanted to make sure he still knew who he was.

"I was actually going to say name, year, and the name of the president, but it looks like you're present and accounted for. Your team's all right, sir. All recovering. You were the worst off."

Zev closed his eyes and nodded very slightly. "Eye?" he said.

"I'm sorry, sir, I don't know. You'll have to wait for the doctor for that."

"Where?"

"Bethesda. You came in from Landstuhl yesterday."

The nurse helped him drink some water, and Zev slept.

~~*

When he opened his eye again, light was battering against drawn blackout curtains, and one sliver of sunlight wavered across the foot of the bed. Julian was asleep in the chair in the corner, folded into it like a pile of sticks and rags. Zev turned his head just enough to watch him.

After a few minutes, Julian blinked his eyes open and then uncoiled all at once and nearly fell out of the chair. "Hey! You're awake! Do they know you're awake? Why didn't you say anything? Can you talk? Do you know who I am?"

"I know who you are, dipshit," Zev croaked. He tried not to smile. It hurt his face.

"Wow, you sound terrible. Water?"

He had more water, which was exhausting, and then lay back down flat while Julian told him about driving down to Maryland with TJ and the argument they'd had over how long you were supposed to rest cookie dough and how much AC/DC he'd been forced to listen to.

"Like, I don't even know, he says I'm too young to understand it, but he was two when that song came out! I made a cooking video with him on YouTube. All his subs love me. He's mad 'cause I'm cooler than he is."

Zev had almost drifted back to sleep listening to him when a doctor came in and ejected Julian from the room for an examination. She checked Zev's eye and the dressing and gave him the tally of his injuries. Burns over the right side of his face, likely to scar, concussion, cracked ribs, dislocated shoulder, orbital fracture.

"That's your eye socket," she added. "And it's not surprising, given the impact. The fracture will heal. There was substantial damage to your retina. We won't know about your sight for a few weeks yet. Keep the dressing on. You could compound the damage if you try to use the eye too soon." She paused. "I can send your guest home if you want me to. You do need to rest."

"He's restful."

"Well, you did just come from a war zone."

She left, and Julian returned. "They put your stuff in a bag in the closet," he said. "You kept the shoelace."

"I'd just read it before we headed out of camp."

"What happened?"

Zev took a breath and then decided he wasn't up to talking that much yet. He shook his head a very little bit. "You should be in class," he said instead.

He fell asleep to the sound of Julian listing all the reasons why he shouldn't be in class, explaining why the amount of tuition charged by even state colleges was criminal, and how this would lead to the downfall of America and probably the rest of the world and a hostile takeover by dolphins. He might've already been asleep for the last part. It was hard to tell.

~~*

Eventually, Julian had to go back to school. TJ and Felipe had work, and so Zev was able to leave the hospital quietly when the doc okayed him. He took the train, arrived back at Beni's apartment, and slept for six solid hours on the floor because he was too tired to move Julian's textbooks off the couch.

He woke up with Julian looming over him, worried eyes, a dripping umbrella in one hand. "I would've picked you up," Julian said.

"I'm fine."

"I'll get pizza," Julian said, turned abruptly, and marched out the door.

Zev blinked after him.

He got back in record time, slapped the box on the table, and went to change out of his wet clothes. When he returned, he stood with his hands twisted awkwardly into his sleeves. "I didn't know you'd be back so soon. I was going to fix things up. Clean or something."

"It's fine like it is."

"You left pretty fast before."

"Not because of the place," Zev said.

Julian looked down at the floor.

"And not because of you, okay? Sit down and eat."

Julian shuffled over to the table. They ate off of paper plates. The pizza grease stained them in uneven blotches like a map of unknown lands. Afterward, Julian cleaned up the mess and then cleared off the couch to unfold it.

"I changed the sheets yesterday," he said.

They both looked toward the bedroom. Zev could see where dust had gathered on the floor in front of the door in the time he'd been gone. "Fine by me," he said.

It wasn't much past nine, but Zev's body had developed an inexhaustible appetite for sleep. He was between the sheets half an hour later, watching while Julian poured over a biology textbook at the kitchen table.

"I hated that stuff in school," Zev said. "Physics made way more sense."

"Physics sucks," Julian said, without looking up. "It makes it seem like the universe plays by the rules when really it's just this big ball of entropy and anarchy and chaos."

"I like rules."

"Is that why you joined the Navy?"

"I joined because I needed the money and I like the water."

Julian wandered over, book in hand, and flopped down next to him on the bed. "You didn't know you were going to be a SEAL?"

"Nah. I just wanted a job."

"So you didn't always have your life together?"

Zev would've laughed, but he knew it'd hurt his ribs. "I've never had my life together."

"Seems like it from here."

"I'm the one who's supposed to be half blind, not you."

Julian sighed and inched closer. He dropped his head to his folded arms, shoulder pressed to Zev's hip. Zev lifted a hand and let it hover over the back of Julian's neck. Julian made a soft noise and bent his head further, like a plea for touch. Zev stroked down his neck and let his hand rest at the base, fingers just inside the loose neck of his T-shirt. He could feel the hitch of Julian's breath.

Julian snaked one arm out and caught hold of his elbow. "I worried all the time when you were gone."

"They won't put me back in the field after this. Desk job, maybe."

"You'll hate that, won't you?"

"Probably."

"I'm sorry. Except not. TJ called and said you were hurt and not even conscious yet, and I know I barely know you, but I want to."

Zev rubbed over the tight muscles at the base of his neck and felt his own start to ease, too. "There's time," he said.

Later that night, they lay close under the covers. Zev could hear Julian's breath and the pop of his neck as he twisted it from one side to the other.

"I saw a guy for a couple weeks while you were gone," Julian said.

"How'd that go?"

"You're not mad?"

"I don't run your life."

Julian scooted closer. His foot touched Zev's calf. "It was okay. He felt sorry for me, though. When I told him some of the stuff that happened. I don't want people feeling sorry for me. I'm doing fine."

"I get that."

"Yeah. I know you do."

~~*

Zev spent a morose three weeks walking the neighborhood around Beni's apartment with the dressing taped in place and the temptation to tear it off steadily growing. He tapered off the painkillers. His ribs no longer felt like they were stabbing him when he took a deep breath. His constant headache faded and finally disappeared. He could use his arm more or less normally.

The burns on the lower half of his face were pink and tender, and he had to wear a scarf over them against the bitter wind outside. The doctors said they would scar, but not as badly as they'd first thought.

He'd had two visits from a psychiatrist while he was still in the hospital and had been encouraged to set up further appointments, which he had no intention of doing. Beni's apartment, though boring, was at least safe from rogue shrinks.

It was not safe from Julian, who was in some ways worse and much more persistent. Also, harder to avoid, given that they lived together, ate together, and slept side-by-side on the now-sagging fold-out couch.

"Pasta for dinner?" Julian said, as he slammed through the door with his backpack over his shoulder, a grocery bag in his arms, and a rush of cold air trailing him up the stairwell.

"I don't know, can we have it without the interrogation this time? More salt, fewer questions?"

"How am I supposed to find out anything about you if I don't ask? You're not volunteering anything on your own."

"Why do you think that is?"

Julian dropped his bag and left his scarf and coat piled on top of it. "Because you're a manly man who only talks about manly things, like—No, wait, war is pretty manly. So maybe it's because you're worried I won't like you anymore if you talk about the stuff you've done."

"Or maybe it's because most of the stuff I've done is classified."

"Did you topple small governments? Can you topple ours and set me up as dictator for life?"

"That doesn't sound very democratic, Mr. President."

"Do you want turkey meatballs with this?"

"Who the hell makes meatballs out of turkey?"

Julian turned around and gave him a look over the tops of his glasses. "The guy making you dinner makes meatballs out of turkey and it is delicious and nutritious. Your line here is 'yes, please, thank you'."

"Yes, please. Thank you. Sir."

"Good. You'll like them, I swear. It's a *Splendid Table* recipe."

"Of course you listen to public radio."

"I grew up on *Car Talk*. It was the fixed point in an uncertain universe. I can't believe there's no new episodes anymore. I'm still in mourning."

"Did you learn anything about cars?"

"I don't even know how to drive. Come and chop garlic."

Zev came and chopped garlic. The meatballs had dried cranberries in them, but somehow they were good anyway. After dinner, they set up Zev's Afghan chessboard, which had been shipped home with the rest of his things a week or so after he got out of the hospital. He lost, as usual.

Julian surveyed the board and scrubbed both hands through his hair. "How are you not even getting any better? I don't get it. You're like the opposite of a prodigy. And you plan military operations!"

"Military operations are nothing like chess. In chess, you know all the pieces and you know how they move, and you're operating in a fixed area. There's no improvisation. Nothing unexpected."

"Fine. What if it was a military operation? How would it go in real life?"

Zev looked at the board. He set up all the pieces again and then grabbed a paperclip off the coffee table and gave it to one of the pawns in the front line.

"What's that?"

"It's an RPG." He moved it in an arc across the board and took out Julian's king. "Bang. You're dead. Game over."

Julian frowned at him for a second. "Are they really that accurate? What about all the guys in the way?"

"Okay. Fair point." Zev put the king back and took out four pawns instead, leaving the king, queen, and bishops exposed.

"But now my guys can fight back, right? What can they do? Do I have RPGs?"

"Automatic weapons. Smoke grenades." Zev's mind was drifting inevitably back toward the last ambush, the one that might have cost him his eye, and the one before that. The one where he'd lost Tom.

"What are smoke grenades for?"

"They cloud the air. It's much harder to hit what you can't see."

"Okay, okay." Julian hunched over the board with an expression of fierce concentration.

Zev moved all of his pieces to the left side of the board.

"Hey, wait! It's my turn."

"You don't take turns in combat."

"Don't I get any time to think?"

"No. No time. And your guys are getting shot at." Zev knocked down a couple of Julian's pawns. "People are dying while you think. Better hurry it up."

Julian spammed the far side of the board with RPGs, probably more than he could reasonably have, but Zev didn't complain. He knocked over a few of his own people, including the king, who had gotten a paperclip right to the head.

"So I win anyway?" Julian said, wary.

"You think we stop fighting if someone kills our team leader?"

"No," Julian said quietly. "So what's next? You're outnumbered."

"Air support. Cobras with Hellfire missiles." He shrugged. "But probably you heard them coming and fucked off somewhere."

"So no one wins."

"Welcome to modern military strategy."

"I like chess better."

"Can't really blame you."

Julian set up the pieces again. He moved slowly and turned each piece over, fingertips rubbing over sharp metal and rough stone. "Which one's you?" he asked. "In this last mission. Which piece were you?"

"The king."

"So you got all your pawns out, but you almost died."

"If anyone's going to get hurt, it should be me. I'm responsible for them."

"But that's not always how it works."

Zev swallowed. "No. Everyone runs the same risks. You can't protect people. Not really."

Julian leaned across the chessboard and kissed him. His hands on Zev's face still smelled like garlic, and his proximity was comforting after so many nights spent sleeping in the same bed. Zev pulled him close, and Julian folded his arms around Zev's shoulders.

"I'm sorry," he said. "I'm sorry your friends died. I'm glad you didn't, even if you're not."

"I'm not sorry I didn't die."

"You kind of seem like it sometimes," Julian said quietly. "It scares me."

Zev closed his eyes. Maybe he'd been wrong about the psychiatric appointments. He'd thought it was better not to be so angry all the time, but this might be worse.

Julian didn't try to kiss him again. He eased around to sit by Zev's side in unprecedented silence. Zev put an arm around him and concentrated on the places where their bodies touched, the warmth, Julian's pointy bones and awkward angles.

"Do you want me to move out?" Julian said, after a minute or two. "Because I probably have enough money, maybe. If I got some roommates."

"I don't want you to move out. If anyone's leaving, it should be me. Beni wouldn't have kicked you out."

"He wouldn't have kicked you out either. He was your brother."

"He did kick me out. The night before I left for training, he threw a tomato at my head and said if I was really leaving I shouldn't come back." Zev smiled. "I never heard him raise his voice to anyone but me."

"You are really good at being infuriating."

"Thanks."

"But you did come back."

"Of course I did. He was my brother. So no one's getting kicked out, okay?"

"Okay."

Zev listened to the hum of the fridge. Julian twisted himself up smaller somehow and put his head on Zev's shoulder.

"We should get a bed," Zev said.

"One a dead guy hasn't slept in?"

Zev smiled. He'd missed a number of things about Julian that had surprised him, and his tactless honesty was one of them. "Yeah. One of those.

Tomorrow. When you get out of Political Bullshit 101 or whatever that class is."

"It's actually Advanced Political Bullshit. And no one numbers classes anymore, Grandpa."

Zev pinched his ear. Julian grabbed a pillow from the couch and hit him in the back of the head with it.

~~*

The next morning, he completed his fifth circuit of the block—walking, since he wasn't allowed to run because of the eye—and dug in his pocket for his keys. Someone called his name and he looked around to see Beni's rabbi hurrying toward him.

He hit an icy patch on the sidewalk, and Zev took his arm to brace him.

"You okay?"

"Yes, yes, fine. Thank you." He looked Zev over and then took a piece of paper from his pocket. "I imagine you're not okay. Don't worry. I won't ask. This is all the information I could find on your family in Israel."

Zev looked at the paper. Two addresses written under the list of names. Three names crossed out. "They're dead?" he asked.

"I don't know. I couldn't keep going without contacting the ones I could find an address for and, well. That seemed like something you should do."

"Yeah." Zev stared down at the paper a second longer and then folded it. "This was... Beni would've appreciated it."

The rabbi smiled a little. "But you don't?"

"I didn't mean that."

"What did you mean?" the rabbi asked, not offended, simply curious.

Zev made himself meet the rabbi's eyes. "I guess I meant his gratitude's worth more than mine."

"Even though he's gone?"

"Yeah. Even though."

"I'll take yours anyway, if it's on offer."

"Thank you," Zev said, and shook his hand.

"You're welcome." He turned to go.

"Hey," Zev said. "Is it bad manners to ask for two favors back to back?"

"I'm happy to help if I can."

Zev let out a slow breath that turned to steam in the cold air. "I think I should talk to someone. A shrink. A psychiatrist. I don't want someone from the Navy. You know anyone?"

"I can get you a few names."

"Thanks. I owe you."

The rabbi shook his head and smiled. "Doesn't work like that."

"Yeah. That's what Beni always tried to tell me."

Down the street, he heard someone singing "Feliz Navidad," badly. He looked past the rabbi's shoulder and saw Felipe and TJ coming toward him, waving like madmen. Zev groaned.

"It's fucking March. Why are all my friends assholes?"

"Birds of a feather," TJ said, and noogied him so hard it felt like his knuckles drilled an inch down into Zev's skull.

Felipe caught up with him, along with Rush, and Tom and Tina's oldest son, Luke. Zev froze at the sight of him.

"Julian called," TJ said. "Said you were getting a new mattress and you'd probably try to get rid of the old one yourself if we didn't help, so we're helping. Who's this?"

"Beni's rabbi."

"Does he have a name?" TJ said.

He did. Zev had no idea what it was.

"David Brafman," the rabbi said, with an amused glance at Zev.

Handshakes all round, and then Brafman took off and left Zev with his friends, who were doing their best to look innocent. They definitely had more than heavy lifting planned.

"They'll take the old one away when they deliver the new one," Zev said. "No helping necessary."

"We're here now," Felipe said cheerfully, grabbed his keys from him, and let everyone into the building.

TJ and Luke followed him. Rush hung back. "I was around when Felipe got the call," he said. "I just wanted to come along and say thank you."

Zev shook his head. "Nothing to say thank you for. We were all just doing our jobs."

Rush was looking at Zev's bad eye, still covered in gauze. "You told me to stay in the vehicle. It could've been me out there. It should've been me."

"I was lead. It was my decision, and it was the right one. If it'd been you instead of me, who would've patched us up while we waited for CASEVAC? Don't do this, Doc. It was my call, and I don't regret it."

"Even if you lose the eye?"

"Even if."

Rush stared at him for a second and then set his jaw and gave one short nod. "Okay. If we're hauling furniture for you, you should get us pizza."

"It's eight in the morning."

"Probably won't be by the time we get it done. And has anyone thought about where we're going to dump it? Pretty sure you can't leave it out with the trash."

By the time Zev had swapped his sweatpants for jeans and changed the dressing on his eye, they'd gotten the mattress stuck halfway down the stairs. Zev sat down on the top step and watched until Luke flung himself bodily at the top end in an effort to force it.

He played varsity football and he wasn't a small kid, but the mattress just deflected the force he put into the tackle and bounced him back. If Zev hadn't caught him, he would've had an uncomfortable landing.

"Why don't you take a break?" Zev said. "Let the brain trust down there work it out."

Luke nodded. He sat on the step next to Zev, arms folded around his knees, not looking at him.

"You don't have to be here," Zev said. "I can take you home if you want. Or call your mom."

"No, I wanted to come."

They listened to TJ and Felipe and Rush argue about angles and rotation and bungee cords for securing it to the truck once they got it outside. If they got it outside.

"My mom said they want to give you a medal," Luke said, fast, all the words running together. "For what you did when you were over there with my dad. Is that true?"

"Yeah, that's true."

"But you don't want it?"

"I was just doing my job. Same as everyone else."

"TJ said they'll talk about what happened at the ceremony. Some, at least. More than they told us."

Zev nodded. Part of the reason for the closed ceremony was operational security.

"So if you accepted it and invited me and Mom..." Luke looked down at his feet.

And it became clear why TJ and Felipe were here, clear why they'd brought Luke, and clear that they'd won before they even arrived. Zev nodded and squeezed Luke's shoulder once. "I'll put you on the guest list."

Later that day, Felipe and Zev watched TJ, Rush, and Luke hoist the mattress down off the top of truck where it had been precariously secured for their trip to the recycling center. Luke was still growing and almost too short to reach, up on his toes to try to do his fair share.

"You're all assholes," Zev said.

"Luke talked to you?"

"Like I said. Assholes."

"It was his idea, man. Smart kid."

"Just like his dad."

TJ, Rush, and Luke all whooped as they flung the mattress onto a pile of other sad discards. Fist bumps and high fives all around.

"Are you and Julian together?" Felipe asked.

"Hell if I know."

"You should be. He's good for you."

"I don't think Naval Intelligence is going to feel the same way."

"Don't tell them."

"He won't be happy keeping it quiet."

"You don't have to keep it quiet forever. Just give yourself a break for once, Z. Take some time. Take a trip. Maybe to a country where no one wants to kill you. When do you get that thing off your eye?"

"This afternoon."

"You want company?"

"Rather do it alone."

"You're never alone. We've always got your back."

Zev smiled, ostensibly at the victory dance currently being performed around the pile of fallen mattresses. "Shut up, you're embarrassing yourself," he said.

~~*

He didn't go alone, as it turned out, because Julian met him at the hospital and refused to be sent away.

"You have class," Zev said. "I know you have class because I scheduled this thing on purpose so you'd be in class."

"Canceled. The professor ran away to Bermuda."

"Liar."

"Maybe it was Cuba. I forget. It definitely had a U in it. Uzbekistan?"

"You can stay in the waiting room. You're not coming in with me."

The doctor sat him on an exam table and removed the dressing. He clipped out the few remaining stitches. "Open," he said, and shone a light into Zev's eye.

Zev closed it again almost immediately and then forced it open. The light felt like an ice pick being shoved directly into his brain, but at least he could see it. He'd been afraid he'd open his eye finally and find that half of his vision just as dark as it had been with the dressing in place.

"There's less damage to the retina than I'd expected. How's the vision?"

Without the light blinding him, Zev looked slowly around the room, good eye covered. He could see shapes and colors, not much more. "Blurry," he said.

"How many fingers am I holding up?"

"Seventeen."

"Sometimes I question my decision to join the Navy," the doctor said. "You're all frustrated comics."

"Maybe four?"

"Try two. But you could've done worse. Honestly, this is better than I was expecting." He tossed Zev a cardboard box containing a black eye patch. "One hour on, one hour off. No bright lights, that includes sunlight. Don't cheat, and don't strain your eyes. You'll just delay your recovery. I'll see you again in two weeks."

Zev put it on before he went back out to the waiting room. Julian stood right behind him while he made the next appointment with the receptionist, nearly bouncing with impatience.

"Well, how is it? Can you see? Are you blind? Are you gonna look like a pirate forever? Did he take out your eyeball while you were in there? Come on, talk!"

"Let's buy a mattress."

"Zev!"

He managed to keep a straight face all the way to car. Julian pinned him against the driver's side door when they got there, both hands on his shoulders. Zev wondered how it looked from the outside, if it looked as intimate as it felt. He wanted to kiss him.

"I can see, but it's blurry," he said. "Doc says wear this thing and come back in two weeks. Less retinal damage than he thought."

Julian's face lit up, and he hugged Zev hard enough to make various still-healing parts of him protest. "That's great! Can I see it? Did he take the rest of the stitches out?"

"No sunlight, so not till we get inside, and yes, he did. I don't look any less like Frankenstein's monster though."

"You look fine. You look good," Julian said, with a stubborn set to his jaw that made any argument useless.

It wasn't true. Zev knew that, and if he hadn't, the subtle recoil of the salesman at the mattress store would've told him. The burns would look better when they finished healing, but they'd never look good. Sometimes it bothered him, though he'd never say that out loud to anyone. Sometimes he preferred having some outward sign of his past.

He bought a new bed frame as well as the mattress and walked out of the store reeling. "That's the most money I've ever spent in one place," he said.

"But we're getting it today! Hey, we should get sheets. And champagne."

"Unless I missed something important, like a year, you're still not old enough to drink."

"I've been old enough to drink since I was twelve."

"I'm sure your liver loves you. We'll get sheets."

They got sheets. Zev bought blue striped ones. Julian lobbied for leopard print and then bought them with his own money when Zev refused.

"Those aren't going near my bed," Zev told him.

"It's our bed, so I get a fifty-percent say in all sheet related decisions."

"They're going to have a nasty encounter with a bottle of bleach."

"I can buy more. I got promoted at work. I'm assistant manager of hotdog orgies now," Julian said.

"For real?"

Julian shrugged. "It's not like it's a big deal. They just pay me a little more."

Zev was torn between kissing him and punching his shoulder and making some smartass comment, but living with Julian's occasionally painful honesty these past weeks made him see another option. "I'm proud of you," he said.

Julian peered down at him, glasses sliding toward the tip of his nose. "You are?"

"Yeah."

"Enough to buy me champagne to celebrate?"

"How about cake?"

"Oh, cake! Yeah! Can we get them to write assistant manager of hotdog orgies on it?"

"If they won't do it, we can do it ourselves."

They had to do it themselves in the end. The lead time on decorated cakes at the grocery store was three days. They bought little tubes of icing, and Julian squeezed out the letters along with a number of oblong pink things that might or might not have been hotdogs. He took a picture and sent it to all his coworkers.

"You're gonna get fired," Zev told him.

"Are you kidding? I'm going to be employee of the month. I'll be Mr. March in the hotdog orgy calendar."

"I desperately hope that's not true."

Julian squirted icing at him. It landed in a large pink blob in the center of his chest. Zev went after him with the purple and got it in his hair. It blended in with fading purple of his last dye job, and he got it all over his fingers trying to pull bits of it out. He turned toward Zev and wiped both hands down his shirt front before he could step back.

Zev picked up the tub of white frosting. Julian's eyes widened, and he ran. Not fast enough. Zev got it on his neck and then down the back of his shirt, Julian squirming to get away the whole time. They fell onto the couch.

The frosting can wedged awkwardly between them and hit Zev in the ribs. He grunted and tossed it across the room. All of this was an excuse. He hadn't known he'd needed one until this second, when he finally had Julian spread out under him, looking hopeful and uncertain.

Zev kissed him. They inched backward until they were lying fully on the couch, Julian's long legs spread and Zev settled between them.

"I thought we'd do this in bed," Julian said.

"We're covered in frosting, and the sheets are clean. Besides, we got this far on the couch."

"Right. Better finish here. And then again in the shower. And then in the bed."

"Stop talking for two seconds," Zev said, but he didn't mean it.

The next kiss silenced Julian all the same. Zev could feel how hard he was already and rubbed a hand over the hot bulge in his jeans. Julian moaned and pressed up into the touch.

Zev stroked him and popped the button of his jeans open. He looked down at Julian's closed eyes and flushed cheeks. "When's the last time you did this?"

"Coffee shop asshole boss. Never got this far with the other guy. Zev, come on. Don't stop, please don't stop."

Zev unzipped him and tugged at his jeans. Julian wriggled out of them and kicked them to the floor and ground up hard in a way that finally brought home to Zev how long it had been for him as well. A lot longer than a few months. He slid off to the side a few inches and yanked down Julian's boxers to get a hand wrapped around him.

Steady strokes, palm wet already with pre-come, Julian squirming under him and asking for more. Zev bit his own lip and watched the flick of Julian's eyes behind closed lids. He bent and kissed him, softly at first, and then with a hand tight in his hair and his tongue pushing into his mouth.

Julian arched up hard against him and tried to say something as he came, but the words were muffled. He wrapped both arms around Zev's neck and held onto him, panting.

"You want me to blow you?" he said after a few seconds. "I'm really good at it."

"Don't believe you. I don't think you can stop talking that long."

For once, Julian didn't reply. He flipped Zev over and slid down between his legs, unzipped him and got his cock free, just enough parting of clothes as was necessary to get it in his mouth. His tongue slid over the head and up the underside. His lips followed and took him deeper, until Julian had swallowed him nearly down to the base.

Most of Zev's previous blowjobs had either been from women or done in a rush and looking over his shoulder. Julian's wet lips and open eyes locked with his almost pushed him over the edge too fast. All the lamps lit and no need to hide, all the time in the world. After a few seconds, his own eyes slid inevitably shut as the sensation swallowed him up. He grabbed behind him at the arm of the couch and fought not to clutch Julian's hair. He settled for a grip on his shoulder, maybe too tight as he lost himself in heat and suction. He came silently, with his mouth open, and fell back onto the couch so hard he jarred his head.

Julian crawled up his body and kissed him and kissed him with no apparent plans to stop. He lowered himself down against Zev with a mumbled question about the integrity of his ribs. Zev pulled him close.

"S'fine," he said. "Good. Wow."

"Shower," Julian said.

"Go ahead. I'm not moving."

Julian settled down, head on his shoulder. "Can I come to your medal thing?"

"Yeah. You're on the guest list. They're running a background check on you."

"I am not now nor have I ever been a member of the Communist party."

"Glad to hear it," Zev mumbled, about thirty seconds away from sleep.

"Are you gonna tell them I'm your boyfriend?"

"No. Not at the ceremony."

"Why not?" Julian asked, but he sounded more curious than confrontational, which was a relief.

"The medal's for everyone who was there that day. Or it should be. It's not for me. I'm not going to distract anyone from that with my personal life."

Julian was quiet for a few seconds. "I am pretty distracting," he said.

Zev smiled and kissed the top of his head. "Yeah."

"We've been living together for like a month. Your friends are going to figure it out."

"Felipe knows."

"Oh," Julian said softly. "Really?"

"He thinks you're good for me. Don't know what gave him that idea."

"Jerk," Julian said, through a yawn.

"I think I'm going to leave the Navy."

"You should join the Secret Service," Julian mumbled against his neck. "So you can protect me when I'm president."

"Sure. I'll get right on that."

Zev pushed his patch up and stared at the ceiling with both eyes open. The world was already clearer than it had been.

Coffee Boy
AUSTIN CHANT

CHAPTER ONE

Kieran really thought that a political campaign office would involve a fancy building. A stern exterior. Heavy security. Something intimidating, or at least austere.

Nope. Heidi White's campaign office is on the top floor of a completely average commercial building. The elevator is slow, the floor is plasticky, and fluorescent lights flicker out of a speckled gray ceiling. The sign on the office door is crooked, and inside there's a jumble of cramped desks and cramped people mixed in with printers and filing cabinets. The windows are open, letting in a trickle of summer breeze, but it's still agonizingly hot.

Kieran stands in the door for a long moment, his work-appropriate satchel clasped under his arm, feeling altogether more anxious than he wanted to. His pronoun pin gleams on the lapel of a shirt he neglected to iron, and his binder's already sticky with sweat on the inside. A few people turn to look at him.

Kieran clears his throat and leans against the door. "Excuse me? I'm the new intern?"

A middle-aged white lady sitting at the desk nearest to Kieran gives him a benevolent smile. "Oh, that's right! I forgot we were getting someone new. I'm Marie. Finances."

"Kieran." He stretches across her desk to shake her hand, then settles stiffly back against the door. "Uh, I don't know about finances, but I'm excited to get started." And if he says it often enough, maybe it'll be true. "Nice to meet you."

Marie nods, smiling. "You'll want to talk to Seth, dear. He's in his office."

"Thanks," Kieran says. A few people are still staring at him, but not enough that he feels like introducing himself to the room at large. "Is Marcus here? I thought I was supposed to see Marcus."

Marie shakes her head. "No, no, Marcus won't be in until later. Seth handles everything when he's not here."

"Okay." *Not* okay. Kieran feels his insides freezing a little. Bad enough that Marcus got him into this whole internship situation—now he's not even around to handle the introductions? Kieran swallows down his nerves and scans the room, catching sight of the one other door. "Is that Seth's office?" he asks, starting toward it.

Marie tuts and waves him back. "Now, wait a minute. He's on the phone. You don't want to interrupt Seth when he's on the phone!" She chuckles, and a few people nearby laugh uncomfortably. "Have a seat. He'll be out soon."

There's really nowhere to sit except at a chair across from Marie's desk, like he's settling in for a consultation. Kieran sits, unwillingly. He's hoping Marie will go back to work and let him fade into the background, but she keeps watching him. He smiles vaguely and averts his eyes.

But she leans forward anyway, clearly intent on engaging him. "Now, Kieran, you *are* the administrative intern, aren't you?"

"That's me."

"Oh, that's so funny." Marie beams. "Marcus thought you were a *boy*." She winks, like they're sharing a joke. When Kieran stiffens and stares at her, the smile slowly slides off her face. "I'm sorry. I'm sure it was just a mistake—"

"He wasn't wrong," Kieran snaps.

He waits for some kind of clarity to dawn on Marie, but she just looks more and more confused. He feels himself blushing. "I'm a guy," he says, loudly. "Thanks."

"I'm sorry," Marie repeats, bafflement written all over her face. She's studying him. Like she just can't make the pieces fit.

Kieran grips his knees. Trust Marcus to promise him a *trans-friendly workplace* and not even bother to find out if anyone around him is trans-friendly.

"It's your hair," Marie says finally, with hopeful satisfaction. "I'm just not used to seeing such long hair on boys—"

"Yeah. I get it." Even to his own ears, it sounds sharp and mean. Kieran can feel people turning to look at them, probably as bewildered as Marie, and he needs to get out of this room. He squares his shoulders, gets up, and stalks over to Seth's door. He ignores Marie's hurried protest and knocks, hard.

Because honestly, fuck this guy's phone call.

It feels like approximately forever as he stands with his back turned to the entire office, but the door finally opens. And a tall, nasty-looking dude—Seth, presumably—glares down at Kieran from inside the other room. He has a landline phone pressed to his ear, the cord stretching away toward a desk across the room.

Kieran feels an internal shriveling when Seth looks at him, and if he were a lesser man, he'd clutch his satchel to his chest to put a barrier between them. But Kieran is not a lesser man, so he slings his satchel over his shoulder and adopts a presumptuous smile. "Morning," he says. "Kieran Mullur. New intern." He looks past Seth to see three desks and a couple of table fans working overtime. Perfect. "Mind if I put my stuff down in here?"

The look on Seth's face says that he does mind, but he jerks his head angrily toward the middle desk and retreats from the door.

Kieran scoots inside and shuts the door with a shudder of relief. Okay. Not his best first impression ever, but no one's ever pegged him for the friendly type.

At least this office is quiet. Bigger and better aerated than the other room. One desk—Kieran's, presumably—is barren; Seth's is painfully neat, with stacks of paperwork separated by colored tabs, matching sets of pens and highlighters arranged in precise rows, everything squared and symmetrical. The third desk has stickers stuck all down one side and a shiny desktop computer somewhat marred by a peeling "Hello, my name is MARCUS" label on the back of the monitor. Typical Marcus.

When his heart has stopped pounding, Kieran crosses the room and sinks gratefully into the chair at his new desk.

Although it might not be his desk for long, if Seth kills him.

Seth, luckily, looks like he's too busy tearing somebody to shreds over the phone to spare much malice for Kieran. His thin mouth is bunched up in a frown. Every time he stops to listen to whatever the caller is saying, his nose wrinkles contemptuously. He's keeping his voice down, but Kieran catches something about "funding that was promised to us" and "pulling all mention of your business from our campaign materials".

Kieran thinks he looks kind of like a Boy Scout—that straight-laced, proper, honest look—but also kind of like a snake. He has hair trimmed short and blunt, long on top but slicked down, and in spite of the heat he's wearing in a crisp blazer. The only part of his look that seems out of place is a single steel stud in his right ear, and even that is vaguely intimidating.

Awesome.

Seth smacks the phone down in its cradle, and Kieran jumps in spite of himself. "So," Seth says. He swivels toward Kieran in his chair and stands up, offering his hand without approaching Kieran's desk. Kieran has to scramble out of his chair and across the room to shake it, while Seth stares imperiously down at him.

Kieran isn't surprised to find Seth's handshake firm and unforgiving. "Hi," Kieran says, forcing a smile. "Sorry for, um, barging in. I was expecting Marcus." Which is only half a lie.

Seth raises his eyebrows. "Marcus mentioned that he knew you. From the university?"

"Yeah. He taught a bunch of my classes." Kieran does his best to sound calm, smooth, anything but as shaky as he feels. "So—who're you? The manager?"

"Marcus is the manager," Seth says, like Kieran should have known. Which probably falls into the category of "things Marcus could've bothered to tell Kieran ahead of time". "I'm Seth Harker, the senior campaign manager."

The way he says *senior* makes it sounds like he has power over Kieran's life and death. "Nice to meet you. Is, um, is Marcus going to be here?"

"He had a family engagement. Have a seat, and we'll talk through your responsibilities."

"Okay." Kieran scrunches himself into the chair in front of Seth's desk.

Seth sits across from him, studying Kieran with an awkward level of scrutiny. "What is that button?" he asks.

The pronoun pin. Kieran feels a sharp blush rise in his face again. He's not ashamed of needing to wear it—he's annoyed that he has to. "My pronouns," he says, as casually as he can. "I like to wear it when I meet new people."

Seth gives a mere nod. "I see. As a reminder?"

Kieran flips his thick, curly hair angrily over one shoulder. "Well, most people make the wrong assumption when they meet me."

"Marcus has been very specific in calling you 'he' whenever he mentioned the new intern," Seth says, "so hopefully there won't be any room for wrong assumptions."

Crisp and cool. Like it isn't an issue at all. Kieran lets out a breath, startled and relieved and annoyed. Because it *is* an issue, but at least he's not going to have to repeat the conversation he had with Marie. "Great. You might wanna clear that up with the rest of the office."

Seth raises an eyebrow. "Why? Did something happen?"

Kieran is *not* going to fall into the trap of complaining about his coworkers on his first day. "No. It's fine. I just—I didn't get the impression that they knew."

"I see." Seth actually turns and scribbles something down on a pad of paper in front of him. Kieran can't imagine what he's writing. "Remind everyone in the office that new intern is a dude"? Or, probably more likely, "Fire whiny trans guy at earliest opportunity".

Seth turns back to him. "Let me know if you have any problems. Now—Marcus said that he knew you before you applied for the internship. He was impressed with your undergraduate coursework."

More like Marcus is a bleeding-heart Ph.D. candidate who thinks all trans people are brave and inspiring, and he'd been willing to overlook Kieran's often lackluster college coursework and pretend it was a sign that Kieran wasn't being challenged enough by the material. Which is why Kieran has the internship. "Yeah, he thought I was okay." Kieran shrugs. "Of course, I'm guessing I'll probably do less campaign strategizing and more... getting coffee and making copies?"

Seth almost smiles. It's a flicker at the corner of his thin little mouth. "You aren't wrong. But we need you for more than that. This is a new branch of Senator White's campaign, and things are just starting to get off the ground. You'll be assisting

Marcus with whatever he needs to keep us organized, and taking on whatever additional duties we might need an extra hand with. Especially social media and the new campaign website—Marcus said you have some skills in that area, and we're lacking staff who have digital experience."

Kieran translates that to "everyone who works here is old". "Uh, yeah. I can help with that."

Seth nods approvingly. "I think you'll find the experience rewarding. Our internship program offers you a chance to learn the types of skills it takes to run a campaign. Working on our digital outreach puts you at the intersection of a lot of departments. It might help you see what kind of a real job would suit you."

"A real job?" Kieran laughs in spite of himself. "I have one of those already."

"Oh?"

"Flipping burgers," Kieran says. "It comes with real paychecks and everything."

Seth frowns. "There will be opportunities for advancement here. Paid advancement. *Assuming*, of course, that you fit the position."

Kieran is pretty sure he won't.

~~*

Seth finds a substantial amount of busywork for Kieran to do, which means that Kieran manages to hide in his office for the next two hours before Marcus arrives. That's when things get interesting.

Marcus breezes in wearing a logo T-shirt and the same thick-rimmed, nerdy glasses he always wore when Kieran took his classes in college. Kieran peeks out of the inner office to see Marcus wandering between desks, exchanging personal greetings and chit-chat with every person he passes. He smiles easily at everyone in the office, and everyone smiles back, relaxed—except Seth, who actually stands up at his desk when Marcus walks in, like they're in the goddamn military. Kieran half expects him to salute.

"Good morning!" Marcus beams, though it's half-past two. "Kieran! It's so good to see you again. Seth, I can't believe you're wearing a *blazer* in this weather. Take that thing off. You look like you're frying."

Seth looks away with a huff and sinks back into his chair. He starts unrolling his perfectly crisp cuffs and pulls off his blazer. "I've been getting Kieran set up."

"Good, good, good." Marcus flops into his chair. "I know it's the internship cliché, but everyone's roasting out there. I think a round of iced coffees is in order—Kieran, would you mind getting some?"

"Not at all, sir," Kieran drawls. Marcus winks at him.

"I'll give you the company card," Seth says coolly. "I do track the purchases made on this, just so you're aware."

"Seth!" Marcus chides. "When has an intern ever robbed us on the way to Starbucks?"

Seth purses his lips and doesn't look up from his desk while he hands Kieran the card. From what Kieran has gathered so far, Marcus is actually the one in charge—not least because he's the senator's nephew—but Seth is the power behind the throne, and like the jaded uncle in a Disney movie, he covets Marcus' authority.

Which is why the next thing out of Seth's mouth is so weird. "Marcus, do you want your coffee with caramel?"

"Oh, that would be nice."

Seth fixes Kieran with a look. "It's the Starbucks down the block. Take a right when you exit the building. Call the office if you get turned around. Get twelve sixteen-ounce iced coffees, and get one of them with soy milk and two pumps of caramel syrup."

"Okay," Kieran says, unable to stop himself from smirking. "You must've been the intern before me."

"I was not." Seth glances meaningfully at the door and Kieran gets on his way. He probably shouldn't antagonize one of his superiors on day one.

But who's he kidding? What else would he do?

~~*

Kieran is, briefly, the most popular boy in the office when he comes back with iced coffee and circles around the desks, dropping off icy plastic cups for everyone. It's a good way to let them see his pronoun pin, too, and to firmly introduce himself by name. A couple people still look confused, but they don't say anything.

With the last three coffees in hand—including the very special one with soy milk and caramel—Kieran wanders back into Marcus' office.

Marcus is standing behind Seth's desk, leaning over to study something on his laptop. "I think it's a good start," he's saying, with his usual broad smile. "I like the new angle." And speaking of angles, Seth is angled all away from him, reclining back in his chair in a pose so carefully arranged that it looks, from the doorway, incredibly uncomfortable. Like he couldn't stand to touch Marcus at all. And he's running his fingers around the collar of his shirt like proximity to Marcus makes him sweat. And while Kieran watches, unobserved, Seth rearranges his perfect hair until it's oddly unkempt—and then averts his eyes when Marcus glances at him.

Unfortunately, when he looks away, Seth notices Kieran standing there with three coffees and an inquisitive eyebrow raised and his expression changes to one of steel. "Were you planning on distributing those coffees?"

"Of course," Kieran says. "I just didn't want to interrupt whatever you were looking at. But, uh, it sure looks like you could use a cold drink."

Seth's face colors. "It's hot in here," he says defensively.

"Yeah, that's what I meant."

"We were just looking at the new campaign lawn flyers," Marcus says brightly, straightening up. "Is that my coffee? That was speedy! I think you beat our last intern by at least a minute."

Kieran offers him the caramel coffee and Marcus takes it with a beaming smile. "Now get settled back in and I'll walk you through the systems we use for organizing our mailing list—it'll probably be second nature for a young guy like you!"

Seth has flipped open a hand mirror and is smoothing his hair back into place. He doesn't look up when Kieran places his coffee on the desk; he barely mumbles a *thank you*.

Kieran shakes his head and gets ready for a riveting lesson in campaign administration.

CHAPTER TWO

Jillian calls him up that night, as he's boiling water for ramen. "Hey, you!" she says. "Guess who's a little jerk and didn't answer my texts all day?"

Kieran rolls his eyes at the ceiling, smiling. "I was at work."

"Yes, and I was worried about you. So how was it? Was I right and it was totally fine?"

Kieran pauses, because he hates disappointing Jillian. She's the one who bullies him into doing all the things he should do but doesn't want to—like this internship, for example—and she's his first line of defense against total apathy. It was mostly for her sake that he finally agreed to take the internship, and resigned himself to sticking it out at least long enough that she won't be crushed when he gives up. "Yeah, it was okay."

"*Okay?*" Jillian says. "I need the full story." With her usual optimism, she ignores his silence. "How's Marcus? Still handsome?"

"Ugh, Jill, he's never been handsome."

"You have no taste! I had such a crush on him, back when I was going through my hot professor phase." She waits for him to reply, but Kieran is short a witty answer. He's exhausted. "All right," Jillian says. "I'm coming over and you can tell me *all* about it."

"You don't have to," Kieran says, although he already knows—before he even says it—that Jill's only answer will be to scoff into the phone and hang up. He adds more water to the pan and tosses in a second brick of ramen. Jillian gets hungry when she plays counselor.

They met in college. Kieran was the lonely, angry back-row queer who glared at his professors but never called them out on anything; Jillian was the gorgeous butch who would chew her professors out for failing to mention queer people in their human rights curriculum, who walked around wearing a Bi Pride pin on her bag every day for four years and sneered at anyone who gave her shit for it. And, for the brief but intense period where Kieran was panicking over the revelation that he was gay *and* trans—like, how doomed to failure could he possibly be?—Jillian was his rock.

Well, *is* his rock. Which she proves by stomping up to his door with an enormous jug of sweet tea under her arm, and cooing sympathetically while Kieran complains about his day. "Oh, babe," she says, when he's finished. "I hope it gets better."

"Me too," Kieran says. Mostly for her benefit, because he's a pessimist. "Crazy thing, though. I'm pretty sure Mister *Senior* Campaign Strategist has a thing for Marcus."

"Nice," Jillian says. "See, I'm not the only one!"

Kieran pokes the side of her ramen bowl with his toe. Not enough to make it slosh. Just enough to make her shriek and slap his foot away. "Is that not *weird* to you?"

"Why? Are you saying mean, bitter people can't be queer?" Jillian pats his foot. "Look in the mirror."

Kieran grumbles, draping his arms over his face. "I just don't get it."

"Hey, on the topic of that guy—if he's ready to go to bat for you with your coworkers, that's cool! You should tell him what happened with Marie. He'd probably crack down."

Kieran loves Jillian, but sometimes he wonders which version of the world she lives in. "Yeah, no, I'd rather not start this trainwreck off by ratting out my coworkers. Also, no offense, but I don't trust a cis guy to know his shit when it comes to *educating the office staff*."

She doesn't say anything, which probably means he's being a bitter pill and she's run out of reassuring words for the night. Kieran sighs into his arms. "Sorry. Wanna watch stupid movies?"

"Sure," Jillian says. She squeezes his foot. "Promise me you're not gonna quit tomorrow."

"I promise," Kieran mutters. It's how she used to get him through class when he threatened to drop out. Just one day after the next, till the end of the semester.

He wonders when he'll get to the end of this job.

~~*

In the first month of his internship, Kieran learns five important things:

> A. People who work on political campaigns have ridiculous Starbucks orders and yeah, being the intern means learning them all and balancing twelve cups of coffee on his way back up to the office.

B.   Kieran's duties aren't extremely specific. They're more general, like, "Do everything that Marcus sucks at doing".

C.   Marcus would honestly be better off as a kindergarten teacher or a knitting instructor than as a campaign manager. He is, for starters, the least organized person Kieran has ever met, and he doesn't like bossing his subordinates around. So Kieran is there to organize shit for him, and Seth is there to give orders to the troops. Marcus mostly seems to think his job is raising morale, approving of everyone's work, and making sure they all get enough coffee. He's clearly only employed because he's Heidi White's nephew. Although, to be fair, Kieran is only employed because he was Marcus' favorite student.

D.   Seth is pretty much a cold fish. Which is a shame, because he's kind of hot, and he's the only one in the office who's never screwed up Kieran's pronouns. He calls Kieran "he" with military precision, each time with a careful moment's pause before the word.

E.   Seth isn't as intimidating as everyone else thinks, because he's crushing on their boss.

E is Kieran's favorite point. If he's being entirely honest, half the reason he studied politics in college was because he liked the drama. If it wasn't enough that Seth can't seem to deal with being physically close to Marcus without turning red as a tomato, he also gets distracted any time Marcus comes in to work wearing something sleeveless. And while he stares intensely at anyone else when he's talking to them—like he's daring them to waste a second of his time—when it's Marcus, he gets suddenly quiet and humble and barely makes eye contact.

As disappointed as Kieran is in Seth's taste in men, as annoyed as he is that the other apparently queer guy in the office is smitten with Kieran's boring ex-professor—it *is* pretty entertaining to watch. Plus, Kieran likes the fact that being queer makes him a good sleuth; he's sure that Seth's painfully obvious crush is invisible to all the wide-eyed cis heterosexuals working at this office, but Kieran is pretty old hat at noticing when people aren't straight.

Unfortunately for Seth, Kieran also notices that there's a picture of a smiling woman and a starry-eyed baby sitting on Marcus' desk. "Is that your girlfriend?" Kieran asks.

Marcus beams. "My fiancée, Glenn," he says. "We're getting married in December. After this campaign is finished, one way or another. See my baby girl? Her name is Ashlynn, and you've *never* met a smarter kid."

Kieran casts an eye over at Seth's desk while Marcus rattles on about how his infant gurgles in complete sentences, just like Einstein, and is probably going to grow up to be a genius architect because she *loves* stacking blocks on top of each other. Seth is staring at his laptop with the intensity of a man who is trying so hard to look nonchalant that he can't even see what's in front of him. His face is an entertaining shade of pink.

Ouch, Kieran thinks. The next day, he gets Seth an extra pump of peppermint in his mocha in sympathy. Then he's circling around the office to give everyone their ridiculous, expensive coffee, when Seth emerges from Marcus' office, looking—as usual—kind of pissy.

"Kieran," he says. "You should bring Marcus his coffee first."

Some idiot part of Kieran's brain keeps thinking that Seth is *joking* about being a) this far up his own ass or b) this far up Marcus' ass, so his automatic response is to laugh.

Then he looks at Seth's face and realizes it's never a joke with this guy. Seth is making needle eyes at him. The part of Kieran that should simper and obey like a good little office rat is also absent today—and every day—so he shrugs at the needle eyes and says, "Okay, Seth. Mind if I give you *your* coffee on the way in to see Marcus? Or would that be inappropriate?"

"Go ahead," Seth says icily. He accepts his triple-shot peppermint mocha with extra peppermint.

Kieran leans in and plonks Marcus' drink on his desk. "Sorry to keep you waiting, Your Highness."

Marcus smiles benevolently. "You don't have to serve me first, Kieran. Everyone's working hard."

Everyone except you, Kieran thinks. He goes back out to give everyone else their coffee. Seth is hovering in the doorway, frowning faintly as he sips his drink. "This tastes sweeter than usual," he says. "Are you sure this is the right order?"

Kieran regrets ever feeling sorry for him. "I think so. Might've ordered a hundred shots of syrup in that one instead of ninety-nine."

Marie giggles. "Watch out, Seth! She's got a mouth on her."

Kieran stiffens, but Marie doesn't seem to notice. Neither does anyone else, for that matter. Kieran's still handing out coffees, and he can feel the appropriate timeframe for him to correct Marie rapidly closing, but he can't bring himself to say something. For all that he has such a mouth on him, his throat closes up.

"*He's*," Seth says, loudly. "*Him*."

Kieran doesn't look around, but he hears Marie's startled acknowledgement. "Oh, excuse me, Kieran. Just a slip of the tongue."

"It's fine," Kieran mumbles. His expectations were never exactly high.

"I expect you—and everyone—to make more of an effort in the future," Seth says curtly. "None of our employees should have to wear a label to remind the rest of us what to call them, but Kieran has been, so the least we can do is get it right."

Shut up, Kieran thinks, his face burning. "It's *fine*," he says. And Seth is apparently perceptive enough to notice that he's embarrassed. He goes back into his office without another word.

Nobody says anything more than a quiet thanks as Kieran distributes the coffee and vanishes back to his desk. He feels Seth glance at him a few times, but doesn't pay attention; he's got an inch-high stack of data to enter that Marcus forgot about until yesterday, and a reasonable quantity of un-sugared black coffee to drink.

~~*

Kieran doesn't know if he feels more resentment or vague gratitude toward Seth. He could have been more graceful with Marie. Now everyone in the office is going to avoid using Kieran's pronouns at all for fear of Seth's wrath descending on them, and that'll make Kieran feel like a ghost floating around the office.

Near the end of Kieran's shift, Marcus suddenly stretches out and grabs his bag. "I've got to head out early today," he says cheerfully. "My little girl's going to a birthday party!"

Even Seth, for a moment, looks pained. Marcus never remembers to mention how long he'll be staying for the day, or how late he'll be in getting there. "All right," Seth says, with characteristic calm. "Say hello to Glenn for me."

"I'll have to bring her and Ashlynn around to meet everyone sometime," Marcus says, pulling on his coat and adjusting his nerdy glasses. "Ash is so curious about my job!"

Then he's gone, and Kieran opens his mouth before he remembers that he's avoiding talking to Seth. "Do you think his one-year-old child is really curious about his job, or was that another gurgle he mistook for intelligent language?"

Seth nearly smiles again. After a second, he manages to smother that glimmer of positivity with a disapproving stare. "*Excuse* me?"

"Never mind," Kieran says, and goes back to categorizing voter polls.

People's shifts started ending a while ago, and most of the workforce has shuffled off; conversations have ended and the sun is setting, leaving the office quiet except for the clicks and taps of fingers on keyboards and the hum of the fan and the breeze rustling papers on Kieran's desk.

Seth stops typing suddenly.

"I apologize if I put you on the spot earlier," he says.

Kieran isn't prepared to respond to an apology. "It's fine."

"I'm happy to talk to the other employees individually about the importance of respecting your pronouns."

The importance. That's a first. "They're getting used to it," Kieran mutters. "Don't make me the most hated guy in the office."

Seth goes uncomfortably silent.

"I talk a lot," Kieran says, at length. He does. He likes the sound of his own voice. He just knows what it sounds like to other people. High, affected—*girly*. The *Mean Girls* voice he cultivated in high school. "I'm shrill, you know. It tricks their brains. I can tell them to call me *he*, but I can't change what's going on in their heads when I talk to them."

"Don't make excuses for us," Seth says quietly. "You can expect better here."

Kieran glances sidelong at him and accidentally makes eye contact. Seth gives him a faint, sincere smile. Kieran clears his throat, startled. "Yeah?"

"Yes."

Why would you do that for me? Kieran wants to ask, but the question won't take shape in his mouth.

Instead he mutters, "Okay, Mister This-Coffee-Is-Too-Sweet-Does-It-Have-Extra-Peppermint—"

Seth's brows knit together. "I didn't say you could get my coffee order wrong."

"I didn't get it *wrong.*"

"I could taste—"

Kieran groans. "You looked like you were having a rough day, so I asked for extra syrup. I figured you wouldn't mind more of a good thing, since you get the most over-sugared shit anyway." He probably shouldn't swear in front of his superiors. But his shift ended two minutes ago, so technically this is off the record. Ish. "Sorry. Won't happen again."

Seth looks stuck between confusion and disapproval. It's not a good look on him. It makes him look older—something about the crinkles around his mean, glinty eyes. "I—" He swivels his chair around to face Kieran. "I appreciate the thought. But the— At a certain point, the peppermint overwhelms the chocolate. It upsets the balance of the flavors."

"Oh." That's probably the most reasonable thing Seth has said today. "So ask for more chocolate as well?"

"If I'm having a rough day," Seth says, "chances are what I need is an extra shot of espresso. But I'll ask, thank you."

Kieran throws him a lazy salute and bows his head over his desk. He keeps working, for an excuse not to look up.

"Your shift is over," Seth says.

"There's twenty pages left."

"I'll finish up here. Go home."

"I don't have anything better to do at home."

"You don't get paid overtime."

"I don't get *paid*."

Seth sighs. "Give me half of the stack."

Kieran is pretty sure Seth has his own work to do, but he hands him the ten pages, and by their powers combined, the work goes remarkably fast. In fifteen minutes, the last numbers have been entered and Seth runs a few dozen papers through the shredder while Kieran stuffs his laptop into his bag.

"Good work today," Seth says.

"Thanks. See you—" Not *tomorrow*, though that catches on his tongue for a moment. "Uh, next time." He doesn't have another shift until the weekend.

While he's meandering to the bus stop, it occurs to him that maybe Seth is so set on correcting the office workers on his pronouns because *Marcus* cares about trans stuff. Because Marcus was all excited about hiring a skinny, testosterone-free trans guy straight out of college, but Marcus doesn't have the personality or the attention span to pay attention to how everybody around him uses Kieran's pronouns. So Seth sits there listening with his obnoxiously sharp hearing and making sure everybody gets it right, so Marcus' office can be the fluffy safe space he wants it to be.

Yeah, Kieran thinks, that would explain a lot.

~~*

As the launch of the new campaign website creeps closer, accompanied by some alarming funding deadlines, the work piles up on Kieran's desk. He has more to do than he has time in his shifts; everyone does. At first Kieran keeps clocking out as usual, right on the hour, but he feels weird going home to watch Netflix when he knows the job isn't done. Like it or not, he's caught a little of the energy of the workplace.

So at first he hangs around fifteen minutes past the end of his shift, then thirty. Seth is always there, and Kieran gets used to the quiet solidarity of working long into the evening with him. Heck, it's not like he has anything better to do.

One night, when Marcus is flitting between desks out in the main room and trying to keep the cogs of the enterprise moving, Seth leans across to Kieran's desk. "Kieran. What time does your shift end?"

"Ten minutes ago," Kieran says. "What do you want? Blood, sweat, or tears?"

"I think Marcus is going to need another coffee. His usual. Do you mind running to the cafe?"

Kieran stretches, savoring the idea of a walk. "Nope. Company card?"

Seth tosses it across to his desk with a minimum of suspicion. Progress.

The usual barista is startled to see Kieran in so late, but appreciates the tips. Kieran wishes she didn't call him *sweetie*, but he puts up with it, like he puts up with the weird customers who call him *baby* and *miss* at his other job. He returns to the office to find the lights on but the desks empty, except for Jake—the web developer, who has his own pot of coffee sitting half-drunk next to his computer—and Seth.

Seth looks up as Kieran walks in and frowns at the sight of the coffee in his hands. "Ah. You're back."

"Where's Marcus?" Kieran asks.

Seth massages his temples. "He went home. Apparently his daughter has a cold."

Kieran can't even fault him for that, really. Sick babies are probably scary even for normal, well-collected parents. "What now?"

"I'm going to finish what I can tonight," Seth says. "The new site needs testing." He blinks when Kieran sets a cup on his desk. "What's this?"

"Dude, it's a triple-shot peppermint mocha, like it is every single day."

"I didn't ask for anything," Seth says, doing his best to look irritated by Kieran's consideration.

"You always stay late if he does," Kieran says, nodding over at Marcus' desk.

Seth glares at his coffee cup. Either Kieran's imagining things, or he's blushing at the mere implication of Marcus. Kieran wants to shake him. "Well—thank you. I don't usually have caffeine after six."

Kieran pats him on the back. Seth's shoulder is bony and warm, and something about noticing that feels too intimate, so Kieran stuffs his hands into his pockets and backs off. "Just, uh, think of it as slamming an energy drink before a final."

Seth picks up his coffee and takes a prim little sip. He doesn't say anything about the shoulder pat, which probably means it was only weird and intimate for one of them. "It's been a long time since I had a final," Seth says.

"No kidding," Kieran says. "What are you? Fifty?"

Seth sneers. "You're too kind, young man."

Young man. A faint warmth settles in Kieran's chest, and he looks away, grinning. "So… sixty?"

"Thirty-five, thank you."

"And you don't look a day older. Think I can have Marcus' drink?"

"I don't see why not." Seth glances after him as Kieran goes and settles at his desk again. "You can go home, Kieran."

"Split whatever work you've got halfsies with me," Kieran says, waving an inviting hand. "You'll be here till midnight otherwise."

"I'm going to be awake past midnight anyway," Seth mutters, with the contempt of an eighty-year-old.

"Whatever. Lemme help out and you can get home to—" Kieran has no idea what Seth goes home to at night, actually. He envisions loneliness. A clean, well-kept void. "Your loving wife and children?" he suggests.

Seth makes a noise that is almost a laugh, carefully muffled. Like he knows it's a joke. "All right. If you can test the links on the new website, that would be helpful."

Kieran slurps at Marcus' gross caramel syrup drink and gets to work on the website. There are only about nine hundred broken links, so that's great. "So what's her name?"

"Marian," Seth says. "And my loving child is Dragon."

Kieran stares at him.

Seth catches his look with a raised eyebrow. "Marian was my wife. We separated years ago, of course. And we never had children."

"Dragon?"

"My cat."

"Oh." Kieran feels the embarrassed recoil that comes of accidentally asking a more private question than he meant to. Seth doesn't seem sad enough to merit an apology, but Kieran doesn't want to leave the subject there, hanging in the air. "Hey, it's probably good for the campaign. If you and Marcus both had kids, you'd both be out every day with a kid's birthday party or soccer practice or whatever."

Seth gives a tiny sigh. Acknowledgement, Kieran thinks.

"I feel for him," Seth says. "It must be hard to come to work at all. I think he'd spend every moment at home with his daughter if he could."

"He might as well bring her to the office," Kieran says, draining the last of the caramel monstrosity.

"I don't know that a crying infant would increase anyone's productivity," Seth says, and now the curl at the corner of his mouth is at least eighty percent of a smile. "Did you finish that already?"

"I had to get it over with," Kieran says, gagging slightly. "How can you stand that much syrup?"

"I don't know. I labor through it, somehow." Seth gives him that sideways look. "Are you working?"

"Yes! *And* I'm logging errors. Check the bug tracker if you don't believe me."

"I believe you."

The silence between them is comfortable now, when they settle into it. And if Kieran keeps sneaking looks at Seth, trying to decide if he's just striking or actually really handsome. He does have a bit of a permafrown going on, but other than that, Kieran likes his face: high, sharp cheekbones and a long swoop of a nose, skeptical eyebrows, and bright brown eyes. Seth doesn't seem to notice him staring.

"Have the other employees been working on your pronouns?" Seth asks after a while. Despite the triple-shot of caffeine, he looks tired.

Oh, are we going to talk about this? Kieran thinks sourly. "Avoiding them."

"Hmm," Seth says. "I was hoping they'd get better over time. I know Marie is struggling, so I've been trying to keep an eye on her. Marcus slipped up the other day, but I told him—"

"Can we not?"

That's all he can muster, for a moment. Seth pauses, staring at him, startled and expectant. Kieran swallows and fumbles for politer words. "You know—like—if you get a splinter or something, it doesn't hurt until you fucking press on it?"

"Ah," Seth says.

Kieran keeps his eyes fixed on his screen, hunching his shoulders. "I know people make mistakes. I hear them. I don't need a report of all the other times it happens. And I don't really want to talk about it unless you've got a great plan for making sure nobody ever misgenders me again." It occurs to Kieran that he's, as usual, probably out of line. "Sorry if that's blunt. But it stresses me out."

"No. I apologize." Seth hesitates. "I've only handled changing pronouns for friends before, never employees. I'm not entirely sure how to handle it." Another pause, and Kieran doesn't know what to say. He's busy thinking, *friends?* Seth has trans friends? So maybe he isn't just doing this for Marcus' sake. "Your comfort is the most important thing. If I've made you uncomfortable, I've mishandled things."

"It's fine," Kieran says. "I just don't want it to be a big deal."

"I understand."

"Yeah?"

"Well, I empathize."

"Yeah."

Kieran wishes he still had a drink to sip. Something to do with his hands besides type. Something to do with his eyes besides work, because then it would be easier to distract himself. So much for the comfortable quiet.

Apparently Seth is aware of the atmosphere in the room, because he quietly asks, "What did you study in college?"

"Political science. I met Marcus in Poli-Sci 101."

"How was he? As a teacher?"

"Terrible," Kieran says, before his brain can catch up with his mouth.

Seth frowns at him. "That's a little harsh."

"Er. Don't tell him I said that? And hear me out. He was great for getting this internship, and he was the nicest prof I ever had. But he forgot half of what he was supposed to lecture about, every day. Then he'd forget to rewrite the tests to take out all the things we didn't cover in class. He fixed people's grades when they complained about the exams, but then he'd do it again."

Seth purses his lips. "That does sound frustrating."

"He *was* nice."

"He is very nice."

Seth is back to staring at his computer. But he's got that look again, like he isn't really seeing it. Kieran smiles. So they've talked about Kieran's transness. Maybe they can talk about the other thing. "At least he's handsome, right?"

Seth's head snaps up. "What?"

"He's a good-looking guy. In the nerdy way."

"I hadn't noticed," Seth mumbles, running his fingers around his collar.

"Oh, come on. I get that all the straights don't pay attention, but—"

Seth cuts him off, loudly. "I *don't* know what made you think that was an appropriate topic," he says, voice sharp and angry. Kieran snaps his mouth shut in surprise. "It isn't."

Kieran can't quite wrap his head around the sudden change in Seth's tone, from practically amiable to frigid. He's baffled. And kind of hurt. "Wait, so—I was assigned female at birth, and that's okay to talk about, but your crush on our boss isn't appropriate?"

"Excuse me?" The color in Seth's face is seriously intense. "This is a professional setting, Kieran."

Okay, so maybe he did cross a line. *Maybe.* But the possibility makes him bluster harder. "Yeah, that's why Marcus shows up in a T-shirt every day and blows off work to plan parties for his toddler. And that's why we're here chatting about my pronouns!"

"None of that is an excuse for bringing up any employee's *sex* life or for reading into the interactions between me and—" Seth fumbles his way free of that sentence without quite finishing it. He slaps his laptop closed and rises, grabbing his laptop sleeve. "That's enough. I can finish the work later. Go home, Kieran."

"Who said anything about sex?" Kieran protests. "I didn't say—"

"*Enough,*" Seth snaps. "Go. Home. And for your reference, I do expect a better grasp of workplace etiquette from someone Marcus *personally* selected to intern here, even if they have such an apparently poor opinion of him."

Kieran stands, shaking, but he can't really think of anything else to say. He shoves his shit in his satchel and leaves the office.

~~*

He'd just been miserably sure, for half a second, that somebody might get it. That somebody else might be as exposed as he is, every fucking day. That somebody else might be wearing a secret on his skin, glaringly obvious. He thought maybe that was a thing he and Seth had in common: an inability to hide whatever made them different. Whatever made them queer.

Failing that, he'd at least been sure they were getting along. But, okay, maybe his standards for "getting along" are kind of low.

He's embarrassed to admit that he got his hopes up, even to Jillian, so he complains to her about Marcus and pretends that's why he's upset.

When he's done being mad, it occurs to him to worry that Seth might tell Marcus something. Probably Seth would leave out the part about his own crush on Marcus and just say how Kieran was behaving inappropriately for the office and said he was a shit professor. That would probably do it.

He shows up to his next shift unsure of whether he's about to be asked to leave. Instead, all that greets him is Marcus' usual cheery grin and Seth's familiar chilly indifference. Well, it's chillier than before. Seth doesn't look at him except to give occasional orders, and doesn't even lift his head when Kieran talks to him.

Fucking asshole. His relief quickly drains away to irritation.

"The mood in here seems a bit low today," Marcus says gently. "Kieran, why don't you get some donuts with the coffee? There's a great donut shop a few blocks away, if you wouldn't mind going out of your way."

Seth doesn't say anything, but he lets out an audible sigh.

"Sure," Kieran says. That gets him about a half hour of freedom before he's back in the office, chewing on some (very good, very fresh) donuts and logging infinite bugs on the campaign website. Marcus is, unsurprisingly, also terrible at bug tracking. He has a habit of thinking everything is perfect long before it's fixed.

Eating donuts doesn't improve Seth's personality. But there is something heartwarming about watching Seth scowl at the sugar stuck to his fingers and trying to subtly lick it off. He catches Kieran watching and glares at him.

Kieran quickly averts his eyes, but he feels a strange jolt of relief. Then he realizes it's because it's the first time Seth has given him that nasty look all day—and he'd gotten used to receiving it about twenty times an hour. The bland silence is infinitely worse. It's weird to realize that maybe Seth hasn't been that annoyed with him all along. Maybe his face just does that. Maybe the pissy glare is Seth's version of amiable.

What a shitty way to find out.

CHAPTER THREE

The first thing Kieran hears when he gets to the office on Saturday is a wailing infant. And he has a moment of bitter apprehension before he walks in and realizes it's coming from behind Marcus' door. Everyone in the room is wearing headphones, and several of them glance at him with vague sympathy as he goes to join Seth and Marcus and Ashlynn in the other room.

Except Marcus isn't even there. The little girl is parked in a stroller next to his desk, screaming. And Seth is hunched over next to the baby, awkwardly cooing and shaking a rattle at her.

It's like Christmas in July. Kieran grins so hard his cheeks hurt. When Seth looks up, he frantically tries to rearrange his face into something appropriately repulsed or sympathetic, but it doesn't quite work. "Uh," he coughs. "Marcus ditched you with a baby? That's harsh."

"He stepped out," Seth says coldly. "He said he thought she was crying because she's hungry."

Kieran edges closer to the stroller. It's like approaching an ambulance with its sirens blaring. Inside is a small, fairly adorable baby in bright green pajamas. Her face is twisted with rage, and she's not paying any attention to Seth's feeble rattling. "You're probably just pissing her off."

"Would *you* like to try?"

"Yeah. As long as you don't give me any shit about having *mom instincts*." Kieran pulls Marcus' cozy office chair over by the stroller and scoops Ashlynn carefully into his arms. She stops crying with a startled, teary gurgle and glares at him in confusion. "Hi, kiddo. Give your dad a minute. Please."

"Should you be holding her?" Seth asks, leaning over with great concern.

"I have a baby brother. Got pretty used to carrying him around for my mom when she was busy." Ashlynn's grimacing at him like she might start screaming again, but he starts rocking her back and forth and she seems to reconsider. For the moment, anyway. "Babies are so weird."

"Yes," Seth agrees.

"She does look smart, though."

"I was just thinking that."

Kieran glances at Seth. He's staring at the kid like… well, not like he wishes he had one. But like he wishes for *something*.

Seth catches Kieran looking and frowns.

"How long's she been screaming for?" Kieran asks.

"About half an hour."

"Uncool." Kieran jiggles Ashlynn gently. He hears the office door open and scoots back to the stroller, returning her. She starts screaming again the moment Marcus walks in, but gets quiet as soon as she's being cradled in his lap and spoon-fed baby food.

"Glenn's at a recital today," Marcus explains. "She asked if I could bring Ashlynn to meet everyone at work. I was hoping she'd sleep, but she has a real appetite these days!"

"Sure seems like it," Kieran agrees. He exchanges a look with Seth. Seth does not look good. Which is to say he seems as pissy as usual, but also sad and frazzled. He keeps glancing wistfully at Marcus, and then ducking his head and focusing all too hard on his work.

Which can't be easy. Even after Ashlynn is fed and appeased and resting peacefully in her stroller, Marcus keeps jingling a rattle at her and cooing and trying to get her to play with him.

Kieran has never met anyone more capable of making everyone else's work harder while doing nothing.

Kieran doesn't usually take a lunch break because his shifts are so short it's barely worth it—and definitely not one hour after arriving at work. But this is an exceptional case. "I'm gonna grab something to eat," he says, and Marcus nods with a distracted smile. "Hey—Seth. Want to come with me?"

"That's all right," Seth says faintly.

Come on, idiot. I'm giving you an out. "Come on, man. I heard your stomach gurgling."

Seth eyes him. Eyes Marcus. Eyes the baby.

Kieran raises his eyebrows.

"Fine," Seth says. He rises stiffly and follows Kieran from the office.

"You looked like you could use a break," Kieran says, as they start down the stairs.

Seth sighs. "Thank you. I appreciate the concern."

Kieran swallows, feeling oddly nervous. He didn't know how much he liked feeling vaguely friendly with Seth until he suddenly didn't, and the friendliness seems fragile now. "What do you want for lunch? Mister Opinionated."

"Korean barbecue. There's a good place a few blocks down." Seth glances at him. "Any objections?"

"None at all."

Seth leads the way, steering them down the sidewalk. His hair must be slicked in place, because it doesn't move, even in the breeze that sends Kieran's blustering in every direction. Kieran's mouth feels gummy with the absence of something to say, with trapped, half-formed sentences. He keeps watching Seth instead, noticing that the crinkles around his eyes are still deep, something tense in his step. At least he doesn't seem to notice Kieran watching him; he's absorbed in whatever's going on in his brain.

The barbecue place is hot and crowded, and smells like heaven—meaty heaven. To Kieran's surprise, Seth asks for a table, not take-out. "They're busy," he says. "We might as well be sitting if we have to wait a while." So the two of them cozy into a booth in a cramped corner of the restaurant; the surrounding tables are split between families having lunch together and other workers on their lunch break.

Seth pulls off his blazer and sits primly. One elegant swipe of his hair comes loose in the heat and tries to lie across his forehead. He smoothes it back into place—which is a shame, because he looks more human, more touchable, when he's a little bit rumpled.

Touchable. That's apparently a place Kieran's brain is going. Great.

"Penny for your thoughts?" Seth asks.

Kieran does his best to look casual and not lustful. "Ever met Marcus' aunt?"

"Senator White?" Seth asks, blinking. "Yes. She visited the office once, for the ribbon-cutting—such as it was. This office isn't terribly important."

"I figured. Marcus wouldn't last if it was."

Seth starts to look disapproving.

"Come on. I *like* the guy, but all he wants to do is be a stay-at-home dad. Can you imagine if the office *needed* a manager to devote all their time to it? He'd quit. Or he'd get fired."

Seth purses his lips and glances out the window, but he doesn't seem to have anything to say in Marcus' defense. "You don't believe in softening the truth, do you?"

"I believe in it. I just get tired of it. Believe me, I spend too much time not talking."

"*Do* you?"

"At my other job." Kieran shrugs, carding his hands through his fluffy curls, still wind-rumpled. "Flipping burgers, I don't care. I tune out. Basically I pretend like I don't even exist at that job."

Seth raises his eyebrows. "So you have to do the opposite in a *professional* setting?"

"Hey, it's super easy to be a robot when nobody really wants you to be anything. But Marcus was always happy when people talked in class. He got nervous lecturing alone, so even if I talked too much, he'd thank me. I figured his office would be the same way. And I'm not great at shutting up when I don't have to."

"I've noticed," Seth says.

The waiter shows up and Kieran hasn't even looked at the menu.

"Uh," he says.

"It's your first time here," Seth says. "Try the galbi."

Something about Seth ordering for him makes Kieran feel pampered. He rubs the back of his neck, face flushed. "Sure."

Then they're alone again.

Seth looks out the window for a long time. He fixes a tiny wrinkle in his shirtsleeve.

Then he runs his fingers under his collar absently and sighs. "I'm glad we're having lunch," he says.

"Uh?"

"I wanted to apologize."

Kieran frowns. He's not sure what to do with his face.

"I shouldn't have snapped at you the other day. It was... *wasn't* about professionalism. It was about my own comfort. Or lack thereof." He doesn't look at Kieran, which is fine. "I'm afraid I don't have your ability to be so open. I don't like to discuss certain personal matters at work."

Kieran could gracefully accept his apology. Or he could open his fucking mouth, and guess which one he does. "Neither do I," he says, and even to his own ears he sounds sullen. "For some reason it always seems to come up, though."

Seth blinks at him for a moment before it dawns on him. "Ah."

"Yeah, sorry. I do get it. You'd rather not have to be queer at work."

Seth winces. "I'm not overly fond of the word queer, either."

"Sorry. Again." And Kieran still doesn't sound sorry at all. He *wants* to sound sorry. But everything that comes out of him is bitchy and bitter. "I guess I forgot that people *can* keep that to themselves. That sometimes even if something's obvious it doesn't mean you want to talk about it."

To his credit, Seth looks less offended and more concerned. "I—hadn't thought about it like that. I'm sorry if I—"

"It's not you. It's my situation." And he wishes he didn't sound so *mean*. "I'm just trying to tell you where I'm coming from, because—" Why? Why is he saying this to his most supportive employer ever? "I get that I kind of overstepped and it was shitty of me, but that's why I did. I didn't want to be the only one who was *out*. But I'm sorry for making you come out to me. I'm sorry."

Kieran's surprised to realize that he means it. And for a moment the realization feels like a knot in his stomach coming undone, finally. Except that the conversation is still happening.

Seth is fiddling with his collar again, and he's gone red in the face, which is reassuring. What a terrible talk they're having. "That's all right," he says. "I can imagine it would be very uncomfortable for you. I didn't think."

"No, it's—"

They're spared from an infinite loop of apologies by the arrival of the food. The food is delicious. Kieran really doesn't notice that it's delicious until it's mostly gone, because he crams three ribs into his mouth so he can stop talking.

Seth picks at his food, though. The waiter brought tea and side dishes with the meal, and Seth nibbles at the content of the little plates, as if he can't quite get around to the main course. And then he does. "Kieran," he says, and sighs. "I don't want you to have to apologize to me. I won't compare my problems to yours. All I have is terrible taste in men."

Kieran doesn't know of a graceful way to agree that Seth's life is less shitty than his (and/or that he has terrible, terrible taste). But he could probably come up with a better way than grunting affirmatively into his galbi.

"I don't think Marcus would ever guess," Seth adds, in a quiet voice. "And I wouldn't want him to."

"God, you are *the* tragic gay man."

Seth smiles. "I'm bisexual."

"Oh." Kieran swallows his food. "I guess that's more original."

"It's crossed my mind that I'm a cliché." Seth shrugs. "I live alone with a cat."

Kieran grins. "Is this the part where you start showing me pictures of your cat?"

"Are you asking to see pictures of my cat?"

"Yeah, show me the—" *Pussy* is what his brain wants to say, but "*Kitty*" is what he manages to cough out. Saved from his own mouth, for once.

Seth gives him an odd look, but he fishes out his phone and holds it out for Kieran to see as he scrolls through, predictably, dozens and dozens of photos of a fat and baleful black cat.

"Dragon?" Kieran asks.

"Yes." Seth smiles fondly. Which *is* a good look on him. It deepens the wrinkles at the corners of his eyes, but in a nice way.

"Eat your lunch," Kieran mumbles, looking away, because his mouth wants to smile back.

~~*

Seth pays for the food, over Kieran's weak objections—like hell he's actually gonna *argue* with someone buying him lunch—and they're on their way. They get coffee on the way back to the office, and Seth insists on sitting for a moment. He's really embraced this whole *skipping out on work* thing.

They grab drinks and a table in the corner, and Seth keeps looking at him. "What's up?" Kieran asks, uncomfortable.

"Can I say something?"

"Yeah? Go for it."

"I don't mean this as an insult."

"Great start."

Seth sighs, pinching the bridge of his nose. "It's only an observation. Kieran, you're very good at this job. Very organized. Very quick to learn."

"*Ouch*. The truth hurts."

Seth needles him with a look. "*But*—you aren't taking it seriously. With the attitude you bring, it's like you wouldn't mind if we fired you."

Kieran's first instinct is to protest, but—why bother? "Well, uh."

"I'm not saying that because I plan on firing you. I just don't understand."

"Can *I* say something?"

"Of course."

Kieran squares his shoulders. "It's 'cause I have a hard time thinking of it as a real job. I mean, the work's real, but I don't see myself in politics. Marcus offered me the internship, I took it. Good resume material. But not good enough to be fake for."

"What about it isn't *real*?"

"My chances of ever getting people to take me seriously?"

Seth looks exasperated. "I take you seriously. So does Marcus."

"Marcus thinks I'm *brave* for getting out of bed in the morning. He doesn't take me seriously. He takes my *problems* seriously."

He expects Seth to defend Marcus, but instead Seth's brow furrows and he nods. "Well, I never thought I'd make it anywhere either," he says. "But here I am."

"Is this where you wanna be?"

"It's somewhere." Seth fixes him with a look. "And you? Are you where you want to be?"

"I guess? Theoretically?"

Seth lets out a patient sigh. "Theoretically."

"I mean, yeah. I graduated college. Got a fancy internship. Got my burger-flipping gig."

Seth just looks at him like he can hear Kieran's confidence waver, and for the first time since walking in to the internship, Kieran feels himself shrinking under that stare.

I don't feel like I'm anywhere, he wants to say. The restaurant, with its shitty customers and the management that doesn't even try not to misgender him, that's the only part of his life that feels real. It's the part that's every bit as shitty as he expects the world to be. And, of course, it's the part that pays rent.

And there's nothing to do about it. Because who he *is* means that no matter what, any kind of success will only set him up for being seen, being dissected. He already walks into the office at his nice fantasy internship and feels a dozen pairs of eyes fix on him as their owners desperately try to remember, *oh yeah, this is the girl I have to pretend is a boy*. Only if he does something bigger, if he makes it big somehow, it won't just be the twelve people he hands coffee to. It'll be the city. The state. The country.

Way better to cut himself off from the possibility. Make a token effort and squander what opportunity he has, so he can say that he tried and failed—he wasn't cut out for it. So he can resign himself to flipping burgers.

"Are you all right?" Seth asks, his voice uncharacteristically soft.

Kieran's stomach feels like it's full of hot lead. For once, the blunt, honest answer sticks in his throat. He wants to say he's fine, but tears fuzz at the corners of his eyes when he tries to say so. And the silence between them stretches out too long for him to just dismiss the question.

"Not really," he chokes.

Seth doesn't say anything, but he's watching when Kieran glances at him. No hint of a glare or annoyance or anything, but there's no pity, either. Just calm concern. Like maybe he's seen people melt down over coffee before and it's not going to be a big deal to him if Kieran does now. Which feels like permission.

"Look, I..." And Kieran lets it out. In careful, clipped sentences so people sitting at tables nearby won't notice that he's on the verge of crying, in language so detached that he could be talking about someone else. In a quiet voice, not the voice he uses to mouth off at his superiors, not the way he talks to his friends, but maybe the way he'd talk to someone who could help. Everything he felt in college when Marcus would treat him with admiring pity;

everything he feels when Marie pauses for a long, awkward moment to restructure a sentence around avoiding his pronouns. Everything that looms in his mind when he imagines the future.

It takes half an hour. He's wondering if it's appropriate or okay to mention that it's hard to breathe sometimes when he's binding his chest in the baking heat of that top-floor office, when Seth's phone chimes.

Seth jumps and brings it to his ear. "Hello? Oh, yes. Yes, sorry, there was—quite a long line. Some kind of lunchtime rush. We'll be back soon. Goodbye."

Kieran glances at his phone and realizes they've been gone for close to an hour and a half. He scrubs his eyes. "Shit. We're on the clock."

"Unfortunately, yes." Seth gets up. "I'm sorry. I should head back. But if you'd like to go home, you're welcome to."

"Huh?" Kieran stands, realizing how shaky he feels. It's not the caffeine, as much as he'd like to blame it for his hands trembling. "Nah, I should..."

"Kieran. You've never missed a shift, and you've worked late at least half a dozen times. Nobody will begrudge you taking the day off. And Ashlynn was crying again when Marcus called. I doubt it's going to be a relaxing shift." The way Seth speaks, it's all so perfectly reasonable.

"Yeah," Kieran finds himself saying. "Okay. I'll, uh... I'll come in for some extra hours some other time. Could you tell Marcus I was sick or something, not that I'm—" *Having some kind of disproportionate emotional collapse because somebody asked if I was okay?*

"Of course," Seth says. He sees Kieran out to the curb, and that's where they go their separate ways, Kieran to the subway and Seth to the office. Seth catches his arm before Kieran can leave. "If you'd like to talk about this again, you can. Don't worry about being on the clock. You do more work in a shift than Marcus does in the average work week."

He smiles. Kieran is startled by it, only used to seeing this particular smile directed wistfully toward Marcus. It's nice. He smiles back, almost too big. "Now you're talking."

"Don't tell him I said that," Seth says.

"Your secret's safe with me."

Seth lets go, and Kieran rubs his arm as he walks to the subway, trying to keep the feeling of Seth's careful grip.

Weirdly, he feels better. He's all cried out, and relieved for having dumped the emotion somewhere other than on Jill or his supportive and long-suffering collection of stuffed animals. His possibly-shitty future seems more real and shitty than ever, but at least he knows, now, why he felt scared.

Admittedly he spends the next six hours watching Netflix and eating a pint of ice cream, but that's his standard self-care routine.

CHAPTER FOUR

Kieran feels a little guilty about how startled and happy Jillian is when he agrees to go see a movie with her. He's not usually *that* bad at leaving his house, but thanks to his jobs, he's been pretty awful lately, and he buys her dinner afterward to apologize. She bounces in her seat all through the meal, chattering about a new girl she's seeing, and Kieran is a little surprised himself at how easy it is to smile along with her. How much he *doesn't* feel like a lifeless loser in comparison to her, for once.

Then Jillian starts grilling him about the internship, and Kieran launches into the story of his semi-disastrous lunch with Seth and the awkward-but-cool weeks since then. He's just getting into the nuances of Seth's coffee habits when Jillian holds up her hand to stop him. "Babe," she says, "I'm really not sure I understand what the problem is?"

Kieran blinks. "Huh?"

"You keep talking about Seth and I keep wanting to say 'Congratulations, kiddo! That's awesome!', but you sound mad about it."

"Well—" Mad isn't quite the right word. Frustrated. Kieran is frustrated. And yeah, everything he's said out loud to Jillian is pretty overwhelmingly positive: Seth continues to be prickly but nice, keeps correcting people on Kieran's pronouns so Kieran doesn't have to, and hasn't been weird about the whole crying-on-him-at-lunch thing. He's allowed Kieran to grouch about his restaurant job and terrible customers. He's even requested the occasional non-peppermint coffee, after Kieran started making fun of his lack of variety.

The fact is, though, that Kieran can't talk about him without getting animated. And annoyed.

"It sounds like your job is going better," Jillian says carefully, "and your supervisor is also great, so—"

"He *is* great," Kieran mumbles. "That's the problem."

"Ohhh," Jillian says. "Kieran. Are you mad because he's cute?"

"Check, please."

~~*

The other part of the problem is that Kieran resents Marcus. He always has. From the beginning, Marcus' attitude annoyed him; it was useful, but still obnoxious, when he realized that Marcus would put up with Kieran's shit as long as he never outright admitted to being a lazy asshole. At least Kieran no longer has a grade riding on Marcus' good graces, but now there's another problem: he's irrationally irritated by the fact that Marcus has Seth, a reasonably hot, eagerly devoted bisexual guy, mooning over him and doesn't even have the decency to notice. Like, how hard is it to tell when a guy is uncomfortably (and *visibly*) turned on by your bare arms?

It's not that Marcus isn't attractive, but he's so incredibly dense that Kieran can't understand what Seth sees in him. And the nicer Seth is to Kieran—to both of them—the more annoyed Kieran gets. "You could do better, y'know," he says, after Marcus goes home one night.

Seth shoots him a sidelong glance, but he doesn't even muster up a glower, even though Kieran is trash-talking his crush again. How times have changed. "There you go again," he says. "Trying to get fired."

Fair enough. The truth is, Kieran feels comfortable talking to Seth, even if it's stuff he probably shouldn't say. "Hey, this is off the record. This is man to man."

"All right," Seth says. "Explain. How could I do better?"

"I dunno, you could swing by the nearest gay bar and pick up literally anyone."

"Marcus is a Ph.D. candidate with a stable job and the ability to hold down a relationship."

"Yeah, *with somebody else*."

"That still gives him an edge over some of us," Seth says lightly, and Kieran remembers that he's divorced. And not, presumably, because of any lack of attraction to women.

He doesn't feel like it would be nice to admit that he's remembering that, so instead he puffs up his chest and says, "Are you saying I can't keep a guy happy?"

Seth laughs faintly. "I didn't mean you."

Well, fair enough. If they're going to go there. "You can't be that bad. You still deserve better."

"I don't tend to think that anybody deserves a relationship."

"I meant better in general."

Seth gives him an odd look. "Thank you," he says.

"And hey, guys at the gay bar aren't that bad."

"Which gay bar is that?"

"You want a recommendation? Aiden's is pretty cool. More of a club than a bar, though." And the owner happens to be a big butch trans guy, which is half the reason Kieran always feels safe there. The other half is that he had an amazing one-night stand in a gender-neutral restroom at Aiden's once, and going back there—even just to dance—always feels like afterglow.

Not that he needs to tell Seth any of that. "I'll think about it," Seth says. He clearly doesn't mean it. Kieran doesn't push; hot or not, he probably shouldn't invite his supervisor to a nightclub.

Kieran's shift is eight minutes over and he's getting ready to clear out when Jake, their long-suffering website guy, leans into the room. "Hey, folks? Got a problem."

"What?" Seth asks, with weary resignation.

"Something blew up when I migrated the site over to the new server. The pages are mostly intact, but a bunch of data got scrambled. I'm guessing we've got all of it backed up somewhere, but I dunno where. Marcus always sends me whatever I need, so I don't dip into your organizational folders much. I took the site down, but if we're gonna have it live tomorrow, I'm gonna need some help figuring out what's missing." He pauses, and then with the reluctant sympathy of someone who already works harder than everyone else in the office, says, "Sorry."

"That's all right," Seth says, firmly unruffled. "Kieran, could you...?"

"Roll up my sleeves and slave away long into the night?"

"Exactly."

"Yeah, boss."

"Thank you."

Kieran makes sure to gripe as he gets settled back in at his desk, but secretly he's pleased; staying late at the office is more fun than staying at home with Netflix. Specifically, being around Seth—goading him, watching his face get all scrunchy and annoyed at the work, listening to him talk—is more fun than anything.

Seth quickly assesses which pages on the site are in the direst need and assigns them to the two of them. Kieran glances at the clock. Eight-thirty p.m. And he's thrilled to still be at the office. Maybe he is cut out for this shit after all.

Or maybe, his traitor brain whispers, *you really enjoy Seth's company.*

"Does Dragon miss you when you stay late?" he asks.

Seth laughs softly. "More like she's furious with me. However late I get home, I'm up for another hour apologizing to her."

"Wow. What a needy baby. Hey, you got any wine under your desk?"

"Do I have *what*?"

"Wine. Y'know, for celebrating after we're done here."

"I don't drink at work."

Kieran snorts. "Whatever. You probably don't drink ever."

"I *do* drink. When it's appropriate."

"Okay, where and when? Home alone with your cat?"

Seth looks annoyed, which probably means *yes*. "At bars. Occasionally."

And okay, Kieran *shouldn't* invite his supervisor out, but the opportunity is right there. And they haven't had a good talk since Kieran got all weepy on Seth, and Kieran's kind of craving another conversation. "In that case, you wanna get a drink afterwards? Because I'm not gonna want coffee after this, but I could really go for a big fruity girl drink."

"I keep thinking that you're too young to drink," Seth says, carefully.

"Dude, I graduated college. I'm twenty-three. I've been boozing it for years."

"Yes, well, for *me* it's been a decade and a half."

"Is that a no on the drinking?"

Seth looks pained. "It's not a no. As long as we're done before midnight."

Kieran spends a few precious minutes researching the nearest nice bar; he'd love to take Seth to Aiden's or another crowded gay club, just to see the look on his buttoned-up face, but on the other hand, Kieran doesn't wanna ruin his life. So a classy, quiet bar it is.

Then he gets to work, determined to power through the data before midnight.

Seth seems startled by his work ethic, especially when they finish at a quarter to eleven. Jake is overwhelmingly grateful and thanks both of them profusely, and Kieran is so pleased with the time they've made that he doesn't even care when Jake stumbles over his pronouns. Seth, though, draws himself up like he's preparing to defend Kieran's honor. Kieran pats his arm and pulls him toward the door, because honestly, he doesn't give a shit about pronoun quibbles right now.

He texts Jill—*taking him out for drinks??*—and stuffs his phone into his pocket, grinning when it buzzes almost immediately with her incredulous reply.

"I was thinking of ways we could make the office more comfortable for you," Seth says, distracting Kieran from his phone. "I was thinking of some kind of mandatory training for the rest of the staff. Most of them haven't received any kind of safe-spaces training, let alone on trans issues. What do you think?"

Kieran thinks that it's kind of hard not to want to kiss Seth when he's being unassumingly nice and competent. He clears his throat. "That would be cool, I guess. I don't want it to be a big deal."

"It shouldn't be. If we make it a matter of fact, then it should seem like a simple social convention to follow. And Marcus and I would enforce the policy, of course."

"I feel..." His throat is all gummy again. "I feel weird. Having all this for me. I feel like everyone's going to hate me for making them go to all that trouble."

"It isn't just for you, Kieran. I hope you aren't the only trans person this campaign ever employs. Or the only person whose gender could be misunderstood. It's a matter of policy. Of making sure all our employees are treated well. Besides, it could change how they all treat other people in their lives who don't have the protection of a supportive employer." Seth's hand brushes his arm, like a careful overture toward comfort. "Don't think of it as special treatment. Think of it as an investment we'd like to make."

When Seth puts it that way, some of the butterflies in Kieran's gut go away. But not all. He doesn't know if he's flattered or mortified. "You wouldn't make it if it weren't for me."

Seth huffs. "That's our fault."

Our fault. It weirds him out how Seth takes responsibility for all this shit, like it was his call. How he shoulders the blame for things he didn't do. "Yeah, well... don't beat yourself up about it."

"I'm not. I'm asking for your permission to schedule a safe-spaces training."

Kieran freezes, rubbing the back of his neck. "Oh. Uh. Go ahead. Do I have to be there?"

"No. Of course not."

"Thanks."

"If you think of anything else we could do—anything at all that would make the office a place you'd be happy to be—tell me." Seth pauses, glancing around as they walk. "Where are we going?"

"Classy bar." Kieran's glad he changed the subject, because his cheeks are burning in the cold night air. He can't shake the feeling of being a nuisance; he's miserably embarrassed and excited by the thought of Seth doing this for him. But he can't argue, either. "Figured you'd want something upscale."

"I assumed you were taking me to—what was that gay bar?"

"Aiden's? Nah. Didn't want to scare you. Why, do you wanna?"

"No, thank you."

Kieran grins. He leads the way to the place he picked out, a fancy downtown cocktail lounge overlooking the river that runs through the middle of the city. It's the kind of place he'd never go himself, a swank and expensive joint, but with Seth, he thinks he can make an exception. Even if it means he'll only be able to afford one drink.

"This looks nice," Seth says, offensively surprised.

"Hey, I told you it was!"

"Well, it's *very* nice."

Kieran elbows him. "You fucking bet it is."

They get a booth by a window; the lounge has serious mood lighting, soft purples and blues and candles stacked at the end of the table. Outside, the river is lit up bright, bands of roving locals and tourists mingling on the riverwalk. The waitress checks both their IDs—Seth looks startled and flattered when she asks for his—and goes away with their drink orders. A frozen strawberry margarita for Kieran, and a scotch on the rocks for Seth, because apparently their alcoholic drink choices are the opposite of their Starbucks orders.

"See, man?" Kieran says. "You're young enough to look like a college freshman trying to drink at a bar."

"Fair enough," Seth says. The purple-blue lighting makes him look younger. Smiling does, too. "Would you like something to eat?"

"Oh, uh..." Kieran glances at the appetizer menu and wants to cry. Who the hell spends fifteen bucks on "gourmet fries"? "That's okay. They're pretty pricey."

Seth shrugs. Probably because he makes more than seven bucks an hour at his job. "I don't mind," he says, and before Kieran can argue he's flagged down a waiter. "What do you want? I'll pay."

Kieran cannot deal with Seth buying him dinner on top of everything else he's done today. "You don't have to. It's fine."

Seth frowns. "Call me an old man, but it's better to eat something with alcohol. You have a young liver, but I don't. What do you want?"

Kieran chews on his lip, face red. "Uh, the fries. I guess."

Seth orders the fries and a plate of tiny, egregiously expensive crab sliders. Kieran tries to remember that the money doesn't mean anything to Seth, that he doesn't need to feel so mortified by the guy buying him dinner.

Then his margarita arrives, and it's huge. Big, red, and juicy, with a ripe strawberry on top. Kieran whoops, forgetting his mortification. "Don't know why you ordered scotch," he says, sucking the strawberry between his lips. "Fruity drinks, man."

Seth clears his throat and looks away. "I get enough sugar in my coffee."

"No, really?"

Seth smiles a little, and the conversation lapses, but Kieran can't let that happen, because he'll have to think about all the nice shit Seth keeps doing for him and then he'll feel weird. "Hey," he says, in desperation. "Tell me something about you."

"Like what?"

"Like anything. Tell me about Seth: the guy, not Seth: works for the Heidi White campaign. I feel like all I know about you is that you have a cat and spend way too much time staring at Marcus' guns. I'll say this for the guy—at least he works out."

Seth pretends not to hear that last part. "Well, you and I have the same degree."

"Where'd you get yours from?"

"UC Berkeley."

"How was California?"

"I liked it," Seth says. He looks out the window at the tourists wandering by. "It was hard to find a job I wanted. I had friends in San Antonio, so when I found work here, I came to join them. They all wound up moving away eventually. I'd been following Heidi White for a while, and I liked her campaign, so when I had the opportunity..."

"Wait, wait, wait." Kieran takes a bold swig of margarita and leans forward, elbows on the table. "I didn't dive into your life story just to wind up back at the campaign office. What'd you do before? Hell, what do you do now?"

"Apparently I go drinking with the office intern," Seth mutters, looking out the window.

"Yo, you go drinking with the only other queer— uh, sorry—non-heterosexual dude in the office. Not with *the intern*. Unless you're into interns." As usual, words come out of his mouth and the words are stupid. "I mean, into drinking with interns. Which is not cool. But drinking with me, that's very cool."

Seth's face goes through several emotional shifts, from bewildered to concerned to vaguely amused. "I suppose?"

"Yep." The food shows up then, thankfully, and Kieran gets to cramming fifteen dollars' worth of fries into his mouth. "And way to avoid the question," he adds, through a mouthful of potato. "What do you do? Marathon soap operas? Laser tag?"

"History," Seth says. "I go to a lot of museums. And read. And occasionally I marathon documentaries, if that counts as a marathon."

"So you spend a lot of time at home with a TV. Knew it."

Seth frowns. "Well..."

"Me, too. Except I don't have a cat. It'd be nicer if I did."

"I can introduce you to Dragon," Seth says, relaxing.

"Yeah?" Kieran's heart jumps, and for a moment he doesn't know why. Then he pictures going over to Seth's place, invading whatever squeaky-clean little bachelor pad he lives in, and snuggling Seth's cat, and... what?

Then he realizes. In his ideal world, this ends with *going back to Seth's place.* He's so fucked.

"These fries are great," he says. "Thanks."

"You're welcome." Seth is doing the thing again where he nibbles around the edges of his food, like he's waiting for them to get to a certain point before he digs in. "Thank you for staying late."

"Whatever. Not like you deserve to face a late-night campaign apocalypse alone." Kieran knocks back the rest of his margarita, which is objectively the best-tasting thing he's ever had. Even if it is fucking expensive. But hey, if Seth's buying the fries, the drink prices aren't so bad. "Wow. I'm so getting another one of those. Sure you don't wanna graduate from scotch?"

Seth swirls his boring-ass grown-up drink around in his glass and has a dignified sip. "No, thank you."

"Loser." Kieran waves the waiter over and orders another margarita, licking his lips—strawberry-tasting and sticky. And warm, from his throat all the way to the pit of his stomach.

"All right," Seth says. "Tell me something about *you.*"

"Huh?" Kieran coughs. "Uh, you kind of know everything."

"Do I?"

"Everything important."

"I don't know what you do outside of work."

Kieran groans. "I told you. TV. Alone. Sometimes my best friend invites herself over to make sure I'm alive. Occasional clubbing. If you really want to know something new, I've been told I get off on Facebook arguments."

Seth smiles like he isn't being told that Kieran is lonely and pathetic. "And? What are you watching these days?"

"Uh, I went through this whole phase where I wanted to watch every gay movie. I didn't realize I was queer till college, so I had a lot of time to make up. But that got old, so now I—" Kieran cringes. "Watch a lot of cartoons? I know, I could stand to get out more. I dunno, since I graduated I've been so busy trying to pay rent that I haven't exactly figured out the rest of *having a life*."

"You'll get there," Seth says. At least one of them sounds confident.

Kieran rubs his face. "So… you're a history nut. What kinda history?"

"Well, ordinarily I'd say 'the history of political movements'."

"Ordinarily?"

"Since it's you—I study gay history. The social movements, and so forth." Seth carefully cuts a wedge out of one of his sliders with a knife and fork. "I like to stay connected with the—with *our* history."

"But you don't go out and dance? Ever?"

Seth shakes his head.

Kieran purses his lips. Accepts his second margarita from the waiter and takes a gulp. "Maybe you should. Y'know, lots of guys could be lured in by the promise of a good-looking single man with a cat."

Seth waves a hand as if to silence him, and it's hard to tell in the colorful lounge lights, but his face looks hot. Like, warm. And also the other kind of hot.

"I'm just saying," Kieran says. "You'd have better luck at a bar than you're gonna have with Mr. Straight-and-Disorganized."

"I know," Seth says. And punctuates it by draining the rest of his scotch. When the waiter circles back again, he orders a glass of water for each of them. "I'm not holding out any hope that Marcus will suddenly abandon his fiancée and child and—"

He doesn't seem capable of finishing the sentence, so Kieran gives it a shot. "Make you his new Mrs. White?"

Seth scowls at him. "Yes, thank you. I would never want him to. He's happy as he is, and I have a great deal of respect for his fiancée. So I have no hope of getting anything from him."

"So let him go! Go moon over other guys. Cuter guys. Smarter, less heterosexual, more single guys. More organized guys. Or gals."

Seth pinches the bridge of his nose and stares down at the table. "I don't know if that would help."

"Come on, why not? You already dress sharp—all you need to do is loosen that tie, go swagger into a club somewhere, and take your pick of the nice, interesting people in there."

"Is that how it works? In your experience?"

Kieran huffs and flips his hair over his shoulder. "Obviously. Do I look like a guy who doesn't get what he wants?"

Seth sighs. He reaches up and loosens his tie a fraction. "Well, maybe it isn't an issue for you."

"Are you kidding? I'm trans. If *I* can go out, you can go out."

"I—" As expected, Seth can't argue with that. He frowns instead, and finally eats his sliders.

Kieran triumphantly drains his margarita. It's like swallowing a mouthful of candy. "Oh my God, I could drink ten of these. Except I'd go broke."

"Do you have work in the morning?"

"At my shitty day job," Kieran says, scrunching up his face. "Don't remind me."

Seth smiles. "As your supervisor, I think I should recommend that you stop drinking."

"I'm not a *huge* lightweight." Never mind that he feels floaty and content in a decidedly un-sober way. On second thought, maybe Seth has a point. "But uh, I guess. To be responsible." He does want Seth to think he's responsible. In a weird way, he's always wanted Seth to think he's good at what he does.

Seth checks his watch. "It's getting late."

"Yeah, yeah. Lemme stuff these fries in and you can get home to your damn cat."

"I don't mean to rush you. Take your time, and I'll take you home."

Kieran blinks. "You don't have to. The bus runs late."

Seth gives him a pointed look. "I'd feel better if I gave you a ride."

Which, all right, it'd be better than huddling at the bus stop, half-drunk in the dark and hoping this isn't the day that some weird asshole decides to mess with him. "Thanks."

Seth nods, sipping at his water. The waiter comes; Seth gives them his card.

Kieran gazes after their server. "Hey, uh—what about my check?"

Seth shrugs. "Don't worry about it. If we were paying you, you'd have worked overtime tonight." He smiles. "Consider this your payment."

The margaritas alone definitely cost more than he'd have earned in an hour or two, but Kieran doesn't argue, because he's not sure what'll come out of his mouth if he opens it. The words in his mouth are all *I'm usually a cheaper date than this*, and he's not, *not* gonna say that out loud.

Instead he winds up mumbling, again, "Thank you."

Seth makes another dismissive noise. He signs the check, tips their server, and offers Kieran a hand out of the booth. It's all Kieran can do to wipe the potato grease off his fingers before he grabs Seth's hand. The room is definitely on the unsteady side, and he's maybe more than half-drunk. Still, when he focuses hard, he manages to walk after Seth in a straight line.

Outside, it's a nice temperature—cool, but still mild from the heat of the day. Seth takes him by the shoulder gently to steer him toward the inside of the sidewalk, away from the street, and keeps himself between Kieran and the occasional cars that roll by. Kieran rubs his shoulder. He could deal with being drunk and having Seth steer him around more often.

"Why're you being so nice to me?" he asks, half-laughing, half-serious. "What's in it for you?"

Seth smiles. "To be honest, I'm glad you came along."

"Tired of being the only one?"

"You could say that. It's almost a relief that someone finally noticed how I—" Seth squares his shoulders, looking away peevishly. "How I feel about Marcus."

"You mean your big bisexual crush on him."

"If you have to call it that."

"But you're glad?"

"I forgot what it was like to be around people who notice." Seth makes a strangled noise that might be a laugh. "And I appreciate your bluntness. Otherwise I never would have known."

Kieran finds himself grinning, rubbing his face in an effort to wipe off the blush. "That's a first."

They get to Seth's car, and Seth shepherds him briskly into the passenger seat. Kieran curls up and listens, barely following but interested, as Seth tells him about the early origins of the gay liberation movement and occasionally asks for clarification on the GPS' directions to Kieran's apartment.

Home is all too soon. And Seth, of course, nice dude, gets out of the car to see Kieran up to his door—only he stops Kieran, catching his sleeve as Kieran starts to turn away from the car. "Just a minute," he says. "About the office. There's—something I wanted to ask you."

"Ugh." Kieran makes a face. The office makes him think of *safe spaces training* and *Seth being nice* and he doesn't want to contemplate either when he's this tipsy.

Seth frowns, clasping his hands behind his back. "I had a word with Marcus. This office is expected to grow as the campaign carries on, and we could use a larger full-time staff. I understand you'd need to quit your restaurant job, so don't feel like you have to rush to a decision, but—" Seth pauses when Kieran reels back and stares at him. "If there were a position available, would you take it?"

"Are you kidding?" Kieran wheezes. He doesn't know what his chest is doing, but he can barely breathe. "Are you serious? *Full-time?*"

"I told Marcus that your work ethic already makes you invaluable, and he agreed. If we have the funding—and I believe we will—we'd like to hire you properly. Real paychecks and everything." Seth smiles tentatively. "If you're interested, that is. After our conversation the other day, I wasn't sure if this was what you wanted."

There are either hearts or dollar signs dancing in Kieran's eyes, or maybe both. "I—*yes*. Of course I'm interested!"

Seth's anxious smile relaxes into something relieved. "Good. I'll let Marcus know."

"Thank you. Thank you, thank you, I mean it." Kieran can't believe Seth is shaking his head, like he expects Kieran to let him brush this off too. "Seth, this is nuts. I can't—"

"You deserve it." Seth clears his throat. "You don't need to thank me. But for the time being, you have work in the morning, so you should go in."

"Okay. Sure. But I'm *gonna* thank you." Kieran lets Seth take his arm and help him up the stairs, because he does feel like he might fall over otherwise. "Holy shit."

"Remember to drink enough water."

"Yeah, yeah, I will. You know—" Kieran ducks his head, because his face is all red and they're about to walk under the light of his porch lamp. "When I showed up on that first day, I thought you were an asshole," he mumbles. "Like, stick-up-your-ass and everyone was scared of you."

Seth's face pinches up. "Well. I'm sorry."

"No, that's the point. I was wrong. Even though I'm always right." Kieran slumps up the last stair to his apartment door, Seth trailing after him, and fumbles through his satchel to find his keys. "You're great. You're so great. That's why I keep saying you should go clubbing. You should have fun. Be happy. You deserve to be happy. I don't think you're an asshole at all, just, like—just a guy who doesn't have enough fun."

In the weak glow of the lamp above Kieran's door, Seth smiles, but he looks tired. And lonely. "Thank you."

"Thanks?"

"For the recommendation." His lips twitch. "And for the categorization of my faults. I appreciate it."

"No, no, *no*. That's not what I mean." Kieran forgets about his keys. Instead he grabs for the banister next to where Seth's hand is gripping and winds up gripping his hand instead, Seth's skin startlingly hot under his fingers. "I meant what I said earlier. You *deserve* better. Like, way better. Like m—" Words. Fucking falling out of his mouth. But now he's said them, so he might as well keep going. "Like me. For instance. For example. If you'd rather not hit up the club. I'm just saying there are guys who would date you. Like me."

Seth blinks, and for a moment his nice, mean, glinty eyes are wide and startled. Then he starts to back away, hand slipping out from under Kieran's fingers. "Go to bed, Kieran. I'll see you at w—"

Kieran grabs his tie by the knot and reels him back in. The warm flush of the margarita seems to be rolling through his head now, and when his knuckles brush against Seth's skin past the one undone button of his shirt, his pulse jumps. "I'm serious right now."

"You're drunk right now," Seth says sharply.

"Like that makes a difference," Kieran retorts, and kisses him. He has to lurch up on his toes to kiss him, and he's wobbly, so he grabs the rail for balance and pulls Seth against him by the tie. And wow, he could get used to Seth's disapproving little mouth in this context. His lips are really soft—

And then Seth isn't kissing him anymore, he's pulling Kieran's satchel from his shoulder and locating Kieran's keys and jamming them into the door with more force than necessary.

Kieran leans dizzily against the banister, a sinking feeling in his gut. "Hey. Seth."

"Good night," Seth says, holding the door open, Kieran's keys and satchel in his other hand.

Kieran opens his mouth, and for once, nothing comes out. He takes his stuff and slinks inside, past Seth, flattening his body against the door so he doesn't have to touch him.

Door closes. Kieran sits on the floor. Listens to Seth's shoes scrambling down the stairs, and the car's engine starting. He hugs his satchel to his chest and listens to Seth drive away.

He feels sick, and it's not from the booze.

CHAPTER FIVE

Kieran is spared the total indignity of returning to the office for three whole days. Which, instead of savoring, he spends being furious and sullen at his shitty restaurant job, and marathoning the dumbest cooking shows he can find, and getting irrationally angry every time Jillian posts a cute selfie with her new girlfriend.

Speaking of Jillian, after he fails to reply to any of her demands for details about his "hot date" with Seth, she gets the hint and just comes over with booze and hugs. She doesn't make him talk about it. She's good like that.

Rejected by his *supervisor*. His supervisor who barely liked him, anyway, who he decided to kiss for no fucking good reason, who offered Kieran the opportunity of his life, who probably wants nothing to do with him now.

Kieran's not sure if he feels more humiliated or stupid or—maybe just sad. And he's not sure how to deal with feeling sad. Sure, he deals with a lot of bullshit in his life, the kind that should make him weepy on a regular basis—but mostly he gets by, by feeling annoyed and superior and like he'd rather drink alone than suffer the company of fools.

He's not used to feeling disappointed. His expectations are usually so low. But for half a second, they'd been so high.

The night before he has to go back to work at the office, he almost convinces himself to quit—to totally commit to never seeing Seth again, sparing himself the uncomfortable silence. He'd be doing Seth a favor; Seth must regret that job offer now, must be trying to think of a way to retract it. Well, it wasn't official anyway.

But Kieran can't quite bring himself to pick up the phone—he's not *quite* that dramatic—so instead he lies face-down on his bed for hours and wishes he at least had a cat.

When he gets tired of suffocating in a pillow, he goes back to his other major form of recreation: scrolling through Facebook and glaring at his happy friends. Halfway down his feed, though, Aiden's has an ad. "Go-Go Boys Night Out at Aiden's... Saturday Only, No Cover!"

Kieran chews on his lip and stares at the attached photo, a burly dude in a thong, posing under bright pink lights.

It's an idea. What if, instead of quitting, he strolled into the campaign office tomorrow with a mild, sexy hangover and a bunch of hickeys? Whoever said the cure for loneliness wasn't grinding on a bunch of cute guys?

Before he can talk himself out of it, he's rolled out of bed and into his clubbing eyeliner. He doesn't text Jillian, because she'd worry. He pulls his hair back in a loose ponytail, leaving a few sultry curls hanging down the side of his face, and puts on the most revealing tank that doesn't show his binder. He admires himself in the mirror for a while, then stuffs the pockets of his skinny jeans with his ID, cash for drinks, and—on second thought—a condom or two.

~~*

Aiden's is a cute little shack, a typical unkempt bar with a rainbow flag hanging over the door, windows plastered with flyers advertising the nightly drink and dance specials. The first floor is the bar proper; usually quiet, with older and shyer patrons clustered around and sipping their drinks. But the floor hums underfoot: down a flight of practically medieval stone stairs is the basement dance club.

Kieran snags a piña colada from the bar and makes his way downstairs, brushing past a couple of tall, pretty girls he recognizes from another night at Aiden's. The basement dance floor is hot and loud and dark, pink disco ball spinning above the floor, the strobe chopping up the moments between pulses of light. There's a good-sized crowd dancing, and a cluster of people around the bar against the far wall. The DJ's playing some questionable dubstep, and Kieran works his way around the edge of the dance floor, planning to lounge attractively at the bar until the music improves for dancing.

As he gets closer to the bar, he notices an obstruction in the midst of the tipsy club-goers trying to get their drinks. Someone square-shouldered and out of place, flattened against the bar but not ordering.

He knows it's Seth by the body language alone. The neat Boy Scout hair, staying stubbornly in place despite the heat and the people jostling around him. And the shirt and tie, so intimidatingly crisp in the office, so stiff and weird for a club. Still, Kieran doesn't want to think it's actually him, so he keeps wandering closer, dubstep pumping in his ears like a second heartbeat, waiting for the image to resolve itself into someone else, some total stranger.

By the time he's close enough to admit the truth, Seth sees him, too. And Kieran's one consolation is that Seth looks as horrified to see him as Kieran feels.

Kieran thinks about turning his back and walking right out of Aiden's. He could make a dramatic exit, flip his hair and stalk off into the night, and no one would even have to know that he was going back to a lonely, shitty, empty apartment to watch TV dramas with a sad assortment of stuffed animals.

But his drink is still ice cold in his hand, and this is *his* fucking club.

So instead he stalks up and grabs Seth by the sleeve, yanking him forward. "Don't stand at the bar if you're not gonna order, jackass," he snips, not caring if Seth can hear him over the music. Seth, wide-eyed, lets Kieran tow him off to the hallway that leads to the bathrooms, which is about the only place not packed with dancers and relatively quiet.

Once they're alone, Kieran drops Seth's sleeve, disgusted. "What are you *doing* in here?"

Seth stares at him, prim and lost. "I'm sorry. I didn't think you'd be here."

Ugly disappointment settles in the pit of Kieran's stomach. "Wow, so you show up at the club *I* told you about? Nice plan, asshole."

"Kieran, I..." Seth breaks off with a huff of nervous breath, running his fingers through his neat hair, roughing it up. "I should apologize for—for a few nights ago."

"Are you fucking kidding? No. You don't need to apologize for *that*. You're not into me, I get it. Whatever. Plenty of guys don't like me. I feel pretty stupid about kissing you, honestly. But what you *don't* do is barge into my favorite club, looking for—" He can't imagine. "What *are* you doing here?"

Seth looks so miserable. He presses his back up against the wall, glancing down at the floor as a few dancers shuffle past them toward the bathrooms. "Finding a distraction."

"A distraction from *what?*" Suddenly Kieran remembers his own damn advice. "Oh. Finally going to find a guy to tear you away from Marcus?"

"No," Seth says. "From you."

Kieran blinks. He frowns up at Seth's face for a minute, while Seth stares at the wall, his shoulders hunched.

He steps back, leaving Seth to lean against the opposite wall while he takes a steadying slurp of his piña colada.

"Are you saying you *like* me?"

"Yes," Seth says, and he swallows, and then— "And I'm aware that it's—it's inappropriate, and as your supervisor I shouldn't feel this way, and as your *supervisor*, I don't. I respect you very much. And as a person, as a man who made me think about the possibility of being with someone again..."

"You like me?"

Seth breathes out. With his hair askew, he looks torn down. "Yes. And I'm sorry. I never meant for you to have to find out. I was hoping to find someone—"

"Hey!" Kieran doesn't know if he's feeling more elation or outrage, but luckily, he has the volume and lung capacity for both. "Go back to the part where you like me and explain why you ran off like a punk bitch when I kissed you."

146

Seth is almost definitely blushing, and staring at the ceiling. Staring anywhere but at Kieran. "You were drunk."

"Oh? Yeah? Well, I'm sober now."

"I'm *old*," Seth mumbles. "I'm an old man who can't hold down a relationship."

"Not with *that* attitude. When was the last time you tried?"

Seth looks at him. Sort of sideways, but it's a start. Is this how Marcus feels? Going through life every day with Seth totally unable to look him in the eye?

Nope—because Marcus has no idea what he's missing out on. "Look, asshole. I'm kinda into you, too. And we're here." Kieran crosses the hall to him, grabs one of his hands and presses against his chest. "And if you're young enough to show up at a club and dance, you're young enough to try dating me. Okay? That's my rule."

Seth hesitates. "Is it?"

"I made it up. For you." Kieran tosses back the rest of his drink and pitches his empty plastic cup in the direction of the nearest trash can. "And I chugged my piña colada for you. So—let's dance."

"I really don't know how to dance," Seth says softly, letting Kieran draw in closer to hear him.

Kieran grins. "Fuck, you think I do?"

He leans up and kisses Seth again. For the first time, maybe, because this is the first time Seth has let Kieran coax him into kissing back, following when Kieran tugs gently at his lip. One of Seth's hands lands on his waist. Light, careful.

Kieran reaches up and undoes the top button of Seth's shirt. Bumps his nose against Seth's and asks—"Dance with me?"

Seth's fingers curl, just so, into the hem of Kieran's shirt. "All right."

Kieran grabs him by the hand and pulls him out of the hallway and onto the floor, where the heat of the crowd rolls over him as he presses back into the cluster of dancers. Seth follows, but he's only watching Kieran. Not the crowd. Not the lights. And he doesn't even seem to mind that the DJ's still playing terrible dubstep—deep, shuddery bass that Kieran feels in his toes when he leans up to wrap his arms around Seth's shoulders and pull him in.

And yeah, it's awkward. A bit weird to be kissing in the middle of the crowd, bumped and jostled by passing dancers. And he feels like he's grinning too much, too happy to feel Seth wrap his arms around the dip of Kieran's back and hold him close.

A decent song with a decent beat comes on and Kieran wriggles loose, throwing his hands in the air and dancing like a fucking idiot. Seth gapes at him like a fish out of water, and Kieran grabs him by the tie, dragging him into a nice deep kiss and rubbing up against his chest, feeling Seth's startled little gasp when Kieran's packer rubs against his junk. Then Seth's palm is squeezing his ass, and they're back to half-dancing, half-grinding, and Seth is laughing helplessly against his mouth.

Kieran's drenched in sweat by the end of the fifth song—binding and clubbing is *never* a good combo—and Seth, overdressed as he is, doesn't look much better. His hair is a mess, all scrambled up by Kieran's hands having combed through it, and his mouth is flushed under the lights. The disco ball overhead sends silver spots glittering across his throat, and Kieran leans up to follow them with his mouth, pressing kisses all the way up to Seth's ear and nuzzling against his one tiny earring. And the next song is Britney Spears, so Kieran summons the last of his dancing energy, working his body against Seth's and feeling Seth's hands map out the curve of his back.

When the track ends, he makes a gesture toward the stairs, and Seth nods, squeezing his hand as they work their way out of the crowd.

Upstairs is freezing by comparison to the dance floor, a merciful chill that has Kieran shivering and leaning on Seth's shoulder as they stumble through the quiet bar seating and out the door to the street. His ears are ringing, still thrumming along to the bass they left behind.

"Not bad for a first-timer," Kieran says.

Seth is pink under the streetlights. "That was—it was fun."

"Yeah? Think you could stand to go again sometime?"

"I could try," Seth says, with a smile.

Kieran goes up on his toes for another kiss, and this time Seth leans down, catching his mouth and gently winding an arm around Kieran's back. Once Kieran is kissing him, he doesn't want to stop, never mind how smart it isn't to make out in the street at night. The cold air starts to seep into his clothes, which is one more reason to press closer, curling his shivering fingers into the collar of Seth's shirt.

He definitely notices when Seth gets hard. Of course, that's apparently another thing that Seth is bound to feel bad about, because he abruptly extracts himself from Kieran's arms and starts to back off. "I—"

"It's cool," Kieran says. "If my dick could stand up on its own, it would've by now."

Seth stares at him, adorably off-balance. He relaxes a little when Kieran reaches out and grabs his hand, squeezing it, but he still doesn't seem to know what to say.

"Just to be clear," Kieran says. "I'm up for whatever's in your comfort zone. Like, for example, sex."

Seth clears his throat, his thumb running over Kieran's knuckles in nervous circles. "I—I want you to know that this won't impact your employment opportunities. In any way."

Kieran leans in close. "I didn't think it would."

Seth swallows. "My car isn't very far. If you'd like to come over, maybe have a drink—"

Kieran grins.

~~*

Seth's car is nice. Kieran was too tipsy to appreciate it before, but now he does, splaying in the passenger seat while Seth—face pink, lips red—starts the car, his eyes fixed on the road.

"How long've you liked me?" Kieran asks.

Seth's throat works nervously. "Oh, I don't know."

"Totally unromantic. Try again."

"I didn't realize until you told me you knew I was interested in Marcus."

"Wow. Well, with the crush you had going for him, I guess I don't blame you for not realizing early on how irresistible I am." Kieran grins when Seth shoots a look at him. "I always thought you were hot. It was just a matter of realizing that you weren't a total dick."

"I'm glad you realized," Seth mutters. He drives for a minute in contemplative silence. Kieran can see him working himself up to something, and finally he does. "Look, are you really all right with this? I won't be angry if you'd rather not even think about a relationship with me. I'm twelve years older than you, and believe it or not, I try *not* to date my coworkers, let alone—"

"Whatever," Kieran interjects.

Seth scowls incredulously at him.

"I like you. So the least we can do is try this out." He leans over and bumps his shoulder against Seth's. "And I don't give a shit about you being old and weird. Obviously."

"Thank you, I think."

They pull up at Seth's place a few minutes of comfortable silence later. Seth's apartment is, of course, nice; it's in a bland neighborhood, but Kieran's not surprised. Not by the interior, either: a neat, sparse little one-bedroom with a TV and a couch and not a lot else.

Except, that is, for the glowering lump of black fur huddled on top of the sofa when they come in. "Dragon," Seth coos, leaving Kieran's side to pet the lump, which makes a squeaky meow and begins to purr.

"Cute," Kieran says, with trepidation. But Dragon lets him scratch her under her chin and behind her fluffy tufted ears, while Seth gets a pair of glasses and pours out wine for the two of them. Kieran's starting to feel gross, sweaty and clubbed-out, but then again Seth's in the same boat—unkempt, and smelling like the combined sweat of a hundred tipsy dancers. Kieran cozies onto the couch with him anyway. "Where were we?"

Seth blushes and takes a steadying sip of wine. "I think—I think I was in the middle of leading up to the Stonewall Riots."

Kieran snorts. "Oh yeah? Did you live through those?"

"That was *nineteen sixty-nine*."

"Wow, not so old now, old man."

Seth huffs, and launches into the epic tale of mid-century queer politics. Kieran gets comfy—because he is interested, in spite of himself, and because it's fun to watch Seth try to focus on history talk when Kieran is running his fingers along the inside of his thigh. But as soon as they're done drinking the wine, he grabs Seth's hand, cutting him off mid-rant. "Hey. You're disgusting."

Seth blinks.

"And I'm disgusting, too. So what say you show me around your shower?"

"Oh," Seth says, blank. And then he seems to recover, and smiles, almost shyly. "All right."

~~*

"Do you need any pointers?" Kieran drawls, sitting on the bathroom counter. "Or a pep talk?"

Seth gives him a strange look, loosening his tie. His fingers work elegantly into the folds of the knot, already slightly askew from Kieran yanking on it. "Why do you ask?"

"I dunno, you don't act like you've ever taken your clothes off in front of somebody else."

"I was *married*."

"I mean, I guess, but I don't like assuming what you did with your ex-wife." Kieran eyes him, up and down. "So. Have you?"

"It's funny you should ask." Seth folds his tie and leaves it next to the sink. Unbuttons his shirt with a nimble touch. "This is usually the part of relationships I'm good at." His mouth quirks up when he says it, but it's not quite a smile.

Kieran doesn't know what to do with that look, other than pull his own shirt over his head and look inviting. Fortunately, Seth takes the bait. He comes in close and smoothes his hands along Kieran's sides, making no distinction between the binder and his skin. His hands stop at Kieran's hips, and he hesitates. "Is there anything I should know," he begins, "about what you—how you prefer to be touched, or called, or anything like that?"

Kieran shrugs, pleased. "I'm not big on 'girlybits' or 'ladyparts'," he says. "Other than that, whatever. I like my body."

Seth smiles a little. "I do too."

There's still a part of Kieran that bristles with nerves as he unbuttons his jeans and kicks them down, but Seth's watching him with careful intensity, with a restrained admiration that makes Kieran's skin prickle with appreciation. So he wriggles out of his binder and leans back on the sink, letting Seth look at him as he reaches down and squeezes his packer through his underwear.

Seth swallows.

"How are you with, uh—?" Kieran has said this to guys before, is not a blushing virgin, but his face starts to turn red anyway. *Spit it out. The worst he can do is freak out.* "How are you with bottoming?"

Seth sucks in a breath. "I—I prefer it. Actually."

"Cool. Because I sort of, uh, prepared for that situation, if you wanna."

"But it's—it has been a while. I'm not sure I have any condoms. Do we need one?"

"Safety first." Kieran ducks down and squirrels his condom and lube packet out of his jeans. "Got you covered. You were gonna go find a guy in a club and you didn't buy condoms?"

Seth takes them delicately. "I didn't really think it through. You're... much more prepared for this than I am."

"I kinda hoped I'd find someone to mess around with tonight." Kieran straightens up, hooking his fingers through Seth's belt loops and tugging gently. "Trying to take my mind off, y'know, you. But I guess I dodged that bullet." He has to smile at the flash of startled, soft emotion that jumps into Seth's eyes. "Hey, are you gonna take your pants off any time soon?"

Seth blinks. "Yes. Sorry."

He unbuttons his pants and lets Kieran pull them down. His legs have a certain gangly charm, but Kieran is honestly more interested in his dick, pressing hard against the front of his underwear. Kieran tugs his briefs down, glancing up at Seth as he wraps a hand around Seth's cock, letting its weight settle in his hand. Seth makes a strangled noise.

"Nice," Kieran says.

"Thank you," Seth says, stiffly. "Will you—in a minute I'm going to be too embarrassed to do anything. Can we get in the shower?"

"No problem, boss."

"Thank you, *coffee boy*."

Kieran laughs and shoves off his own underwear, absently gripping his own dick, the packer slung around his hips on the harness he bought specifically for those nights out at the club. Seth switches on the water, and Kieran scoots underneath the showerhead with him, the hot water cascading down his back and washing away the sweat of the club. Seth is breathing carefully, like he's doing his best not to appear overly excited, although his dick is communicating that on his behalf. He also can't seem to keep his eyes off Kieran, which is exactly what Kieran revels in.

"Deep breaths," Kieran reminds him. "I know. It's a lot to take in. I'm pretty hot."

Seth makes a sour lemon face. "I'll try my best to handle it."

"Lemme know if I'm going too fast on you. Don't wanna blow your mind too hard."

"As I said," Seth grumbles, "this is the part I'm *relatively* comfortable with."

Kieran grins, reaching up and tangling his fingers in Seth's hair. "Then I'd hate to see you uncomfortable."

Seth mutters indignantly and kisses him, hands coming up to cradle the back of Kieran's head as he pushes Kieran against the wall of the shower, his cock brushing Kieran's thigh. Kieran reaches down and squeezes his dick, gently working it in his hand as Seth shudders and pushes his tongue into Kieran's mouth. The soft, muffled sounds Seth makes at the back of his throat while they're kissing are the hottest things Kieran's heard in a long time, and okay—for a guy who acts like his last relationship was several centuries ago, Seth is a pretty good kisser, eager and coaxing all at once.

Seth's half-smiling when he draws back, his hair spiky and punked out from Kieran's hands combing through it. "Can I—? Would you like it if I—" Seth pauses for a moment too long, and then the words jumble out of his mouth all at once. "If I sucked your cock, would it be—good? For you?"

"It'd be a good show," Kieran says, cracking a grin. "Go on, show me your skills."

"It's been a while," Seth mumbles. "I don't know what *skills* I have left."

But he's remarkably eager to get on his knees, water dripping down his face as he settles between Kieran's legs and wraps a hand around his cock. He glances up, and Kieran's throat jumps, a jolt of arousal leaping through him at the sight—Seth, wet and rumpled, leaning in to slide his lips down Kieran's dick.

"It's probably like riding a bicycle," Kieran says, shaky. "—Haha. Hey. *Bi*cycle."

There's nothing quite like seeing a guy try to glare at you with a mouthful of silicone cock.

Kieran can't help laughing, slumping against the shower wall, tossing his head back. Then Seth presses forward, his hand twisting around the base of Kieran's packer, pressing it against his clit—and Kieran hears himself groan, loud and sharp, his back going stiff against the wall. Okay, maybe Seth isn't the only one who hasn't gotten laid in a while. The gentle, grinding pressure gets Kieran's nerves on edge, and he ruts against it, nudging his cock deeper into Seth's mouth. Seth tightens his grip and pushes Kieran back against the wall; Kieran whines, running his nails along Seth's scalp.

The pressure's not enough, and not at the right angle to make him come—not quite—but it's enough to send a flush crawling up his chest, pleasure spiking through his abdomen. Seth's eyes are closed, eyelids fluttering as he mouths at Kieran's dick, and the need, the bliss in his face is suddenly too much for Kieran to handle.

"I gotta fuck you," Kieran gasps. "Seth, c'mon. Let's go."

Seth glances up at him, a slow look that makes Kieran's stomach churn with craving for him. He pulls off Kieran's cock with a final long suck, which he punctuates with a twist at the shaft that makes Kieran shiver all the way to his toes. "Bed?" he asks, hands on his knees, dick hard between his legs.

"Yeah. Bed."

Kieran barely dries off with the towel Seth tosses at him, squeezing the water out of his long hair but stumbling out of the bathroom with trails of water still rolling down his chest and legs. Seth's bedroom is sparse, clean, blue—that's all Kieran bothers to absorb before he's falling into the bed, straddling Seth's cock and running his hands down his chest. He grinds against Seth's stomach for the way the packer rubs his clit, riding it while Seth kisses him. Then Seth tips him over and crawls on top of him, hair dripping, and picks up the condom and lube.

Kieran gazes up at him, sweeping his eyes over Seth's long, skinny frame, the soft flecks of dark hair on his chest, his nipples hard and pink. His expression of intent concentration as he rolls the condom down on Kieran's packer and rips open the packet of lube. "Hey," Kieran says, "no rush—don't you need, like, prep?"

Seth pauses and looks abashed. "I, ah. No, I don't."

Kieran scoffs. "Are you sure? Because most guys do, and I'm not gonna hurt you."

"It's not that." Seth clears his throat. "I—I took care of that earlier, before... before I decided to go out."

"Wowww." Kieran can't choose between amused and turned on, and he hopes his tone conveys a little of both. He grabs Seth by the hips. "Okay. Then get your ass on my cock, boss."

"Please stop calling me that," Seth groans. But he slicks up Kieran's cock and lowers himself onto it, nice and slow, with a careful hiss as he sinks down to take it in completely. The pressure takes Kieran's breath away for a moment, and he forces himself to stay still, to not chase after the sensation by rolling his hips up and fucking into Seth before he's settled.

Seth runs his hands down Kieran's chest slowly, bracing himself, breathing deeply. "Oh." He mutters, half to himself, "I forgot what this is like."

"You're so *hot*," Kieran groans. "I'm so fucking glad."

Seth wipes his hair out of his face with a shaky smile. "Glad?"

"That you're not screwing some other lucky guy at the club right now?" Kieran runs his hands down Seth's legs, liking the soft scrape of Seth's hair under his palms. "That you're into me?"

"I'm glad you came and found me." Seth bends down and kisses him, one of those deep kisses Kieran just wants to sink into, and then he starts to rock his hips, sliding up on Kieran's dick and taking him deep again. He moans into Kieran's mouth with the motion, and bites his lip, enough to sting. His hands squeeze Kieran's chest, stroke his sides, and Kieran wraps his arms around Seth's back, pushing up, groaning when the base of the packer rubs all along his clit.

He's so *wet*, and so hungry for it—he almost yelps when Seth works himself deep on his cock, grinding into him, rutting him toward an orgasm that feels like months in the making.

Kieran reaches between them to palm Seth's dick, tugging it, matching the slow rolls of Seth's hips. Seth shudders and hangs his head, pressing his cheek to Kieran's shoulder, his stubble scraping at Kieran's collarbone. "Fuck," he whispers, barely a breath. His hips stutter, push back hard.

Kieran's not really interested in making this last; they've both been waiting a long time, and he wants to come, wants Seth to come with him. He grips Seth's cock and jerks him off, arching his hips up and grinding himself to completion, a white-hot burst of pleasure that makes his whole body squeeze tight, tight, tight—then feels Seth moan and come across his stomach, sticky and hot.

"Fuck," Kieran says. He deflates into the bed, head spinning.

Seth lets out a long sigh that seems to indicate agreement. He climbs gingerly off of Kieran's cock and collapses into the sheets at Kieran's side, his head landing on Kieran's shoulder.

Kieran sighs. "We gotta shower again."

"Mm."

Kieran turns his head, bumps his forehead against Seth's. "Can I, um... can I sleep here?"

"Of course." Seth draws a hesitant breath. "You're still interested in the job?"

"Of course I am. The only way I wasn't gonna say yes is if you changed your mind about wanting me there."

"I would never. And..." His voice gets so quiet, like he's scared to ask. "Will you stay for breakfast?"

Kieran cozies against him, grinning as he closes his eyes. "As long as you're cooking."

~~*

Of course, Seth turns out to be a real adult. The kind who gets up fuck-early in the morning.

Luckily, he doesn't try to rouse Kieran at whatever gross time it is. Even his slow and careful wriggling out of the bedcovers disturbs Kieran's slumber enough that Kieran groans at him, but Seth just presses a kiss to his forehead—Kieran grumbles sleepily—and slides out of the sheets, and then he's gone.

Kieran doesn't appreciate Seth being gone. He tries to go back to sleep on his own, but after an indeterminate period of trying to cuddle with one of Seth's lumpy pillows, he gives up and crawls bleary-eyed out of bed.

His clothes are folded politely on the bedside table. Definitely Seth's doing, because Kieran is sure he abandoned them on the bathroom floor last night.

As he's struggling into his shirt and underwear, Kieran looks around, taking in the clean but homey state of Seth's bedroom. There's a framed photo of Dragon on the bedside table, along with an old couple who might be Seth's parents; there's a UC Berkeley diploma and historical maps of San Francisco and New York hanging on the walls. A glance inside Seth's dresser confirms that he absolutely does fold his socks and sort them by color.

Then there's a desk, as painfully neat as the one he keeps at the office, but stacked with books and DVDs—Kieran catches sight of *Before Stonewall* and *The Celluloid Closet*. But further investigation reveals that the DVDs are mostly a collection of super schmoopy and decidedly un-historical gay movies.

Honestly, he's never met a guy more in need of a boyfriend.

Kieran hopes he's up to the task.

He pokes his head outside the bedroom, and the first thing he notices is the smell of bacon and eggs floating out of the kitchen. Seth is humming to himself, and the pan is sizzling. Something soft bumps against Kieran's ankle. He jumps, and looks down to see Dragon curling around his feet, purring like a garbage disposal.

"I think she likes me," Kieran calls.

Seth peers out of the kitchen, a pair of nerdy reading glasses perched on his nose. Kieran grins at the sight of him. "Well," Seth says. "Good. I don't know what I'd do if my cat didn't warm up to you."

"Kick me out on the spot, probably."

"Probably." A flicker of something—insecurity—passes across Seth's face. "Are you staying?"

Kieran smiles. "Yeah." He crouches down and scoops up the cat, wandering into the kitchen as she purrs into his shoulder. "Yeah, I think I am."

Breakfast comes served on fancy plates with a cup of coffee, black, no sugar. Seth has a cup of peppermint tea, and scrunches up his face when Kieran points out that he has a peppermint problem. But under the table, his foot rests against Kieran's ankle.

Kieran thinks about how every time he brings Seth a coffee, he's going to think of this. The smell of peppermint and diner food, Seth smiling, self-consciously pulling the collar of his pajama shirt up to hide the hickies on his neck. Kieran's never going to be able to look at his weird boyfriend across the office without grinning.

He could get used to that.

One Last Leap

HELENA MAEVE

The lane warped and snagged on sharp corners, as capricious as a length of yarn blown by the autumnal breeze. Down we went, flung through bends, clipping sidewalks with our rear tires, May's cackle overtaking the pounding in my ears.

"What's so funny?" I bit out. That I hadn't lost my supper yet was a modest sort of miracle.

That May still remembered where the brakes were blew my little triumph out of the water.

The Ford screeched to a halt, rubber burning into the asphalt as she raised a hand to point. "Look, darling. The sky is *shot with crimson. A splash of blood*! It's just like in that horrid book you keep quoting!"

Summoning what little self-control I had left, I pushed back from the dashboard where May's demented driving had flung me and flashed my most imperious sneer.

"You can piss right off, *darling*."

Typically, May found my comeback worthy of doubling over with laughter. Wispy white hair fluttered into her eyes...

I had a sudden image of us as the neighbours might have seen if they chose to peek out their window at five in the morning: prim and posh May with her snowy head and viciously rouged lips and red-nose, and me with my tie askew and shirt collar undone. What a pair we made!

I desperately hoped some industrious teen had dug out his smartphone and had started to film our antics. We could be YouTube gold. We could blow those suburban grandmothers sampling pot for the first time clean out of the water.

With the car blessedly at a standstill, I groped for the door lever and hauled myself from the passenger seat.

May's laughter followed me out. "What are you doing? I said I'd drive you to your door!"

"If you're starting to confuse my house with Manderley, you've clearly had too much to drink."

"Manderley!" she cried. "That's it! Now I remember! Oh, don't be such a bloody fool. You'll break something. It's still slippery out... Philip, get back in the bloody car!"

An early frost had settled over Hastings since last night, silvering hedges and houses alike, covering the sidewalks in treacherous black ice. BBC Weather had forecast it well in advance, but May and I decided they must be wrong. It was only September.

I held onto the Ford as I tested my footing. The BBC was not wrong. At this rate, we'd be going to the opera on sleighs.

"Well?" May asked, and I looked despondently at her. "Are you going to let me break my neck?"

"Ask me nicely and I might break it for you!"

May barked out a laugh, but I could see her considering it. "All right. But you're a daft old man. Can I park in your driveway?"

"You won't have room. Try down the street."

Left to her own devices, May put the car in gear and shot off like an arrow in search of a parking spot that wouldn't block the many garages on either side of the lane. The red lights at the rear of the Ford winked even as the rest of the chassis became one with the thick, black night.

I sucked in a frigid breath. Negotiating the slippery asphalt to the sidewalk was more or less feasible, but once there, I had to grab hold onto the nearest hedgerow to keep upright. My feet had a mind of their own. No matter how I tried to tighten every muscle south of my waist, I still felt on the brink of a tumble.

Because I'd drunk too much and because there was no one around to hear me, I chortled.

"You all right there?"

The voice came out of nowhere, as though the night itself was speaking to me.

I spun around, half certain I was hallucinating, and my right foot went skidding out from under me. My stomach pitched.

So much for effortless grace.

I reached out blindly.

Two meaty hands grabbed mine. Miraculously, I didn't hit the ground, nor break anything, nor find myself crying out in pain like so many extras on *Casualty*.

"Careful!"

Wind batted away the cloud and a shaft of moonlight snagged on the sharp angles of my rescuer's face. It was a good-looking face. Medieval and handsome, proud in some strange, arresting way that beckoned rather than repelled me.

"Ivan? What—what're you doing here?"

165

My builders hailed from Eastern Europe and worked with a hunger I'd never seen in any tradesman I had ever worked with. But their zeal was matched by the inconvenience of having their trailer parked behind the house; both they and I were stuck living on a building site.

Ivan nudged me a few paces away. With his help, I found a patch of sidewalk that had escaped the ice.

"Needed the phone," he answered as he released me.

He was a big guy, with biceps the size of tree trunks, but his voice was soft despite the faint trace of a Polish accent. Whenever we had reason to talk, I found myself thinking of suede or velvet—and then of nothing at all.

Ivan was my employee for the duration of the refurbishment. I couldn't afford to think of him in any other terms.

"The phone?" I frowned, thinking of the red booth at the bottom of the street. I hadn't realized it was still in use. "What's wrong with your mobile? Or the landline?"

"Landline is out of order. No more cables."

"Oh."

Ivan stuck his hands in his pants pockets, shivering. His breath misted when he spoke. "And no credit. But you're out late, too..."

Heat rose to my cheeks. "Ah, yes, I was..." I glanced in the direction of the house. There was no sign of May yet. "We should, um, we should go inside. You'll catch cold."

Christ, could I sound any more mumsy? I turned before I let myself be drawn into scrutinizing every twitch of Ivan's lips. Was he mocking me? Was he amused? Did he think he'd lucked out with a client who didn't know the first thing about construction work?

Providentially, May joined us on the doorstep before I inserted any more of my foot into my mouth.

"Bloody hell, it's freezing. I feel dreadfully sober—Oh, Ivan. I didn't see you there."

"Mrs Summers."

"How many times must I tell you? It's *Miss*, love." She emphasized the word with a conductor's flick of the wrist. "What were you doing out in this wretched weather? I hope you haven't started the day yet. Philip's working you to the *bone*, isn't he?"

I had the uncanny feeling that she was looking Ivan up and down for far more reason than to attest how overworked he was. My skin prickled with envy. Of course, *she* could get away with such a blatant show of interest; if I tried it, I'd probably get my teeth punched in.

"Mr. Irwin is a good boss, Miss."

Ivan's answer was so diplomatic that I instantly regretted the envious path my thoughts had taken.

At last, I fit the key into the front door and we hurried out of the cold. The hall was barely wide enough for all three of us and our cumbersome coats. The sullen gleam of a single light bulb made the space seem narrower than ever. As with the remainder of the house, Ivan had assured me that he knew what he was doing and I would be pleased with the result. I fervently hoped so. If asked in that moment, I would've liked nothing better than a functional kitchen and a modest conservatory, just as they'd been before I decided to invest thousands of pounds into ripping out all the floors and scraping the walls clean.

"Now, since you haven't started work yet," May cajoled, "I think you should join us for a drink, Ivan. What do you say?"

He swung his gaze from May to me and back, hesitating.

Overcompensating with an encouraging smile, I held up the whiskey. "Johnny Walker Green?"

Ivan arched his eyebrows. "I did not know they made it in green..."

"Oh, the things we could teach you about liquor," May boasted as she exchanged her gloves for a trio of heavy tumblers.

I poured and she distributed the glasses, retaining the tallest for herself. "Let me think. How do you say cheers in Polish, darling?"

"*Na zdrowie*," Ivan and I said nearly in unison.

May grinned. "Oh, I see. This isn't the first time you two indulged, is it? My, the secrets you keep, *Mr. Irwin*..."

If we'd been alone, I would have flipped her off. I bottled the impulse and let Johnny Walker soothe my prickly pride.

"How's the work advancing? I can't trust anything Philip tells me," May added, with a lackadaisical wave. "He doesn't know the difference between spackle and plaster."

"And you do?"

May shot me a withering stare. "I'll have you know I renovated six houses... All of them my husbands', granted, but I do believe that makes me something of an expert." And to prove it, she launched into one of her interrogations, holding Ivan up to account for every choice of material and technique.

They might have been speaking Chinese for all I understood.

Our night out slowly catching up to me, I soon tuned out their back and forth. My favourite armchair was comfortable and the whiskey worked quickly to banish the chill of the outdoors.

I watched May and Ivan through lowered lashes until my eyelids became too heavy to keep open.

I wasn't going to nap. I just needed to rest my eyes.

Just for a moment.

~~*

I jolted awake to the sound of laughter somewhere on the other side of the wall.

Light streamed through the sitting room windows, a crosshatch slanted across the rug. The clock on the mantel read nine-fifteen.

Ivan's team was already ripping away at the kitchen.

A quilt had been draped over my knees. There was no trace of May or Ivan.

Shame washed through me. I was fifty-two years old, not seventy. I was a man in my prime, for god's sake—napping at nine o'clock in the morning, in his favourite armchair.

Who was I kidding? The sheer fact that I had a favourite armchair was over-the-hill enough.

I quickly ripped off the quilt and stood, stretching my tired limbs. I almost would have preferred a hangover to the faint throbbing in my knees. At least hangovers reminded me of being on tour.

I gave up all hope of a surreptitious escape as I stepped over the sitting room threshold. A central hallway connected the front door of the cottage to the kitchen at the back. To cross to the stairs, I had to traverse a scant six feet of original Victorian tile.

Laughter aborted as soon as my tread echoed through the ancient house.

"Good morning." I tried for cheer and nonchalance, but standing in the kitchen doorway I had a hard time feeling anything but awkward.

Ivan's team was made up of four muscular men. Three of them spoke a little English. The fourth spoke none at all. But they all managed to muster a polite "good morning" when they saw me.

I had the uncanny feeling they'd stopped to stand at attention while I glanced over the destruction around us. May was right; I hadn't the first clue what to look for in the wreck of the room and there was only so much we could do with embarrassed smiles.

"Ivan around?" I wondered.

"In the garden," one of the builders told me.

I thanked him and turned away. It would have been awkward to head up to my room at once. Although the thought appealed and I was tired, I made a beeline for the mudroom, with its array of wellies and macs and so far undisturbed floor.

Better to rip off the bandage now than fret about what May might have said while I dozed away like an old geezer.

"Morning, Ivan," I called out. The flagstone path had once bisected rows and rows of azaleas. Now it was strewn with cement dust and in bad need of a scrub.

Ivan looked up from where he was measuring a slab of orange tile. "Mr. Irwin."

"One of these days, you'll have to start calling me Phil, you know..." I hugged my sides, my suit jacket and vest providing poor insulation against the cold. "How're you getting on?"

"Good. Everything is good." He pointed the measuring tape to the work bench, where a map of the kitchen sat beneath a trio of garden stones. "I think we might finish this today."

As I approached, I saw that it wasn't one of the plans I'd printed out for him, but a hand-drawn copy, the dimensions marked out in blue pen.

"What, the whole kitchen? I should get you drunk more often."

The words slipped out before I fully grasped what I was saying. By then it was too late, the joke hanging between us, as inappropriate as it was sobering.

"I didn't mean—"

"One little glass of whiskey is not enough to make me drunk," Ivan replied before I could get the apology out. He grinned, gaze lingering on mine for a long beat.

I swallowed and thought, absurdly, that his eyes tracked the bobbing of my Adam's apple.

There was liquor still in my bloodstream. I was hallucinating.

"I'll, um. I'll leave you to it." I made to retreat, but Ivan's voice brought me up short.

"Miss Summers is a nice lady."

"She is." Where was he going with this?

"And she is not married?"

171

"Not since her seventh divorce." Which I had predicted but regretted on May's behalf. "I must have missed some interesting stuff if you two got to talking about marriage..."

Ivan ducked his head, saying nothing.

Some interesting stuff, indeed. May was a beautiful woman. What she lacked in youth she made up for in charm and sophistication. I shouldn't have been surprised that Ivan had noticed as much, yet the thought of them together stuck in my craw.

"I'll ask if she wants her kitchen remodelled," I said. "I know for a fact she keeps a better liquor cabinet than me."

Ivan blinked at me, bemused. "That would be... kind."

"Don't mention it." I could feel my cheeks numbing with the cold. Hunger growled in my stomach. "I'll get out of your way." This time, I turned on my heel and did not look back.

Ivan said nothing to make me stay. I was an idiot to hope he might.

~~*

Under a leaden sky, the pier stretched out into the Channel waters like a lolling tongue. I watched seagulls swoop and dart through its metal supports, going in on one side and coming out on the other, their wings tight as they ducked under the whitecaps.

The morning chill had not abated by the time I sat down for brunch at a small café two doors down from the White Rock Theatre. In my pig-headedness, I'd picked a table on the sidewalk, hoping a cup of Earl Grey would warm me from the inside out.

No such luck.

My fingers were pink with the cold as I finished the last of my pulled pork sandwich. Doctor's warnings against red meat could not compete with my love of the very thing I'd been forbidden. Anyway, I wasn't going to live forever.

Bitterness would not surrender its grip. It had been my companion since leaving the house. Strolling through Hastings like a ship with no rudder, carting it around like a ballast as I settled the bill and started back down the seaside route toward home, did nothing to shift the chip on my shoulder.

I'd never been an outdoorsy sort, but today I was in no hurry to get back to the cottage. The thought of calling May for a chat rose and fell from my mind like the sea surf.

She'd pick at me like a heron if she saw me moping and I wasn't in the mood for her clucking and pitying sighs.

It wasn't May's fault that she was a magnet for all the men I fancied.

It wasn't Ivan's fault that he preferred her to a retired dancer whose knees clicked when he walked.

A shop window clouded as I passed before it. The reflection was foggy, my features superimposed on buff mannequins wearing low-slung jeans and garishly colourful hoodies. From the neck down, it wasn't so bad. I'd always been slim; it was a necessity if I wanted to fit into skin-tight leotards and not be shown up by my partners or the sixteen-year-olds in the chorus line. But my hair was thinning at the temples, black strands shot with more grey every year. And I could still see the scar at the corner of my right eye snaking down the cheek to disappear into my hairline.

Lucky, the doctors had called me. Half an inch closer and I would've lost the eye. As it stood, I only lost my nerve.

I turned away from the shop window.

The road home was largely devoid of pedestrians. Hastings in September was no one's idea of a holiday venue. Sometimes I wondered what had possessed me to come back. I could have lived anywhere in Britain—even bought a house in Spain now that the prices were so low.

But what would be the point? Terry was gone.

I stopped in at Waitrose for some precooked, pre-packaged greens before putting the town square behind me and allowing that I'd run out of places to hide.

The cottage was not the cacophony of Radio One and whirring saws I'd come to expect. As I stepped through the front door, I was astonished to discover a new floor laid out in the kitchen, tiles blending seamlessly into the ancient hallway flooring. A new lamp dangled over my head in the foyer—it was cast iron and blue glass, old-fashioned enough to fit the general feel of the house but new and functional all the same.

The men were outside, smoking and talking. I saw only a couple through the kitchen windows, but the rest couldn't be far.

Rhythmic thumps of the hammer put paid to that theory.

I tracked the sound into sitting room.

"Someone's been eating their spinach," I drawled, trying desperately not to let the sight of Ivan laying down laminate floorboards affect my tone. "Your lads're taking a break. Shouldn't you...?"

"I will."

Ivan reached for another board. They'd been cut to size already, I noticed, longer pieces laid out in one stack, shorter ones piled in another. I might not have known much about construction work, but I understood preparation.

"You know there's no prize for working twenty-four-hour days, yes?"

Without looking up, Ivan gave an acquiescing hum.

Oh, for God's sake. "Stop," I said, imbuing my voice with a sense of authority I hadn't felt in years.

To my surprise, Ivan did. His brows furrowed when he saw me begin to unload the shopping bag.

"Chicken salad. Grilled shrimp in bacon. And kale." I laid out one plastic container after the other. "There must be something here you like."

"You're very kind, but—"

"No buts. I don't want you hammering your fingers into my floor." When Ivan made no move to oblige me, I grabbed the kale. It would serve as my penance for the pulled pork sandwich.

Ivan sighed. I opened the lid and stabbed my plastic fork into the crinkly greens.

Eventually, still glaring, he reached for the chicken salad.

The tension between us didn't quite fade as we sat down to eat, me on the edge of the coffee table, he in the jungle of laminate boards.

"Kitchen's almost ready," I noted between bites.

"Mhm."

"And the conservatory's painted."

He nodded, pressing the back of his hand to his lips as he swallowed and said, "Should be done by the end of the week."

"What, with everything?"

"It is almost a month."

I knew that well. The kitchen had to be stripped down to the brick and cement, plumbing replaced and gas mains removed. My back garden bore all the evidence of the destruction that had been wrought— on my orders, with my money. But soon I would have the kitchen Terry and I had once talked about.

I saw myself eating clean, home-cooked meals while Tchaikovsky played in the background. I nearly choked on my kale.

"Good," I said, clearing my throat. "That's good. Excellent." *Overcompensating much?* "Here's hoping there are no more surprises."

Ivan offered one of his rarer smiles, the corners of his eyes crinkling with genuine amusement.

"Can't make promises."

"Just... let's not have any exterior walls collapse again." His mirth rallied my smile, no matter how I struggled to maintain the blasé façade. "I like my bedroom upstairs. I'd rather not end up at ground level."

"I will try."

"Do." *And while you're at it, try to stop looking at me like I'm a cool drink of water.*

I made my exit as quickly as I'd finished the kale, under the pretext of stowing the shrimp in the fridge. Ivan did not follow. He was done with his chicken salad by the time I brought him a cup of tea.

Our eyes met briefly as he thanked me, but whatever strange electricity had sizzled in the air just minutes before was now gone. I'd probably conjured it up out of melancholy.

It was just as well that the build would be finished by the week's end. This couldn't go on.

Four more days. I only had to behave myself for four more days.

~~*

I kept to my room for the rest of the day, snatching handfuls of sleep here and there when my third reread of *Rebecca* failed to retain my interest. When I blinked awake, the sky was a dark bruise mottled with thick, low-hanging cloud. More rain, I guessed, fumbling for the remote control.

The flat-screen television went dark at the touch of a button, the six o'clock news cut off midstream.

I scrubbed at my eyes as I swung my legs over the side of the bed. In the dark, the bedroom was a hoarder's paradise with a nostalgic flavour. All the knickknacks I'd been able to carry up the stairs had fetched up here.

My eyes swept over trophies and statuettes, framed photographs I hadn't the heart to throw away. Echoes of my former life stared back from shelves and boxes, as accusing as a pointed finger.

It was a relief to tug on a shirt and close the door behind me.

I washed the grit from my eyes in the bathroom, avoiding my reflection in the glass. Bad enough I could feel the scar beneath my fingertips; I didn't need to see it to know it was there.

On the landing, I hesitated. There was light in the yard—the men must be inside their caravan, relaxing after a busy day's work. It wouldn't be long now before they packed up their tools and restored my little cottage to its former quietude.

But a light streamed from the sitting room. I saw it clearly as I plodded down the landing in socked feet.

"You're not working still."

Ivan startled. He must have been entranced by his plans and calculator if he hadn't heard my descent. This house was like a megaphone, every sound magnified, replicated with a ghostly echo.

"Mr. Irwin. Phil," he amended. "I'm sorry, I was just—"

"Working."

"Not for this." He'd covered his scribbles with a splayed hand, but even his wide palms couldn't disguise the cornucopia of precise lines and hand-scrawled digits. "Working for myself. In my spare time. I'm sorry, I would be in the trailer but the football is on and it's very—"

Uproarious laughter trickled through the slightly ajar conservatory windows as though to offer proof.

"Noisy?" I guessed.

"Yes."

Flustered, Ivan had begun gathering his things, movements herky-jerky.

"Please don't stop on my account."

"I am in your home."

"You're in my home most days," I pointed out. "Sit. Work on your... thing." A smile tugged at the corners of my mouth. I sucked my cheeks in to conceal it. The last thing I wanted was for Ivan to think I was taking the mick.

The fridge had been moved out of the kitchen to make room for re-tiling and would soon be replaced with a newer, better version. I circled the dining table—relocated from the dining room after a portion of the exterior wall gave out—and rummaged inside for something to eat.

"So no football for you?" I pitched over my shoulder.

"Arsenal is playing."

"You don't like Arsenal?"

"If I watch, Arsenal loses."

I turned, the chill of the fridge rippling under my shirt. "Huh?"

Ivan's back was to me, shoulders slumped, but he'd stopped drawing.

"You'll say it is superstition."

"Well, if the shoe fits…"

Ivan flung out his hands in a minute, helpless gesture. "But it is true. Whenever I watch a game, Arsenal loses. If I don't watch, they win."

"Uh-huh." I let the fridge door swing shut. "Does Arsenal know about this?"

I regretted the joke when Ivan thinned his lips and looked pointedly down at the papers strewn over the dining table. I held out my box of bacon-wrapped shrimp.

He shook his head.

"I'm not judging you, I swear. Look, before I went on stage—back when I still went on stage, that is—I'd swallow toothpaste."

"Why?"

It was my turn to feign indifference. "It worked. I swallowed toothpaste, I'd give a good show. I didn't and disaster struck. Nikiya would knee me in the groin coming out of her *rond de jambe.* Or the Wilis would drive me to the edge of the stage. I remember one time I had a full-on diva moment and sent Terry home for it..." Breath snagged sharply in my throat.

I'd sent Terry home. I'd been such a pain.

Ivan waited me out, his brown eyes intent. "You danced?" he asked, when I failed to pursue my trip down memory lane.

I smiled stiffly. "A long time ago."

"Ballet?"

I braced myself for his ridicule as I nodded.

"Oh. That's hard."

"It is." Where was the snickering? Wasn't he going to ask me about the tights?

"My sister wanted to do ballet," Ivan recalled. "She's a schoolteacher now."

Probably for the best. I looked down at the table. "I didn't know you had a sister."

Ivan held up two fingers. "One younger, one older."

"No brothers?" I couldn't imagine Ivan with siblings. I couldn't imagine him as part of family unit, laughing and chatting at the table, passing plates of *pierogis* around. He might as well have sprung fully formed from the ether, and to the ether he would return when he finished refurbishing my kitchen.

He had no brothers, he said, but all his cousins were boys. Most were already fathers themselves. I quickly lost track of the nephews and nieces, his extended family as complicated as a Russian epic. But I didn't need to remember each name to enjoy his sudden effusiveness. I wasn't sure quite how I'd driven Ivan into speaking so freely. It hardly mattered.

"What is it?" he asked, stopping midway through a story about Christmas two years ago.

"I've never seen you so animated. It's nice."

Ivan folded his hands at once, scratching idly at his nose.

"I'm sorry. I didn't mean to make you uncomfortable—"

"You don't."

I appreciated his saying so, but I could tell when a man was self-conscious; it was a bit of like calling to like, I supposed, something familiar in the dart of his gaze, the arch of his shoulders.

"You don't," he said again, quieter.

"Do you miss your family?" I deflected.

"Yes."

"Will you be going back, then? When you finish here."

Ivan snatched a grilled shrimp. "I may."

"Unless you find another job?" The scribbles on the dining table suggested that he'd already been hired; I didn't recognise the house he was working on in the exquisitely realistic drawings that peeked from beneath plans and sheets of additions and divisions.

"I think... I would like to build. Next."

"Build?" I frowned. "You mean from scratch?"

He canted his head. "I have a little money. I know how... Why not?"

In his voice, I heard my twenty-year-old boasts. Why not try my luck in St. Petersburg? Why not assume I was good enough for New York?

I had a glimpse of what it meant to be young and fearless again, and my insides gave a guilty, nervous quiver.

"Why not, indeed... I should put this in the trash before it starts to smell fishy."

Ivan's hand covered mine on the box. "I will do it."

"Don't be silly." My voice cracked. I was suddenly acutely aware of his touch.

His palm was callused and warm, fingers all hangnails and frayed skin. Did I imagine him squeezing my hand? I knew that some Eastern European cultures were more touchy-feely than others, but surely he'd worked enough in the UK to know that wasn't the case here.

But Ivan simply rose from his seat and, with his free hand, grabbed the container. "Will you make tea?"

"Um, sure."

"I can never make it taste as well." He towered over me, a big, imposing mountain of a man, but his brown eyes were soft and crinkled at the corners.

He was still smiling as he left the room.

Lightheaded, I let out a breath I hadn't realised I was holding. There was every chance he was pulling my leg. The urge to call May leapt inside me. I reached for my mobile.

But May would never let me live this down.

She'd want to know why I even assumed my contractor had any interest in playing games. Why I cared.

I set my mobile back onto the side table; I was a grown man in full control of my faculties. It took more than a few taunting apropos to rattle me. *It must.*

I stood on wobbly knees and went in search of the kettle.

~~*

Ivan was only too appreciative of the Earl Grey. He drank his with honey rather than sugar, two spoonfuls stirred into a blend so murky that the bottom of the cup no longer showed. Each sip was prefaced by a soft exhale that stirred the steam rising from the surface, and followed by a delighted moan.

I shifted uncomfortably in my armchair. Eighty quid worth of whiskey hadn't generated anything close to this reaction.

Perhaps we should have stuck to hard liquor.

"Do you still dance?" Ivan asked out of the blue.

"Hmm? Oh, no." I held the teacup to my lips, a makeshift shield against the harsh truth. "I'm too old for that." I'd been old since I turned thirty-five.

"Teach?"

I shook my head, skin prickling. Why did he want to know? "Too old for that, too."

A wrinkle deepened the furrow between Ivan's thick eyebrows. "Why? You're still fit."

Language barriers being what they were, I chose to believe he didn't fully grasp the meaning of the expression.

"I'm in good health," I agreed, "but you need more than that to put up with parents who expect you to turn their daughters into the next *prima ballerina assoluta*."

"Good health," Ivan echoed, "except for whatever happened here..." He jerked his chin, gaze zeroing on a point just slightly to the right of my eye.

I dropped my hand hastily. I hadn't realised I was worrying the scar.

"Sorry," he said, noticing my flinch.

"It's all right," I lied. I'd already said too much.

"No, it is none of my business."

"Don't be daft. It's fine. You can ask." My answer came out sharper than intended. I scowled into my cup.

We'd moved to the armchairs by the silent hearth. A single lamp was lit in the corner, splashing Ivan's silhouette over the rug, the dining table lost to the shadows of the room.

I felt both furious and petulant, and both sentiments annoyed me in equal measure. "It's a matter of public record. It was even in the papers." I waved my hand as though dragging the headline into the air between us. "'Disgruntled mother attacks former star dancer in injured child dispute'. This was in the days before *Dance Mums*, of course... *The Daily Mail* had a ball. Suppose it was a slow news day."

It was also, like so much of what the *Mail* printed, an unambiguous lie.

"What happened?"

"We opened the dance school in London. All very posh, very exclusive. First week of classes, girl complains of pain in her hip while she's practising at the bar. I tell her to push through it, that's what real dancers do... Twenty minutes later, she's on the floor, her hip's dislocated and, oh yes, the BBC is here to film a special for their breakfast show." I grimaced at the memory. "Suffice to say we didn't get the kind of press we'd hoped."

"Was she all right?"

I nodded. "She was diagnosed with Ehlers-Danlos. It's not life-threatening, but it tanked her mother's dreams of a ballet career by proxy." And my dreams of life after the stage.

With my reputation in tatters, I'd closed up shop, salvaged what money I could from the investment, and retired. I still felt the sting of failure.

"You said we."

"Pardon?" I was slow to crawl out of the deep well of memory. By the time I realised my mistake, it was too late to claim I'd misspoken. "Oh. I had a partner. Terry."

"Was she a dancer, too?"

"No..."

"Money?" Ivan guessed.

Blood whooshed in my ears. My fingertips numbed around the teacup. Suddenly I was pinned beneath Ivan's inquisitive stare, unable to extricate myself. I wasn't sure I wanted to. The last person I'd talked to about any of this was May, and that was ages ago.

"*He,*" I corrected, "was my... romantic partner."

Here it comes, I thought. Now for the thinning of the lips, the subtle shift that said *I'm no longer comfortable being alone with you*, the staple of straight men who felt as though they'd been hoodwinked into treating me like one of the guys when I was something else. Something daunting.

I didn't think Ivan would raise a hand to me in my own home, which was more than could be said for years past. The stage had protected me from that kind of treatment at work, but I no longer had the limelight on my side.

"Oh."

"Oh?" I parroted, adrenalin simmering in my veins. "Is that all?"

Ivan set his cup on the coffee table, every movement slow and precise. "Oh," he repeated pointedly, "I thought May and you were a couple."

"Sorry to disappoint." Acerbic beat anxious any day.

Ivan clenched his jaw, stubble shifting to a darker tint beneath the dim glow of the halogen bulb. "I should go back to the caravan."

"What about Arsenal?"

"The game will be over."

"All right." I flicked my fingers in mocking goodbye, turning the camp up to eleven. "Don't let the bedbugs bite."

"Good night," Ivan said, rising. He didn't bolt from the room as though afraid my queerness might rub off, but he wasn't exactly sluggish in putting one foot in front of the other.

Yet much to my surprise, he lingered just inside the mudroom door, the wall between hallway and sitting room nearly hiding him from view.

"You are lucky."

"Excuse me?" I must have misheard.

"To be able to say it. As you do."

I frowned. Say what? That I was a poof? It wasn't as though I shouted it from the rooftops. I was no activist; I'd never been to a gay pride parade in my life. "Well, I'm glad *you* approve." Condescension was preferable to revulsion, but I would've happily done without either.

Moonlight streamed through the mudroom window, casting a shaft of light across Ivan's rugged features.

"You are lucky," he said again. "We cannot all be so brave."

A muscle slid in his jaw, and for a moment I thought he might say more. He didn't.

The back door opened briefly and then swung shut with a quiet click. I caught a brief glimpse of Ivan stalking away toward the rear of the garden before the darkness swallowed him whole.

I took a sip of my lukewarm tea. Had he just said what I thought he'd said?

~~*

May picked up on the second ring. "M'ello?"

"It's me." We'd long given up on names. As we aged, the number of people who willingly called us early in the morning had dwindled to a tiny handful, plus telemarketers.

"Call back later."

"Are you still in bed?"

"It's seven o'clock on a bloody Thursday," May grumbled. "And I *hate* Thursdays."

"Since when?"

"Since they come before Friday and drinks on the waterfront with my least favourite person."

In other words, me.

I heard the rustle of sheets and imagined May pushing herself up to lie with her back to the mountain of pillows she could afford to keep in her bed now that she no longer had to make room for a husband.

"Well? What do you want? It must be something important if you're disturbing my beauty sleep."

"You know how I conked out the other day?"

"You'll have to be a little more specific. Old men and their kips..."

187

I rolled my eyes, impatient. "After the opera. Johnny Walker might have been involved—"

"Ah, yes. I remember. Mr Walker, Mr Ivan and I had a jolly good time while you snored."

Oh God, had I? I'd slept surprisingly well in my armchair, something I attributed entirely to the alcohol in my system, but that didn't make it any less awkward.

"You and Ivan talked... Right?"

"Are you asking if we talked about *you*? How self-centred you are, darling!" May snorted, trailing off on a yawn. "If you must know, we did. A little. He asked if *Mrs* Irwin was no longer in the picture. You know that portrait of Dame Margot you've got on the mantel? He thought that was your wife."

I closed my eyes and the view from my bedroom window faded. In the sitting room downstairs, there was indeed a framed original of Margot Fonteyn, one of the greatest ballerinas to ever grace the stage.

"Frankly, I think he was trying to figure out if you and I are doing the dirty," May went on.

"Ugh, never say that again."

"What? Are you too prim to talk about sex? You're *not* that old. And that hunk of yours certainly isn't. Oh, what I'd like to do to him! Perhaps I'll seduce him..."

I opened my eyes, the spill of sunlight like pinpricks beneath my lids. "I'd love to see you try."

"You *would*, you filthy old man... What's this about, Philip?"

"I was just curious."

"About your contractor."

Tongue jammed into the roof of my mouth, I acquiesced wordlessly.

"Phil."

Silence wouldn't spare me May's whip-sharp intuition. "I should go. Lots to do. Did I tell you they're finishing up this week?"

May hummed, dubious. "Are we still on for drinks tomorrow?"

"Why wouldn't we be?" The forced cheer in my voice was about as pleasant as the whir of power tools for once absent from the house.

"I don't know. Maybe you have plans with your hunky contractor?"

"Goodbye, May."

"Now that you mention it, he *did* stare at you a lot—"

I hung up before her taunts could add fuel to the fire roaring between my ears.

Below, in the garden, Ivan had just emerged from the trailer. His overalls hung tantalisingly low at his hips, sleeves knotted around his waist. His bare chest heaved with breath as mine instantly hollowed. He was just shrugging into a T-shirt when, purely by chance, he happened to look up.

Our eyes met through the windowpane.

Oh, no.

Ivan froze, shirt rolled up his arms but upper body still exposed, the veins in his neck showing in sharp relief against pale skin. He swallowed hard.

I felt like a teenager again, caught spying on one of my mates.

I was about to expire, my lungs burning for air. I was about to get my arse kicked.

Then Ivan finished tugging his shirt over his head. Our stare broke. I did the only thing I could and staggered away from the window. What was I doing?

It was one thing to befriend Ivan, quite another to spy on him.

It's not his friendship you want, a voice crowed at the back of my mind.

I couldn't deny it. I pressed the heels of my palms into my eye sockets, as though the sight of a shirtless, buff Ivan was something I could unsee.

~~*

Staying in my room all day was not feasible. I discovered this around eight-thirty, when hunger and thirst finally gained the upper hand on my humiliation. I dressed as though I was preparing to go out and bustled quickly through the boiling of a kettle, the business of sticking teabag into tea mug.

"Good morning."

Ivan's voice startled me from my pretend preoccupation.

"Good morning!" I replied, gratuitously cheerful, tasting ash in the back of my mouth.

His shirt was mercifully *on* when I cut my eyes to him, though he almost seemed to fill the conservatory door with the broad span of his shoulders. Had he always been this imposing, or was I casting him in a new light because my thoughts were running away with me?

"Who won the game?" was the first thing I could think to say. It came out in a rush, my trepidation barely masked by the hiss of the electric kettle.

"Arsenal."

"Good thing you didn't watch, then." *Good thing you stayed to talk to me.*

Ivan smiled crookedly. "Are you going to the shops?"

"Thought I might," I said, glad for a topic of conversation to distract me from his bowed lips.

Neither his—potential—interest in men nor his—potential—inclination to tolerate my leering at him like a pervert meant that he was by default interested in *me*. My romantic history would have been a lot pleasanter if all the good-looking men I'd ever fancied also fancied me back. Life just didn't work out that way.

Ivan held up a two ten-quid notes. "We're out of cigarettes."

"Oh."

Hope shattered. He just needed a favour. *Stupid, stupid.* Perhaps it was true what they said about men of a certain age: we regressed from rational beings to spoilt brats, greedy and cranky when our needs weren't met.

I snatched up my cup with one hand and held out the other for the money. "And brand I should look for?"

Barred from any vices that might interfere with my performance, I'd never picked up the habit in my youth and in this day and age of inch-tall warning labels I found it pointless to start.

"Camels," Ivan suggested. "A pack or two. Nothing too expensive, though."

"Sure. Anything else?"

"No. I mean, if you have time to get the shrimp thing again..."

"Bacon-wrapped?" I smirked. "A man after my own heart."

Ivan's fingers brushed mine as the twenty pounds exchanged hands. A shudder raced up the length of my arm, sparking somewhere deep in the pit of my stomach.

"Thanks."

"Anytime," I answered.

Again our eyes met and held, but whether his gaze was meaningful or mocking, I had no way of judging. I looked away first. There was food enough left in the fridge for a quick breakfast, but I wanted to be out of the house as soon as possible.

Just when I thought I'd gotten away with it and my little foible this morning wasn't going to be mentioned, I heard Ivan's voice from the conservatory. He was humming surprisingly well, his choice of song none other than Rockwell's "Somebody's Watching Me."

My cheeks burning, I couldn't close the front door behind me fast enough.

~~*

Waitrose was only so effective as a distraction. I wandered the aisles for far longer than necessary and still I barely managed to kill an hour before I found myself lugging lunch and cigarettes home in a single shopping bag.

The chill of the last few days had finally broken, and a late summer sun splashed the coast in warm amber hues. I thought of taking the long way back, but it seemed too much as though I was trying to avoid Ivan. My behaviour bordered on the irrational. I wasn't afraid of his reaction; I wasn't going to shy from crossing his path as though I'd committed some great sin.

My eyes had strayed, that was all.

I was willing to bet he'd done it, too, though obviously not for the likes of me.

I didn't let myself slow down until I was well onto my lane and could turn neither left nor right. These daily walks were certainly doing miracles for my creaking joints. Since retiring, exercise and I had mostly parted ways. I had no reason to keep my silhouette, much less work out obsessively lest my arms drop my co-stars mid-performance. I had no one to keep in shape for, my interest in dating having dwindled since Terry.

Had something changed? I turned the key in the lock and was greeted with the whir of a sanding machine in one room, the grunts of straining workers in the other.

Lunch went into the fridge, stowed for whenever the men decided to take a break. The cigarettes I placed on the counter in the kitchen.

Sound trailed me up the stairs. The bedroom door muffled it a little, but not enough to offer me peace. *Just a few more days of this and I'll have peace.* Despite the mess downstairs, I knew the finish line was in sight. It should have been a relief—no more ruckus, no more cement bags or skip in the driveway.

I grabbed *Rebecca* off the bedside table and, toeing off my socks, settled against the pillows to read. Tuning out the commotion was easier when my mind's eye saw only fancy-dress parties and sour housekeepers.

Lunch came and went, the frenzy downstairs interrupted for an hour then picking up again as shadows deepened steadily. I popped down to fetch something to eat but didn't stick around for conversation. Ivan's conspicuous presence played no tiny part in my desire to climb upstairs and close the door on the rest of the world.

Like the old man I'd become, I dozed in the afternoon and woke to find the sky pitch dark. *Rebecca* had somehow rolled under me while I slept.

I pried out the much-abused paperback and did my best to smooth out the bent corners. But as I did so, the photograph I used as my bookmark slid out and fluttered to the floor.

I made to grab it, but drowsiness slowed my reflexes. My fingers closed around thin air.

The photograph found the groove between two floorboards and improbably slotted right through the gap. It was a narrow portrait frame, one of those tacky photo-booth affairs I'd gotten at the mall, back when such things were still a novelty.

A cry scraped the inside of my throat.

Bile pitched into my mouth and suddenly I was frantic, on hands and knees by the side of the bed, scratching and pinching with my useless hands at the corner that protruded. Yet for all my efforts, I couldn't grasp hold. My nails dug into the meat of my fingertips again and again, but the photograph remained where it was—stuck.

"Come on, you bleeding, stupid—"

"Phil?" Ivan's voice echoed, muffled, through the bedroom door.

I fumbled for some semblance of self-control. "What is it?" What was he doing up here?

"I thought I heard a shout... Everything all right?"

"Yes!"

"Are you sure?"

"I... No." I sank against the bed frame, too frustrated to lie. My eyes stung.

"May I come in?"

In my private, unacknowledged fantasies, I'd imagined Ivan setting foot into my bedroom for the first time. Of course, I had, though in *my* version of what went on once he stepped over the threshold, the room was spic and span, no clutter in sight, and I wasn't wearing a pair of faded pyjama bottoms with a thin undershirt.

"It's open."

The doorknob turned with a click.

"I dropped something," I explained, reluctantly raising my blurry eyes to his. "I'm not normally this pathetic."

"Under the bed?"

I shook my head and ran my fingertips over the groove in the oak boards.

"What was it?"

"A photograph. It's not... it's nothing important." No one had autographed it for me. I wasn't holding onto it as a family heirloom. If anything, the rush of adrenalin I felt at the thought of losing the photo was wholly mystifying.

Ivan must have come to the same conclusion because after a beat, he turned on his heel and walked out the door. It was such a smooth, uncompromising exit that I nearly laughed. It seemed like something out of a play. My over-dramatic despair no less so.

But a moment later he was back, something shiny in his right hand. Pliers, I realised at once, but with a narrow tip and thin blades instead of the wire-cutters I was familiar with.

Ivan knelt down in the narrow gap between bed and dresser, and skilfully worked the slightly parted blades into the gap of the floorboards. He took my hand as the photograph emerged and deposited his finding safely into my palm.

"There. No harm done."

He didn't comment on the absurdity of the moment, nor ask who the man in the photo was. He could have done—I wouldn't have begrudged him the curiosity. But he didn't.

A smile crinkled the corners of his eyes. "It's good to have a toolbox in the house, yes?"

With Terry's likeness clutched in my hand and half driven out of my mind, I tipped forward. I didn't think. I didn't let myself hesitate. I simply pressed my lips to Ivan's in a reckless, ill-considered kiss.

It took me a moment to grasp the magnitude of what I'd done. Then another to realise that Ivan wasn't kissing me back.

I broke away with a sharp inhale, my insides rioting, my face aflame.

"Oh God, I'm so sorry."

"No," Ivan started, shaking his head as if to clear it.

"*Yes.* I shouldn't have done that. Christ, I don't know what came over me..." I scrabbled to my feet on jelly legs, desperate to put some distance between us. It was one thing to discover we were alike in one improbable respect and another to take advantage of his willingness to share that part of himself with me.

My stomach dropped into my knees. "I—there's no excuse." I pressed my forehead into the still-open door and squeezed my eyes shut. Anyone might have come in and seen us. Ivan's lads were just downstairs.

"You were upset."

"That's not—"

"The picture," Ivan went on, "losing it upset you... I understand."

With some effort, I made myself meet his gaze. He was offering me a way to save face. Why?

He rose smoothly. "I am not offended."

"Oh."

"Terry, was it?"

I nodded.

"He is a lucky man." Unflappable, Ivan ducked his head and walked out with that strange parting volley, steps creaking as he left me to wrestle with my humiliation alone.

I sank to the bed and put my head in my hands. The edge of the photo scraped the scar on my temple. I clutched it tighter. *Lucky.*

Had Ivan said as much to Terry, he would have laughed in his face.

~~*

An evening and a night, and there was still no sign of Ivan when I left the cottage on Friday morning to go on my usual stroll. I had hours to kill before May came down from London, so I went along my habitual route—market, pier, castle, then market again. But where I would have turned toward home, I spurred my steps and passed into the grounds of St. Agnes.

197

The church and I were barely acquainted. I'd been invited to a couple of weddings there, the odd christening. By now the couples I'd watched tie the knot under the solemn gaze of ancient Norman effigies had likely split up, remarried. The babies were adults christening their own children.

I took a seat in a pew at the very back, where some mason had made a hash job of repairing St. Paul's stony likeness. Silence reigned in the cavernous interior. St. Agnes was a small house of worship—intimate, I'd seen it described in guidebooks—but with its plethora of statues, it also seemed perpetually overcrowded.

At eleven in the morning on a Friday, parishioners were few and far between. Most, like me, sat in silent contemplation beneath some apostle's unseeing eyes.

The last time I'd set foot inside St. Agnes, I had worn a black suit and black tie, neither of which I remembered purchasing. The clothes just appeared inside my wardrobe on the day of the funeral. I'd done my bit by tugging them on and walking to church. By saying my goodbyes.

Guilt hooked its talons into my chest. How many years had it been since I'd visited the cemetery next door? Three, four? Surely no more than five.

Today was as good a day as any to break that streak.

I didn't move from the pew. My limbs would not obey.

He's just next door. He's waiting. You've been a terrible husband.

The old litany came back slowly but steadily. The moment my lips brushed Ivan's, I knew it was only a matter of time before I turned remorse into self-flagellation.

I reached into my breast pocket and carefully removed the photograph I'd nearly lost to a crack in the ground. In it, my face was only a sliver—one blue eye, a long nose, the jut of a pointed chin—but Terry grinned back from the glossy snapshot with leading-man good looks. I ran my thumb over the smooth-shaven shelf of his jaw. My palm still remembered the texture of his curly hair.

My lips remembered his mouth.

But other parts of me remembered other parts of him. The yoke of his digits had eaten into the flesh of my wrists. My hair was paradoxically thinner at my nape, where he liked to tear out strands because he said it calmed him. If I walked my fingertips two inches right of my bellybutton, I could feel the crenulated jab of his bony knuckles.

You earned that one in the end. You had it coming.

Kissing strangers in the bedroom we'd shared counted as a trespass against vows we never took. But Terry was gone and my secret relief at losing him had finally found its outlet.

I grabbed hold of the pew in front and hoisted myself to my feet. With pockets empty, it was easier to walk out of the church than it had been going in.

~~*

"Don't take this the wrong way, darling, but you're a great big bore tonight."

I huffed as I turned to May. "Is there a *right* way to take that?"

"You know what I mean. You're so..." She lifted her hands from the steering wheel and waved them in a distracted arc. "You're not your usually loquacious self."

"We were at the theatre. Should I have talked through the performance?"

"You normally do."

I frowned. "Do I? How rude of me."

But May wasn't about to be driven off the scent. As we idled at a red light, she turned to me, drumming her fingernails on the wheel. "Is it the hunky contractor?"

"Would you stop calling him that?"

"Well, he is, isn't he?" May pursed her lips. Tonight, she'd gone for a dark shade of purple that would have been more at home on the mouth of a teenager. The contrast with her snow-white hair was slightly eerie, but like everything else about May, she made it work. "Just tell me you're not hung up on him and I'll leave off."

"I'm not hung up on him."

"Then *what?*"

I raised my eyes to the sky. "Really shouldn't have walked into that one."

"Did something happen? You sounded off on the phone yesterday. He didn't intimidate or—?"

Her guess couldn't have been further from the truth. "I'm a grown man, May. I can take care of myself. And the light's changed."

A car behind us honked, as though in agreement.

May's mouth flattened into a thin, displeased line as she put the Ford into gear. The motorist tailing us decided we still weren't going fast enough for his tastes and overtook us in the next flat stretch. The

roar of his—and I was almost certain it was a *he*—
revving engine raised the hair on my arms.

Was this how bad May and I got when we'd had a
little bit too much to drink? Contrition found me,
constantly months and years late.

"You couldn't always," May said into the ensuing
silence.

She kept her eyes on the road and her hands on
the steering wheel, but still I felt the weight of her
words as though she'd seized my shoulders and given
me a shake.

I opened my mouth to contradict her. *Rubbish!
Don't you remember the hell I put Terry through?
What about my pre-show rituals, eh? I drove him
bananas.* The lies stuck to my tongue like honey. I
swallowed them back.

"How long have you known?" I asked instead.

May swallowed audibly. "Since the academy."

Seventeen years. A gut punch would've winded
me less.

"Why didn't you say anything? Why...?"

"You would've told me I was crazy, stirring
trouble." She cut her eyes to mine. "Do *you* think you
would've reacted well?"

At thirty-five, my ego had been the size of the
Royal Opera House.

My silence was an answer in itself.

Sighing, May pulled to a stop outside the cottage.
"I know you're going to say it wasn't what I think—"

"It was." I couldn't look at her.

The house was dark but for a single light peeking
through the sitting room curtains. I thought of Ivan at
the dining table, his broad form squeezed into a too-
tight gap, his back against the wall. I imagined him

industriously calculating dimensions and sketching out ideas.

He was by far the most patient man I'd ever known. He always said what he meant—bluntly, perhaps, but in the short six weeks I'd known him, he hadn't gone back on his word once.

"We don't have to talk about it," May told me softly. "It doesn't change anything."

"I'm still your least favourite person?"

Her smile was tepid. I reached across the gearshift. "I want to tell you."

"Okay."

We made plans to meet again for Sunday brunch. Hastings boasted enough waterfront tourist traps to tempt even someone with May's eclectic tastes, but I had the uncanny feeling she agreed mostly for my sake. She thought I needed to talk.

She wasn't wrong.

I stood on the sidewalk until the Ford had disappeared from view, then turned and made my way into the house.

It was no longer unusual to step into the cottage and find the lights still on. But today the builders were not at work. From the entryway, I saw that the new kitchen cupboards had been fitted into place, a new table slotted into the breakfast nook. To my right, the dining table had been moved back to its proper place across the hall, all six chairs arranged around it.

I looked to the light, then, into the sitting room where Ivan had just jolted to his feet.

"Hi."

"Hi," I echoed.

The conservatory was finished, too. My potted herbs and vegetables had recovered their place under the newly sealed double-glazed greenhouse windows.

"You've been busy." I kept my tone light.

Ivan glanced around himself, as though uncertain if every piece of furniture had regained its place. There were still gaps, of course, mostly owed to the boxes I'd taken upstairs, but I discovered I liked this minimalist design better.

It was enough to have Dame Margot preside over the room from the portrait on the mantelpiece. Perhaps the rest of my junk could stay in storage.

I hauled my gaze back to Ivan's. "Does this mean you're finished?"

"The skip will be moved in the morning and we still have some cleaning to do outside, but... yes, for the most part." His eyes met mine, the ring of brown so thin against the inky black of his pupils that I could barely tell the difference.

"Then I suppose I should get the chequebook..." I doffed my coat and hung it up on the hook in the foyer, the cage of my ribs suddenly tight around my lungs. There was no point delaying. I started down the hall toward the safe built into the cupboard under the stairs.

A fickle hope shot through me when I heard Ivan's footsteps, but he hung back, waiting for me in the sitting room. Chequebook in hand, I nudged the cupboard door shut with my socked foot.

"Do you have a pen?"

If I didn't look up as I filled out the dotted lines in clear ballpoint print, it was as though we were client and supplier, employer and employee. Nothing more.

The heat that prickled at my nape as I straightened was best ignored.

"The remaining fifty percent of your fee. Pleasure doing business."

Ivan took the cheque gingerly, looked at it for a moment, then extricated his wallet and folded it neatly inside.

"So you'll be leaving tomorrow?" My voice cracked. It had been a day for emotional ups and downs. I'd be right as rain by morning.

And Ivan would be gone not long after that.

"I think so."

"Any idea where? I know you said you want to buy a plot of land—I hear prices are low in Cornwall. Of course, that's coming from May, so do take my input with a grain of salt..." I busied myself with rearranging a few lamps that had been relocated from their proper places during the refurbishment. Any excuse was good to keep me from staring at a man I couldn't have.

Ivan's hand had alighted on my shoulder.

I wasn't a good enough actor to pretend I didn't feel it. I dug my fingers into the blue ceramic vase I'd decided I liked better on the credenza. "What is it?"

Ivan tightened his hold. I felt the strength of his grip, his calloused, hardworking builder's hand, and let him turn me around. The urn was a poor shield between us, but I was too anxious to let it go.

"We shouldn't," I started, wishing my voice didn't quake.

"Why?"

"You're leaving." It was the first excuse that crossed my mind, nowhere near to the foremost objection I could bring to bear. "You're working for me—"

"Not anymore." Ivan's gaze was mild. "Why else?"

"You're far too young." *And far from home. And from a different world.*

Ivan knew about cement and plaster, the correct way to lay down tile or insulate a bathtub. He dreamed of building a home with his bare hands.

I knew *grand jetés*, pointe and *revoltades*. My dreams belonged to the past.

"Does it bother you?" he wondered.

"It should bother *you*."

"Why?"

"Because... because..." My mind a blank, I could do nothing but stare at his mouth. I'd noticed the bow of his lips before, but I'd never allowed myself to imagine kissing it—even once I had.

I closed my eyes, lightheaded with the urge to touch him.

Ivan curled his hand around my nape, holding me in place. "Because what, Philip? If you don't want... I can stop. I will go."

No, I didn't want that. The very possibility lit a spark of urgency in my chest. *Don't go.*

My last ounce of common sense expired as I hooked my own fingers into his shirt and hauled him closer.

Our lips met in a sloppy, tooth-clacking kiss. It was as graceless as yesterday's attempt, but infinitely better because this time—this time Ivan kissed me back.

He cupped my cheek with his broad palm, angling me into the kiss, and took over. I let him do it, so desperate for his touch that I could hardly do anything else. I opened my mouth to his when I felt the probing stroke of his tongue against my lips and my whole body melted, tension leaching out in a sudden rush.

I groped for purchase on the credenza at my back, then when that wouldn't do it, on Ivan's shoulders, his tapered hips. I wanted him close, closer than this.

"Bedroom," I choked out, breaking the kiss.

His breath gusted against my cheek. "Are you sure?"

It wasn't the response I'd counted on, and my first thought was that he asked because *he* wasn't.

"Don't you want to?"

Ivan kissed me again, his hand fingers carding into my hair. I had my answer.

We staggered up the stairs in an awkward shuffle, hips and shoulders striking furniture and walls along the way. I spared a thought for Ivan's underlings, but when I broke our kiss long enough to check that they wouldn't venture into the house, he assured me they'd gone down to the pub to celebrate.

"They'll think you're weird," I panted. "First the footie, now the pub..."

"Don't care what they think," Ivan said and pulled his shirt over his head.

If I lived to be a hundred, I'd never stop feeling ashamed of the squeak I made at the sight of him bare-chested.

Ivan grinned. "You've seen me before."

"Not up close." I ran my fingertips reverently up his flanks. I was hardly celibate by nature, but it had been years since I'd touched a man. Years since I'd wanted to.

I pushed away from the door and nudged Ivan back, my eyes on his, until his calves hit the mattress. He dropped with a soft *whoop*, the corners of his mouth threatening to quirk into a smile as the bedsprings bounced him up.

He looked like something out of my private, unmentionable fantasies: Adonis sprawled, shirtless in a pair of heavy-duty jeans—no ripped denim for him. *In my bed.*

I tore off my suit jacket, for once not terribly bothered about leaving it to wrinkle on the floor, and sank to my knees. The last time I'd been there, Ivan had found me neurotic, on the verge of a panic attack. I did my best to erase the memory as I slid my hands up his splayed thighs, zeroing slowly on his pelvis.

His chest heaved, a vein pulsing in his neck, but he didn't speak and neither did I. There was no need for words.

Slowly, I popped the button on his fly and lowered the zipper. I should have felt nervous; everything else about Ivan spiked my adrenalin and made my hands quake. Not this, though. In this, I was calm. I knew what I wanted.

As I bent forward to mouth at the jut of his hipbones, I stroked him lightly through his underwear, teasing us both. Butterflies flapped restless wings in the pit of my stomach as I felt him harden against my hand.

"Phil..."

My name on his lips was all the encouragement I needed. I curled a hand around his cock and gently pulled him out. He wasn't small, but I'd expected him to be bigger—a porn star cock, perhaps, to go with the rest of the fantasy.

"All right?" he asked when I hesitated.

I smiled. "Very all right."

It was a relief to take him into my mouth and know I wasn't running the risk of gagging. Even so, I went slowly, savouring the taste, the silky texture. I matched the motions of my mouth with a hand around his shaft, pulling the foreskin back to reveal the slick-shiny glans.

Breath left Ivan's lungs in a rush. His Adam's apple bobbed, a cork in water. "Oh, fuck... *Phil*."

I hummed. *Yeah, you like that, don't you?*

Giving head had never made me feel in control, but suddenly I thrilled with a sense of power. I could tease him if I wanted to. I could graze his slit with my tongue or mouth lightly at the length of his erection, relishing every moan he made in response. I could grip his foreskin between my lips and play with it until he squeezed the sheets in his fists tightly enough that they creaked.

He was close. It didn't take long to get him there—*youth*, I thought with a touch of amusement, and let him slip from my mouth.

"You can come," I breathed.

Ivan picked his head up from the bed and looked down at me through his lashes. "In—inside?"

I thought about it for a moment. "Hang on."

The box of condoms had been relocated from bedroom to medicine cabinet in the bathroom a few short months after Terry's passing. I checked the packaging quickly. They expired in October of this year. I grabbed a couple and made my way back into the bedroom.

Ivan blew out a breath. "I thought—"

"That I left?" I smirked. "What kind of monster do you think I am?"

His cock hadn't softened at all for the interruption. I resisted the impulse to reacquaint myself with his taste as I ripped open a foil packet and slid the latex sheath down his erection.

Ivan rolled his hips into my hand, a helpless moan catching in his throat.

"*Now* you can definitely come in my mouth."

I expected him to crack a joke about my being prepared, or finicky, or any of the things Terry would've done in his place, but Ivan only whimpered as I slid my mouth down and picked up the rhythm. He seemed reluctant to touch my head, but his hands fluttered over my shoulders, my elbows. I felt his knees quiver against my shoulders as he tried to keep so very still for me, and my own trousers suddenly felt a little tight.

I redoubled my efforts, sucking him as deep as I dared and running my tongue along his shaft as I pulled back.

Once, twice more, and that was all it took. Fingers clamped around my forearm, he nearly jack-knifed on the bed as he found his peak, moans fading into guttural pleas.

I knew the feeling—too much, not enough, the itch to let a lover's sweet torture go on and on coupled with the muscle-seizing fear of what that might entail. I chose to be kind and slid off, stroking him through the translucent latex.

"Okay?"

He nodded, limp against the mattress.

A thought came to me, unshakable and absurd all at once. "Was that your first?" I wondered, half kidding. He was thirty years old, not sixteen—and thank the heavens for that. Surely he'd had other lovers.

He had a pretty face and a striking physique. The thought of him going through the world without attracting a few admirers seemed preposterous.

Ivan nodded, his eyes shut as his breathing returned to normal.

"Oh…" An entirely inappropriate warmth rushed through me. "I've never been anyone's first."

"Was it as good for you as it was for me?" His voice was rough with exhaustion, but a smile quirked at the corners of his mouth.

The sight of it buoyed my fledgling confidence.

"It was good… but I think we can do better than that," I said as I bent a knee to the mattress and climbed onto his lap.

I didn't expect Ivan to kiss me square on the mouth, tongue curling against my teeth. If he minded the lingering flavour of the latex condom, it didn't show.

"You want to fuck me?"

He winded me with a single, blunt question.

"Christ, Ivan."

"If you don't, that is also—"

I kissed him again to shut him up. Did I want to? What did he think? That because I was middle-aged I was also out of my mind? Of course I wanted—I'd fantasised about it often enough.

"Are you sure you don't… I mean, the other way around would be easier." *On you. For your first time.*

Ivan blinked. "Do you only do it that way?"

"No," I answered honestly. I was slighter, though, and when I'd hitched up with Terry, it was a rare night I wasn't the one with my face in the sheets.

Running his hands up and down my spine, Ivan considered this.

"I don't want it the other way."

"You want me inside you?" It was my turn to sound hoarse.

"Yes."

"Sure?"

"Yes."

Some doubt would've gone a long way toward making me shoot down the idea, but with Ivan so secure in his desires, I had little choice. I wanted it, too. The thought alone was heady.

Our kisses grew increasingly more frantic as Ivan's orgasm faded. We all but tore each other's clothes off, my shirt and tie landing somewhere at the foot of the bed, my trousers pooled on the floor next to Ivan's jeans. Haste was suddenly of the essence. If I dithered, if I delayed, I might lose my nerve.

We had no lubricant—that *had* expired and I'd seen no point in buying more—so hand lotion would have to do. Ivan didn't seem to mind. He turned onto his side when I bade him, the skin along his thigh rippling with goose bumps.

"Nervous?"

He shook his head. It was a white lie and, I suspected, for my benefit.

I kissed his shoulder. "Relax for me."

"I know it will hurt." He let out a shuddering breath. "I have done it—myself."

A vision flashed behind my eyes: Ivan with a hand between his legs, pressing his fingers into his hole. Grimacing, perhaps, because he did it dry.

"It doesn't."

"How—"

"Trust me," I pleaded and began to stroke the tight rosebud of his entrance with my slick fingertips. If I thought he could withstand it, I would've gone down on him, maybe opened him up with my tongue. But that was almost too intimate.

Next time.

"Just relax. And if you don't like it—"

"I will."

"If you don't, it doesn't make you weird. Or less gay." I hadn't used that word before, not with Ivan. And for one brief, irrational moment I feared it might be our very own Beetlejuice.

Ivan rocked back onto my finger after a few seconds and I let him have half an inch, just to try it. He made a sound halfway between a plea and a sigh, so I did it again. By the time he had two of my digits inside him to the third knuckle, I was well past doubt. Ivan was right. He did like this. The third slid in easy as he sighed.

"That's it," I murmured in his ear, tempted to drive him to the brink with my hand alone.

But the offer I'd made went a step further. Reluctantly, I eased my fingers free and fumbled for the other condom. It took me a moment to slide on, my hands shaking and slippery.

Ivan laughed when I swore in frustration.

"Here—" He took the condom from my hands. "My turn, yes?"

It took everything I had not come right then and there, with Ivan's solid fists rolling the condom down my prick.

"Roll over," I told him roughly. I needed him now.

Ivan hastened to obey, this time pulling both of his knees up so that he lay curled with my front spooned against his back. My fingers weren't as thick as his, but I'd opened him with three. It should have been an easy fit to work my cock inside him.

His whimper startled me into stopping.

"Did I—"

"No, no." Air shuddered out of Ivan's throat as he exhaled. "No, I like—I like it. Please—"

Whatever he said after that was incomprehensible to my uncultured ears, but I grasped the intent. He wanted me to finish what I started, to fuck him in earnest. Seizing his hip in one hand, I angled my hips and resumed my forward momentum.

I was inside him for maybe a moment or two before I had to pull out, do it again. His inner muscles squeezed me like a vice. I was terrified as I thrust into his body, reluctant to rock back. As far as my rhythm went, it was sloppy, uncoordinated. I clung to his shoulder and hip, anchoring myself as best I could against the torrent building in my bloodstream.

Ivan cried out again, whole body going rigid, and I realised I'd found his prostate. In an ideal world, with a body that was twenty years younger, I would've known how to replicate that fortuitous accident. But my attempts faltered, the pace of my thrusts falling to pieces.

"Oh, love, I'm gonna... ah!"

Orgasm washed over me, obliterating all thought. I jounced against Ivan's body, rocking us both a few inches up the bed as pleasure swept through me, wave after wave.

I became aware of Ivan's arm moving after a moment or two and, confused, raised my head from his shoulder blade for a better look. His hand was a blur between his legs. He was stroking off, turned on by my climax.

"Don't stop," I breathed. "Come for me, that's it..."

I wasn't arrogant enough to think it was my voice that tipped him over the edge, but Ivan spent himself just a moment later, gasping as bliss shivered through his body.

I felt it too, each convulsion telegraphed from one of us to the other in an endless feedback loop of hedonistic delight.

My limbs heavy, my mind empty of thought; I would have been content to lay there for another hour.

Ivan reached between us, though, and slowly eased himself off. *That* snapped me awake quite effectively.

"You all right?" Anxiety pitched in my chest.

Ivan nodded. He grimaced a little as he settled onto his back. "It feels... strange."

"Good strange or—"

He met my eyes and his grimace became a grin. "You worry too much."

"I don't want to hurt the people I lo—I mean." *Shit.* I really was useless after a fuck. I had no filter. My face warming, I tried to shrug off the near-confession. "I don't want you to have any regrets.

That's all. Think well of me when you're with your future boyfriends and all that."

"Future boyfriends?" Ivan hitched his bushy brows. "I don't understand."

Post-coital bliss would be hard to hang onto if we did this now, but I forced myself to answer. "I know what this is. We had lovely time, but I'm not—This is where it ends, right? I'm not exactly relationship material for a man your age."

Ivan rolled all the way over to face me. "You keep saying that. 'A man my age'. Am I too young to know what I want?"

"No—"

"To know when I am attracted to someone?"

I scowled. "Stop it."

For once, Ivan didn't listen. "To know when I love someone?"

A hollow opened in my chest, fetters cinched in place over the course of many years unlocking. I told myself that was just the endorphins blurring the line between physical satisfaction and something more profound, more life-altering. I couldn't quite believe it.

I reached for Ivan's hand and clumsily twined his fingers with mine. "What did May tell you about me?"

"That you're a good man." Ivan shrugged the shoulder he didn't have pressed into the sheets. "I already knew."

"There's a lot you don't know." *A lot that's ugly and wicked, a lot that I wish I could take back.*

He squeezed my fingers with his. "So tell me."

I looked at him, this man who didn't belong in my world, who I might never have met if I hadn't decided, on a whim, to gussy up the cottage; who claimed to love me. Whom I thought I might be able to love back. The sky behind him was shot with the red of some distant cruise ship gliding along the Channel.

I thought of Manderley and the flames that consume the ghost house in that horrid little book I'd read again and again since Terry passed. And suddenly I could taste something of that freedom.

"All right," I murmured. "I'll tell you everything."

A Corgi Named Kilowatt

C.C. BRIDGES

CHAPTER ONE

Evan stared at the pack of papers the department secretary—Judy, or maybe Jane?—shoved at his chest, a dawning horror creeping down the back of his neck. "But I'm supposed to teach Comp I."

"Right, and you still are." She pushed the stack harder. "You're Professor Leaverman's TA, and she's out with the stomach flu—"

"Gross."

"—so you need to take her classes this morning. It's the first day of the semester, and I don't have time for this." She let go of the papers, and Evan had to catch them to avoid strewing syllabi across the office floor.

Before he even had time to catch his breath, another student took his place, pulling the secretary's attention away. He backed up, knocked into someone, and apologized before slipping out of the crowded office.

Evan braced himself against the wall of the hallway and glanced down at the syllabus. Intro to Poetry? Something in his belly flipped at that. It was the kind of more advanced class he hadn't expected to be allowed to teach until much later in his PhD program.

He might have entertained fantasies of himself sweeping into a lecture hall, the flaps of his coat fluttering behind him like a cape, as he commanded the attention of every single student in the room. With a sentence, he enraptured them. As he completed the poem, he ensnared them. By the end of the class, they were his.

The flutter of the papers brought his attention back to the present, and Evan finally noticed the class start time. 9:30 a.m. That left him—he checked his watch—fifteen minutes to trek to the Kestrel building on the other side of campus. Hardly enough time to become familiar with the syllabus before presenting it to the class.

"Calm down, it's no big deal." He shoved the copies into his messenger bag and took a moment to straighten his tie. At least he'd dressed for success today, wearing what he'd taken to calling his 'professor uniform': pressed white Oxford shirt, pale blue tie, and khaki slacks. Part of him wanted to go for it and wear the bow tie, but he didn't think anyone else would get that he was trying to be ironic.

Maybe if he hurried, he'd have time to look over the syllabus while the class filed in.

Evan hadn't counted on having to navigate around students who were finding their own way. He'd been in town for a few weeks before the semester started, and he was used to the campus being relatively empty. They'd done a nice job of separating the university from the town around it, using strategically placed trees and half-walls. It gave the campus the feeling of being in a park full of green, hidden from the outside world.

Still, that meant he didn't know any short-cuts yet himself, so when he made it to Kestrel, he was sweaty and out of breath. *So much for making a good first impression.*

The sense of dread only increased when he made it to room 302, pushed open the door, and found it full of expectant students who all looked up and stared as he entered. Sweat slid down between his shoulder blades, making him feel unpleasantly cool in the air-conditioned room.

"Good morning, class." Evan made his way to the professor's lectern and set down his messenger bag.

The whispers started.

"Excuse me?" An older man in the front row raised his hand.

He must have been a non-traditional student. Evan couldn't help but be districted by the good-looking stranger, with his thick, dark, wavy hair and sleepy bedroom eyes. He had stubble shading his cheeks, the kind that begged to be stroked. To top it off, his voice was deep, like whiskey over gravel. All those features had long been part of Evan's mental image of the perfect man.

Evan held tight to the lectern and his attempt to be a professional. Of course he'd have the dumb luck to meet someone just his type in one of his lectures. "Yes?"

"You can't be our professor. You barely look old enough to be out of preschool."

"I'm twenty-three." Evan felt his face heat, and he realized he'd already lost control. "That is, I mean, Professor Leaverman is out sick today, so I'll be handing out her syllabus."

It should have ended there. Evan should have given out the syllabus and left. But he kept trying. Poetry was important, and the more he tried to talk about it, the worse it got.

Finally, a kid in the back said, "Yo, man, I'm just here for my lit requirement. I don't give a shit about Shelley or Kelly or whatever."

That was it. "Fine. Read the syllabus. Buy the textbook. Do the readings for next class!" His last words were shouted because most of the class had gotten up and left.

That could have gone better.

~~*

After the chaos of the first day of classes, Evan sought solace in the library. He bypassed the line of undergrads looking to set up their accounts at circulation and went downstairs to the archives. Here he found the quiet he'd been seeking since he left Kestrel that morning.

Evan kept replaying the disastrous moment in his mind, trying to figure out how he could have salvaged the situation. Sure, the older guy had caught him off-guard, but Evan should have been able to take control of the class. Perfect eyes and a sexy voice were no excuse.

He stopped by the card catalogue, only used down here because no one had ever bothered to digitize the archive's records. Evan knew that wouldn't last forever, but he took solace in flipping through the cards, the tiny slips of cardboard firm against his fingertips. He knew what he wanted, and soon he was turning over his card to the librarian at the desk.

"Davis papers, please. Collection I."

He settled at a table, pencil in his white-gloved hand. Evan lost himself in the letters of his favorite poet, long-forgotten Paul Davis. Davis had taught at Winston, which was why the university had custody of all his papers. Something about the crisp writing grounded him, brought him back from the edge.

But he couldn't shake the sense of failure, even after he'd read through his favorite works and had to return the box. He'd completely lost it because of a handsome face and a voice that could have him turned on in seconds.

Maybe a walk off-campus would help. At least he could forget he didn't even know Handsome's name.

~~*

Evan had explored much of the small town surrounding the campus after moving in. He'd already found his favorite coffee shop—not a chain, but one of the tiny, off-the-beaten path shops that seemed to only exist in works of fiction. It even had built-in shelves of books along the walls and couches instead of chairs.

He looked forward to having a latte. As he moved toward the entrance, Evan could almost taste the creamy goodness on his tongue, but something tangled between his legs. Evan found himself falling, and he managed to catch himself on one of the patio chairs before he hit the ground, although his messenger bag slammed against the cobbled sidewalk with a bang.

"Well, fuck, are you all right? No, down, Kilo—down."

It couldn't have been. That voice, again?

Evan looked up, but his vision was blocked by a happy dog face with a long tongue. The reason for his fall, he presumed. The dog had long pointed ears and looked like he was smiling.

"Sorry, sorry, we're working on socializing him. He's getting better with a leash, but so far I haven't been able to train that herding instinct out of him."

Yes, it was that voice again. Evan looked away from the dog and into the face of his handsome heckler from class. Dazed, he let the guy pull him to his feet. "You."

Apparently he still couldn't say anything worthwhile around this man.

The guy ducked his head and rubbed his hair, making him look much younger. "Uh, yeah, me. Look, it was a shitty thing I said. I'm sorry. I should've apologized after class. Can I get you a cup of coffee to make it up to you?"

The dog bumped into Evan's calves, catching him off-guard. Evan knelt and stroked its ears to give himself time to think. Coffee wasn't too inappropriate, was it? He wasn't technically this guy's professor. Evan wouldn't even be grading that class's papers. "Um, sure. But, uh, can you tell me your name?"

"Marc. Marc Romano. And this little guy is Kilowatt. Kilo for short."

~~*

Marc damn well knew that adopting Kilo was going to get him in trouble. He never worked with corgis before, had assumed they were like any other herding breed. 'Course this little guy had his own too-big personality.

Now Kilo reminded him of how much of an ass Marc had been that morning. What were the odds that his leash would get tangled with the one man Marc had been thinking about all day?

"What would you like?" Marc tilted his head in the direction of the café.

"Oh, um, regular coffee is fine." The kid—no, 'Professor Andrews'—picked up his messenger bag and started flipping through its shuffled contents.

"Now, see, I don't think you're a regular coffee kinda guy." Marc cocked at eye at him. "Here, hold on to Kilo. I'll surprise you."

"Wait, what?"

"No dogs allowed." Marc pointed to the sign in the window before hopping into Loretta's shop. She laughed at him from the counter.

"You up to no good?" She knew him too well. They'd both set up shop in town around the same time. If he'd been of any other persuasion, he'd have asked her to marry him a long time ago. Her coffee was that good.

"Always. Whip me up a couple of your specials? On ice?" Despite being the start of September, the wicked heat still burned outside.

She winked at him. "You got it. Trying to impress the cutie?"

He tapped the counter while she worked. "Trying to apologize."

"Started off on the wrong foot already?" She tsked, her hands deftly mixing the drinks.

"Don't you know it."

She handed off two tall plastic cups, each topped with a generous amount of whipped cream. "Be good. It's not right for you to be alone."

"You sound like my mother," he teased, dropping cash at the register. If he didn't move fast, she might offer the drinks on the house, and he knew better than anybody what running your own business was like. Marc wouldn't do that to her.

Leaving the dog had been a good idea. The kid looked ready to bolt, still standing where Marc had left him with Kilo wrapped, literally, around his legs. Marc laughed.

"I think you should have named him Spider-dog."

Marc set the cups down on one of the patio tables and got the kid untangled. "You got a first name, Professor?" He couldn't keep on calling him the kid in his head.

"Oh, uh." He stepped out of Kilo's leash and nearly fell into his seat. "Evan."

It fit him. "Evan." Marc slid in the seat across from him, wound Kilo's leash around his hand, and told the little dog firmly to sit.

"Yeah, I tried that." Evan frowned when Kilo listened to Marc and dropped onto the sidewalk, his tongue hanging out happily.

"You have to sound like you mean it." Marc winked.

"Mmm." Evan had taken a sip from his drink. He closed those pretty eyes, which were such a clear green even behind those gold-rimmed glasses. Pink lips parted and a dainty tongue licked away the excess whipped cream.

Marc adjusted himself subtly. Wouldn't do getting a hard on for his professor. Damn it. "So, ah, you." He cleared his throat. Being tongue-tied didn't suit him. "I'm sorry for being an ass earlier. When I decided to go back to school, I expected the other students to be younger than me. Didn't plan on the teachers being so young."

"Well, I'm technically still a student." There went that tongue again. Loretta used whipped cream on purpose, damn her. "I've just started the PhD program. I'll be a professor eventually."

"If you're teaching, you're a professor." Marc tried to distract himself by working on his own drink. It was sharp and sweet, and cooled him down perfectly. "What are you studying?"

"Literature. Specializing in poetry, mostly."

"That explains the…" Marc raised his hand in the air and winced. Evan had tried so hard in that class, and it was clear he loved his stuff.

Evan looked glum again. "Yeah, well. I wasn't prepared. I'll do better next time."

Marc wanted to erase the frown from that pretty face. Fuck, he had it bad already, and he wasn't even sure Evan was gay. He had a good idea, but it had been a while since he'd cruised anyone outside of Flanigan's in the city. "You new in town?"

"Been here a couple of weeks. I'm renting a room on Fleet Street."

"I know the neighborhood." Students packed those houses, three or four to a townhome not necessarily designed for that.

"It's not quite what it was when Paul Davis lived here."

Marc blinked. "Who?"

"Early twentieth-century poet. All but forgotten in the modern canon." The frown disappeared, giving way to flushed cheeks and bright eyes. "Which is a shame, really because his poetry is absolutely brilliant. He taught at Winston, did you know?"

"I didn't, but I'd like to know more. You light up when you talk about him."

The blush got even deeper. Aw, how cute.

"Um. We haven't talked about you. You said you're back at school?"

"Nothing interesting about me. I quit college before I even started." He smiled, remembering the eighteen-year-old punk he'd been, sure he'd known better than anybody. "I fucked around good and hard till I finally figured out what I want to do with my life."

"And that is?"

Marc pulled one of his cards out of his pocket—he always kept them handy—and slapped it on the table. "Romano's Kennel" it proclaimed: boarding and dog training. "Dogs. Like 'em better than people most times."

Evan picked up the card and stroked its edges. Marc couldn't look away from his long, slim fingers. "You own this place? Why do you need to go back to school?"

Marc shrugged. "Principle of the thing, I guess. Don't like leaving shit undone. Right, Kilo?"

Marc glared at Kilo, who had started to paw at his shoe. Sneaky corgis who liked to match-make. Time to get moving—Kilo didn't like to sit still for long. "I need to head back. Gotta check on the dogs and keep my staff frosty."

"Oh, uh, thanks for the coffee." Evan got to his feet. "Don't suppose I'll see you again?"

That was a leading question, but it wasn't exactly a request for a date. Damn it. "There's a bar I like. It's not near drunken row." You couldn't catch him near the frat boys. "On the edge of town called Lincoln's."

"You certainly know the good places." Evan gestured with his drink.

"Wisdom comes with age." Marc winked and flicked his wrist. Kilo got eagerly to his feet. Clearly he could behave when he wanted to. "Maybe I'll see you there."

"Maybe."

CHAPTER TWO

If Evan hadn't expected to find his roommate lying on a blanket in the campus quad, he might have stepped on her. As it was, he barely managed to keep from tripping before setting his bicycle against the tree.

"You know, you might want to put up some flashing lights. Maybe a flare."

Rae propped herself up on one elbow and flipped him off. "You're the only one who's gotten anywhere near me in the past thirty minutes."

Evan sat down next to her. He wore dark trousers, so he didn't worry too much about grass stains. Something lightened in him as he sat, as if the weight of the week finally eased off his shoulders.

"We survived the first week of classes, man." Rae sat up and held out her fist. Evan laughed and returned the bump.

When he'd been looking for cheap housing, he'd come across Rae's ad looking for roommates on Craigslist. He hadn't expected to find a friend, especially not one who was a science major. But she'd shown up at his bedroom door one night with a tub full of chocolate ice cream and a DVD boxset of BBC classics. They didn't see each other much—her lab schedule was insane—but that was fine for his introverted self. He could have done with seeing less of their other two roommates as well.

Rae wore shorts in deference to the heat that still hammered on this early in September. She sat up and curled her arms around her bare legs. Her natural curls were swept up by a dark violet scarf, which only accentuated the beauty of her dark skin. "We should do something to celebrate. You know, before things get crazy."

"Maybe go out tonight? There's a place I want to try—it's a locals' bar. Lincoln's? Have you heard of it?"

Evan didn't meet her eyes as he spoke. She didn't need to know about Marc or that Evan was angling for a reason to check the place out and didn't really want to go alone. The card Marc had left on the café table burned in his pocket. He didn't know if Marc had left it on purpose, hoping Evan would call, or if Marc was showing off his business.

He wasn't even sure if Marc was gay. Something in that dark gaze had set Evan's instincts prickling, but he knew as well as anyone that his gaydar wasn't perfect. His past boyfriends had always been found in 'safe' locations, like clubs or the LGBT group at his undergrad. Certainly not from subbing a class.

"Lemme text Tangent. She might be up for something new." Rae pulled out her phone and rapidly tapped on the screen.

"When is she *not* up for something new?"

"You have no idea."

Rae's girlfriend studied Fine Arts, and anyone could guess that in a second. This month, she'd dyed one half of her head purple and shaved the other. Last weekend, she and Rae had gone out for new piercings, but as Evan hadn't seen a new one added to her nose, lip, or ear, he didn't even want to guess where. Still, he hadn't met anyone as serious about art as Tange. He figured that was what she and Rae had in common: their passions for their subjects.

"I hope that wasn't a sex reference." Evan grinned. He closed his eyes and let the sudden breeze wash over him.

Rae snorted. "The tales I have to tell."

"Spare me." He covered his eyes, as if her words would make him see visions of the two of them tangled together.

Instead he saw sleepy dark eyes. He'd been obsessing about Marc since last Tuesday. Evan had Googled the kennel, read review after review on Yelp, and then shut it all down in a fit. He needed to be devoting time to his studies, not stalking some guy who bought Evan coffee after being tripped by his dog, and whose first words to him had been an insult.

Still. That voice. That rumbling, whiskey-soaked voice.

"Tangent is up for it."

He came back to earth when Rae's phone buzzed. "So we're on for tonight?"

Rae laughed. "Let's paint this one horse town red, asshole."

~~*

Apparently both Rae and Tangent had gotten it into their head that Evan needed to hook up tonight. Otherwise why the hell would they make him leave his glasses at home and pour him into a pair of too-tight jeans he'd bought by accident? Evan had turned down the offer of eyeliner, because, really? They weren't going out of town, and who knew what kind of place Lincoln's was?

Tangent had only laughed and doubled her own eye makeup. "Sweetheart, wherever I go, it's my kind of place."

He hated it, but yeah, she walked into any situation with a kind of swaggered confidence he could only envy. Tangent wouldn't get shot down by snotty undergrads during her first attempt at teaching. They wouldn't dare.

Tangent also had a car, unlike either him or Rae. It might have been twenty years old and running on fumes, but it suited her. Both front doors had been replaced at some point and were never painted to match. The interior had been patched with fabric tape placed in strategic yet artful positions. Somehow, whenever she hit a bump in the road, the radio station would change. Evan made sure to buckle up. She drove them all out to the edge of town, to the bar that didn't even have a website.

"This is either gonna be awesome or suck monkey balls." Tangent said as she threw the car into park.

Lincoln's wasn't too far from the highway entrance, located on a street with pretty serious traffic. The only sign flickered, as if the owner hadn't gotten around to replacing the lightbulb and didn't care. The building itself reminded Evan of every place in town with its old, dark brick that seeped up the decades of history. The cars in the lot matched Tangent's: old for the most part, lots of pick-ups, and not a single mini-van.

"I can see why the undies don't like this place." Tangent had her own spin on undergrads.

"Maybe because none of them have cars?" Rae snorted. She got out and walked around to hold Tange's door open for her.

Tangent rolled her eyes, but she grinned. "Buy me a beer, sugar?"

Evan got out and stared at the place. He put his hands in his pockets to keep from fidgeting and nearly called the whole thing off. "What if it sucks?"

"Okay, then we get back into the car and go someplace else." Tangent bumped hips with him. "You need to get a sense of adventure, Ev. Get out of the library."

He bristled. "The library is a perfectly reasonable place to spend time if one is a serious student."

"Oh my God." Rae grabbed his arm. "This was your idea, Ev. Embrace it." Her tone softened. "It's gonna be fine."

And that was why they were friends.

They walked into a dimly lit bar, the soft lightening accentuating the dark wood paneling and the green leather seating. The long bar itself took up the length of the room, displaying a truly astonishing array of bottles. Clearly you didn't come here for cheap beer. Every stool was taken, and the room was filled with the tones of soft conversation.

"Hi. Are you here for dinner?" A waitress appeared out of nowhere, wearing subdued black slacks and a green apron. "We have a few tables unless you want a booth?"

"Booth is fine."

There was one problem with Rae and Tangent's clever plan to get him laid. Evan couldn't see well enough to tell if Marc was in this crowd somewhere.

~~*

Marc knew instantly when Evan walked through the door. Something prickled at the back of his neck, and he'd turned around to look, as did half the others in Lincoln's. Winston students didn't typically come out this way, though a few trickled in now and then. The ones that made a nuisance of themselves got kicked out flat.

He had to double take to recognize Evan. It wasn't like Marc hadn't been looking for him since he'd put out the invitation. But this young man who sauntered in paid little resemblance to the uptight professor who'd been shot down in Marc's class. Evan wore jeans and a fitted black T-shirt that set off the golden tones of his skin. He hadn't worn his glasses, which made him look less like an academic and more like a rent boy.

Evan squinted across the room, didn't react to Marc's presence at all, and followed his two friends to a booth in the corner. Huh. Maybe those glasses were for more than show.

Marc took one last sip of his beer before he waved over the bartender and switched to soda. If he played things right, this might be an interesting night.

~~*

They'd loaded up on appetizers. Rae stuck with soda, nominating herself designated driver of the evening. That made Tangent rub her hands together and eye the specialty menu with glee.

"It all tastes the same anyway." Evan fingered the label of his beer. He wanted to get a closer look at the bar and maybe catch sight of Marc.

"You have no palate."

233

"I like to keep my guts intact, thank you."

Evan decided he like this place. Quiet, as bars went, with damn good food.

"Oh, that's a jukebox up near the bar." Tangent made a grabby motion with her hands.

"Keep your quarters in your pocket, girl, there's no music playing now, so it's obvious they don't want it on." Trust Rae to be sensible, possibly because she was stone-cold sober.

"It can't hurt to check. Besides, there's a guy up there who's been eying us since we walked in."

Evan's heart began to thump a little faster. "Oh?"

Tangent grinned at him. "I say that's worth a quarter."

"I will stay here and guard the cheese fries." Rae swung her finger around to include all of their food.

Evan wiped his palms on his lap and then winced, realizing he'd probably smeared French fry grease all over his jeans. He slid out of his seat and followed behind Tangent, who all but skipped across the room.

"This baby is ancient," she crowed, crouching down to look at the music selection.

There was an uprising from the bar. It seemed like everyone turned at the same time and said something.

"What?" Tange asked.

"They're trying to tell you that you need to pass the bartender's test before you can turn it on."

The sound of that slow cadence had Evan's hair prickling. He turned and swallowed at the sight of Marc standing behind them, looking fantastic in jeans and a white T-shirt.

"What's the test?"

"He'll mix you up a drink, and you have to guess the ingredients after a sip." Marc winked at her.

Tangent mimed rolling up her sleeves. "I was born for this." She strode up to the bar.

Evan didn't move. "Hi," he said, and then cleared his throat when his voice came out raspy instead. "I, ah, couldn't see you without my glasses."

Even up this close, he had a hard time seeing the details of Marc's face. He'd recognized the voice before anything else, but that probably had something to do with his hard-on for Marc's rumbling tones.

"Figured." Marc smiled, a wide beaming thing that Evan damn well noticed despite his lack of 20/20 vision. "I've been hoping you'd come by."

"It is a nice place," Evan admitted. "What I can see of it."

"That's not what I meant by the invite." Marc lowered his tone. "Tell me if I've got this wrong, kid, but I was hoping to see you again."

Evan couldn't miss the intensity in Marc's gaze. He licked his lip nervously. "Like, a date? You couldn't ask for my phone number?"

"Wasn't sure you were interested."

Evan did not listen to the part of his brain that wanted to jump up and down and yell 'omg yes I am so interested, please talk to me some more.'

He looked down at his feet and fidgeted, not knowing what to say. Finally, he coughed up some courage. "Yes?"

Before Marc could respond, there was a cheer from the bar. They looked over to see Tangent fist-pumping and slamming the bartop. "Yes! The jukebox is mine."

"Friend of yours?"

"That's Tangent. She's Rae's girlfriend." He tilted his head back over to the booth where she still sat. "Rae's one of my roommates."

Marc winced. "That's her name? Don't they give kids normal names these days?"

"You know, if you honestly want to get into my pants, you gotta stop calling me 'kid.'"

The wicked grin returned. Marc leaned forward, getting real close, his lips inches from Evan's ears. "Oh? Then what do you want me to call you? 'Sweetheart'?"

Before Evan could respond, Tangent brushed past them, brandishing a quarter. "Let's liven this place up a bit."

He feared her selection. It could go one of two ways: something she really wanted to listen to, or the most annoying song she could find on the thing. After a moment of clicking and concentration, the tones of *Build Me Up Buttercup* filtered through the bar. Evan laughed.

"What do you say we continue this conversation somewhere quiet? My place?"

Evan swallowed, still under Marc's spell. He met Tangent's eyes as she turned and gave him a thumb's up. One crazy night before the semester really got underway. That was what Rae said, right?

"Sure."

~~*

It didn't go as smoothly as Evan had wanted it to. Rae wouldn't let him leave, and he finally had to break down and explain that he'd met Marc on campus. She gave him the stink eye. "Fine. But you will text me every hour so I know you're alive."

Evan opened his mouth to argue, but Marc interrupted, "I'll make sure he does, ma'am."

Rae held his gaze for a while, and then nodded. "I'll know if it's not him."

Evan could feel her eyes follow them as they left the bar. He found it somewhat comforting.

"I don't normally do this sort of thing." Evan fiddled with the seatbelt in Marc's truck before buckling himself in. Well, not since the first year of undergrad and before he got serious about his work.

"What? Pick up strangers at bars?" Marc started the engine. "We're not exactly strangers."

Instead of putting the car into gear, Marc reached over and placed his hand on Evan's knee. The warmth seeped through Evan's jeans. How long had it been since Evan had physical contact like this? His body ached to be touched, and he wanted it to be touched by Marc's firm strong hands.

"No, we're not." It took Evan two tries to get the words out.

Marc took pity on him and removed his hand, getting them on the road. "Besides, we don't have to do anything you're not comfortable with. Say the word, and I'll take you home."

"You're a good guy." Evan actually believed Marc would do that.

"Once we get to my place, you'll see how good I am." Marc's lips curved, and—just like that—set the tension back up to eleven.

Evan shifted in his seat, his damn jeans too tight. He wanted to adjust himself, to do something to counteract the denim pressing into his erection, but was afraid that would only make things worse. "I hope you live close."

Marc's answering chuckling did nothing to help Evan's arousal.

Soon, they were turning off the county road into the long driveway past a sign advertising Romano Kennels. There were two other cars parked off to the side. Marc swung around them and pulled up in front of the house: a simple two-story structure with a long front porch. Two rocking chairs sat out front, separated by an old barrel turned planter filled with greens.

Marc led the way, wiping his boots on the mat in front of the door. Evan could hear the barking as he approached. He wasn't surprised when Kilo leapt out, tail wagging as he dived for Evan's ankles.

"Hah." He leaned down to stroke the dog behind his ears.

"Damnit, Kilo." Marc sighed. "He's been getting through the gate somehow."

Evan laughed and followed Marc inside, Kilo at his feet. He stopped when they were greeted by another dog: large and black, with brown markings and gentle eyes. Marc patted her under the chin. "This is Bella."

"She's... big?" Evan swallowed.

"And better trained than Kilo." Marc snapped his fingers and both dogs followed. "Lemme let them out, and then I'm all yours."

"I like the sound of that." Evan stuck his hands in his pockets as Marc led the dogs away. He took the opportunity to look around Marc's living room. It echoed the same country aesthetic as the front porch: simple, wooden furniture, all in a beautiful, rich dark grain. It smelled faintly of dog, and also something else, like evergreen. Pictures on the wall near the fireplace drew his eye, and Evan went to get a closer look.

Family portraits stared back at him, images of Marc with a large family behind him. However, Marc also had framed a good portion of dog photos. Some were dogs next to trophies or ribbons. Others were happy looking doggie faces, some with tongues hanging out, others looking noble and majestic.

"That's Stevie," Marc's voice came too close and Evan nearly jumped as Marc's hands settled on his waist. "She was my first success with agility training. That dog loved to run."

His voice made Evan shiver. He could listen to Marc talk about his dogs all night. There was so much love there. "You've been doing this a long time."

"Near twenty years."

Evan opened his mouth to ask how old Marc was—he'd clearly miscalculated—when Marc turned him around and brought their lips together. He gasped, taken by surprise, his mind still on the dogs.

Marc tasted like summer. Evan couldn't explain it, but something about Marc reminded of him of warmth and light. He opened his mouth and let Marc devour him, their lips meeting like hungry wolves. His fingers caught the soft fabric of Marc's T-shirt.

One of Marc's hands shifted from Evan's waist, to cup Evan's cheek. Evan leaned into it, his heart swelling at the tenderness of the gesture.

Then Marc pushed Evan up against the wall and pressed their hips together, hardness against hardness. He pressed his lips close to Evan's ear. "This okay?"

"Yeah," Evan gasped. Anything to have more of that heat, now. Marc's erection dug against his, a weight with promise.

He moaned when Marc pulled away. "What?"

Marc's hands settled on Evan's hips as he slid to his knees. Oh. Well, that was okay, then. Evan thumped his head against the wall, and decided to let Marc do whatever he wanted. He couldn't resist a peek, and leaned forward to watch Marc unzip the fly of Evan's jeans.

Evan let out a breath. Oh, thank God, those jeans had been killing him.

"Now that's what I want," Marc murmured, words hot against Evan's skin as Marc tugged down his boxers and exposed him to the air. The scent of his arousal filled the room.

He looked down as Marc looked up, those sleepy bedroom eyes pinning him to the wall. Evan bit his lip to keep from crying out.

"Yeah, bite that lip, pretty boy."

Evan shuddered, too turned on to protest being called a boy. If Marc kept it up, Evan wasn't going to care what he called him. He tried to wiggle his hips, but Marc's hands kept him in place.

"Not till I say." His breath was moist against the skin of Evan's fully erect cock. "I'm going to enjoy this. You look about ready to burst."

"It's your voice," Evan choked out. "I can't... it's so hot."

Marc chuckled. "I bet I could make you come like this, couldn't I? Whispering words to your dick? Hello there." His lips grazed the sensitive skin under the head and Evan cried out.

No one had ever made Evan feel like this with nothing more than words and soft lips. His previous boyfriends had been too eager to cut to the chase. It wasn't like they had the time to do more in tiny dorm bedrooms, or on one memorable occasion, the laundromat. But Marc seemed content to make Evan wait for it and Evan never realized how much of a thrill that could be. Arousal thrummed through him, gone past the point where he thought it was too much, and curled down to the depths of his toes.

"Wow," he muttered.

"Oh, we're not quite there yet, sweetheart." Marc trailed his tongue over Evan's length, his teasing eyes still watching. As if he were waiting for something, Evan couldn't know what. But then Marc moved, swiftly, and took Evan inside his mouth.

So hot and warm. Evan curled his fingers against the wall, glad he had something to hold on to. Marc's fingers dug into his hips, a heavy weight that grounded him, even as Marc's mouth took him soaring.

"Please," he begged, unable to be any more articulate than that.

Evan could smell nothing but musk, as sweat beaded across his forehead. He arched his body, calling out as Marc sucked him harder. He was so close, so close, almost...

There.

Boneless, he nearly slid down the wall, but then Marc was propping him up and holding on to Evan's jeans. "Bedroom is this way."

Evan didn't think about walking; he merely let Marc lead him away. "What about you?" He wasn't so ill-mannered as to get off without thought of reciprocating.

"I'm thinking a young one like you has to have enough in him for round two." Marc pushed open a solid wood door, revealing a queen-sized bed with a patchwork quilt on top. "Get yourself naked and under the covers. I'll be right back."

"Huh? Where you going?"

"Gotta make sure everything is okay with the kennels and the night staff is all settled in. I like to double check on the dogs." He leaned down and pressed a kiss to Evan's forehead. "Don't think we're done here."

~~*

Marc needed a moment to get his head on straight. He figured anyone who didn't understand his commitment to his dogs wasn't worth worrying over. Plus, he wanted to give Evan time to get up for round two. He adjusted himself, wincing at the scrape of hard fabric against his cock. Patience, he schooled himself. The thought of those hot little faces Evan had made as he came set Marc's dick throbbing. Marc needed to make this run fast.

By the time he got back to the bedroom, his arousal had flagged only a little, but he knew he'd be up for it in no time. Marc brought a glass of water from the kitchen in case Evan was thirsty, but it was his own mouth that went dry as he opened the door to find the young man naked in the center of his bed, both hands closed around his cock and a come hither look on his face.

Evan propped up one leg, displaying the long, slim lines of his body. His skin flushed a delightful pink under Marc's gaze.

Marc set down the glass and pulled off his shirt, for a moment self-conscious about his own body, older and hairier, though he thought he kept in pretty good shape. His dogs kept him young. Then he decided if Evan hadn't run screaming from the bed yet, he still had a good shot.

His jeans slipped off easily, following his toed off shoes and socks. Marc left his boxers on until he got to the bed, following the way Evan's eyes couldn't move from his hidden package. Before Marc climbed on, he tucked his thumbs in the waistband and slid his underwear down, revealing his flushed cock that bobbed against one thigh.

Evan sat back on the pillows. "Want me to suck you?"

"Got something else in mind." Marc crawled on the bed and over Evan until he reached the headboard, his legs bracketing Evan's thighs. As he leaned down to kiss Evan, Marc let his hips drop until they were cock to cock.

Evan hissed. He felt incredible beneath Marc, all warmth and silk. "I wanna come all over you."

"You can't say things like that."

Laughter threatened to build up and kill the mood. Marc leaned down and bit at Evan's bottom lip, taking it in his mouth and sucking slightly. Evan tasted like peppermint somehow. He continued to lick and mouth until Evan moaned and wriggled beneath him. Old man still had it.

"Let me." Marc backed up enough to get a hand between them. It had been a while, but he'd always liked frot. No stress, just two guys getting off.

Evan reached up and clasped Marc's shoulders, hanging on for the ride. His green eyes widened and

Marc found himself falling into them. Abruptly, out of nowhere, he wanted to be inside Evan, to feel tight heat clench around him, to see this young man utterly come apart beneath him.

A fire lit in his chest, and Marc knew he couldn't let Evan walk out of this room. He wanted more.

"Marc." Evan gasped, his fingernails digging in harder.

Hearing his own name unlocked something inside him. Marc came, striping his come all over Evan's cock and belly. Evan's eyes squeezed shut as he climaxed, biting his lip once more. Fuck, if Marc hadn't already blown his load, that would have done it.

He leaned down to kiss that abused lip. "Hang tight a second."

Marc managed to get up long enough to grab a clean towel from his linen closet and generously wiped Evan down before attacking the mess on his own belly. He climbed up on the bed, unwilling to let go of the moment. They smelled like sex and sweat, and he couldn't help but wallow.

He swallowed hard. "If you want, I'll take you home. But I'd like it if you stayed."

It seemed like an eternity before Evan responded. Marc couldn't even look over at him.

"Sure, okay. Let me text Rae first, okay?" Marc could hear the smile in Evan's voice, even without looking.

"Yeah." Marc grinned back.

~~*

Evan woke up to a wet nose in his face. He sputtered and sat up before realizing where he was. The nose belonged to Kilo, who somehow had managed to hop up on the bed despite his stubby little legs. With a laugh, he dug his fingers into the dog's fur, loving how Kilo narrowed his eyes and leaned into the scratching.

"Kilo, down. You have your own bed." Marc entered the room carrying a tray of food.

Something tightened in Evan's chest. Last night had been incredible. They had this sudden connection, the way their bodies moved together. Evan had never experienced anything like that. He thought he could quickly grow addicted to Marc's body.

"You must think I'm the world's worst dog trainer," Marc grumped as he set the tray down. On it sat a plate of toast and eggs with a large mug of coffee on the side.

Evan scooped up the coffee eagerly, inhaling its rich scent before drinking deeply. "Honestly, I haven't known any other dog trainers to compare you to."

Marc laughed, ruffling Kilo's head as he sat on the bed. He sat and watched as Evan dug into his breakfast. "So, uh, last night was pretty great, right?"

"Yeah." Evan didn't know if he was coherent with his mouth full of scrambled eggs. Marc could cook, too. None of his boyfriends had ever cooked for him.

"I don't know about you, but I figure we might want to make this a regular thing?" Marc tugged at a loose thread in the quilt at the foot of his bed. Evan wanted to tell him to stop or he'd unravel the whole thing.

He had to replay Marc's words in his head. Evan didn't understand, not completely. Did Marc want to be fuck buddies? Or did the way he kept looking away meant he wanted something more but was too shy to ask? Evan had somehow discomfited an otherwise confident man, and he couldn't help but feel a little smug at the thought.

But he had to figure out what he wanted, and quickly. Evan could not let this moment pass. Good sex or the chance for something… more? "You mean, like, a date?"

Marc snorted. "You pointing out that I went about this whole thing backwards?"

At least Marc looked at him again. His eyes smiled when he did, and Evan could feel his heart flutter. "I'm saying, hey, would you like to meet up for coffee sometime?"

"I think I can do that."

CHAPTER THREE

The air that morning had a distinctly cool feel to it. It wouldn't be long until every coffee shop served pumpkin spice lattes to combat the crisp bite of Fall. Evan rubbed his arms, his argyle cardigan not heavy enough. Time to start unpacking his cold weather clothes.

He shifted in his seat, taking a moment to watch the other students disappear into the Rec. Apparently he was the only one willing to brave a table outside. He considered joining them, but he'd promised to meet Marc before his 9:30 poetry class.

This would be their first 'date' since meeting up at the bar last Friday. Evan's cheeks heated at the memory. Marc had dropped him off at his townhouse the next morning. Evan had stumbled inside looking thoroughly well fucked. He'd found Rae waiting expectantly at the door and at first he couldn't tell if she were pissed or if she wanted details.

It turned out to be a little bit of both.

He'd had to explain to her how he'd met Marc and fessed up to the disastrous first class. That thought still embarrassed him, so Evan tried not to think about it. Instead, he felt excited at the thought of seeing Marc again, to try to give this thing a shot. It would be… nice to have a boyfriend again.

"Hey." Marc slid into the seat across from him, carrying a travel tray with two coffees and a bag with the logo of their favorite coffee place. "I brought breakfast."

"That's much better than waiting in line at the Rec." Evan took the cup Marc offered him, the same sweet concoction Marc had brought him before. Somehow Marc knew Evan liked his brew sweet without having to ask.

Marc opened the bag, revealing a selection of pastries. Evan grabbed a muffin and bit into it eagerly. Sweet richness filled his tongue, followed by a slightly nutty flavor. "This place is awesome."

"Loretta is a genius in the kitchen." Marc took a sip of his own coffee.

"You know the owner?"

"I've lived in this town for a while." Marc nodded his head at the pile of books on the table. "Studying hard already?"

Evan frowned. "I'd checked out some extra stuff on theory from the library. It's not easy to wrap my head around." His required reading had given him a headache. Evan didn't know if it was the material or the fact that he'd been distracted.

"Introduction to Literary Theory." Marc picked up one of the library books and thumbed through it. "Okay, I'm gonna leave this stuff to you..."

Evan laughed. "So why are you taking Intro to Poetry?"

"That never really came up, huh?"

"We had other things on our minds." And with those words, the temperature rose a few degrees. Evan felt himself flush.

Marc pursed his lips. It made it hard to resist leaning over and kissing them. "You really want to know?"

"Yeah, I really want to know." Evan leaned forward anyway.

"Once upon a time, I was a snot-nosed kid, not too much younger than you right now. I'd registered for community college up state. Flunked every single one of my first semester classes."

"Ouch."

"But you know what I didn't skip out on? My volunteer time at the local animal shelter. I met a guy there. The less said about him the better, except that I followed him to this little town where I started working at the dog groomer's." Marc took another sip of coffee, looking like he was fortifying himself. "I kicked the guy to the curb as soon as I made enough money to afford the rent on my own. That's when I started learning about dogs. Met up with some other trainers who worked with the shelter. Took me a lot of hard work till I was able to afford the mortgage on my own place and start up the kennel business."

"And then what? You got bored?" Marc had said it was the principle of the thing before. Evan couldn't quite understand it then, but a clearer picture started to form now.

"Smartass." Marc swatted at Evan's hand as he went for another muffin. "No. I regretted fucking up college the first time. So a friend of mine suggested I look into taking some classes here, see what I think about trying again. He recommended the poetry class. Said the professor was fantastic."

Evan flushed. "Only for me to screw it all up."

"Hey, didn't we establish that when I was your age I was failing out of school?"

That brought them to another question, one Evan had been holding off on asking. "So, uh, how old are you?" Evan's own age had been blurted out in embarrassment. He'd kinda wished he hadn't said anything, now.

"I'll be forty-one in March." Marc leveled a heavy gaze on him. "That a problem?"

The question deserved a serious answer. Evan hadn't thought about it when he'd considered getting into Marc's pants. Now he had to face the reality of dating an older man and all that entailed. Sure there were benefits, like being with someone more established, who owned his own home and car. But Evan wasn't exactly at the same place in his life. He had a lot of school to go before he could get anywhere near where Marc was, and odds were he'd never make enough to own the kind of property Marc did.

There were a thousand reasons this was a bad idea. But Evan couldn't help feeling that he'd be missing out on something important if he didn't take this chance now.

"No." Evan said firmly, hands on the table, meeting Marc's gaze head on so he'd know Evan meant it. "Not a problem at all."

Marc nodded and dove into the bag, choosing a chocolate frosted donut for himself. "So what about you? Why are you studying literary theory?"

Evan bit back the semi-sarcastic response he had on the tip of his tongue—*who wouldn't want to study literary theory?*—and instead tried to find the words to explain something so much a part of himself.

He'd been sixteen when his mom lost her job. For a while, it looked like they were going to lose everything. Evan began thinking she'd be better off without having to worry about having to support him or pay for college. He'd been in a dark place.

These were things he couldn't tell Marc. Not yet. Maybe not ever.

"Words saved my life," he said instead, the truth brutal when simplified like this. "If I hadn't had the library to hide in, I wouldn't be here."

He'd spent hours crouched in the stacks, the solid weight of a shelf at his back, the book in his lap, words of poetry speckled across its pages, unparalleled beauty that took him beyond the worries of money and school.

Marc frowned at him, which would be more concerning except for the bit of chocolate stuck at the corner of his lips. Evan suppressed the giggle and leaned forward with a napkin to wipe it off. "Anyway, I knew I didn't want to stop studying literature. I wanted a life of the mind. And I was lucky to get this assistantship. "

"Because that poet you like worked here."

He could see Marc was still struggling to understand. "Partially. Also because it's paying for my education. PhDs aren't cheap."

"If it's worth working for, it's never cheap." Marc crumbled up the empty paper bag. "I need to start walking to class."

"I'll walk with you. My first class isn't until the afternoon." Evan found he didn't want the conversation to end. If he could prolong this little date for a bit longer, he would.

Marc laughed. "Are we going to hold hands and skip?"

"And I'll pin your picture in my locker." Evan joined in the joke, but he kinda did want to hold Marc's hand.

They took care of the trash and then blended into the crowds walking the paths through campus. "Seriously, though, how out are you? In my day, you didn't..." Marc gestured, indicating the two girls with their arms around each other walking opposite them.

"In your day? You're forty, not sixty, Marc." Evan winked at him, delighted at the way Marc scowled back. "I don't know if I've ever been in. I'm not exactly subtle." He tugged at his cardigan to prove the point. "You know Rae and Tangent are a couple, right?"

Marc made some comment that sounded like 'that girl,' but before Evan could press, a balding man in suit was hailing them. It took Evan a moment, but once the man got closer, he recognized the dean of the English department, Henry Wilson.

"Hey, Harry, how's it going?" Marc held out a hand and Dean Wilson shook his heartily.

"Good, good. Marshmallow is fully housebroken now." He rolled his eyes. "Never should have let my daughter name her."

Marc laughed. "Give the dog a nickname. It'll be fine."

"I'll have to call you. We're going away during Thanksgiving break, and I'll need to board her. I know you fill up quickly."

"No worries. I'll save a spot for you." Marc nodded.

Evan stood silently, wondering if he should enter the conversation or not. This was Dean Henry Wilson, the very man with whom he'd interviewed in order to obtain this position. And Marc happened to train his dog?

The dean finally focused his attention on Evan. "Hello, Mr. Andrews. Are you showing Marc around campus? I'm pleased he's decided to return to school here."

"Evan is a credit to your institution," Marc answered when it was obvious Evan was tongue-tied. There was even a little glint in his eye as he said it.

It wasn't until the dean waved and carried on his way that Evan could breathe. "You are friends with the dean of my department?"

"He's a client, really." Marc started to look uncomfortable.

"Oh God, tell me he isn't the guy you moved down here for." Evan's chest felt tight. Had he slept with a guy who'd fucked his dean?

Marc took hold of his shoulder and squeezed tightly. "Breathe, Evan. Listen to me. I know Harry like I know most everyone in this town. I've been here a long time. You're gonna be hard pressed to find someone I don't know. And no, I haven't slept with him. That guy I mentioned... he's long gone. You don't have to worry about running into him here."

Evan leaned into the touch. He wanted more. Physical contact with Marc seemed like a gift, and one he couldn't help desiring. "Okay. Sorry."

"Harry is the one who convinced me to take classes here. So you can thank him for being the reason we met." Marc winked. He threw his arm around Evan's shoulders and squeezed him before carrying on back down the path. "Don't want to be late."

"Do you want to do this again, sometime?" Evan started going through his mental schedule, trying to figure out when he was next free for lunch.

"I suppose the next step would be a fancy dinner someplace, right?" Marc made a face. "I mean, if we're following the dating playbook."

It took Evan a second to realize he was joking. "What if we want to go off-book?" His life didn't lend itself to traditional dating.

"Well, if that's the case, I'd invite you over to my place on Saturday. I can show you the dogs." Marc downright beamed. Evan could detect the hint of pride in the way Marc spoke about his dogs. Of course, he should be proud of the business he'd built. There was more to it than that, and Evan wanted to find out everything.

Evan wanted to see Marc with his dogs. "Should I, ah, bring an overnight bag?"

"You do that."

~~*

"You're going to his place again?" Rae stood in the doorway as Evan filled his backpack.

Evan sank down on his twin bed and spread his hands to encompass the tiny room. "It's not like I can have him here. Besides, he's inviting me specifically to see him working with his dogs."

She crossed her arms over her chest. "That's not what I meant. It's awfully sudden to start spending the night, isn't it? You just started dating."

"How long did it take before you had Tangent spending the night?" Evan didn't ask to be mean. He was honestly curious. His last relationships weren't exactly the best way to model future behavior.

Rae's cheeks darkened. "All right, good point."

That didn't answer his question, although it gave Evan a good idea. He'd never known them separate. Rae came with a girlfriend. He's never gotten to see how they fell for each other. Maybe he was doing this all wrong.

Maybe he didn't quite care?

He admitted he wanted more of Marc, more of that delectable body. Evan's skin prickled at the memory of those capable hands moving against it. However, more than just the desire that exploded between them, Evan wanted to get to know the guy who'd happily suck Evan's cock, then get shy when asking for a date. Marc was a puzzle that Evan wanted to put together.

Evan started shoving his textbooks into his messenger bag. It was always a good idea to bring schoolwork. He also had a ton of grading to do. He double-checked that he had the packet of assessment essays in there, too. Those were going to take forever to comment on.

"I don't want to see you get hurt."

"Hey, relationships are risk, right?"

She sat next to him and tweaked his nose. "And you are the most risk adverse person I know. So this guy must be something special, huh?"

"Yeah, I think he is."

~~*

Marc lifted the lid off of the crock-pot and took a deep breath. The sauce smelled perfect, the hints of oregano and garlic tantalizing his nose. At least one thing seemed to be going right for him today. Calling his mom to double check the recipe had been a good idea.

His last client had run late, more due to the human than the dog. Marc could tell the owner needed a few lessons before the guy would be able to control the dog at all. The problem was, as always, convincing the person they had no idea what they were doing and letting Marc teach them.

Now he was an hour behind schedule, and his clothes stuck to his body. Marc took a whiff and winced. He smelled disgusting. Shower or drive out to Evan's smelling like a horse? He glanced at the clock. Maybe if he made it a quick shower...

"You know, they have this new invention called the phone. It allows you send messages and let people know when you're going to be late," Evan said as Marc rolled down the window of his truck.

"What's that, whippersnapper? I can't hear you." Marc unlocked the doors.

Evan threw two bags in the back—one backpack and his ever present messenger bag, stuffed full with papers spilling out. He slid into the front, looking good enough to eat. The cold nip in the air added a flush to his cheeks and his pretty eyes were bright with excitement.

That light gave Marc hope. He'd figured they'd do this now, before he found out months down the road that Evan didn't like dogs or didn't appreciate the time Marc spent with them.

It wasn't fair to Evan to judge him by Marc's string of failed relationships. There'd been Kurt, the first asshole who'd lured him to this town. Kurt didn't mind dogs per se, he didn't like anything that took Marc's attention away from him. And then there was

Bobby, who couldn't stand dog hair on his pristine law-firm suits. The less said about Lindsay the better.

"I didn't know if I should bring anything." Evan laid his hands flat on his lap.

Marc reached over and took one of those hands in his before pulling out into traffic. "You already did."

~~*

Evan hadn't been sure what to expect to find behind Marc's house. He'd never seen a dog kennel before, and part of him feared a string of cages like the shelters he'd seen on TV. Instead, on the long stretch of property that served as Marc's backyard, a large barn-like structure hid the pens. Marc slid open the front door, and they walked into a cacophony of happy barks.

"It's heated in winter. A/C in summer." Marc pointed to, Evan assumed, the HVAC system in the ceiling.

The pens reminded him of stalls in a stable. All fairly large, and though the floor was concrete, each dog had a fluffy bed to sleep on and a large bowl of clean water.

Evan crouched down in front of a dog with long curly ears and amber eyes. It pawed at the cage door and he held his hand up against it in response. "These are all dogs you're training?"

"Boarding," Marc corrected. "I finished all the training clients this morning. They don't usually stay over. These are dogs whose owners are all on vacation."

Owners like the dean of the English department. Evan winced. He still quite hadn't gotten over that bit of information yet.

"I usually hire students to do things like clean up the dog poop." Marc stopped to pick up a shovel and rake set by the door. "They work cheap and they don't mind working weird hours so I've always got an extra set of eyes on the dogs."

Evan got to his feet and brushed the dirt from his knees. He watched for a moment as Marc worked at clearing out the pens, but always pausing to give a hopeful pup a pat or a scratch. Marc murmured to the dogs, too, something too low to understand, but it seemed to keep them happy.

"I exercise 'em twice a day. I've got a run set up behind the kennel." Marc opened the door on the opposite side of the room. He started collecting leashes from a hook. "You ready?"

"Um." Evan didn't know what to be ready for. He'd been too caught up in watching Marc, how he moved, muscles flexing beneath his tight Henley.

"Here, you take Fluffy. Her owners gave strict instructions. She doesn't run with the other dogs. Lead her around the fence." Marc clipped a hot pink leash onto a regal white poodle before handing said leash to Evan.

Soon all the dogs were outside, barking and running madly around the exercise pen that Marc had set up. There was a crate of tennis balls, and Marc laughed as he threw scores of them into the chaos.

Evan circled them with Fluffy walking primly beside him. Eventually Marc ran back to the house to get Kilo and Bella, who joined in the fun. Evan couldn't take his eyes off of Marc, the way playing with the dogs made Marc's face light up.

Marc's movements did something for Evan, but it wasn't quite arousal. Fierce emotion swelled in his chest, and Evan couldn't keep the smile from his own face.

"You look about twenty years younger when you play with the dogs," Evan told him after they kenneled the pups for the night and made their way back to the house, Kilo and Bella leading the way.

Marc winked. "Then we're the same age."

Evan laughed. His own heart felt light, like nothing could weight him down.

After dinner—and, seriously, Marc could cook— they settled down in the living room. Evan took out a textbook, because he really needed to keep up on his reading, while Marc pulled out his own poetry book. It was only when Marc came over to pull a blanket over him that Evan woke, his book clattering from his hands.

"I'm sorry." He yawned. Marc must have had plans Evan ruined by falling asleep.

"C'mon. There's a big bed waiting for you. No pressure." Marc held out a hand.

Evan followed, finding sleep easy to come by in Marc's soft bed, a corgi at their feet. He woke again to sleepy kisses and gentle murmurs against his lips. He rolled under the covers, spreading his legs to let Marc's fingers press into him.

Evan thought he could get used to this.

CHAPTER FOUR

"This is the worst excuse for academic writing I have ever received in a graduate seminar."

Evan dug his fingers into his knees in an attempt not to reach out and snatch the paper out of Professor Leaverman's hands. She kept waving it around as she spoke, and he could see red pen marks everywhere. When she requested this private conference, he hadn't expected this.

"You must understand how difficult it is to make it in this field. You have to stand out. Get published. This kind of work will not get you there, Andrews." She put down the paper—finally—and her gaze softened. "You're one of the most promising poetry students I've seen in a while. That's why I can't stand it when you don't work to your potential."

"I'm sorry?" It took him a few tries to make up enough saliva to speak. Evan hadn't thought his work that bad, but now he itched to see how it had gone so horribly wrong.

"Sometimes the first semester can be an adjustment. It's a learning curve, really, juggling teaching and your own research. I firmly believe you are capable of this. I wouldn't have signed on as your advisor otherwise." She folded her hands on the cheap metal desk and leaned forward, her glasses sliding down her nose. "Is it true that you've recently begun a... relationship?"

Evan had forgotten about the gossip mill of the English department. It wasn't like he and Marc had been subtle. For the past two months they'd been together, hanging out on campus, eating lunch in the cafeteria when their schedules matched. Every other Friday, Marc would pick him up outside Ridly Hall for a weekend spent at Marc's place. Evan thought he was doing pretty well bringing all his work with him and completing his reading curled up on Marc's couch.

Apparently not.

"Yes," he admitted.

She sat back in her chair and her shoulders fell, as if he had told her the worst news imaginable. "Relationships can be distractions. That's not what you need when you're starting a PhD program. The life of the mind isn't for everyone, Andrews. But I need to know if you're dedicated to this." She tapped the paper, sitting forlornly on the desk. "You can't afford to be distracted."

Evan nodded. "This is all I ever wanted."

She held his gaze for a moment before sliding his paper across the desk. "Good."

He snatched it up before she could change her mind and made his escape. Evan all but ran down the front steps of the building, his messenger bag slapping against his thigh. The red ink haunted him, but he didn't want to stop and look at it yet. The last thing he needed was to burst into tears in the middle of campus. His eyes were already raw, and he blinked hard as he trudged down the quad.

Mostly he couldn't shake the feeling of embarrassment. That was his advisor. She expected the best from him, and what had Evan given her? Some piece of crap, apparently.

He hadn't thought the paper that bad. Certainly not his best, but not red-pen worthy. Maybe that was the point. Every paper needed to be his best.

A car horn honking startled him out of his musings. Evan looked up and saw Marc hanging out of his truck. He'd forgotten Marc was picking him up today, yet somehow his feet had made it to the parking lot without him noticing. Evan stepped off the sidewalk and got in the passenger side.

"Hey." Marc grinned, looking impossibly beautiful with the sun shining through the glass window behind him.

Evan tried to force a smile. "Hey."

"Uh-oh, what's wrong?" Marc turned the key and the truck flared to life.

"That obvious?" Evan looked away, watching the campus rumble by. "I got chewed out by my advisor. Apparently, my work hasn't been up to her standards."

His voice sounded foreign to his own ears. Evan hadn't realized how pissed off he was until that moment. Why was he the only one called out? He glanced at his paper, still clenched in his fist.

What if he wasn't meant for an academic career? If he fucked up so bad on a first semester paper... he could lose his scholarship, his TAship, everything he'd worked for.

"Hey," Marc said, as if aware of Evan's sudden panic. "Whatever's wrong, I'm sure you can fix it."

"Not if I don't stop screwing around at your place," Evan snapped. "I need to focus on my damn homework instead of—"

"Screwing around?" Marc's lips thinned and his hands tightened around the steering wheel.

Evan shut his mouth. His cheeks burned as he stared at the glove compartment. Silence filled the cab like a thick, oppressive fog.

"Maybe I should take you back to your place?"

Evan wanted to protest, to take back every stupid word that had come out of his mouth. Instead he said, "I think that would be a good idea."

They'd had plans for this weekend. Nothing more involved than hanging around, playing with the dogs, maybe watching a movie, but still, plans to spend time together. Evan had ruined all of that with a word.

Before Marc could say anything in response, Evan's phone rang. He shifted in his seat to grab it out of his back pocket.

"Hi, Mom."

~~*

Marc figured Evan needed a few days to get his head on straight. He'd known rough times himself, when he wasn't sure where the next rent check was coming from, or some dog resisted anything Marc tried to do with him. November wasn't an easy time either, judging by the stressed-out college students he'd hired over the years to watch the dogs.

So he didn't take the minor freak out too badly, but the way Evan went white as a ghost when Marc suggested he take Evan home, it was pretty clear Evan did.

"I'm sorry, Mom, I meant to call you this morning." Evan turned away, his phone tucked between his cheek and shoulder.

It wasn't like he could help listening in. Marc eased up on the gas a bit to go a bit slower. Evan didn't live far from campus. He wanted to hear this conversation. Evan mentioned his mom every now and then, but no other family members.

"I told you, I can't afford to fly home for a few days," Evan said slowly, his voice straining as if he was forcing himself to be calm. "It's a busy part of the semester. I'd be sitting around doing schoolwork anyway."

His voice caught at the end, almost breaking. Marc glanced over and watched him squeeze his eyes shut. Were those tears?

"I'm sorry." Evan ducked his head down. "Maybe over winter break? I know, I know."

A minute later, Evan had the phone in his lap and Marc was pulling into a spot on the street as someone drove away. He threw the car into park and shut off the engine. "What's that all about?"

Evan shrugged. "My mom wants me to come home for Thanksgiving. It's not something I can afford on a TA salary."

"Oh."

"It's okay. It's fine. Won't be the first holiday I've skipped out on. Wish she wasn't going to be alone for this one." Evan pushed the car door open violently and clattered onto the sidewalk.

Marc hurried after him. He'd be damned if he left Evan like that. "Mind if I come up? I haven't seen your place."

Evan looked so lost standing there, the wind ruffling his hair and battering his cheeks. He finally shoved the paper he'd been holding into his bag. "It's not much to look at. I have the smallest room in the entire house."

"You should've seen my first apartment. It was the upstairs room of a pizzeria. I always smelled like garlic and oregano." Marc moved next to Evan and put his hand on his lower back, propelling him gently down the sidewalk. They both needed the physical contact.

To his relief, Evan laughed. "Those aren't bad smells. Your kitchen smells like that now."

"Yeah, well, maybe I got used to it."

Evan led him up three brick steps onto a little porch where a lawn chair sat with the decaying remnants of a pumpkin on top. The townhouse was attached to the one next to it, like this entire row. This neighborhood was popular with the students, and Marc thought the university should buy it all up and make it housing anyway. 'Course, based on the pink bicycle sprawled in front of the house next door, there might still be a few local families who'd hate that.

"The first floor is open concept." Evan opened the door and spread out his arm, revealing the cluttered living room that had been furnished with a couch, a couple of bookshelves, and a large TV surrounded by piles of DVDs. Beyond it, Marc could see an eating area and a kitchen.

"Not bad. A bit... dusty." Marc had expected worse, honestly. At least he wasn't tripping over beer cans—just a worn carpet that hadn't been installed properly.

"My room's on the second floor. Rae got the third floor, which is the entire loft. But I pay less for living in the closet." Evan led the way up the carpeted stairs along the wall and past a bathroom with pale blue tile.

"It can't be that bad." Marc clicked his mouth shut when Evan opened the door to reveal his tiny bedroom, barely large enough to fit a twin bed and a dresser.

Evan tucked his bag beneath the narrow desk. There wasn't much room for it elsewhere. "And check out my fabulous closet." He showed off the sliding door and revealed a row of clothes hanging behind it. "It's actually the biggest closet in the building. That's because they carved out part of the room for it."

"You know, these old houses were built during the time they used to tax for closet space," Marc said, repeating some crap a realtor told him once.

"That sounds like some serious bullshit." Evan laughed.

Good. Had to keep him laughing. Marc shut the door to the tiny room behind him, sidestepping to do it. He switched the lock.

Evan watched with a bemused look. "Really? On my twin bed?"

Marc stalked across the room, as best as he could because it only took two steps. "You ever been fucked on a twin bed?"

"I did survive the dorms in undergrad." His lips spread into a real smile, one Marc couldn't help but want to kiss.

"No talking about previous boyfriends." Marc seized Evan by the waist, slipping under his shirt to get at warm skin. "Getting naked time. If I'm not having you to myself this weekend, I want my fill now."

For a moment, he worried his words would make Evan angry. Instead, Evan stepped closer, kissing his way along Marc's jaw, his own hands tugging at Marc's jacket and getting caught in the buttons.

It was easy to fall into familiar habits. He bit down at the spot behind Evan's ear, knowing that would make Evan hard. Evan, in turn, knew how to stroke that spot up Marc's back, the one that tingled and went straight to his groin. If they weren't in this tiny room, they'd be halfway to horizontal by now.

Still, he couldn't help laughing when they bumped into the dresser. Marc never had the kind of dorm experience Evan talked about, but he sure knew about having sex in cramped conditions. Least this was better than the backseat of a car.

"I'm glad..." Evan started to say, and then looked down.

"Go on." Marc didn't stop, his fingers dancing down the line of Evan's fly, feeling the hard bulge there.

"That you're laughing."

"Aw, Evan." Marc didn't say any more than that. He caught Evan's lips once more, sucking the bottom one into his mouth, gratified to hear an answering moan.

Marc took one last savoring kiss, tasting the peppermint gum Evan always seemed to have on hand. Someday he wanted to know Evan's true taste. At this point the merest hint of peppermint got him hard. Marc pulled away and started attacking his own clothes. The close quarters made anything else too difficult.

Evan followed suit, stripped out of those layers, unwrapping himself like a gift. Marc drank in every inch of smooth, pale skin. As soon as he kicked off his own pants, he moved, getting his hands on Evan, stroking down his back and cupping a buttock in each hand.

"Supplies?"

Evan shuddered in Marc's arms. "Top drawer." His voice came out raspy with want. Good.

Marc found the lube and condoms easily. Neither had been opened before. He was the first to deflower Evan on his twin bed. The thought had him grinning.

"Hands and knees. On the bed." Marc pointed.

"Not like there's anywhere else to go."

"Hey, you've got a perfectly good wall over there." Marc slapped Evan's ass as he moved into position.

Evan turned back to look at him over one shoulder. "I was just concerned for your knees, old man."

Marc let out a growl, loving the way the sound made Evan's eyes go wide. If the kid had a thing for Marc's voice, then he'd damn well use it.

It took a good few minutes to uncap the lube and prep Evan. Marc liked to be thorough, but he kept one hand on Evan's cock throughout the proceedings to keep it interested.

The room got almost unbearably hot, smelling like sweat and the slightly plastic scent of the lube. Marc decided he wanted Evan's bed to smell like him, so even when he did as Evan wished and left, there would be something of him remaining.

He grabbed a condom, slipping it on before sliding into Evan's heat. Fuck, he was tight, no matter how long Marc stretched him. Evan cried out and Marc soothed him with kisses along his spine.

After that, he found his rhythm, rolling his hips in a familiar motion. Marc held on to Evan's waist, fingertips digging in hard enough to leave marks. He lost control for a moment, lost in his own pleasure as Evan moaned beneath him. Marc came with a shout, spilling into the condom.

He pulled out, rolled Evan over, and moved between spread legs to finish Evan off with his mouth. Marc was addicted to this taste, so raw and pure—Evan's true essence.

Evan grunted low in his throat, a hand on Marc's head the only warning before he climaxed. Marc swallowed, licking his lips as he climbed up Evan's body.

"Can we end every fight like that?" Evan kissed a line down Marc's jaw.

Marc closed his eyes, enjoying the post-sex glow. "I wouldn't call it a fight. I know what it's like to need time to get your shit together."

"Mmm. Right." Evan moved away, leaving cold where there had been warmth. "Lemme get a wash cloth."

He slid out of bed, grabbed a pair of boxers, and eased the bedroom door open. After throwing Marc a thumbs-up—the hall apparently clear—he disappeared, closing the door behind him.

Marc sat up and stretched. Out of the corner of his eye, he saw Evan's phone on the floor. It must have fallen out of his jeans in their mad dash to get naked.

He picked it up, and the screen came to life with the details of the last caller. Marc looked at the contact marked 'Mom' and frowned.

Evan wiggled his toes. Even with the extra blanket he'd thrown over his feet, the weight wasn't quite right. The downstairs couch had come with the townhouse, so he felt every inch of those previous inhabitants in the coils that dug into his ass and back.

He shifted again, sending his notebook and pen tumbling onto the rug. Evan stuck a post-it to mark his place in the text and let it rest on his lap.

Nothing he did could give this place the same sense of comfort he felt while at Marc's.

The front door opened, revealing Rae with a pair of goggles propped on top of her head and a backpack filled to the brim. He shouldn't be surprised—she lived here too, after all—but they'd both been so busy with classes and work that it felt sometimes like he didn't have a roommate.

"Evan? What are you doing home?" She dropped her stuff before shutting and locking the door.

He sat up and rubbed at his gritty eyes. How could he feel so tired after only a few hours of work? "Long story. Thought I could concentrate better here, but I was wrong."

"Don't move, I'm getting both of us something to drink." She held up one finger before disappearing into the kitchen long enough to grab two beers.

Evan hesitated at first but realized he was probably done for the night anyway. He accepted the bottle and took a tentative sip. "You've still got your goggles on, you know."

"Damn it." She reached up and pulled the plastic strap out of her hair. "Safety glasses. Not goggles."

He toasted her with his bottle. "Same thing."

Rae settled in on the empty end of the couch. She took a long draught herself and shifted in her seat. "This thing is uncomfy as hell."

"Right?"

"Which brings us back to the point. Why the hell are you here?" Rae gestured with the bottle.

Evan dropped his head back. "Because I am an idiot." The whole story spilled out, except for the part about having sex on his twin bed. "And it's not like it even helped. I get more work done at Marc's." He missed the warmth of Kilo draped over his legs, the softer scratch of Marc's pen as Marc worked on his own homework, the crackle of the fireplace, and the sheer presence of Marc being in the same room. Of course, knowing that the evening would end in the bedroom helped. It gave Evan incentive to get his work done quickly.

"So you have to answer a question. Is the problem Marc being a distraction? Or..." Rae blew out a breath. "Is the problem with the work itself?"

Heat boiled in his chest. "You think Dr. L's right?"

"I didn't say that. I meant—was there something about this particular paper? Maybe you have a mental block." Rae tilted her head. "Back when I was taking Orgo—Organic Chemistry—I had the hardest time. I could not get it. Dumbest thing helped, too—one of those idiot's guides they have in the library."

Evan gave it some thought. Leaverman's class focused more on theory than anything else he was taking. He'd never been the biggest fan of hardcore theory. Evan would much rather read the words, appreciate their beauty, and then make his own meaning.

"I don't think a library book is gonna help."

She slapped his knee. "You'll figure it out."

He grinned at her. "Maybe."

Rae hesitated, and then finally asked, "So how are things with Marc?"

Evan felt himself flush. "Great, you know? Really great."

"Good. He seems like a good guy."

They hung out for a bit longer, chatting about their week. It had been a while since Evan had the chance to chill out with Rae, and it felt nice.

His phone buzzed and Evan pulled it out of his pocket, smiling to see a text from Marc. Then he frowned at the content:

Hey. I did something you might be mad about. Check your email.

"Evan? What's up?"

Evan swiped his finger along the screen, pulling up his email. The most recent message listed a local airline and confirmed a ticket purchase for the day before Thanksgiving.

He swallowed. "I don't know if I'm going to kiss him or punch him. Marc bought me tickets home for Thanksgiving."

"Told you he was a good guy."

"That's a shit-ton of money." Evan couldn't stop staring at his phone. Were they in a place where Marc felt comfortable doing something like this? Evan couldn't repay him for this, not on his salary.

"Piece of advice. Kiss him. Take the gift in the spirit it was intended." Rae winked. "And then give him the best blow job of his life."

"Rae."

CHAPTER FIVE

"I want to hear all about your boyfriend."

Evan paused in the middle of dishing himself some gravy. He'd flown in late the night previous, after surviving being crammed in on the most crowded flight he'd ever seen. When he'd stumbled into his mom's car, he'd been half asleep. He barely recalled making it upstairs to their apartment, and only woke to the smells of Thanksgiving dinner.

"I can't believe you waited until dinner to ask that." He looked down at his plate and fiddled with his fork. Thanksgiving had always been about the two of them, especially after his father had left when Evan was ten. It had gotten even lonelier after his grandmother died last year.

"Well, what better dinner conversation?" His mother smiled as she dug into her own plate.

Mom looked good. She'd done something different with her hair—highlights, maybe?—and it hung past her shoulders in waves that shouldn't have looked that good on a woman her age. Evan frowned. "Are you seeing someone?"

She flushed, a dead giveaway. "I believe I'm asking the questions here. Your boyfriend is the one who called me."

"That's still a sore subject." Evan took a bite of his mother's stuffing and closed his eyes in ecstasy. Eventually he'd pry the secret recipe from her. "He's… a bit older than me."

"I figured. Most twenty-three-year-olds don't have that kind of money." She leveled a gaze at him. "Evan, does he make you happy?"

Now it was his turn to flush. "Uh, yeah." He didn't have the right words to explain how Marc made him feel. Evan knew Marc was comfort, and passion, and dedication. He was like a whirlwind who'd captured Evan from the moment they met, despite their inauspicious beginning.

"I don't know him," Mom said. "But he spent a lot of money to send you to me. I think that says a lot about who he is."

"Marc. His name is Marc." Evan took a gulp from his glass of water. "He's amazing, Mom. He runs his own business and he works with dogs. He's like a dog charmer."

She let him go on for a while, the smile never leaving her face. Finally, she said. "Don't be too angry with him. But a little piece of advice from someone who's been in a relationship or two. Set your boundaries now. He needs to know he can't do this kind of thing behind you back. And you need to speak up for yourself. That's the kind of relationship you want to have."

"So what made you such an expert?" Evan teased, pleased to hear her laugh in response.

It was her turn to expound on her new flame. His mother rarely dated, so he never saw this side of her.

She was right, though. Once he got back to Winston, he and Marc needed to talk. Marc needed to learn to ask first. Still, Evan really appreciated this gift. Already he felt more settled after talking to Mom.

After dinner, they gathered in front of the TV. Evan typed at his laptop trying to keep up with his work, easily tuning out the soft tones of the old black and white movies his mom favored instead of football. His phone buzzed and he smiled at Marc's text:

Happy Thanksgiving, kid. Missing you. Kilo says hi.

Evan sent a reply and then turned toward his mom curled up on the couch. "You know, I think you should get a dog."

~~*

The tickle in his throat started about three days after Evan got off the plane. He stood in front of his Comp I class, going over the basics of their research paper—again—when he couldn't quite swallow properly. Evan coughed, took a sip of his water, and continued on with his lecture.

He made it through the week, but on Friday afternoon, he stumbled into the townhouse and nearly passed out on the couch. Evan had to admit he had picked up some sort of cold. Rest and soup should set him to rights.

Sleep. He needed to sleep.

Evan put his foot on the first step, and nearly fell when he missed the next one. He blinked at the stairway and it blurred in his vision. Oh, that was not good. He grasped the railing and closed his eyes, making it up to his room by sheer will alone. His legs ached with the effort.

Before he fell on his bed, he remembered that he and Marc were supposed to get together later. Evan tugged out his phone, sent a quick text, and then collapsed face-first onto his pillow.

The next thing he knew, a pounding on the door had him sitting up in shock. Evan wiped his gritty eyes before stumbling to unlock the door. He blinked up at Marc, who stood in the doorway slightly out of breath, like he'd run for a long time.

"Marc?" Evan could barely speak, his mouth was so dry. "Thought I texted you. Sick."

"Yes, Evan. That was yesterday. You didn't respond to any of my texts or calls." Marc put one hand against Evan's cheek and frowned. "Rae let me in."

Evan sat on the bed, unable to keep upright any longer. "Oh."

"You're burning up." Marc crouched near him. "Aches, chills?"

Evan nodded. The room started to spin. He curled his fingers in the covers of his bed, hoping it would stop.

"I think you caught yourself the flu." Marc turned around. "You get his stuff. I'll grab him."

Before Evan could question who Marc was even talking to, Marc scooped Evan up in his arms, as if Evan weighed no more than a baby. That made the spinning even worse, so Evan ducked his head against Marc's shoulder. "What?"

"You're coming home with me, where I can take care of you properly."

There was something he needed to talk to Marc about. The urgency bloomed in his belly, but Evan couldn't remember what. "I'll get you sick."

Marc laughed, a rumble that Evan felt down to his toes. "That's the advantage to dating an old fogey, kid. I had my flu shot."

Evan felt too sick to even laugh. The sounds of Marc and Rae talking faded to murmurs of nothingness. He'd let Marc take care of things this once.

~~*

Marc left Evan tucked into his bed, with the lights dimmed and some quiet music playing. Kilo had planted himself at Evan's feet, despite damn well knowing he wasn't allowed on the bed. The dog had declared his preferences, and his presence seemed to comfort Evan, so Marc didn't make a stink of it.

He crept to the kitchen and started up a kettle of water. Only then did he pull out his phone and key in a number. "Hi, Carol. It's Marc."

"Marc? Is Evan all right?" Evan's mother sounded worried, and he couldn't blame her. Last time Marc had called, it had been before Thanksgiving when he had bought the airplane tickets. He had to know where he was buying a ticket for, after all.

"He's fine. Managed to get himself sick, though. Pretty sure it's the flu." Marc ran a hand through his hair. He hated seeing Evan liked that, so pale and shaky.

"Oh, no."

"It's okay. I brought him over here. I'll make sure he's right as rain." Marc opened his cabinets, checking that he had everything he needed to make his mother's chicken soup. "And his roommate stopped at the campus nurse, got him some Tamiflu.

He'll be fine. I wanted to let you know where he was."

She hesitated for a moment, but he caught it. "Marc, thank you. Really. But I think it's important that you don't baby him."

For a moment, he was offended. Did she think he went around looking for young college students to take advantage of? "Look," he started, "This isn't some fling for me. He's not my boy toy or whatever you think is going on. I care about him."

"Do you think you're trying too hard to prove that?"

"I'm trying to do the best I can, ma'am. It's not like they sell a manual for these things."

To his relief, she laughed. "All right. Keep me updated, okay?"

"Of course."

~~*

They managed to survive the next few days. Marc called in some favors to make sure the dogs were covered. The holidays were always his busy season, and he could afford to hire some more students, at least in the short term.

He skipped his own poetry class on Tuesday, figured he could miss at least one. Evan tried to keep working, but more often than not fell asleep at his laptop.

"Last week before finals," he said. "I've got to get this grading done, so I can work on my stuff."

Marc kissed his forehead and then went back into the kitchen to brew more tea. That mixed with honey seemed to be the only thing Evan could stomach right now. When he came back, he found Evan asleep once more, the laptop sliding off onto the bed.

Leaving the tea on the end table, Marc moved to grab the computer before it crashed to the floor. He saw the familiar grading screen and frowned. Last month, Evan had gone on and on about how much easier it was to grade online. He didn't have to scrawl comments in between lines of text anymore. He could type it in.

For a moment Marc watched the rise and fall of Evan's chest, so grateful to see him breathing easy at last, after several nights of hard coughing. Evan needed to focus on his own work, not waste his time grading papers when he was so sick. It wasn't that long ago that Evan had been so upset after his meeting with his advisor. Marc knew how easy it was to fall behind and never be able to catch up. He couldn't let that happen to Evan, not when Evan was so sick.

Marc sat in his easy chair, propped the laptop on his knees, and proceeded to grade.

~~*

Evan woke to generous doggy licks on his face. He laughed as he pushed Kilo away. Throughout his entire illness, the little corgi had kept to Evan's side. His warmth had been a comfort, even when Evan was shivering so hard he couldn't get warm.

For the first time in what felt like forever, he felt... not that bad. Evan pushed the covers off of his lap and swung his legs around. He took a deep breath and got to his feet. He swayed a bit, but was able to take shuffling steps.

Where was Marc?

Kilo barked at the door. With a laugh, Evan opened it, and slowly made his way into the living room. Marc sat in his favorite easy chair and looked up from typing. "Hey. You're up."

"Yeah, I'm starting to feel a little more human. What day is it?" Evan rubbed at his forehead, which throbbed. "My classes..."

Marc held up one hand. "It's Wednesday. I called the department secretary. She got your classes covered this week, and your professors are emailing you the lecture notes and final review sheets."

Evan slid onto the couch and snuggled between cushions that never felt so comfortable before now. He still had a million things to catch up on, but at least there was a little room to breathe. "Is that why you're on my laptop?" Now that he'd gotten close, he'd noticed it was his black Dell, not Marc's silver Toshiba.

Marc stopped typing. "You'd left the program open when you passed out. I thought I could help a bit."

"Help with what?" It wasn't like Marc could be doing any of his papers for him. Evan tried to remember what he'd been working on before he fell asleep. There'd only been grading for Comp I. "Tell me you're not grading my students' papers."

Marc looked up. "Um."

Evan got up and grabbed the laptop. Marc had the grading program open, and all thirty-five of his students had comments logged and ready, although not submitted, thankfully. "What the hell is wrong with you?"

"I was trying to help."

"Have you even heard of FERPA?" Evan's heart raced. "This could get me fired and the university fined."

"Evan, it's not that big a deal." Marc had gotten up from his chair and held out one placating hand.

Evan stepped away, the back of his legs brushing the edge of the couch. He held the laptop close to his chest. "Losing my position isn't a big deal?"

"That's not what I meant. Nobody has to know that I was helping you out."

"I would know." Evan licked his dry lips. "You can't keep doing this."

"Doing what?"

"Everything, Marc. The plane ticket. Literally sweeping me off my feet to bring me here. Doing my work for me. I'm not a stray pup that you have to take care of."

"You couldn't even get out of bed. What was I supposed to do?"

"You were supposed to ask. You do not get to make decisions for me."

"I'm supposed to be a mind reader? You don't ask for help, Evan. I don't think you know how. Hell, your own advisor had to pull you in for a talk."

"We're not talking about my academic performance here."

"Why, am I too stupid to understand it?"

Evan pointed shakily with his free hand, so frustrated that he couldn't put it into words at first. "Well, you're definitely not qualified to grade my students' papers."

"Back to that again."

"Oh, for fuck's sake, Marc." Their voices overlapped. Kilo stood between them, looking from

Marc to Evan, his ears twitching. Evan paused to catch his breath, his lungs protesting. He felt better, but clearly not good enough for this fight.

But one thing he knew, he wasn't getting back into Marc's bed.

"I think you should take me home."

Marc eyed him. "If that's what you want."

"Yeah."

It didn't take long to pack up his stuff. Evan stuck his laptop in his messenger bag and his extra clothes in his overnight bag. He couldn't help the prickle at the back of his throat as he worked, and he knew it was more than his illness.

Kilo protested the entire way to Marc's truck. He refused to be left behind, hopping up into the passenger seat and curling into an immovable ball. Marc bit off a curse and grabbed the leash off the porch.

Evan squeezed next to the corgi and sunk one hand into his thick fur. He knew abruptly that he couldn't let this dog go. "I think Kilo wants to come with me."

Marc, who'd slid into the driver's seat, grasped the steering wheel so tightly his knuckles went white.

"Okay."

CHAPTER SIX

The snow fell in fat fluffy clumps before dissolving on concrete still too warm to hold more than a dusting. Kilo let out a little whine as he stared out of the window. Evan looked up from his laptop and flexed his fingers. He deserved a break anyway.

"Course you want to go outside. You've got your own fur coat." He clipped on the leash, laughing at the way Kilo's entire butt wiggled with glee.

He still didn't know what possessed him to steal Kilo as he walked out of Marc's house last week. Evan knew he couldn't let the dog go. Hell, he wasn't sure he was ready to let Marc go. Many times over the past few days, he'd had his phone on his lap, the cursor blinking at him as he wondered what he could possibly say.

Maybe the problem wasn't only with Marc.

Evan coughed as he made his way down the stairs. Kilo bounded ahead of him. Luckily none of his roommates had a problem with the dog, and it was a secret they were all keeping from the landlord for now.

"You sound like shit."

Crap. He didn't realize Rae and Tangent were down here. They had the TV on so low he couldn't hear it from upstairs. "I'm still recovering."

"And yet you're taking your dog out for a walk." Rae and Tangent exchanged a look. Then she detangled her arm from around Tangent's shoulders. "I'm coming with you. I need to stretch my legs."

"Fine." Evan grabbed his coat from the rack near the door and waited as Rae bundled up. Kilo sat patiently for once. He was getting what he wanted. Evan tucked a plastic bag into his pocket, picked up Kilo's leash, and opened the door. He didn't care if Rae followed or not.

"You can't keep avoiding talking about it."

"Sure I can. Watch me." They let Kilo lead, sniffing his way down the block from tree to tree. "It's not like I don't have other shit on my mind." Two papers, one presentation, and then forty research papers to grade. Thinking about it made him tired.

That was the problem, wasn't it? Being so tired.

"Evan, come on." Rae punched his shoulder. "You gonna tell me what Marc did that was so bad you took Kilo and noped out of there?"

"It's not what he did." Though, yeah, that sucked. But Evan could forgive him for that. He should have had that talk with him after Thanksgiving, if he hadn't gotten caught up in work or picked up the flu. "He's got his life figured out, you know? He owns his business. Hell, he'd got enough money to buy me plane tickets. I'm a piss-poor PhD student who can't even cut it."

"Evan..."

"It's true." He could feel wetness on his cheeks and knew it wasn't the snow. "I knew I'd have to work hard. I get that. But I thought I'd enjoy it more, you know?"

Marc had been the bright spot in this semester. Not Evan's work, not getting to work with premier poetry scholars. All the things he thought he wanted, well, it turned out they weren't so delightful after all.

"You're not gonna quit, are you?"

Evan opened his mouth to deny it, but what came out was, "I don't know."

Rae didn't say anything as they continued around the block, Kilo trotting happily between them now that he'd done his business. Evan appreciated the silence. It had been so long since he'd had a moment to gather his thoughts. Jumbled words flitted through his head, and nothing made any sense.

"Sounds to me," she said as they turned the corner toward home, "that you need to get your shit together before you can even involve Marc."

"Yeah." Evan pulled Kilo back up the stairs to the townhouse. But how would he even begin to do that?

~~*

Evan started at the library. He left Kilo at home with Rae and Tangent, and felt odd as he walked the campus without his little buddy by his side. Kilo had accompanied him on his errands the past week, but Evan knew animals were not welcome inside the library unless they were certified service dogs.

He felt a little naked as he strolled into the archives, still expecting a furry form snuggled against his legs. Evan cleared his throat and went up to the counter.

"Hey, I haven't seen you in a while." The librarian at the desk grinned.

It reminded him how this once had been his sanctuary, getting lost in the words of his favorite poet. Evan wondered if the words would give him the same comfort now. "Yeah, I had the flu." The librarian took a step back at that, making Evan laugh. "I'm healthy now. Mostly. Could I get the Davis letters, please?"

"Sure. Student ID and fill out this card, please."

Evan knew the drill. He'd done this often enough, but never with fear before. His hand shook as he pressed the tiny golf pencil to cardboard. "You know, you're always here," he joked. "Do you ever leave the library?"

"I need the hours if I have any hope of paying off my student loans." The librarian didn't look to be much older than Evan, but that might have had something to do with the polo shirts and khaki pants he favored.

"Well, at least you get to work with all this." Evan made a gesture, encompassing the entire archives, but also meaning the three floors of the library above them.

To his surprise, the librarian snorted. "Yeah, I'm a glorified clerk. Not what I set out when I went to library school. Nobody ever told me how hard it would be to get a real librarian job." He stopped, as if realizing what he was saying, and snatched the card from the counter. "I'll be right back with your box."

The conversation disturbed him long after he sat down with his box of papers. Evan knew he didn't want to be stuck in a dead-end job, hoping for his chance.

He swallowed and lifted the lid to reveal the loose papers inside. His heart thudded loudly in his chest as he pulled out the precious letters. This letter—where Paul Davis had sketched out the first draft of what would become his famous "Sonnet to my Lover"— never failed to move him. Evan feared that this time he wouldn't have the same emotional experience.

"Dearest Alise, I hope you don't mind my scribbles," Davis began in his firm hand. "Here are the first few lines..."

Evan mouthed the words as he read them, having committed this imperfect version to memory, loving it despite the rough meter and near rhyme. He caught his breath as he murmured the final line, "... of my love..."

Yeah, still had quite the impact. Evan trailed his fingers over these words from the past. For the first time he noticed the little sketch Davis had included at the end. He'd always been so focused on the words, he never paid attention to the stylized little dog in the footer of the stationary. Was that...? Had Davis drawn a corgi?

He couldn't help but laugh. Talk about getting a sign.

Evan still loved these words. They meant as much to him as they ever did. The problem wasn't the poetry itself, but what he chose to do with this love. Evan needed to find another path.

He packed the papers away carefully with one last tender stroke. Now, he needed to make an appointment with his advisor.

CHAPTER SEVEN

Marc refilled the pitcher from the water purifier on his sink, and carefully carried it back to the table laden with food in what used to be his living room. He still watched his footing, even though Bella was crated in the kennel for the evening, because some part of his subconscious expected Kilo to be dancing underfoot.

"Put that down and help me with the spaghetti." His mother waved her wooden spoon at him.

He laughed. "Yes, Mama." Marc trekked back to the kitchen for several bowls of hot steaming pasta. The aroma of the sauce rushed over him: rich tomato and the tang of the fish used only on Christmas Eve. It took him back to childhood with a sniff. Mama might have been getting up there in age, but nobody could hold a candle to her cooking.

His sister Gloria got up from the table to help serve. The cacophony of voices swelled, becoming almost like a choir of noise, broken only by the sound of his infant niece crying. For once they were all together for the holiday, and, despite the chaos, he should have been glad.

"Marco, is that your doorbell?" His other sister, Anna, had cocked her head to one side. She always had freakishly good hearing.

He set down his bowls. "I'll check." Marc shuffled to fit between the folding chairs and his couch to make it to the front door. It swung open to reveal a familiar face.

"Evan," he breathed.

Evan looked better than the last time Marc had seen him. Color tinged his cheeks and that sunken look had disappeared from his eyes. He stood wide-eyed on Marc's porch, hands tucked into the pockets of his coat, the wind whipping at his hair.

Best of all, Kilo barked happily beside him.

"Hi. I, um, saw all the cars out front, but I didn't want to chicken out after borrowing Tange's car to get here."

"Let's go out back." Marc turned back long enough to shout, "Start without me!" before grabbing his coat and joining Evan outside.

"Hey, boy." He crouched down to scratch behind Kilo's ears. Marc couldn't help it. He'd missed the little troublemaker. "C'mon. The kennel is heated. I probably should check on the dogs."

Evan looked at the house. "What's going on? Are you having a party?"

"That is Christmas Eve dinner with the Romanos." Marc stuck his own hands in his pockets and shivered slightly as they walked toward the kennel. Once he'd had hopes of inviting Evan to meet his family. That might not have gone over entirely well—none of his relatives could be called shy—but he still fantasized about it, presenting Evan as his significant other, not hiding out here in the dark.

"Um." Evan bit his lip, looking as cute and desirable as ever. "It's not Christmas Eve. Right? I know I lost track of days, but..."

"Relax. You're not crazy. We had it over the weekend this year because it's the only way everyone in the family can make it. I ended up hosting because I can't leave the dogs." Marc undid the lock on the kennel door and opened it. Happy barks greeted them as he flicked on the lights and moved to check the water bowls. Evan shut the door behind them, cutting off the cool blast of air that had followed them inside.

He knelt before Bella's cage, sticking his fingers in between the wires. She had her favorite bed in there, but he hated having to lock her out of her home. There were too many people inside, and he'd never had her around a baby before.

"I got an A in that poetry class, you know. I didn't think I'd like it, but it turned out not to be that bad. Doesn't mean I'm signing up for any more classes. Except I saw a flyer for a program on dog first aid, and I think I could use a refresher course. That's always something you want to be fresh on."

"Marc," Evan interrupted. "You're rambling."

"Yeah." Marc sat back on his heels, watching Evan who still stood in front of the door. The ball was in the kid's court.

Evan ruffled his hair. "It's cute to see you flustered for once. You're always so... perfect." He shrugged.

"I'm human, Ev."

"Yeah, but you're also doing what you always wanted to do." Evan spread out his arms, encompassing the kennel before crossing them over his chest. "You're, like, a real adult, with a house—"

"And a mortgage," Marc couldn't help adding.

"The point is that you're living your dream. I think I was a bit jealous of that."

Marc had no idea where this was coming from. He'd never gotten any hint of that from Evan before.

Did Evan not understand his own worth? He was a genius, and Marc could never compare with that.

"So when you went and graded my papers, it's like, is there anything you can't do?"

"I shouldn't have done that." Marc pushed himself to his feet. "I was wrong, and I'm sorry."

"You were right about one thing. I don't know how to ask for help." Evan looked so lost. "I couldn't even see how much I was in over my head."

Marc wanted to put his arms around him, but he didn't dare move, afraid he'd spook Evan.

"I'm sorry." He didn't know what else to say. He hoped, but he couldn't speak

Evan shook his head. "Rae told me to get my shit together and she was right. So I went to see my advisor. I'm not quitting school, don't worry. But, we're going to work on my program, see if we can figure out what's making me so unhappy."

"Oh, kid."

"You're the best fucking thing that happened to me this semester, Marc. Tell me I haven't fucked it up completely?"

Now Marc moved, closing the distance between them and cupping Evan's face between his hands. He could hear the raw emotion in Evan's voice, and his own throat felt tender. He ran his thumb along Evan's cold cheek.

"No, you haven't. I had a lot of time to think. Too much time. I kept second guessing everything." He'd lain in bed, staring at the ceiling, too conscious of the empty space beside him. He'd missed Evan: his smile, his enthusiasm for everything, the way he beamed as he watched Marc work with the dogs. Every conversation ran through his mind, and he wondered what he could have said differently. "I'm not real good at this relationship thing."

"What? You mean you try too hard to be helpful?" Evan snorted. He leaned forward and pressed a kiss to Marc's lips—a hint, a promise, nothing more. "Can we try again? I think maybe this time we should go on more dates."

"What, hanging out on my couch wasn't enough for you?" Marc couldn't help it. He moved in for more than a taste. He parted Evan's lips with his own, drinking in Evan's flavor, so sweet, no peppermint this time. Evan groaned, and Marc could feel the stirring of arousal.

No, no sex in the kennel. There were some things he couldn't do in front of stranger dogs. Besides, he figured they needed to do a whole hell of a lot more talking before things were straight between them.

They separated as Kilo started to bark and dance between them. Damn dog started this whole mess. "I haven't forgotten about you."

"He missed you." Evan swallowed. "I missed you."

"Yeah, me too." Marc took one of Evan's hands in his. "So, uh, are you up for meeting my family?"

Evan hesitated. "Well, I think it's only fair, since you apparently are good friends with my mother."

"Oh, she's a pussycat compared to mine." Marc set the lights on dim. This was going to be fun.

The Memory of You
ERICA BARNES

The popcorn bag sat atop Maddie's lap, greasy butter sticking to her fingers as she tried furiously to wipe it off without getting her blonde hair in the way. The napkins were never thick enough to do the job. Often, she was left with a small mountain in an empty cup holder by the time the movie finished. She looked up in time to see the next piece of movie trivia pop onto the screen. Maybe she should stop eating and save herself a trip to the concession stand.

Checking her watch, there was only five more minutes until the film started. No one would've guessed by the way the theater was emptied of any life form, save for the lone woman sitting at least six rows closer to the screen. Maddie asked her best friend Lorraine if she wanted to come along, but Lorraine's wedding was occupying most of her time.

Maddie supposed she should have been attending to her needs, but Lorraine was what some might call a control freak. Maddie would suggest something to help calm her nerves, and Lorraine would promptly tell her a better alternative to what she suggested and then why they shouldn't do it. Maddie tried chalking it up to wedding jitters, but Christ almighty, she was pretty much always like this. Time apart was damn near mandatory.

Maddie tossed a piece of popcorn into the air, successfully catching it with her mouth. The lights began to dim then, the first preview starting. Something for some new romance movie that looked uncannily similar to a Nicholas Sparks film. Ten points if it actually *was* for a Nicholas Sparks film. She waited two minutes, body leaned forward, anticipating that little announcement that said it was based on his books.

"Based on the best-selling novel by Nicholas Sparks—"

Ha! Who was right? She was right.

"Shocking," the woman from the front deadpanned, loud enough for Maddie to hear over the next preview.

Her brows furrowed. Did the woman know she wasn't alone? Maddie looked around. It was still only the two of them. She ate another piece of popcorn, taking extra care to stay quiet.

"You're just gonna blow the place up," the woman said, propping her booted feet up on the empty chair in front of her. The next second, a flashy explosion filled the screen. "Knew it."

"That doesn't mean *he* blew the place up," Maddie finally said. Really, if she was going to give commentary the whole time, it might as well be a two-way street.

The woman jumped. Her head whipped from left to right in search of the voice's source. Maddie giggled, effectively helping the woman spot her.

She let out a heavy sigh. "Oh, honey. You scared the shit out of me."

"Sorry," Maddie winced. "I didn't mean to."

"It's all right. I just didn't think anyone else was here. Were you gonna let me go the whole movie doing that?"

"Would you have done that the whole time?"

The woman let out a hearty laugh. "Yeah. I would have."

"Again, sorry." Maybe she shouldn't have put in her two cents.

"No, it's fine," she said as another trailer ended. "Might as well sit up here, though. Don't want to almost pee my pants again."

Maddie hesitated. Sure, good conversation was fine, but the woman was a total stranger. What if she was, like, a serial killer hiding in a supposedly empty theater? No, that was more like some weird nightmare Maddie had sometimes. Everything was fine. She was just a friendly lady.

"You coming or what?" the woman asked.

"Just… let me get my stuff," Maddie said, grabbing her popcorn, purse, and coat before walking out to the aisle and down to where the woman sat. She had a split second to decide if she was going to leave a seat between them or sit completely beside her. After the woman pat the seat beside her, the decision felt made. She sat down and made herself comfortable.

"I'm Claudia, by the way," the woman said, not taking her eyes off the screen.

"Maddie. Nice to meet you."

"Nice to meet you, too," she grinned.

They continued to talk despite the previews playing in the background. Apparently Claudia had lost a bet to a friend, so she'd waited until the last possible minute to hold up her end of the deal, which was to see this movie. When she told Maddie the bet was over who could drink the most daiquiris without puking, Maddie about choked on her popcorn. Those contests never ended well for her, either.

Maddie wanted to keep the conversation going, but the screen faded to black, and an open pasture appeared on screen. Maddie ignored the beginning of the romance movie she'd waited at least a month to see. Her eyes couldn't help glancing over to Claudia. It was harder to tell from where she was sitting before, but Claudia was actually very, very pretty. She had short black hair that curled into a sharp jawline. Her eyes were wide as she watched the movie, either with wonder or a liveliness that didn't match the crow's feet at the corner of her eye.

"He'll cause problems later," she commented.

Maddie looked up and saw a guy who wasn't the one from all the posters flirting with the lead girl. "He might not. Maybe they're misleading us."

Claudia scoffed. "Yeah, right. These movies stick to a strict, boring formula. He'll be trouble. And that girl there is gonna discourage her friend from seeing him. So predictable."

"That's not a bad thing," Maddie reminded her. "Sometimes people are in the mood for predictable. Predictable can be good."

Claudia chortled. "Predictable is overdone. Shake things up a bit. Make me excited to see what happens next."

"Aren't you?" she asked. "We don't know how it ends. You're just guessing."

"Wait a few minutes. We'll see if I'm wrong."

So they did. They continued watching the movie, Maddie waiting to see what it would produce. The trailers for it always seemed good, predictable plot or not.

Unfortunately, the events that Claudia predicted would happen did come true, much to Maddie's chagrin. While perhaps it was part of a formula, Maddie found herself enjoying the scenes nonetheless. Claudia would scoff, but Maddie would roll her eyes at the reaction. So what if they could see it coming from a mile away? That also meant there would be a happy ending. She didn't know about Claudia, but Maddie looked forward to those endings.

It wasn't until after the main couple had gotten into their ultimate argument for the film that Claudia spoke again. "He'll come to the gala and make a spectacle of himself in front of everyone to reconcile with her. She'll be so touched that they just *have* to kiss."

"It's not that fun watching movies with you," Maddie finally grumbled. "So what if that is what he does? It's cute and I want to see them together again."

Claudia turned to Maddie. "I wasn't trying to ruin your fun."

"Well, you are. Being unpredictable might be fun to you, but trying to guess everything that happens before it does isn't why I bought a nine-dollar ticket to see this."

"Wouldn't you want more for your money?"

Maddie was dumbfounded. "I would be getting what I wanted if you weren't so busy trying to sound like a know-it-all."

"That's not what I'm trying to do," Claudia laughed. She turned her body more so that she was facing Maddie better. For the first time that night, she saw both of Claudia's eyes clearly, illuminated by the massive screen. There were wrinkles in places where Maddie had yet to get any, and a depth that could only be acquired by years of living. It didn't make them any less... enthralling. That was a good word for it. And God, were they ever enthralling. "Don't you think life would be more exciting if you didn't know what happened next?"

Maddie didn't even know what she was having for breakfast tomorrow. "Sure."

Claudia inched closer. They were close enough now that Maddie could feel Claudia's breath ghosting along her skin, warm and minty. She did her best not to fidget. Strangely, it wasn't because she was uncomfortable with the lack of personal space. "In a movie, what do you think would happen right this second?"

"I don't know," Maddie answered quietly. "You murder me and muffle my screams?"

A giggle escaped Claudia. Her hand then went from covering her mouth to lying on top of Maddie's. It caused Maddie's breath to hitch. "Not that," she said, resting her chin in the palm of her free hand so that a slender pinky finger lay against her pink-tinted lips.

She wasn't leaving much room for any other interpretation but one. "I guess you'd kiss me."

Claudia leaned in closer, and goddammit, Maddie wanted this to be a movie. Whatever perfume she was wearing made Maddie want to leave the theater smelling like it. Her eyes closed and she waited for the inevitable, the movie long forgotten. Except nothing came. She opened her eyes and saw Claudia watching her intently, a hint of surprise written over her face. Had Maddie been mistaken? Maybe. But the look of shock was gone almost instantly and Claudia was smiling again. "Doesn't that seem a little boring, though?"

Boring wasn't the word Maddie would use, but okay.

"What if the twist was that we didn't kiss?" she continued.

"That's not new either," Maddie said. Movies always teased the almost-kiss.

"No, but not kissing, and then never seeing each other again after tonight. Just knowing that there was *this*," she said, waving a finger between the two of them. "*That* would be real."

"That sounds terrible," Maddie said seriously. Why would anyone ever walk away after finding out there was chemistry with someone else? If there was a girl she had a moment with, she got that girl's number. And right now, she really wanted Claudia's number. Although she was fairly certain of what her answer would be if she asked.

"Hate it all you want, but that happens in real life."

"Sounds like an awful real life to have."

Claudia chuckled, the light on her face disappearing. The moment went with it. Maddie looked around as she saw the end credits begin to roll.

"Movie's over," Claudia said. She hesitated only a moment before grabbing her purse and standing up. "It was nice meeting you, Maddie."

With that, she sidled past Maddie and out toward the exit, leaving Maddie to sit alone and stare at her retreating form. She wished the movie wasn't over.

~~*

"You promised us the venue!" Lorraine shouted into her phone, cheeks flaming red. "Yes, I know you made a mistake. Now *fix* it."

Maddie sat with wide eyes on Lorraine's couch, while her soon-to-be-husband, Richie, stood in the kitchen and popped the Tylenol bottle open. He walked into the living room to sit beside Maddie. "She's been like this all morning," he whispered.

"She's been like this for ten years," Maddie said. "You should've seen her Sweet Sixteen."

"Her dad filled me in," he chuckled, albeit a bit nervously. Maddie watched him place a hand to his temples.

"You're not getting cold feet, are you?" She wasn't going to let Lorraine get left at the altar. Not that Lorraine would let anything or anyone mess up this wedding, but still.

"No, I'm getting a migraine," he said, giving her a small grin afterward. "Don't worry. I'm in this for the long haul."

Maddie nodded, accepting his answer. She began to twiddle her thumbs, eyes downcast. "Do you ever wonder what would've happened if you never saw Lorraine after that first day you met her?"

"I'd be a lot lonelier," he told her casually, leaning further back into the couch. "I'd probably still have those sideburns."

Maddie smiled. "I mean... I don't know what I mean."

"I think I do," he assured Maddie, giving her a playful push. He took a deep breath, a thoughtful expression crossing his face before he answered. "I would've gone through life wondering what that hottie with the legs was doing. After a while, though, I probably would have forgotten about her and moved on to the next one."

"You don't think it's sad that it could've been completely different?"

"Well, no, since it isn't, and I *am* marrying her," he said, giving Maddie a funny look. "You okay?"

Maddie sighed. "I feel like I missed a really big opportunity."

"Like what?"

"Like being with this girl who seemed amazing," she said. "I met her a couple weeks ago, and there was something there, I could feel it. But no, she wanted to be exciting and different." Maddie groaned. "I just want a chance to date her, and she could be anywhere by now. I mean, what if she was only visiting town for a few days? What if she's halfway across the country?"

"Sounds like you want to date the idea of her," he laughed. "She could've been a total loser for all you know. Hell, you might have dodged a bullet."

Maddie fell back onto the couch, mirroring Richie's position. "I know, but it would've been nice to find out for myself."

"Do you even know this chick's name?"

"She said her name was Claudia, but that's all I know. If that's even her real name."

Richie pursed his lips for a moment before shaking his head. "Yeah, name doesn't sound familiar. The only Claudia I know is the one making our cake, but she's gotta be as old as my mom."

"Well what does she look like?"

He gave some sort of a shrug, seeming to search for a description. "About average height, short black hair, looks like she might jog a lot in her free time," he listed off. "Wish I could help more. Sorry."

"It's okay," Maddie said, trying to make her words as steady as she could. Claudia hadn't stayed long enough for the lights to completely turn back on, but everything sounded like how Maddie remembered her. The wrinkles had made Claudia look older, but maybe she was even older than Maddie anticipated. Could this be the same Claudia? "That reminds me, did you guys ever decide on a flavor?"

"No," he scoffed. "We're actually going back for another tasting today. Wanna come? You have this way of helping Lorraine make decisions that I don't have yet. I could really use your help. If not for me, come for my sanity."

"What about your sanity?" Lorraine asked as she perched on the edge of the couch beside Richie.

"Nothing," he said quickly, voice sugary sweet.

"Mmm," Lorraine hummed, rubbing Richie's shoulder. She looked at Maddie. "We could use you today if you want to go. There'll be raspberry."

"You don't have to twist my arm. I'll go." She felt bad for keeping the reason she was really interested in going to herself. Not that tasting cakes didn't sound like a blast, but she mostly wanted to see if her mystery woman and their baker were one in the same. Other than that, she was dreading the trip a little. She already felt like Claudia, guessing how long it would take for Lorraine to decide between two flavors of cake or icing. But this was real life, not a movie. Predictable movies were fun. Watching

Lorraine complain that her grandmother could make a better carrot cake was not fun.

It didn't matter, though. Four hours later, after they'd eaten a light lunch, she was getting out of the car with Lorraine and Richie to walk into the Sunflower Bakery. The shop windows were decorated with little sunflowers, cakes, and cupcakes. She must have passed this store a million times and never once thought about going in.

A small bell chimed when they walked in. The blonde girl behind the counter looked up and gave them a bright smile, all pearly whites. Small tables were scattered around the shop, a couple of which were occupied with customers. A variety of different treats sat behind a long glass display. Tarts with glazed fruit over a creamy custard, small cakes with whipped icing and elegant decorations, cupcakes piled high with piped frosting, cookies that looked like they would melt in her mouth, and much more were all perched on shelves, waiting to be devoured. Maddie's mouth was already watering. The white walls and floors of the bakery only made it look more upbeat.

"Hi! How can I help you today?" the woman behind the counter asked, smile still plastered on her face.

"We're here for a cake tasting. We have an appointment under Thompson," Lorraine said as she approached the counter.

The woman, Danielle, checked a small book, giving them a smile after her finger landed on their appointment. "Just in time! Congratulations on your engagement, and if you'll follow me, I'll lead all of you back to our tasting room. Miss James will be out momentarily to help show you our various flavors, as well as our different icings, fillings, and decorations."

"Thank you," the three of them said as they took a seat at a small white table. Danielle nodded, walking back out to the front without waiting for Miss James to arrive. Maddie looked around, but she didn't see signs of cake anywhere. There was another opening off to the side that was covered only by a white curtain. It was all very neat.

"I'm leaning toward half of it being chocolate, and half of it being carrot cake," Lorraine said.

"Why not half vanilla, half carrot cake?" Richie asked.

"More people like chocolate than vanilla," she said, sounding only slightly unsure.

"What about coconut?" Maddie asked.

Lorraine made a face. "No, that doesn't sound good."

"Most of my clients taste the cake before making a decision," a voice said from behind them. They turned around and Maddie could've sworn the breath got knocked out of her.

It was Claudia.

Her short hair was somehow tied back into a ponytail, an all-white uniform covering her body. In the light of day, it was obvious by the dark circles under her eyes, and the few extra wrinkles, that Claudia was much older than she previously suspected.

Claudia smiled until her eyes landed on Maddie. Briefly, she forgot to keep up with appearances, her grin fading. Within a matter of seconds it was back, however, and her falter seemed to have gone unnoticed by the other two. Maddie didn't know how to act, much less how to remember simple gestures like smiling. Half of her was jumping with joy, but the other was worried as hell.

"I know you don't like to wait," Claudia said, addressing Lorraine, "so let's get straight to business."

Claudia pushed the white curtain aside and walked inside the tiny room it had concealed. She came out with a large tray that held four different slices of cake on a large plate.

"I have the four flavors you requested. This first slice is our Chocolate Decadence cake, a chocolate cake with a chocolate fudge icing. We can also put any filling of your choice inside. The complete list of choices can be found here," she said, laying a laminated sheet with a long list beside the plate.

Maddie took a bite, slowly chewing to savor each flavor. Not that she expected anything different, but the cake was delectable. The icing was sweet, but not so rich that she would still be able to taste the sugary coating in her mouth half an hour later. By the look on Richie and Lorraine's face, they were fond of it, too.

"This is amazing," Richie said through a mouthful. Lorraine nodded in agreement.

"Save room for the rest," Claudia laughed, jotting down notes while they tasted the cakes. She pointed to the second slice. "This is the carrot cake with our signature cream cheese icing."

Lorraine, of course, was in love with it. Maddie knew that despite the two cakes left to taste, this would probably be the one they went with. Richie didn't look like he was suffering, so Maddie was positive he'd be okay with it.

The third cake they tried was a simple vanilla cake with a white chocolate mousse that didn't taste simple at all. The mousse was like velvet in Maddie's mouth, and the cake was just fluffy enough without falling apart. The fourth and final cake was also vanilla, but with a raspberry filling and icing to top it off. Lorraine chuckled when Maddie made a happy noise while chewing.

"Told you it would be good," Lorraine said to Maddie.

"You're just getting my hopes up," Maddie said. "I know what you're picking."

"You think I should?" Lorraine asked, looking longingly at the spot that had held the carrot cake before the three of them finished it off. "I want it, but I want something everyone will eat."

"It's your wedding." She should be able to have whatever she wanted.

"We can get the carrot cake," Richie smiled, taking Lorraine's hand in his. "I thought it was great."

"Then we want the carrot cake with the cream cheese icing. And for today, can we get a small vanilla cake with that raspberry filling and icing?"

"Absolutely," Claudia said, making more notes. "Now we have a few more specifics to work out, like design, etcetera."

Claudia had another employee prepare the raspberry cake while she continued working on Lorraine and Richie's cake. Maddie chimed in occasionally when Lorraine was stuck between choices, but she mostly listened to them decide on three tiers, a simple but elegant design with branches and blue flower petals draping down one side of an all-white cake. They decided to have a smaller version of the vanilla cake with white chocolate mousse in the end, since Lorraine was still worried she'd have to hear her mother talk about no one eating the carrot cake.

Most of the time while they were deciding between this and that, Maddie found her eyes drifting to Claudia. A baker. That was not what Maddie expected her profession to be. She seemed so spontaneous, so adventurous. For some reason, she imagined Claudia was a worldly traveler, always the mysterious woman to passerby. She would draw attention, and people would wonder what her life was like, what she was like. Maddie still did. Was she crazy for it? Was she missing some sign that said Claudia wasn't into her? Had she read everything at the theater the wrong way?

"Thank you so much for this," Lorraine said, standing with Richie and Claudia. Maddie did the same.

"It's no trouble at all. Thank you for choosing Sunflower Bakery to make your wedding cake," Claudia said, extending her hand to shake Lorraine and Richie's hands. When it came time to shake Maddie's hand, she could've sworn Claudia lingered, but it could just as easily have been in her head.

The four of them walked out to the front so Lorraine and Richie could purchase the take-home cake, Danielle smiling all the while. Once finished, Lorraine handed Maddie the neatly wrapped yellow box.

"A thank you for dealing with me," Lorraine said.

Maddie smiled, giving her friend a hug before they turned toward the door. She didn't want to leave just yet, but she couldn't let Lorraine and Richie stay if she expected to get a word in privately with Claudia. Thinking fast, she touched Lorraine's shoulder. The next place they planned to go was the hotel, and that was only four blocks away.

"I think I might get a few things myself. If you want to go on, you can. I'll meet you there."

"If you're sure," Lorraine said, giving Maddie a hug. Richie did the same, the couple walking out afterward.

Now, to see how well this went.

She turned around and saw Danielle helping a couple of girls who had come in after Lorraine and Richie paid for their time. Looking toward the backroom, she saw Claudia leaning against the wall, arms crossed as she watched Maddie. She looked somewhere between surprised and fidgety when Maddie started walking toward her, which didn't make any sense whatsoever.

Maddie placed the yellow box down on a nearby table, and then turned back to Claudia. Where did she start? What was she supposed to say?

"It's good to see you again," Maddie said, shifting from one foot to the other. Claudia only looked at her. "I thought you'd be out of town or something."

Claudia sighed. "I wish I was. I wouldn't have to stand here and do this if I could leave."

Ouch. Maddie tried to keep her face from falling. "I thought you were just trying to make things exciting. I won't bother you again. Sorry."

She turned to grab her cake, but Claudia spoke up. "No, wait. That's not what I meant."

Maddie stopped, looking expectantly at Claudia. "What did you mean?"

She scoffed. "I meant I hate being stuck in town. And before you start, whatever happened in the theater is best left there."

"So you think there was something there, too?"

"Yes, but what do you think can come from it?" Claudia groaned, wiping her hands over her face. "Listen, you've been great, and I would love to get to know you more, but it won't work. I can tell you that now. You're just a kid."

Ouch again. Kid-zoned. "I'm twenty-five."

"And I'm forty. But unlike you, I have an ex-husband and a ten-year-old son. That's not a life someone your age knows how to handle. Whatever might be here can't grow. It was better left to our imagination."

Maddie could feel her blood begin to boil. Richie was right. She didn't know anything about Claudia. She didn't know what she liked, disliked. She didn't know she had a son, but it wasn't something she couldn't handle. Claudia just assumed she would run the other way. "You don't know anything about what I can handle."

"And you don't know anything about me, or my life."

"At least I'm willing to find out," Maddie retorted, crossing her arms over her chest. That was why people dated, to see if it was something worth trying long-term. "You're just a hypocrite."

"Excuse me?"

"Yeah. You act like you're better than predictability and normality, but that's your life. You judge everything and everyone before you even know what in the hell you're talking about because, what, you're old? Wise? I'm twenty-five, not five."

"Could've fooled me," Claudia said coolly. It infuriated Maddie to no end, and she didn't know why.

"I'm sorry, should I be respecting my elders?" she asked sarcastically. "You know what, tell me that this isn't something you want. Tell me you're not looking for a relationship or ready for one. Tell me you don't like anything about me, or that you're worried about what your son will think, or that you're not even into girls. Can you say anything like that, or are we going in circles because you think you know how this ends?"

"See? Too young to get it," Claudia said, wearing the smuggest smirk on her face as if she'd won some goddamn contest. That was it for Maddie. This was too much of a hassle, and if Claudia wasn't going to open up or stop making Maddie feel like an idiot, then there was no point in staying. It was just a stupid moment in an empty theater.

"I guess you're right, and I'm wrong," Maddie said, grabbing her cake box. "And I guess you did know all along how this would end. Congratulations."

When Maddie turned to leave, she never once looked back. This was all a stupid escapade by a stupid kid who believed in romantic endeavors working out. Maybe she didn't understand how the world worked, and she was being too optimistic when it came to how they would have turned out. Maybe Claudia was more right than Maddie wanted to admit. But they would never find out, would they? They would be stuck with their imaginations. At least, Maddie would be stuck with hers.

~~*

"Stop it," Lorraine said as she stared into the mirror, hands brushing out the invisible wrinkles in her wedding dress.

"Stop what?" Maddie sat with her legs crossed on a plush chair, watching Lorraine try out the new fitting.

"It was a one-night stand that happened months ago. You've done better than her."

"It wasn't a one-night stand. I know what those are," Maddie chuckled.

She'd had many one-night stands in the six months since the incident at the cake shop. Nights spent with someone else her age, or close to. And it wasn't as if it was always on her mind. Time helped eased some of that embarrassment. But every once in a while, she'd let her mind wander to what ifs. It was evident when her mind slipped; her nails would often sink into her skin out of anger at the memory. She looked down and saw the red outline of her nails indented into her forearm.

Lorraine took the chair next to her, ruffles going every which way. "I promise that if I can't find you a good bridesmaid, I'll get someone else at the wedding."

Maddie laughed. "Really, I'm fine. It's just weird to think about."

"Why?"

"One night can be so impressionable. It's weird."

"Impressionable night my ass. She tried using a B.S. excuse so she didn't have to give you her number. And it wasn't even that good! She lives in town, did she think you'd never want a cupcake?"

"Could she have been right, though? With the age difference being a problem?"

Lorraine shrugged. "Richie and I only have five years between us, so I don't know from experience. But it might've caused issues down the road."

Maddie nodded. She sat back in her chair, staring at the floor. "I think I could have done it."

"Done what?"

"Handled her having a kid. An ex-husband."

"Are you sure?"

"No," Maddie said outright, "but I would've tried. That's what matters, right?"

"A little, but there's a lot more to it than that. Like... okay, you couldn't even tell *me* about this woman until three months ago. Imagine trying to tell your parents. What would they say when you're dating someone who isn't much younger than they are?"

"They could warm up to it," Maddie pondered. Then again, even she hadn't yet adjusted to all the different aspects of being romantically involved with someone that much older than her. She wasn't used to someone having an established profession rather than an internship to help them climb the work ladder. She wasn't used to someone taking care of a kid instead of drunken friends that smelled like cheap vodka because that's all they could afford. So what would it be like for her parents to shake hands with a woman who was more likely to be mistaken for one of their friends than one of Maddie's? Her brows furrowed at the thought. "I think."

"All right. Say they do. Then what happens when you start noticing the little differences? She makes a reference you don't get, or she wants to stay in when you want to go out and have fun. Maybe she turns to an oldies station in the car, and you want to listen to something newer. Won't you get embarrassed?"

"Just because she's older doesn't mean we don't have anything in common. I don't even know what she likes to listen to. And if she liked something I haven't heard, I can give it a try. I'm sure it wouldn't be hard to do the same for me. I mean... I'm sure I wouldn't get every reference she made, but that doesn't mean we couldn't give it a try. I don't base my current relationships on how well they know a T.V. show or not."

"Well, it's not something you think about with someone our age. And this isn't even *touching* on how she has a family already. Are you ready to mature that fast? I haven't heard you ever talk about settling down."

Maddie sighed. "I know."

She'd met plenty of nice girls since Claudia. They'd gotten along or agreed it was better left to a night. She was single, and ready to mingle at Lorraine's wedding in a month. She needed to stop worrying about who would or wouldn't be okay with her dating someone much older. It didn't matter. What mattered was the bride.

"Do you think Richie and I are doing the right thing?" Lorraine asked unexpectedly.

"What? Getting married?" This was why it was important to focus on the bride. Even someone as stubborn as Lorraine wasn't immune to cold feet syndrome.

"Yeah. Do you think it's right for us?"

"You're asking me this *now*?" Maddie chuckled, shaking her head. She took a moment to formulate

313

the proper response. "I think you guys are good together. I think he loves you, and you love him. So whatever's making you second-guess this, I think it'll pass. You'll see. You guys will grow old together and annoy me with your slow walking."

"Loving him isn't the problem. What if we get divorced later? What if we cheat on each other? What if we aren't annoying you together?"

"My guess is he's not thinking about this kind of stuff," Maddie said. "I bet he hasn't even thought that far down the line yet."

"How do you know?"

"I don't. But Richie seems like the kind of guy who lives in the now. He doesn't worry about what could be. He just knows what is. And I think he knows how smitten he is with you."

Lorraine giggled. "Smitten."

"What? It's true."

"No, I like it," she assured Maddie. "He's smitten with me, and I'm smitten with him."

"See? If you guys keep up that mindset, you'll have grandkids together before you know it."

"Yeah, I guess so. Thanks," she said, giving Maddie a grin before standing. "Be ready to go when I get out of this," Lorraine ordered with a smile, heading back to the dressing room. "The florist is next."

Maddie did as she was told, and she continued to for the next month while the wedding drew closer. Last-minute details were always a bitch, but she was ready for Lorraine to be off on her honeymoon and no longer worrying about which guest is sitting where, or how often her parents would come up to her and annoy her with some minute concern that only added more stress. To say the month flew by would have been a lie, but they got through it without too many casualties.

The day of the wedding was chaos, but not completely in a bad way. There was excitement buzzing in the air, the promise of love blossoming. Guests were ushered to their seat as everyone prepared for the big moment, and the reception that came after. The bridal party consisted of six girls in aqua blue strapless dresses, including Maddie, and all were fluttering around Lorraine as they prepared her appearance and simultaneously tried not to ruin their own—Lorraine would've killed them if they had. It had taken her a couple months of planning to decide which dress they would wear, and another couple months after the date had actually been set to know how their makeup would be done, and if their hair would be curly or straight—ultimately, it was light on the makeup with the bridesmaids' hair falling in waves down their back.

By the end of the preparations, Lorraine looked stunning, her white off-the-shoulder lace gown fitting perfectly to her body, while her partially pinned back curls shone brighter than any from a shampoo commercial ever could. It was hard not to think of what Maddie's wedding might be like someday. Would it be this elegant? Would Maddie's partner be dashing for the door or for her? It made her giddy just thinking about it.

Time whirred by before the procession, and soon enough, she was marching down the aisle with her bouquet in hand. The wedding march began to play once all the girls were standing at the front, and she tried to evenly distribute the weight on her heels, being careful not to step on the floor-length maid-of-honor dress. *Don't cry, don't cry,* she thought to herself. Lorraine gave her a wink as her father walked her down the aisle, slipping her hand into Richie's. It was a beautiful ceremony. She thought she caught a tear running down Richie's cheek, but Maddie knew he would never admit it to anyone but Lorraine.

It took a couple hours, and one very nerve-wracking speech, but they eventually got to the more relaxing portion of the evening. The one where the DJ played his songs, and everyone danced either with or without a drink in them. Maddie had at least two drinks in her, but they were nothing strong. Lorraine had mentioned to her that none of the bridesmaids were viable choices for her, but there were at least two other girls attending the wedding that she might be interested in.

Girl number one, Sienna, was nice enough, but she liked talking extensively about her math courses and what jobs she already had lined up. "What is your profession?" Sienna had asked, voice nasally. Maddie told her she worked at a bookstore. "I mean, what are you studying to do?" she asked again. That was when Maddie realized this wasn't going to work out. Maddie had long since been out of college, and working at the bookstore was all she knew how to do. It was a stable job. It made her happy.

Girl number two, Jessica, wasn't any closer to someone she could connect with. Jess was too drunk to get anything coherent out. She relied heavily on Maddie to get her from point A to point B after she said she wanted to go visit with some old friends. Maddie had helped her, of course, but she hightailed it out of there as soon as Jess was sitting down.

Maddie stuck close to Lorraine and the other girls after that. It was okay if she didn't meet anyone. The wedding was going perfectly, Lorraine was having fun with Richie, and holy hell, the food was fantastic. Even the cake that she wanted to hate so badly tasted like it was carved from a cloud.

She had seen Claudia around at some point during the beginning of the night. Claudia and a couple staff members were assembling the cake when Maddie had jogged by to fetch Lorraine's mother. They never met each other's gaze, and Maddie was glad they hadn't.

By the time midnight rolled around, Maddie knew she couldn't take any more. Her feet were killing her, the dress was starting to rub all the wrong places, and the party had mostly died down by now. Not to mention Lorraine and Richie were preparing to leave for their honeymoon. Maddie waited until Lorraine was finished showing her gratitude and saying her goodbyes to one couple before gently grabbing her arm.

"I think I'm gonna head out," she said, leaning in to give Lorraine a hug. "I'm tired."

"Thank you for everything," Lorraine said, arms wrapped around Maddie's body tightly. "I couldn't do this without you."

"I'm always here for you. Now go. You have a long night ahead of you," Maddie said, giving her a sly wink. Lorraine returned the wink before being pulled away toward the desolate dance floor.

Maddie laughed, moving to grab her belongings. The night had been fun, but she was ready to take a much-needed break.

~~*

For some reason, once Maddie was in her car and driving down the road, she found herself heading straight for the bookstore. One of the perks to having keys and being on good terms with the owner was being able to enjoy the place after midnight. Many long, quiet nights had been spent pouring over volumes of books.

She parked her car just outside the store. Her heels had long since been discarded with no intention of putting them back on tonight. Walking around barefoot would be better than putting those monstrosities back on. Gorgeous shoes, but never had a blister been easier to get.

No bell chimed when she entered the store, purse and coat in hand. Maddie locked the door behind her and went behind the counter to put her stuff down, heels clacking as they hit the hardwood floor. She let out a long sigh, soaking in the silence. No buzz of conversation, no loud music pumping in her ears, or the strong smell of alcohol when someone tried talking to her. It was just the blissful quiet.

The store itself looked like an antique on the outside, one of those mom-and-pop bookshops on the cover of a tourist brochure to make the town or city look homier. Inside it looked fresher, renovations having been done here and there, making the dark wooden shelves stand out against the white walls and ceiling. The newer books were placed near the front, but if anyone traveled far enough into the back, over half the books had dust on them.

She turned on a light away from the door so no one mistook the store for being open. Now, what to do? She could tidy up, read something she hadn't read before. Maddie wasn't sure. All she knew was that she didn't want to go home and watch late-night television. The night had been too wonderful to go end it.

Just as Maddie was about to settle onto the floor, there was a knock at the door. She jumped, not expecting anyone to want in at this hour. What was more unexpected was the face she saw staring in.

"What the hell," Maddie whispered to herself as she stared blankly at Claudia. She was as pretty as Maddie remembered her being. Eyes that looked worn out, a slender frame hidden under a burly coat, and black hair that was only a tad longer than she remembered it. After seven months, the sight of her still affected Maddie physically.

She didn't want to unlock the door. The store was closed anyway; it wasn't like she had to give a reason. Yet Claudia still stood there, a soft expression on her face. How Maddie kept running into her, she didn't know. Claudia held up a piece of paper about the size of a notepad. It read: "I'm sorry."

Maddie inhaled deeply. Dammit.

Luckily, she was in a good mood. Maddie could let her inside and say whatever it was she wanted to say, or get whatever it was she wanted to get. It didn't have to be long.

She opened the door and stepped to the side, allowing Claudia to walk in before shutting it behind her and relocking it. Maddie swept by Claudia, turning to her afterward. The air between them was thick. Suffocating.

"I, uh… happened to see you walk in from across the street," Claudia said, hands stuffed in her coat pockets as she started to meander through the room. "Hope you don't mind."

Maddie shook her head. "I'm surprised you aren't at the wedding."

"I left after they said 'I do'." Claudia stopped next to a shelf with cookbooks. "I've been to enough receptions to know how the rest of the night goes."

"Yeah. My feet probably wish I'd left earlier."

Claudia chuckled, plucking a book with a pot of stew on the front from the shelf. "You'll want to ice those later."

Maddie leaned against the front counter, watching Claudia flip through the book's pages. There was still the matter of what was written on that paper. "Why did you really come?"

Claudia stopped looking through the book. "I owe you an apology." There was a pause as she closed the book and set it down, finally turning to look Maddie in the eyes. "You weren't wrong."

"About what?"

"The connection we had at the theater. I felt it. I did. I shouldn't have been so cruel when you pointed it out, either."

"It's all right. I should have taken the hint better," Maddie said.

"No," Claudia said, putting a hand to her forehead. "No. This isn't your fault. I—"

"Look, let's just put it behind us. It was months ago," Maddie shrugged. She walked toward the back of the store. "Is there anything else I can help you with? Did you want one of those cookbooks?"

Another long silence while Maddie straightened up some of the books. It still felt tense, like there was something unresolved there. But Maddie had gotten her apology. That was more than she could've hoped for.

"I've been divorced for seven years," she said without warning. Maddie stopped messing with the books to look back at Claudia. "My favorite color's yellow. I eat cobbler like no one else could possibly want a slice. For the past five years I've wanted to go to California, but I can't because I have my bakery and my son to worry about."

"What are you doing?"

Claudia wrung her hands, staring with wide eyes at Maddie. "This is what you're supposed to do, right? Get to know each other on dates?"

"Is that what this is?" Maddie lifted a confused eyebrow.

"I don't know, but I figure I owe you a few tidbits," she said.

"You don't owe me anything," Maddie said, sliding down a nearby bookshelf so that she was sitting on the floor after situating her dress. Claudia followed suit, sitting down next to her.

"I think I do. I've been sitting at home, lonely and berating myself for being an idiot. Truth is, I'm scared. I'm scared of what liking you means about me."

"It means you like me," Maddie said, trying to hide her smile.

"It means I'm cradle robbing. *I'm* the horrible person for going after someone so much younger than me. You're just the poor girl who doesn't know any better. And my family doesn't even know I find girls attractive. That's still new." Claudia paused, staring down at the floor. "It wouldn't be the easiest thing to explain."

"I think if they really love you, they'll be okay with whatever makes you happy. My family was." Maddie might have known since she was seven that she liked girls, but her family never made a big deal out of it. Well, her immediate family. Her aunt continuously pointed out cute boys to her when she was a teenager, no matter how many times she told her guys wouldn't do the trick.

"My family isn't yours," Claudia scoffed. "They're old-fashioned."

"I'm sure your son would understand."

"That I'm interested in someone so young? I don't know."

"You always think reality is so bad. It doesn't have to be. They might get it."

"My marriage ended terribly. My dreams to be or do anything beyond this city have been gone since I had Lance. Reality ain't a dream."

Maddie shook her head. "Have you ever considered that you're being the most pessimistic person on the planet? You've got a really good bakery, and a son who I'm sure loves you very much. Your marriage ended, but now something new can start. With whomever that may be."

"You are annoyingly optimistic," she grinned.

"When one door closes, another opens. I didn't make up the saying, I just enforce it." Maddie smiled, earning a bright one from Claudia as well.

"I sure wish I could see it your way. I'm a little set in my ways," Claudia chuckled.

"Gee, I couldn't tell."

Both women went into a fit of giggles that slowly died down as time passed. Maddie leaned her head back against the books, staring at nothing in particular. This had been what she expected to happen a few months prior, this ease that came naturally between the two of them. For the first time, it felt like there were no limitations. It was high time Maddie test how open Claudia was willing to be.

"Why did you and your husband divorce?"

"I was wondering how long it'd take to get there." Claudia sighed, clasping her hands together. "It might've had something to do with the co-worker he was sleeping with."

"Oh. I'm so sorry."

"Yeah. Never saw that one coming."

"That's not your fault."

"Do you know what it's like to feel that kind of humiliation? To think your husband thought the world of you when he really, really didn't?"

"No. I don't know what that's like," Maddie frowned. She hoped she never had to deal with that. Finding out someone she loved was unfaithful would be a cruel trick.

"We only talk because of Lance. I'm not interested in being around him or his new wife."

Maddie scooted closer to Claudia, placing a hand overtop hers. "It'll get easier."

"I've been telling myself that for seven years. It never gets better."

"You haven't been with anyone since your divorce?"

"I've been with men, but it's never more than a few weeks. It's how I found out I liked women. Men just... didn't do it for me."

"I bet it has something to do with you pushing people away," Maddie smirked. Claudia gave her an eye roll. "I'm serious," she continued. "You're too afraid to take a chance on someone, so you wallow in misery."

"Great. Now I'm gettin' advice from a—"

"Don't you dare say 'kid,'" Maddie warned.

"I was gonna say 'stranger.' Relax." Claudia's expression made Maddie think that was the opposite of what she was going to say, but there was no point in arguing it.

They didn't talk for a while, listening to the cars drive by outside or watching how the street lights lit up the other shop windows. Maddie turned her head to see that Claudia was looking down at the hand still touching hers. It left Maddie wondering what to do next. Her fingers itched to do more the longer they stayed there, whether it be to curl around Claudia's fingers or to reach up and brush her cheek. The feelings she hoped for the longest time would be gone only seemed to be stronger. The connection between them wasn't lost. And contrary to what Claudia might or might not have believed in the moment, something so special wasn't better left to the imagination. It had to be acted on.

She inched her face closer to Claudia's, not wanting to surprise her. When people said that time stopped, sometimes Maddie found it hard to believe. There had never been a moment like that in her life for all that she remembered. But now, with the stillness of the night and the silence that pervaded the bookstore, it felt like the hands weren't ticking. Whatever they did tonight might be all there was. Morning wouldn't come and the 'closed' sign would never be turned to 'open'.

Claudia minutely turned her head so that her eyes could flick up to meet Maddie's. They could have heard a pin drop it was so quiet. Maddie wanted to wait for a reaction, for Claudia to meet her halfway, but did she want this? Even after their long talk, Maddie still didn't know if this was only an apology or if it was meant to be the first step of something more.

Maddie's breath caught in her throat. Claudia was moving closer. Her eyes involuntarily closed, but half of her expected a repeat of their first night. She would be waiting for one thing, and something totally different would happen. Except that didn't happen this time. With baited breath, she felt Claudia's lips touch her own.

As often as Maddie wished this happened sooner, there was no preparing for the sparks. Her talk with Richie made her worried that maybe she was sad over nothing. That there would be no chemistry beyond the night, that quite frankly, Claudia would be right and their night was one best left for daydreams. Oh, but were they wrong. They were so wrong.

When Claudia and Maddie finally parted, Maddie could feel the heat rise in her cheeks. It was the way she could remember all her first kisses being, with butterflies fluttering away in her stomach, and her head spinning as if she didn't know which way was up or down. The electric sensation that traveled over her body and made her skin tingle. A smile spread across Maddie's lips before she even opened her eyes. And when she did, Claudia was blushing, doing a terrible job of not smiling back.

"Am I ever going to hear the end of this?" Claudia asked.

"That would mean I'd have to see you again," Maddie grinned, much too proud of herself. "Will I?"

Claudia's smile fell the tiniest bit. "This doesn't change what I said before. All of it still applies."

Maddie sighed, nodding. She would still be stupid to walk away from this without doing something, though. "All right. Then after you gather up the courage, I want your number."

"Is that all?" Claudia asked. Maddie's eyes widened, but Claudia only laughed. "I'm kidding. I think that's a promise I can make."

"Good," Maddie said, looking down at her feet. "Now where does that leave us tonight?"

Claudia's smile faltered again. "I think that means I should get home and release the babysitter. I've stayed out long enough."

Maddie nodded, standing and helping Claudia to her feet. She was hoping their time apart wouldn't be as long as the last, but the fact remained that she didn't know. She just didn't know. Claudia gathered her things and lingered by the door, fingers barely grasping the knob. Maddie crossed her arms, leaning against the counter. "Thanks for stopping by. Come again soon," Maddie recited playfully, giving Claudia a wink.

Claudia opened the door, letting the cool air inside. "I hope I can."

With that, Claudia was gone. Maddie waited a little before locking it behind her, partially hoping she would come back. This was the end for now, though. While she hoped Claudia would appear sooner rather than later, the only thing she could do was wait and see if she appeared at all.

~~*

"We're gone a week and I've suddenly married a lobster," Lorraine sighed, staring at Richie as he attempted to move around the store without irritating his skin. Maddie chuckled, wishing she could have sunburn instead of frostbite.

"I'm surprised you didn't force the suntan lotion on him," Maddie smirked.

"I bet he wishes I had now," she muttered. "We were busy with... other lotions."

"More than I need to know," Maddie frowned. Her sex life had been nonexistent for a month, but she wasn't desperate enough to start living vicariously through Lorraine.

"Don't be a baby. I've listened to you go into gory detail about some of your encounters. I owe you more than enough honeymoon stories."

"Fair enough," she conceded, attending to a mother and child who came to the counter to purchase a couple of brightly colored children's books. After she said thank you and watched them leave, she faced Lorraine. "So what are you and the husband doing later?"

"Going to dinner. Want to come?"

"I don't want to intrude on you newlyweds," she grinned, walking out from behind the counter to put away a few books that some customers had returned.

"All right, then you're going with us. End of story," Lorraine shrugged, following Maddie. "I haven't seen you without the looming threat of wedding stress over our heads. It'll be our treat."

It was true. Now that Lorraine was back from her honeymoon, they could probably celebrate the hell of wedding preparations being over. Plus, a free meal was a free meal. "Where are you guys going?"

"That sports bar across from the flower shop where I got my bouquet. Richie and I are craving wings."

"Oh, sounds great. I could go for some chili cheese fries."

"Well, that was easy," Lorraine grinned merrily. "When do you get off?"

"When I see a pretty girl," Maddie smirked.

"Ha ha."

"Seven," Maddie laughed.

"We'll pick you up at seven-thirty. Don't be late, or I'm dragging you out of whatever hole you're hiding in."

"Yes, ma'am." Maddie shoved a hardcover book between two others. She turned, giving Lorraine a quick hug before returning to her spot behind the counter.

"Husband," Lorraine called, spotting Richie behind a shelf of brochures. "We need to let Maddie do her job."

"I'm not the one pestering her," he retorted, placing a pamphlet about Mexico back in its place.

"See you tonight," Lorraine said, walking out with Richie when he came to the front.

"Bye, Maddie," Richie said from over his shoulder.

Maddie shook her head. It was nice to have Lorraine back, but her week of peace was officially over. She knew better than to be late to anything Lorraine invited her to, so when seven-thirty rolled around, Maddie was dressed and standing on the sidewalk. Lorraine and Richie were there right on the dot, too. Together, the three of them went to the sports bar Lorraine told her about earlier. It looked like every other one she'd been to in the city, with a black iron fence enclosing the outdoor patio, and a green canopy to keep the sunshine and rain off the people outside. They would have to enjoy that another time, however, when it wasn't cold enough to cool their meals down in two seconds flat

All of the TVs were tuned to either a basketball game or hockey game. Maddie was interested in neither, though Lorraine was stealing glances now and again at the screen with the hockey game. The hostess greeted them with a smile, taking them to a booth near the back.

"This place is loud tonight," Lorraine noted once the hostess had gone.

"What did you expect?" Richie laughed, perusing his menu.

"Something a little quieter on a weeknight," she replied.

"No one cheers like this," Maddie whispered. Lorraine glared at her, so she continued at a normal volume. "It'll be fine. Promise."

The waitress visited their table after a few more minutes, profusely apologizing for taking so long. It was Maddie's turn to glare at Lorraine when she looked put out for a millisecond. Thankfully, the waitress didn't seem to notice and began taking drink orders. When she was gone, and they'd ordered a large appetizer to hold them over, Maddie noticed Lorraine looking around at more than the television screens.

"Are you okay?" Maddie asked. "You seem more weird than normal."

"I'm looking for a bathroom," she said, eyes widening when she stopped looking. "There it is."

"Want me to go with you?"

"I'm fine," she grinned, giving Richie a kiss on the head. "Someone needs to keep him company."

"All right," Maddie said, watching Lorraine leave. She turned to Richie, who was still busy searching his menu for an entrée. "Is she really okay?"

"You're acting like you haven't known her longer than I have," he said. "She's fine."

Maddie bit her lip, turning back to her menu. He was right. She was overanalyzing it.

But after ten minutes passed, she began to wonder if Lorraine fell into the toilet and got stuck. She was about to go check when she saw Lorraine walking back. Maddie sipped on the lemonade their waitress had brought to them in the meantime, staring at Lorraine.

"The line for the bathroom is so long," Lorraine said, picking the menu up. "Might want to hold it if you have to go."

"Lorraine, are—"

Maddie was cut off when a small child who looked no older than eight walked up to the table. He held a small notepad in his hand, the biggest brown eyes she'd ever seen staring at her.

"Are you Maddie Hall?" the boy asked, his fingers pressed tight against the booklet.

"Yes," she said, looking at Lorraine and Richie. They looked just as confused as she was. "Who's asking?"

"I'm supposed to give you this," he said, handing the notepad to her.

Maddie took the book carefully, unsure of what she was about to see. Did someone think using a kid as a messenger to ask her out would make the chance of success better? She stared down at the pad he handed her. Yup. It was a phone number. She looked back at the boy. "Who wanted you to give this to me?"

"My mom," he said, hands clasped behind his back.

At first she didn't understand, but then she wanted to smack herself for not getting it sooner. Maddie couldn't help the grin that spread across her face. She'd know those eyes anywhere. "Is your name Lance?"

"Yeah," he nodded.

She laughed, looking down at the seven digits again. Huh. Claudia actually did it. Maddie extended her hand to Lance. "It's nice to finally meet you. Your mom's told me good things."

"It's nice to meet you, too," he smiled, taking her hand.

"Are you with your mom?" She hadn't seen Claudia when they came in. Though she was a little more than worried how she knew Maddie would be here tonight. The bookstore was a pleasant coincidence, but the thought of Claudia following them to the restaurant made her want to reach for her phone. She wanted to give Claudia the benefit of a doubt, however. Maddie never got anything close to a stalker vibe from her, so there must have been something else at work here.

"Yeah. You want to see her?" he asked.

"I'd like that," Maddie smiled. She looked at Lorraine and Richie. "Order some Cajun wings for me if I'm not back before the waitress."

"Can do," Richie said.

Maddie nodded, following Lance as he led her through the restaurant, sidling through people after almost every step. By one of the windows in the front, Claudia stared out at the street, chin held in the palm of her hand. She turned around when Lance touched her shoulder, eyes immediately finding Maddie. Lance pulled out a chair for Maddie, waiting anxiously for her to take a seat.

"Why, thank you," she said to him.

"You're welcome." He smiled, sitting down next to Claudia.

"You could have just stopped by the bookstore," Maddie said.

"I was going to. Then I ran into your friend over there. She said I couldn't just 'stop by.' So she told me I should do something better. She thought of the restaurant, and I thought it might be an opportunity for Lance to meet the girl I told him about."

Now Maddie knew why Lorraine had seemed off tonight. She hoped Lorraine never had to keep a *really* big secret in the future. "I'll have to thank her for this later."

"Mom said you work at a bookstore. Do you sell comics there?" Lance asked.

"We do. You should stop by some time and pick some out," Maddie smiled.

"Can we?" he asked Claudia, all big eyes and excitement.

"I think that'd be fun," she told him.

"So we'll see each other again?" Maddie asked, watching Claudia expectantly.

She nodded. "You have my number."

"Good," Maddie grinned. She rubbed her hands up and down her thighs. "Well, it was nice to finally meet you, Lance, but I don't want to intrude on your dinner. I should—"

"You can sit with us if you want," Lance interjected. He looked to Claudia. "Can she sit with us?"

"I think she has friends to get back to," she told him. "But another time. If you'd like," Claudia said, facing Maddie. "Maybe we can catch a movie."

"I'd love that." Maddie stood, careful of the people around her. "I'll see you around. Okay, Lance?"

"Okay," he said, sounding disappointed.

"Bye," Maddie waved, turning around and diving into the throng of people.

She was about halfway through the crowd when she felt someone tap her shoulder. A pair of big brown eyes stared back briefly before their lips touched. Maddie was taken by surprise to see that Claudia followed her, but she wasn't about to argue with the hands holding her waist. They pulled apart, Maddie's hands still on Claudia's shoulders.

"What was that for?" Maddie asked.

"A reminder to dial that number," she smirked. "And a thank you. I feel better now that Lance knows."

"What about your friends?"

"Later," Claudia said. "Lance is who matters. If he knows, then I think this might work out."

"Good. I want it to." Maddie gave Claudia a quick peck on the lips before pulling out of her grasp completely. "See you around, old timer."

Claudia smiled, turning around to go back to Lance. Maddie did the same, walking in somewhat of a daze back to Lorraine and Richie. This felt different compared to her other relationships. Something felt more thrilling. Whatever it was that had her in such a tizzy, she knew it sure as hell would never be dull.

Runner

SAM SCHOOLER

CHAPTER ONE

It was raining in the mountains.

"You'll cook for him, obviously," Boris MacClair told Eden, swinging his ridiculously expensive car around the next muddy bend in an endless labyrinth of muddy bends. Gravel and dirt sprayed to either side of them, splattering the pine trees they passed.

Eden kept his eyes on the side mirror and his hand on the door.

Kept his jaw clenched tight, because if he didn't, he was going to throw up.

All he could think was, *It's happening again.*

Only this time it was completely out of his control.

"You'll clean his house. You'll keep the outside as much as you know how. He doesn't go outside, as far as I know. He, *heh*, doesn't like neighbors much. Or anyone. He probably doesn't get out of bed much." Boris shot a toothy smile Eden's way, and Eden forced himself to keep his hand still. If it looked like he was tensing to jump, he would be caught in two seconds flat. "And last I heard, he didn't like pussy anyway. Aren't you glad you won't have to worry about that? You'll have a cushy life now, kid." Boris reached over and rubbed the back of Eden's head, sending ugly, scared shivers down his spine. "You get to be a pack wife and you don't even have to suck cock for it."

Eden thought for a second about killing him. But no. It would be less messy to leave both the car and Boris behind and make his way on foot through the mountains. He'd trekked in from the forests in the south, but if he headed west through the mountains that separated Wildwood, Washington, from the rest of the world, he could get to Seattle.

And in Seattle, he would be able to do anything he wanted. Get a job. An apartment. Tap the underground and see if anyone else had escaped the police sweeps in Denver. Maybe find someone who could locate his mom and his sister.

He just wanted to make it to somewhere safe. Somewhere that didn't allow the cops to arrest every homeless werewolf in a city because of a stupid rumor.

He'd been so desperate. So hungry and so tired. He should have listened to his gut and turned tail and run as soon as Boris shook his hand too hard, put a pre-packaged sandwich down in front of him, and asked if he was over eighteen.

Boris gripped Eden's shoulder in that same firm hold. Eden didn't have time to flinch away. "Pay attention, kid. Can't have you drifting off. Don't make a habit of that, either. Who knows what kind of temper Mickey has now that he's..." Boris took his other hand off the wheel to gesture at his leg. Eden didn't know what that meant. "Anyway, you'll see. He's not... well."

He patted Eden roughly, then took his hand back. Which was good, because Eden had been considering biting it, and damn the consequences.

"That makes you one heck of a pair, huh?" Boris murmured, almost to himself. "I'm sure you'll get along swimmingly."

Whatever type of "not well" Michael was, it was enough to constitute him living isolated outside the MacClair pack territory, something Eden hadn't seen before, in any pack.

It was enough that when Eden had marched into the pack's cover address—a decrepit office building close to the river—and held up the newspaper ad offering a caregiver position in exchange for free housing and food, every person in the place had stopped to stare at him.

Now he knew the ad had been running for two years in the Sunday papers. No one else had answered it.

Because everyone in Wildwood knew all about Michael MacClair.

Everyone except Eden, who'd been in town for a whole half a day before he got stopped in the middle of the street by a mounted police officer hounding him for his ID. It was far from the first time he'd been pegged as a runaway.

He should've been old hat at it, joking with the officer and confirming yes, he was glad to be somewhere that had hot showers, but the thought of being plucked out as a troublemaker so soon after Denver had paralyzed him. He'd had to stand there and wait while the officer's horse tossed its head and showed the whites of its eyes, the proximity of a predator making it nervous. Finally, the officer had let him go, but the scrutiny was enough to convince Eden that he had to find some form of legitimacy if he wanted to lay low for a while.

Eden hadn't exactly put "get married" on his list of possibilities.

He'd thought it was a genius move, answering Boris's ad. He hadn't cared what kind of money or benefits or problems the job would give him. He'd just known it was a position that would grant him the protection of a powerful pack. A pack too big and too well-established for the human police to make them disappear and not face questions on the national level.

No one cared if a bunch of street people were bullied around, or went missing. Eden had assumed that Boris, who was a lawyer at one of the biggest firms in the northwest, would be a different story.

He was. Turned out he did the bullying.

And Eden *still* didn't know anything about Michael MacClair.

Except that the two of them were married now.

"Almost there," Boris said.

Time to move. Eden pressed the bottoms of his worn kicks to the floor and curled his fingers around the door handle.

Rain drummed on the windshield. It'd wash him clean, wash his scent away. No one would find him, if he didn't want them to. He could run into the woods and lose himself.

"How much farther, Boris?" he murmured.

"That's *sir* to you."

Eden licked his teeth. "*Sir*, how much farther is it?"

"Five minutes."

"Bless me," Eden murmured. *Bless me, Mother, give me strength.*

Then he threw himself out of the car.

He hit the ground hard, water and mud filling his mouth as he rolled, one arm wrapped around his head and the other holding his backpack to his chest. Distantly, he heard the Chrysler screech to a halt, heard Boris's angry shout, but he was already orienting himself and focusing on the change. No time to take his clothes off—he twisted in them, shedding his shirt and the tatters of his ragged jeans as he bent and broke his body from human to wolf.

Boris slid around the end of the car and stumbled like he'd been shot, mouth sagging open. "You—you're..."

He took a step back, stinking of fear.

Eden ignored him. He snatched his backpack in his teeth and bolted past Boris, relishing his startled yelp, then scrambled up the embankment and bounded across the next stretch of road into the trees.

There were human footpaths leading up the mountain, but Eden passed them by, choosing the thick underbrush instead. Rain soaked his coat and sunk the ground under his paws. It clogged his eyes and dampened his sense of smell, but he could feel something else, something stronger, the same way a bird could feel the currents of the breeze change: he was going the right way.

Rabbits scattered ahead of him. Birds chittered and took to the sky. Back, below, he could still hear the Chrysler's engine rumbling. It wasn't coming any closer.

He almost laughed, thinking about Boris gathering up his superior attitude and lumbering after him.

Something tugged his sense of direction, leading him left. He cleared a log and spun, diving through a copse of trees and streaking around a clearing. The promise of running water, the sweet little bubble of a creek, drew him in, and he stopped to drink, keeping his backpack secure between his paws.

Some wolves couldn't keep their human minds when they shifted. Eden's mother was like that. She said it all streamlined—that the superego bustle was tuned out, washed away with the scritch and squeak of prey and the smell of distant industrial fumes.

Eden wished it was like that for him. But he was rarely able to separate himself and the wolf. His human worries clung to him like a sickness.

He sneezed at a fat bullfrog as it jumped past his nose, then reconsidered and lunged forward, snapping it up by a hind leg. He dragged it onto the shore, pinned it with a paw—*Mother, thank you for this blessing, may I be worthy to take its life*—and bit into its soft belly and chewed a mouthful. He was past the point of squeamishness, and could feel himself sinking into familiar survival mode, where he stopped thinking of "tastes good" and "edible" as synonymous.

After he'd eaten as much of the frog as he could, he rinsed his mouth and cleaned his muzzle in the creek, then grabbed his pack and headed up again. A few yards up, the creek forked off from a larger one, which led up the mountain, hopefully to a lake.

He circled around a tree and loped along beside the creek, his black paws flashing out in front of him, sure and steady as the creek fell away below him and the land carried him higher, until he was keeping an eye on the water from the top of a sharp drop-off.

He heard the snap before he felt pain.

One second he was running, and the next his whole body rebelled and he was crashing down on his back, his head slamming into the ground hard enough to make his vision white over.

Panting for breath, he blinked up at the dusky sky.

When he turned his head, he saw his backpack lying a few feet from him, on the edge of the cliff.

Deep, radiating agony crept into his awareness. It slunk up in the back of his skull like a migraine, dizzying. He whined and dug his back paws into the mud to turn himself over on his front. He'd smacked his head, maybe twisted a paw. That was all. He just had to move...

He looked at his paw.

Bile rose in his throat.

Oh no. No no no.

Crunched into his front leg were the heavy teeth of a huge silver wolf trap. It was hard at work searing away the fur and skin around the wounds. The trap had probably been dusted with silver powder, or filled with liquid silver, for it to work this fast. Soon it would get into his blood and curdle it, if it hadn't already. Soon it would turn all his cells sluggish and make him so weak he wouldn't be able to cry out for help.

What help?

He swallowed down vomit and his panic, trying not to whimper in case one of them was near. If no one came for him, the humans who set this would find him, and the kind of men who set these traps weren't the kind who would take Eden to the police. They would sooner shoot him in the head and take his fur to put their kids to bed with.

Hacking through a renewed gulp of nausea, he stumbled up onto three legs, shaking bitter slaver from his jaws. He wasn't going to lay down here and *die*.

Darkness swam up, crossing his eyes with vibrating dots. He swayed on his feet until the dizziness from the silver forced him back onto his belly.

Fine. He'd lie down and crawl.

He inched himself backward, stretching the silver chain to its limit. The pain made him want to go weak, but he kept going, using the leverage of his body to try to force the trap's stake out of the sucking mud.

Every time he moved, the trap's teeth ground deeper and deeper, until they were scraping— infecting—his very bones with silver. They ate the sinew and skin in a destructive spiral until Eden could see mangled, bloody bone, shining too bright to look at.

Eden closed his eyes and laid his muzzle down. Flexed his back paws in the dirt. Still backing up.

You'd think I would've learned to look where I was going.

At least the rain was making it hurt less.

He wondered what his father would think of him now. Packless. Injured. At least he was married into an upstanding pack, he thought, letting his lips curl in disgust. Yeah, at least he had that, the way his dad had wanted. But he was running away from that too.

Always running from everything.

He could almost hear his father's voice swimming under his fever, taunting him: *"This is what happens when you're not right with the Mother Moon."*

Eden's own mother had defended him, but his father—always a staunch believer in the old worship rituals—had decided Eden's unnatural ability to shift outside the full moon, coupled with his mismatched sex and gender, meant Eden was never meant to be blessed enough to be a wolf in the first place.

He'd probably pay to be here. To watch Eden be hunted down.

He'd find religious matter in all of this: the cleansing rain; the mountains above; the frog's blood still on Eden's tongue; the thuds of—

Footsteps.

Eden gasped in a strained breath and peeled his heavy eyes open.

The person, whoever it was, emerged from the trees straight ahead and slipped into the clearing, easing over a fallen log and crouching in front of it.

The haze of rain made their outline fuzzy. Or maybe that was him dying, Eden wasn't sure. But he did know he didn't want to be touched. Not again. He bared his teeth at the stranger's reaching hands and snarled.

"Shhh," the person—a man, an older man—said, coming closer. "Shh, shh." The sound was stiff, like he didn't get a lot of practice soothing someone. "Shhh. Calm down, boss. Let me look at that. Easy, easy now."

He seemed nice.

Eden needed to run.

He gathered all his strength and lurched up onto three paws, ready to bite whatever he could. But he barely managed a few staggering steps and halfhearted growling before jagged white lines streaked across his eyes and his balance abruptly vanished. He listed to the side and his legs folded under him, only instead of hitting the ground, he was lifted and maneuvered into the man's lap.

No—

He thrashed, turning his head to weakly snap at the man's shoulder. He smelled of human skin and sweat and rain, overpowering soap and grass and clean wood and not wolf. Not wolf.

A hunter.

A hunter who'd kill him at worst and take him to the police at best. And then Eden would end up in prison or shoved in some "rehabilitation" program for disobedient wolves, where he'd be forced to admit the moon was just a piece of floating rock and forced to recite paragraphs that illustrated why he ought to be ashamed of himself because he was a danger to human society. He knew all the stories. He knew what they did.

Something was hissing.

The rain, he realized muzzily. He licked his lips and his tongue felt thick and swollen.

It was the rain hitting his overheated body. Silver fever.

You would've been better off married.

Two traps: that and this.

You would've had a home.

"Hey," the man said sharply. "*Hey*, don't. Don't fall asleep, do you understand me?" He took handfuls of Eden's fur and *yanked*.

Eden disappeared somewhere small inside himself as his instincts swelled up, driven by pure need for self-protection. He felt his jaws clamp on the man's upper arm with a distant crunch of muscle and a burst of hot, living blood. His teeth shredded the thick goosefeather coat the human was wearing.

The blood tasted crisp and he wanted to drink it to purify his own.

Do it, something whispered.

He gasped and tore his mouth away, blinking back to himself. He had to be hallucinating. Not good.

The man breathed out hard. "Ow," he said mildly. His other hand swept down Eden's flank, smoothing away the pain he'd caused. "Feel better now?"

Eden let his growl die away in case it started to sound more confused than threatening. Confused meant vulnerable. He buried his nose in the feathers leaking from the man's ruined coat.

"Yeah, you owe me a new one of those. That's the only one I got." The man twisted to look over his shoulder—at the drop-off, Eden thought. They couldn't be more than five feet from it. "You stay just like that for me, killer. Easy, easy."

He pulled a thick flap of leather from his back pocket and unrolled it on the ground. Eden rolled his head to look. A lock-pick kit?

The man ran his hand up and down Eden's side. "Don't squirm. I don't want to hurt you."

He set to work, tools clinking off the trap, and a low buzz dulled Eden's hearing, shutting out everything but that. He buried his face in the feathers and told himself he was just resting, gathering his strength for when he was free and could run.

"—see. Bite me again," the stranger said, rapping a closed fist gently on Eden's ribs.

Eden jerked awake. *"What?"*

"You heard me. I've got to jam this open, and if you don't pull yourself up and get your paw out, it's your shit luck. I can only do this once, so wake up and help me." He squeezed Eden closer to his chest. "Stay awake. Use my shoulder to get yourself up, or I'll leave you stuck here."

Well, his snotty tone was encouragement enough for Eden to fumble around with his nose until he found where the blood was leaking and buried his teeth in deep, matching new teeth marks to the old ones. He was surprised the man wasn't one of the wackos who thought a bite would turn a human into a wolf. He was surprised at it all, he guessed. Grudgingly.

But not too impressed to realize this guy couldn't want anything good with him. Who walked around in the forest with a lock-pick kit for wolf traps?

People who set wolf traps.

He bit a little deeper out of spite. Warm blood burst in his mouth, berry-soft.

The man just snorted, like it didn't hurt at all. "There you go. Now pull when I say. Ready?" He shifted around, setting his weight and muttering to himself.

The trap squealed around Eden's leg, then crunched deeper, and Eden sobbed out a breath, scrabbling in the mud.

"I know, I know, boss, hang in there. Ready?" Eden nodded dizzily. "All right. *Now.*"

Eden strained up with his three good legs, his loose front paw planted next to the man's hip, and used his jaw to lever himself up. The trap came free of his leg with a sick squelching noise, and the teeth screeched closed on empty air. He slipped, crashing forward, and bowled his rescuer over. The man still had one arm around him, the other holding the trap, and there was nothing behind them and—

And the cliff—

"Stop!" Eden shouted, shoving his front paws down on either side of him. Pain shot up where his injured left rubbed raw over dirt and rocks. *"Stop, stop us, I can't!"*

"I can't either!" the man yelled back, and then they went over.

~~*

The snap of their bodies catching sent hot shocks up Eden's spine, bringing him back to full, terrible awareness. He opened his eyes and saw only air below them, and trees a long way down, the flowers of their tops welcoming as a graveyard. He was crushed to the man's chest.

Rain beat down on them.

"Move," the man panted. He'd found a handhold and was keeping them both from falling.

Which should have been impossible.

It *was* impossible.

"Move!"

"I have nowhere to go," Eden told him, trying not to sound as panicked as he felt. His back paws were midair, the muscles in his back strained to the limit. The only reason he wasn't buried in the earth below

347

was the man's arm wrapped around him, under his front legs. He squirmed, twisting his head to look at the jagged face of the drop-off.

"Stop moving!"

"If you want me to get up, I have to!" Eden gingerly put out one front paw, stepping on the man's wrist and testing the leverage there.

Whatever he was holding on to slipped an inch.

"Shit," the man swore, "shit, shit, just get up and do it fast. Just go!" He heaved himself forward and planted his feet against the cliffside, tensed his arm—slipped another inch—and *threw* Eden, who hit the drop-off with his front paws barely over the top. He gasped and scrabbled in the dirt, shredding his paws. The panic overwhelmed the pain, and he tore his way through rocks and mud and grass and flesh, back into the clearing.

He whirled on his unsteady legs and saw it was the trap's silver chain that had saved them both.

Then he dove forward, clamped his jaws on the man's coat, and hauled him up, too.

They collapsed side by side in the mud, panting. In Eden's silver-foggy mind, he heard their breaths sync up, in and out and in and out together. They'd done this together.

Whether he liked it or not, they'd done it together.

He didn't know any human who'd want to die over a wolf.

"You okay?" the stranger rasped.

He took stock of himself. His paws were bleeding. If he didn't get the silver antidote soon, he'd slip into a coma. But he wasn't speared on the pine trees below, left for the ravens to eat. *"I could be worse,"* he decided.

The man let out a reedy laugh between pants. "That's one way to think of it." He winced and rolled onto his side, unwinding his hand from the chain. It was burning angry red, the places where the chain had rested already swollen and inflamed. It must've cut him, Eden thought, until he saw the graying veins rising fat and poisoned under his skin.

Mother save us.

He lifted his head and stared at him. The man stared back, wary and cool now.

"But you don't smell like a wolf," Eden said.

"Yeah," the man said, "I know."

Discomfort mixed into Eden's cocktail of dizziness and tempered adrenaline. Lone wolves weren't natural. It wasn't an arguable point. Wolves needed others—friends or lovers or family, it didn't matter, they just *needed someone else*. Eden had never felt a disconnection so heady as when he was on the road with no pack to call his own. Lone wolves weren't romantic or brave like those pulpy 1950s human noir novels showed. They weren't happy. Not ever.

Eden would know.

It was almost worse to realize what he was smelling on the man wasn't human, but a sheer absence of wolf.

"We both need the antidote," the man grunted, saving Eden from having to say anything else. He picked himself up carefully, minding more than his injured hand, and waved off Eden's offer of help. Good thing, too, because Eden didn't know how much more he could handle being touched today. "Better change back. I can't carry you."

"I don't need you to carry me."

The man curled a lip at him as he shed his ruined goosefeather coat, leaving him in a ratty T-shirt of indistinguishable color and sweatpants that looked three sizes too long for him. "Well, I wasn't fuckin' offering."

"Good," Eden growled, shaking himself off. His whole head rang. He flattened his ears and padded to his pack, wobbling on his paws. "Turn around," he told the man, nosing his pack open to make sure he had an extra set of clothes with him. He did, but he didn't know if they were his own or if they were handouts from a hostel or motel's lost and found. They definitely weren't from Boris, who'd promised to outfit the "family's new little lady" with anything he needed.

The stranger still hadn't put his back to him, so Eden barked at him. *"I said turn around."*

"Did you come up here with anyone else?"

Eden stiffened. *"No."*

Shifting so his body was in front of Eden's, facing the forest, he said, "Then we'd better move our asses." He started into the trees. "Someone's coming up in a car."

Eden clenched his jaw and looked out over the trees. He could dive off the drop-off and hope he caught branches on the way down—no—or he could run back down the mountain, follow one of the hundred other deer paths, and hope he found antidote before the silver overtook him completely—and before Boris found him on the road. Or put out a notice to look for him.

He'd never make it.

Part of him wanted to say *stop being a defeatist*. But that part sounded uncomfortably like his father. And his mother's guidance said to do what he thought was smart, pride be damned.

"Are you coming or not?" His rescuer's voice echoed through the trees. "We need to move now."

"Wait."

He closed his eyes and reached for the thread inside him that would break all his bones and remake him. The silver made it slippery, hard to reach—but never impossible, not for him. His bones collapsed in on themselves, his fur shedding off him and re-growing to match what it had been before: thick black hair, cut to his jaw and shaved completely down on one side. Dark hair grew on his arms and chest, on his stomach, leading down between his legs. He scrubbed his hands over himself to get used to the feeling of his rebirthed skin.

His trap wound was on his left forearm, and it was already turning an off-color gray, veins winding like railroad tracks down to the heel of his hand. Poisoned for sure.

Damn it.

Whatever clothes found their way into his hands on first grab were what he put on. He slung his backpack over his shoulder and clambered over the fallen log blocking off the clearing from the rest of the woods. Fallen pine needles quieted their movement, and now Eden could hear what the other man had: footsteps, big and heavy, echoing up from where they'd been.

Paranoia made him pause to see if it was Boris MacClair. Or worse—maybe?—whether it was humans, come to check on their traps. He imagined them: hunters, big and broad-shouldered, laughing and jeering at one another over the promise of an upcoming kill. Or maybe angry at each other, taking out their frustrations once they saw the trap had been sprung and its prisoner freed.

A hand touched his arm. "Hey."

Eden jerked away and whipped to face the man. "Don't touch me," he snapped.

"Sorry," the man said immediately. He didn't move his hand fast enough, though, so Eden shook him off brutally, with a low-key snarl. Better to put this person in his place before they got to his cabin. Him rescuing Eden didn't mean he had free rein.

"If you expect me to pay you back for that," Eden said, jerking a thumb over his shoulder, "then we should cut this little charade right now and I'll go back to town."

"You won't make it."

Eden could almost feel his lupine ears flatten to his skull. "Is that a threat?"

The man blinked at him, his pale blue eyes widening. "No? Simple statement of fact, boss." He held up his burned arm. "You and me both."

Right. The skin was bubbling now, starting to peel off. Soon it would show those darkened veins, expose them to the air, and then it was only a matter of time before the rot started gnawing through muscles and bone.

Eden didn't know what to say, so he shrugged. He was half expecting another snappy comeback, but all he got was a weary "Come on," and then, "You wait around here much longer and they'll be using your hide for bath towels or some shit."

The man turned his back on Eden, which was either stupid or faithful or another bid for Eden to let his guard down. Eden had nothing else to do—he followed him, watching the way his wiry muscles flexed under his thin shirt. Only because he needed something to focus on, or the creeping fog at the back of his head might take over. The man knew the forest well, found handholds and exposed roots to ease the way up the hill, but there was an offbeat, uncomfortable nature to the way he walked. Probably he wasn't used to leading random people to his home.

As soon as they reached the place, Eden could see why.

The man looked faintly shamefaced, in a gruff, jaw-clenched way. Eden tried not to stare.

The cabin—if it could be called that—was a *mess*. There were piles of animal bones outside the front door, and in the shoddily maintained yard there were scraps of soaked wood, pieces of tarp, and three old chainsaws. On the far side was a rusted-out Ford truck that had been red a hundred years ago. A storage shed stood behind the cabin, but its roof was caved in, and there were stacks and stacks of moving boxes sitting outside it with a haphazardly erected plastic tent as their only protection from the storm.

A sign was planted where the trees fell away into the overgrown clearing.

STAY OUT. TRESPASSERS SHOT.

He gave his rescuer an uneasy look. Thought about reconsidering who he'd rather face—this man or the hunters.

The man's eyes darted between Eden and the sign. "Anyway," he mumbled, rubbing his good hand over the back of his head and smearing mud all over his hair. He trudged up into the yard, boots squelching in the sodden ground, water and mud-logged purple pants slipping down his hips. Eden didn't get it; if he'd been the one to put the sign up, why make a big sheepish deal of it?

Why come down to help Eden at all?

Curiosity and practicality getting the better of him, Eden hiked his backpack up and followed. The front door of the cabin was unlocked. When the man went in, a warm rush of fire-scented air blasted out to greet Eden. He gasped it in and stumbled inside without bothering to take off his shoes. A huge cooking fireplace was set into the far wall, and the stranger was adding chunks of wood to make the fire larger.

"Shut that damn door," he ordered.

Eden frowned at him but did so, dropping his backpack next to it and coming closer. Even the sudden burning in his arm—the silver reacting to the fire—wasn't enough to ward him off seeking out the heat to chase the chill of rain off his skin.

He leaned next to the fireplace, pressing his face to the warmed wooden wall. It felt like the thing was melting all the stress from the past weeks off him, sloughing it away from his bones like marrow jelly. He wanted to lie down and curl up and forget about running away for a few minutes.

As bad as it was, he thought he dozed off listening to the warm living sounds of being in a house with someone else, because the next thing he knew, the man was clearing his throat in Eden's ear. "Hey, uh." He held up a wet cloth. "You're bleeding."

Eden peered at his arm. No blood—only the sheen of silver rot.

"No, your head." The man gestured at the base of Eden's skull. "There." He offered the rag.

Fighting through fatigue and dizziness, Eden took it and mopped sloppily over his neck, doing it more out of determination than anything. He didn't want anyone else touching him there—or anywhere, really, but especially there, and his throat, and his soft belly, which was so vulnerable right now. All of him was so vulnerable. How could he have fallen asleep?

"I'm gonna get something for that," the stranger said, jerking his chin at Eden's arm. "You have any allergies?"

"Well, yeah," Eden said shakily. He licked his lips and grinned, trying to prove he was just fine leaning here, mopping up his wounds on his own. What was it his sister used to say? He was just holding up the wall, was all. "I have this thing with silver..."

The man pressed his lips together in a way that suggested he either want to laugh or scold Eden. "You *know* what I meant," he chided.

Eden sighed and slumped into the wall, letting the washcloth stick to his neck. "I'm okay. Nothing else."

The man slouched away. He'd put a shirt on, flannel and oversized, and it drowned him in a way the rain hadn't been able to. He was built stocky, but he was even shorter than Eden, and he looked like a kid in his dad's clothes—though the frown lines around his eyes and the gray mixed into his blond hair gave it away that he was probably old enough to be *Eden's* father.

Eden watched him for no particular reason, other than he couldn't really move his eyes much right now. His body was powering down after being strung so high for so long—on the run, always on the run, for miles and miles and what felt like years. Always on the run, always watching his own back because he'd thrown away or left anyone else who would want to. He squeezed his eyes closed, because he would not cry. He *would not* cry, not now. He'd asked the mother moon for her help and she'd given it to him, sent a lonely wolf his way, and he couldn't bring himself to be that ungrateful.

Focus. When he was a child, he used to hate throwing up, so every time he was sick and felt it climbing up in his chest, he'd snatch up a book and read as fast as he could, distracting his mind and body until the feeling passed. He did the same thing now, only he took in the details of the man's house. Well, home. Home?

The house... cottage?... no, *cabin* was one room and just as in disrepair as the outside. There was an unmade bed with mismatched coverings pushed into one corner, piled with books and jars of herbs and who knew what else. And in the opposite corner was the kitchen, which had dinky appliances that had possibly been rescued from a youth hostel or a very cheap university dorm room. A ratty couch had been arranged cockeyed to the fireplace—but the longer Eden stared at it, eyes glazed, the longer he figured maybe it wasn't actually a design choice, but a poor eye for straightness.

Ha, he thought. He also had a poor eye for straightness.

That was when he realized the silver was getting to him more than he'd thought.

"I'm," he slurred.

"I know, I know," the man said. "Give me two seconds. Don't you fall over, 'cause I'm not giving you another washrag if you bust your head on my coffee table."

Coffee table?

Did he mean the sad, stained wooden footstool in front of the couch? *That* was his coffee table? It wasn't straight, either.

"Not straight," he said, rubbing his face on the wall. It was *so* warm.

"Congratulations," his rescuer told him, and oh, he was suddenly a lot closer, and his pupils were so big. Hunting big. Scenting, chasing, rutting, *wanting* big. *Great.*

No, not great. Eden didn't do this anymore. But— "Come on, kid, drink, it's antidote, look, see, I'll drink first"—the cup being lifted to the man's mouth and then to his smelled amazing, warm and healing, so he opened up and drank obediently. The liquid burst on his tongue with brushes of lavender and vanilla that almost covered the bitter bite of witch hazel and silver serum. There was something terribly intimate about drinking after this man. More intimate than all the hundred-dollar motel room and sixty-dollar back-seat sex Eden had.

He gulped it down, swaying on his feet, and thought, *This is bad.*

Then it got worse.

"Can I touch you?" the man asked, moving his open hand to hover by Eden's shoulder. He would touch him. He would hold him up.

Eden shook his head. He'd hold himself up.

The stranger huffed. "Then you need to move yourself to the couch before you fall down."

Eden eyed the distance between him and the couch, which was pulsing with the pounding of his head. "I can nap... here. Right here."

Another huff. But the man didn't try to grab him. "It's only a few steps. You're telling me you can haul your skinny ass up a mountain, but you can't get to my couch? What were you doing out there?" he asked, his voice softening without warning.

And it definitely needed a warning, because it was butter-mellow and melting now. Unless that was the silver serum settling hot in Eden's belly. "I was..." He snapped his drowsy mouth closed before he could give himself away, and stared hard at the wall until he had the perfect explanation: "I was hiking and I got lost."

"Huh," the man said. "Okay, kid. Sure." He waved a hand at the couch. "Anyway. You... go there."

He sounded a little lost himself.

"Where do *you* go?" Eden asked muzzily. It seemed like a sensible question. The couch looked ten times more comfortable than the bed. He didn't know how this man slept on that bed, and he'd slept in *alleyways* before. *Alleyways* looked more habitable than the bed.

Than this whole place, really.

The man was silent for the full length of time it took Eden to disengage himself from the wall and stumble to the couch, which smelled like dust and human skin. No wolf here either. No pack. Just nothing.

He pressed his face into the cushions.

Behind him, the stranger murmured, "I don't go anywhere."

Then he draped something heavy over Eden's shoulders and the whole world zipped away.

CHAPTER TWO

He woke up already moving.

He'd rolled off the couch and landed light on his fingertips and toes, and then he was shifting, tearing out of the second set of clothes in as many hours. Or no—wait, it wasn't day anymore. Outside the cabin's dirty windows was absolute black. Inside the cabin wasn't much better; his wolf's eyes saw in monochrome, and all he could make out was shadows.

The fire had died.

So had his fever.

There was a man standing in the doorway.

Eden panted, drawing himself low and tight to the ground. His foreleg still ached.

"Well, this is convenient," a voice said.

Boris MacClair's voice.

Eden wriggled backward, dragging his sore leg. Once he was past the edge of the couch, he could see the rest of the cabin was empty. His rescuer was gone like the fire and the fever, and he'd left Eden in this box, alone and defenseless.

Any stab of hurt was squashed out by a roaring wave of *you should have known better than to think otherwise*. He forced his ears to unpin from where they'd flattened to his skull and whined.

Defenseless.

That was exactly what he wanted Boris to think.

He whimpered in the back of his throat and put his muzzle down on the floor, letting his ears droop. *"I got lost."*

"I'd say so," Boris sniffed, moving toward him in the clear darkness. Not too close. Not close enough. He smelled like sweat and mud and frustration. "If we've all learned one thing from this little adventure of yours, though, it's that I picked a fitting... *companion* for my brother." Hands on his hips, he pointedly surveyed the cabin. "Everything else around here is broken too."

Eden didn't understand for a few molassesy seconds.

When he did, it came in waves: first, *of course it's your brother*, because honestly, it was becoming more and more apparent he'd run to the end of his luck; then *but he helped me*, which Eden dismissed altogether; and finally *get out now*.

His heartbeat thundered in his ears.

Screw playing pathetic.

He surged up onto the couch, bounding straight over the back. He staggered as he hit the floor. Eden threw himself sideways, around the cabin's single rug. Boris's big body was blocking most of the doorway still, but Eden sized up the gap and then shot between his legs, out onto the porch. He narrowly avoided dropping himself into a gap where a board had once been, spotting it out of sheer luck and gathering all his strength to leap over it. His leg buckled when he hit the ground, and he rolled, scrambling up.

"Fucker!" Boris yelled from inside the cabin.

"What the *fuck*?" a familiar voice said from the trees.

Eden froze, panting with panic. There was that strange tug again, the one that said *you're going the right way*.

Yeah, he was. Away from here.

Boris stomped out behind him, kicking viciously at one of the wooden posts on the porch. Eden whirled to face him. "Little fucker! You signed a contract!"

"Jesus, Boris!" The man from before—*Michael MacClair*—moved into the clearing, an ax resting across one shoulder. He stank of fresh tree sap and shaved wood. He spared Eden a passing glance that was devoid of emotion before turning those same blank eyes on Boris. "What the hell are you doing up here?"

"Looking for *her*." Boris jabbed a finger in Eden's direction.

"For..." Michael frowned, paused.

Eden snarled, *"Him."*

Michael shifted his weight. "Looking for him why?"

As scared as he was, Eden felt a little glow kick up under his ribs, both because Michael had gendered him correctly in the first place, and because he wasn't doing that thing some people did, where they capitulated to the first person to use the wrong terms.

He moved warily toward Michael, almost convinced the man would let him pass back into the woods if he tried for it. And he was going to. He was—

"Stop!" Boris shouted from the porch. "You take one more step and I'll tell every cop in Denver exactly where you are!"

All his muscles stiffened.

"Oh yes," Boris said silkily. He drew himself up now that he knew he had a foothold. "You thought I didn't know?"

"Boris, what the fuck—"

"I know all about you." Boris came off the porch toward them. "You thought you could walk into my city like some pretty little innocent teenager applying for a babysitting job? I always knew exactly who you were. And that you didn't check in with immigration here. Which is why I thought you'd be *grateful* for the opportunity I'm giving you to stay out here." He bared his teeth and gestured at the guarding trees with his soft, limp lawyer's hands. "With a pack that won't abandon you."

Misery speared Eden through the chest. *"They didn't abandon me,"* he hissed before he could stop himself.

I abandoned them.

"Okay, that's *enough*." Michael put himself in Boris's path. Compared side by side, it was obvious they weren't blood-related: Boris had a thin, hawkishly mean face that didn't match his bulk, and Michael had a strong, square jaw and a wide nose, but barely scraped five-foot-five. He clenched his fists and got right up in Boris's face anyway, ordering, "Tell me what's going on and why you're in my fucking cabin and why you know him."

Boris sighed like they were the ones bothering him and dug into his pocket. "Here." He passed over a folded sheaf of papers.

Michael took it and scanned it.

Above them, the half-moon shone.

"What is this, a joke?" Michael flipped through the papers twice. His laugh was flat and hard as a stone.

It hurt, and Eden wasn't sure why.

"Come on, Boris." Michael balled up the papers and tossed them back at him. "Jesus. It's not April for another six months. What do you really want?" He stiffened. "Tell me it wasn't you who set that trap. Tell me you haven't sunk *that* fuckin' low."

"I don't know what trap you're talking about. But this right here? It's yours." Boris slapped the papers against Michael's chest, then jabbed a finger in Eden's direction. "And hers. Marriage certificate and the written—and *signed*, by the way—agreement to go along with it."

The humor sluiced off Michael's face. He paled. "Bullshit."

"Of course it isn't. That is yours. Did you read it? Thoroughly?"

"Oh yeah, I had a lot of fuckin' time to read all the fine print." An icy snarl rode under the words. "Here's the part you missed: I woke up this morning and stayed here all fucking day. Ate breakfast, did some shit. I don't know. But I for damn sure didn't go down to the courthouse and get married."

"Well, no. I did that for you."

The sudden fear in the way Michael stood made Eden hold his ground, watching them from where he was, braced on his three good paws.

Michael smoothed the papers out again with one shaking hand. For the first time, there was real emotion in his voice. "How."

"Remember when your mother died?"

Anger exploded out through Michael's whole body. All the little soothing—if sardonic—moves he'd made to stifle Eden's fear when he was trapped seemed like they'd come from someone else. Even in the darkness, Eden's wolf's eyes could see Michael's ugly scowl in perfect detail. He took an involuntary step back, suddenly glad Michael was on his side in this.

For now.

"Wow, no, you know what, I don't think I do," Michael said, lips curled back. "Howsabout you bring that up to my face again? Maybe give me a run-through too; I don't think I remember all the precious moments."

"Michael, please." Boris pinched his nose. "First her, now you. Can't anyone make this easy?"

"Is he a fucking prostitute?" Michael burst out. "Did you bring him here? Are you trafficking *people* now?" He spun to face Eden, who couldn't help flinching. Michael showed his palms, the wedding papers dangling from two fingers like a dead mouse. His eyes were wide. "No, no, you stay, you stay here—look, whatever he paid you, I'll give you double and I'll get you a plane ticket wherever you wanna go. It's fine. It'll be fine. You don't have to stay."

Boris cleared his throat. "If you'd like to read *some* fine print, Michael, I think you'll see that's impossible. I had Whitton draw that up this afternoon, and it says..." He leaned into Michael's space to thumb through the contract, apparently unaware—or he just didn't care—how furious Michael was.

If it was Eden, he'd bring that ax of his straight down on Boris's head. Problem solved. Wouldn't be the first time he'd done it.

"Ah, here." Boris flipped a page and pointed at something. "See?"

"You mean do I see where that's not my signature?"

"Power of attorney," Boris said.

Michael squinted.

"You never revoked it. I'm still your legal guardian, in the eyes of the pack."

"You're my *what*? I'm a grown-ass man!"

"Your *keeper*, then." Boris's voice was icy. "Who owns the land this shithole of yours is standing on. But that isn't the important part right now. Read that."

Michael bared his teeth, but did read. His lips moved silently with the words until, "... A thirty-day clause."

"Exactly. It's some trendy law now, to prevent skirmishes between packs with unblessed ceremonies. I thought we could try it out."

"I'm not your fucking guinea pig," Michael spat. "And neither is he. Kid—"

"Eden."

Shock crossed Michael's face. Like he hadn't realized yes, Eden had a *name*, even though it was right there on the papers in front of him. Yes, he had a name and his own opinion about all of this. No way was he going to stand by anymore while these two argued over him.

He decided right then to clear something else up, too. *"I'm not a prostitute. I came here on my own."*

"From Denver," Boris added meaningfully.

"I don't care. You can't force either of us into this. I didn't sign, and I *know* he didn't know what he was getting into, or he wouldn't have either."

Boris raised his eyebrows. "Oh no? He came in and asked for your hand."

Michael stepped back as if struck, making Eden swallowed his reflexive disagreement. "You—" He swung his head to stare at Eden. "You what?"

You can use this.

The insidious little thought curdled Eden's stomach. But there was sheltered hope in Michael's voice, hope for something, buried deep in a damp bunker of a place and only now checking the surface for safety. Hope like that could be taken advantage of. Eden had learned that practically as soon as he'd left his parents' place. Had hardened when people had taken him in, a trusting baby of a wolf with no concept of how the world was outside his family's close-knit camp, and turned on him. Robbed him when he wasn't looking. Asked for certain favors if he wanted to stay. Told him to give up his religion in exchange for something a little more realistic.

But he hadn't hardened enough, or he wouldn't be here.

Sucked for Michael. Kind as he was—well, had seemed—Eden wasn't about to waste an opportunity. *"There was a request for a companion for you,"* he said. *"I answered it."*

Michael's expression twisted.

And Eden knew just like that: he was in. All he had to do was cinch the story tight.

"I answered it," he repeated. *"I came out here with him."*

Michael studied him for a few seconds. It was an intense expression, one that made Eden squirm on his paws. One that made him think maybe Michael knew he was lying by omission. Thankfully, it was only a few seconds before Michael's hair-trigger temper rolled back in and he shoved Boris in the shoulder. "You put an *ad* out for someone to marry me? I'm not a used car, Boris, what the holy *hell* were you thinking?"

Boris rolled his lips between his teeth. "I'm thinking it doesn't matter." He dragged his eyes from Eden. "It worked, didn't it? People have been talking, Michael. It reflects badly on the pack, the way you keep this place, and mayoral elections are coming up. You could use a tidy wife around to keep your things in order. She could even come to town and pick up your groceries, so I can stop sending that poor woman up here every week." He patted Michael on the shoulder. "Come now. This is a good thing. And if I'm mayor, well... we'll see if I can't get you something more than a wife, hmm? You want to move back to town?" His voice had gone all schmoozy car salesman, but unlike with Eden, where he'd sounded totally convinced by his own idiocy, his offers were threaded with insincerity.

"You're fucked up," Michael said immediately. "You're fucked up, and this is fucked up, and you need to get away from me right now."

"I'm not taking her—"

"No, you're right, you're not taking him anywhere." Michael squared his shoulders under the handle of his ax. The agreement crumpled in his fingers. "He stays. You leave."

Boris grinned. "So you're keeping her, then?"

"What happens if I don't?"

"To you? Nothing. I'll just repost the ad. To her?" He shrugged and shot a nasty grin Eden's way. Eden wasn't sure whether to be glad or revolted that they'd apparently settled on the same strategy. "You really should get a newspaper or something, Michael."

Michael shook his head. All the fight seeped out of him at once, dragging away in a sheet and leaving just him, small and pale. His shoulders slumped and he let his ax's head drop to the still-soggy ground. "Leave us alone, Boris. He stays with me." He sounded as exhausted as Eden felt.

It was a miniscule victory when Boris left, his expensive wingtip shoes squelching all the way back to the barely visible footpath that led down through a copse of trees.

"Don't think I'm not gonna get that power of attorney shit fixed," Michael called after him. No response. Eden listened with pricked ears until he heard the crunch of gravel under the Chrysler's whitewall tires.

Then it was only Eden and Michael, alone by the cabin.

Escape would be easy.

Michael *would* let him go. He could see that now.

Crossing the mountains with no supplies and lingering silver poison would be harder. And he couldn't guarantee he'd be able to hunker down and find safe shelter with enough food to last him through the inevitable manhunt Boris would bring down on him once he filed an unregistered resident complaint and linked it to the Denver raids. The police didn't play around anymore, not after the new laws had passed and slammed stricter regulations in place. Eden had seen other people get life in prison for a single stolen bag of groceries from a dollar store, had seen teenagers hurt or killed because a cop found them smoking weed and didn't like their attitude.

The idea of an actual cross-country hunt would thrill the police—like a rich man's fox chase, with an equal amount of death but a bigger payroll.

"You won't make it," Michael said suddenly.

Eden realized he'd turned his muzzle up toward the mountains. He lowered it, meeting Michael's eyes.

Michael sighed and dropped his ax right there, letting it land with a thunk in the mud. "Go if you want, but you won't make it. Believe me, I know. And you know too. I know you tried to run from this and I don't care. If it's different for you now, stay. If not, go." He scratched at the back of his head, then grunted and tossed the marriage agreement down next to his ax, where the thin paper instantly soaked through with filth.

And then he just... shrank back in on himself and walked inside. Left Eden out there on his own.

Somewhere down the mountain, a raven cried, lonely and hungry and maybe hunted, too, who knew. Who knew what was prey these days?

Eden limped into the cabin.

Michael was sitting on the muddy couch, head in his hands.

"Don't look," Eden said. He shifted without waiting for Michael to answer, which was okay, because he didn't answer. He didn't look, either. He didn't even sound like he was breathing.

Eden closed the door. There was no bolt on it, but there was a bucket next to it. Eden hung that off the doorknob so he'd at least hear if anyone tried to come in. His backpack was over by the kitchen; he only had one lost-and-found shirt and two pairs of ill-fitting pants left, and no shoes.

Michael was right. He wouldn't make it, not like this. Not with no food, no shoes, weakness from the silver holding on to him, and no guarantee that he'd be able to sneak into another place without scanning his ID. And if he had to scan it and Boris really did flag his ID as suspicious, he'd end up like every other wolf from Denver: stuffed away in some "rehabilitation" prison, collared and tracked for the rest of his probably short life.

He dressed silently, then crossed to the fireplace.

Michael ignored him.

Well, fine, then. "I *don't* like your brother."

"*Step*brother," Michael corrected without moving. His eyes were closed.

"Well, whatever. I don't like him."

"Makes two of us."

Thick silence descended.

Eden cleared his throat and shoved a hand through his thick hair to get it to lie right. He'd undercut the right side once, but after that time, getting money to go to the barber had been too much, and it wasn't worth the staring people did, anyway, so now it was growing out, tufty and soft, barely enough to grip a handful. Dried mud flaked off it into his hand, and he made a face at it. Maybe the first step to feeling normal about all this would be to do something normal. "Do you have a shower?"

"Tub," Michael grunted. He didn't elaborate.

371

"Okaaay," Eden said, shifting from foot to foot. "Can you... show me where it is?"

Michael tilted his head and sighed, opening one eye to look up. That bone-deep weariness from when he'd dropped the ax was back. Like he'd lie down and never get up again if Eden would just stop bothering him.

Eden had seen that before, in plenty of people. People who were ghosts one day and gone the next. People who never quite looked *at* you, only through you, seeing something else or nothing at all.

So he kept needling. "I need a bath. Unless you want me to get more mud everywhere. Look, it's all over your floor."

"Doesn't matter to me."

Okay, Eden should've guessed that one. "Well, I'm stuck living here now too, and it matters to me. So show me where the tub is."

Michael raised his head slowly, his pale eyebrows climbing toward his hairline.

Eden cleared his throat again. "Please, Michael."

"Mick. It's just." He made a sharp motion with one hand. "Just Mick."

Mick was short and brutal and quick. It fit him better than Michael. Eden thought he'd seen a gooey center when he'd freed Eden from the wolf trap, but all that was burned away now and he was whipcord-hard with steel eyes, leading Eden out the front door—with a brief, quizzical pause at the bucket—and into the fine rain.

Turned out there was a second shed behind the collapsed shed, and it wasn't collapsed. Mostly. Mick nudged the toe of one boot against the brass basin in the back of the place. "Water doesn't really get hot-hot," he grunted, "but it's a tub."

It was... a tub, all right. With a rust ring three inches thick and what was possibly a fat and very dead cricket at the bottom of it. "Have you ever used this? No? Once?"

"Once. Maybe."

Eden glanced at him; he couldn't tell if the uptick in his monotone voice was an attempt at humor or if he was annoyed. "Okay. Uh. Thanks."

Mick jerked his head in a nod and turned to go. But he paused at the door. "You don't have to stay here," he said. "Whatever Boris did or didn't tell you about me, I'm not stupid enough to think you did that on purpose."

He was drawn so tense Eden thought he'd snap like a broken bowstring.

"I didn't know it was marriage papers," Eden said carefully. How much of the truth could he tell? How much of his hand could he keep? "But there was an ad for a caregiver. He didn't tell me anything else about you."

Silence.

Rain pounded on the roof.

Mick finally slumped in the door frame and snorted. "Big fucking surprise there." He lifted his left leg off the ground until just the tip of his boot rested on the floor, holding it there like a resting horse. Eden thought he'd leave, but instead he said, "Look, what Boris said about Denver..."

God, Eden did *not* want to elaborate on that. "Yeah? What about it?"

Mick either didn't pick up on or didn't care about the warning snap in his tone. "What happened there?"

Eden blinked. "You don't know? It's all over TV."

"Did you see a fucking TV in my house?" Mick growled.

Actually, no. Nor a phone, nor a computer. It wasn't like there was a WiFi hotspot out among the trees, either. Eden was suddenly sorry for all the times he'd mentally whined and moaned about dealing with slow internet café desktops. The prospect of being totally cut off from pro-wolf message boards and news sites was almost as crushing as thinking he'd have to cross the mountains alone.

He swallowed and scraped his voice together so it wouldn't crack. "Chill out. I just—it was big news, that's all. I thought everyone knew about it."

"*You're* big news," Mick muttered.

Eden gaped at his back. "You do realize that's a three-year-old's comeback, don't you? You're way too old to use that."

"Way too old to be hitched to someone like you, too. Take your bath since you wanted it so much." Mick left without another word. He walked with his head down and his shoulders scrunched in, making his small frame narrower, until he was just a slip in the darkness, barely visible and fading with every step. He navigated his way around the piles of junk in his yard and to the cabin, which stayed dark long after he'd slipped inside.

Once he was sure he had the shed to himself, Eden let himself wobble and reached back for the lip of the tub to guide himself into sitting. He had a million questions he wanted to ask. First of which was why Mick had sequestered himself in this crap cabin when his lawyer sleaze of a stepbrother led one of the largest packs in the country and could definitely afford something nicer. Also why didn't he smell like a pack at all, and why the ad had requested a *caregiver*. Eden had been expecting someone who had a disability, or an elderly person who needed extra help around the house. Mick seemed pretty capable of taking care of everything—he just *didn't*.

Eden had never seen a living person so deadened. Like an exposed, raw nerve that had eventually gone dormant and numb to protect itself.

And, Mother Moon help him, but Eden wanted to know *why*.

CHAPTER THREE

Mick was in bed by the time Eden got back from his bath. None of the things scattered on his bed had been moved. He'd arranged his body around them; books and tools and a coffee cup had all drifted toward him, lured in by the steady gravity of his weight. His breathing was shallow but slow.

There was something wrong with him, Eden thought as he hung the bucket back on the doorknob. He was suddenly sure of it the same way you could smell sickness on a dying person, or see rot in the core of a bad fruit. Something was deeply wrong about this town, and whether Mick was a cause or a symptom, it made Eden itch to abandon his strategy and run again, no matter how rash and dangerous it would be.

Maybe he would have. He didn't know. He was considering it until he walked around the couch and found a plate with a hard wedge of cheese and some questionable brown crackers waiting for him on the couch, along with a cup of something that smelled strongly of lavender. Questionable or not, Eden wolfed down the food, left the cup alone since their fragile treaty didn't mean trust and Mick wasn't awake to act as his taster, then stoked the low fire and dropped onto the couch. It was lumpy and smelled weird, but it wasn't the worst place he'd slept.

Not by a long shot.

Sleep was restless anyway. He kept waking up when the fire cracked, when the cabin creaked around them. Mick never moved, never spoke, never stopped breathing in his lapping rhythm, but Eden had the feeling he was awake and thinking, or waiting, and that sensation sat between them like a physical thing: *You say something.*

No, you.

But neither of them did.

~~*

In the morning, he was woken by the sound of the door slamming, followed by the bucket clanging off the wooden floor. So much for all the junk those human-free nature retreats promised. *SAFETY! RELAXATION! GO BACK TO THE WILDERNESS! LIVE FREE! (ONLY $1,799 PER WEEK!)*

He rubbed his good hand over his face. His hair had dried all over the place, he could tell, and he shoved his fingers through it, peeling himself off the couch to go find a mirror.

Only there wasn't one. The kitchen sink had a nearly empty tube of toothpaste, a toothbrush, and a razor stuck in an empty, scarred-up Campbell's Chunky can, but there was no mirror. Eden settled for sweeping everything over to one side of his neck, knotting it off with a tie made of raven feathers from his pack, and hoping it looked artful and middle-of-the-woods chic.

Which was ridiculous, if he really thought about it. Who was he even trying to look pretty for? The man he'd been tricked into marrying? The one whose brother called Eden his *wife*?

Mick didn't call you that, though.

Eden growled at himself. His stomach growled back.

If he focused hard, he could hear Mick yelling outside. His best guess was it was Boris on the other end of the line, unless Mick was yelling at his truck or his ax or the mountain. Eden wasn't sure he could rule any of those possibilities out. Right now he was more interested in what other food Mick had lying around.

The fire was dead and there was no firewood in the house, so he wrapped his arms around himself and started poking around the tiny stove. Everything in the kitchen was miniature except for an enormous and ancient cabinet that turned out to be filled with jars upon jars of tea blends.

Mick shouted something outside, followed by the distinct sound of wood hitting metal. Eden sighed and bent to investigate the fridge. So long as Mick wasn't yelling at him, he'd ignore it. In general, he found shouting almost comfortable, and definitely preferable to silence, since voices, the noises of living people moving and breathing and fighting nearby, were always better than nothing, and no one. It was messed up, he was sure, but all the experience he was supposed to have as a kid coming out of a messed-up house was backward. His father had never *yelled* at him. Had never hit him. He'd just told him, calmly and in small words, what was wrong with him and why there was no point in treating him like a real person anymore.

Like he ever *had* treated Eden like a real person. Eden was sure that after the very first shift he'd popped as a pup, his father had been done with him.

Had probably blamed it on his mother, since he blamed everything else on her and her "hoodoo curses."

By the time Mick slammed the front door open, Eden had rustled up a—potentially clean?—pan and was cooking—potentially safe to eat?—pancakes made from a dusty box of mix that had been stuffed behind the microwave. The pan was so small he could only fit one pancake in at a time. He was working on the first, sliding a butter knife underneath it to check its doneness.

Mick ground to a halt a step inside the door, a chunky house phone in one hand. "What the fuck are you doing?"

Eden hadn't given a lot of thought to how he was going to handle Mick, exactly, so he defaulted to the same typical teenager attitude he'd used on every adult who'd approached him since he left home. "Making food, miracle of miracles. Miracle of miracles I even found food, I mean." Eden flipped his butter knife in his hand to gesture at the pathetically small dining table and its lone chair. "Sit down before you have a heart attack."

Mick's angry whuffs of breath cut off. "I..." He frowned. "What?"

"Sit," Eden repeated, "down."

He was the one who ought to be worrying about a heart attack, from how hard his pulse was pounding in his ears.

Instead of tossing him out or telling him to stop being a mouthy brat, Mick slowly lowered his hackles and, eyeing Eden the whole way, slouched over to drop into the chair, which wobbled dangerously under his weight.

Eden couldn't put his back to him. He just couldn't do it. So he cooked quarter turned, looking at Mick looking at the table. Gradually Mick's shoulders fell from his ears back to their normal hunched position, and that was when Eden felt comfortable enough to ask, "Was that your brother?"

"*Step*brother."

"Was that your *step*brother?"

Mick jerked his head. "He's got some fucked up ideas."

Eden was sorely tempted to say "LOL" aloud. Gracie, one of the other hundreds of street kid wolves he'd known in Denver, would've appreciated that. But he had a feeling the irony of modern teenage slang would be lost on Mick, who, in the light of a sunny day, still looked pretty old. "Yeah, I got that. Probably around the time he told me he'd tricked me into signing marriage papers."

"Is that how he said it?"

Eden shrugged, flipping a pancake onto one of Mick's mismatched plastic plates, then pouring another one out. It bubbled almost immediately. "We got done with the paperwork and he was driving me up here. As soon as we were out of the city, he told me my position was a little more permanent than I'd been told."

"Fucker." Mick scratched one fingernail over the table.

"Yeah, well, I'm glad we agree on that, 'cause in thirty days, he's going to be the reason I get out of this place." Eden winced at his unintended callousness and poked the edges of his next pancake. It was possible he felt sort of bad after Mick had called him out last night. It had been that obvious he was angling for Mick to take him in for his own purposes, and Mick had just lain down and *taken* it. Taken him in, like it didn't matter if Eden was a bad person or not, was using him or not. "I mean," he tried, "I'm not really the marrying type. So there's that."

"Yeah."

The utter flatness of Mick's voice was starting to make Eden itch between his shoulder blades. "What do you mean, 'yeah'?"

Mick fixed him with a look over his shoulder. "I mean yeah. What else am I gonna say? You think I'm gonna ask you to stay? You think I want some scrawny kid hanging around my house until I die?"

His voice wavered when he said it.

"Mother help me," Eden muttered.

Mick twisted around in his chair so hard it tipped, threatening to pitch him sideways. He paid no attention. "Oh god, you're one of *them*."

"Not really, no." Eden flipped the fourth pancake out of the pan and came over to hand it to Mick along with one of his child-size forks. He didn't have any butter, so Eden had set out a jar of some kind of peachy-smelling spread. "My parents are. My dad is. Mom says she's a heathen."

By "them," Mick could only mean one thing: traditionalists. The wolves who still believed the moon was a sacred being instead of an astrological happening. The wolves who knew in their bones that it was the moon who gave them their ability to turn, and the moon who could take that ability away if they sinned. The wolves who whispered stories to each other, sharing theories of creation and destruction, always coming back to the power of a pack bond and the eventual inheritance of the Earth by those who were part man and part nature.

The wolves who thought Eden was wrong, or tainted, or scarred. And after the lupine population boom and the subsequent lockdown of cities and militarization of human police forces, they were the ones in his hometown who had wanted him sacrificed for better luck. They were the kids at his middle school who had tried to force him to shift in class. His first boyfriend, who'd asked to see and then smacked his muzzle and called him a freak, and told everyone at their high school that he wasn't a boy after all, just a liar.

They were his father, telling him to leave or he'd kill Eden himself.

Eden didn't realize he'd stopped in the middle of the cabin and that his fists were clenched, nails digging into his palms, until Mick's hesitant hand touched his shoulder. He wrenched away.

Blood spattered the floor.

Same as last time, Mick flinched and backed off, lifting both hands in supplication.

Time to get one more thing straight. "Don't fucking touch me," Eden spat, feeling the burn of soap on the back of his tongue for the curse. There was traditionalism for you. He said it again to get the taste out of his mouth: "Don't ever fucking touch me."

He thought, reflexively, that Mick might throw him a "what, you worried about your virginity?" or even a "we're married now, why shouldn't I?"

Only he didn't.

He dropped his hands and walked out.

The front door gaped like an open wound in his wake.

You agreed to this, so why shouldn't I? You signed up, now suck up.

The same reasoning so many of the guys who'd paid him for a blowjob had given.

It's happening again. He'd thought that yesterday, preparing to tumble out of Boris's car. He sold himself all over again, only this time it wasn't for survival—it was because he'd let himself get so desperate, because he'd let himself hold that newspaper in his hands and think, *I could keep someone company.*

The very first time he'd tempted a guy in a bar into paying him forty bucks for a blowjob, he'd been sick with himself, paranoid that after everything it would be *this* that got him shunted out of the moon's favor. But he'd had to do it, because it was the only way he could survive, before he came to Denver. Lots of towns didn't have hostels and he would've felt bad taking up shelter resources, and motels would see someone like him coming in, windblown and road-weary, obviously a vagabond, and jack up the price some. He'd almost never found a place to stay for less than fifty bucks a night, and subpar dollar-menu meat could only keep a wolf healthy for so long. So he'd done what he had to.

Most of them had treated him terribly. Pulled his hair, called him "exotic" and sometimes "colored" and sometimes things worse than that.

And now he'd walked right into the first place he could stop and sold himself again. And it was only hitting him now just how badly this could go. He understood sex better now, didn't buy into the propaganda about the value of his body, especially when all the people who wanted him to preserve it already thought he was a sinner in form, but...

But no matter how kind Mick had seemed back at the wolf trap, Eden had chosen to stay here. Had put himself in this horrible, vulnerable situation, and he'd have no one to blame but himself if Mick turned out to be awful, because he could've run. He could've run and he didn't. The one time he needed to run, he hadn't.

How had he thought this whole charade could work out in his favor? How had he thought he could manipulate Boris *and* Mick and then walk away without a scratch on him? How had he thought he could just get away from this? He'd put himself in such a bad place, and it couldn't be out of naïveté. He wasn't naïve. Was he just egotistical? Convinced he could charm the universe into giving him a little more leeway?

Or maybe he didn't know himself well enough after all to have a handle on when he was in over his head.

Maybe this time he was just *wrong*. Maybe he'd screwed himself over. Maybe Boris would come back up here in a month and decide Eden wasn't the perfect wife he wanted him to be. That he wasn't worth the effort.

If that day came... the second Boris decided Eden was too much trouble, he'd check Eden in at Wildwood's console and flag him as a Denver escapee. He'd said he was running for mayor, hadn't he? What better way to bolster his mayoral candidacy among humans than to drag a wanted wolf criminal in to face the police? If Mick's ad hadn't gone unfilled as long as it had, Eden would probably be sitting in a holding cell right now while the Wildwood news stations drooled all over themselves for the chance at a first interview with Boris.

Suddenly his month here seemed less like a cushion and more like a countdown.

All because Eden had given himself away without bothering to check what he was signing.

It was happening again, and this time it was all for nothing.

And all his fault.

He wanted to throw up.

Then he did. Barely made it to the dented metal trash can before he was bent over and heaving, throwing up everything in his stomach and a couple mouthfuls of bile with it.

"Jesus," he heard Mick say from behind him. "Eden, Jesus Christ." Heavy footfalls. The sink running. "Here." Mick crouched down next to him a careful distance away and offered a washrag. "It's clean."

Eden snatched it and mopped at his face with shaking hands.

"I have a toothbrush if you want." Mick's voice was hesitant.

"What I want..." Eden cut himself off with a rough shake that made his head ache. He didn't understand Mick—one second he was all mouthy roughness and the next he was this, and he didn't seem comfortable when he was either. What if he was the one who got tired of Eden? What if he called his brother—*step*brother—and said he was done? Eden wouldn't stand a chance. Even if Mick did keep him around for the thirty days, who was to say Boris wouldn't decide he'd done a poor job?

He had to get ready for when that happened. He had to be prepared.

"I know what you want," Mick said lowly, like he'd read Eden's mind in the chaos of his panic. "But you can't leave."

That panic fluttered right under Eden's breastbone. He pressed his face to the cool side of the trash can and peeled his lips back off his teeth. "So now I *can't* leave? I'm stuck here? As your wife? What happened to letting me go if I wanted to go?"

Mick faltered. He put a hand on the floor close to Eden, fingers flexing. He wanted to touch him.

Well, too bad.

"Look," he said. "I'm sorry I tried to play you last night." He kept his eyes closed so he couldn't see the inevitable thunderclap of temper was making its way onto Mick's face. "I'm sorry I stayed here—" *I'm sorry I did this to myself,* "—but that doesn't mean you get to take me out of one trap and put me in another one. Both our names are on those papers. Not just mine. If I want to leave, I—I get to leave."

"Jesus," Mick said after a while. No storm in his voice all. Eden looked at him, teeth still bared, and Mick looked away, dodging eye contact. His eyes were red. "That's not what I meant. Not for one second did I believe you answered that ad because you're a woo-woo tree spirit, good-deed-doing, flower-child Samaritan who wanted to marry me out of the good of your heart. We're not actually married, kid. I know that. I'm a hermit. I'm not fucking naïve."

Eden picked his head up. "... 'Woo-woo tree spirit'?"

"You know what I mean. Hippie save-the-world kids." Mick sat down and leaned back against the kitchen wall. Stared at his hands. He sucked in a deep breath. "I don't care why you want to stay here. I don't care what happened to you before. None of that's up here. Just the forest and shit. I just can't figure out why you want to be all the way up here with an old man when there's a million other things for you to do. You decided you wanted to stay here. That's what I meant. *You* told Boris you wanted to stay. I went along with it because I was tired of listening to him whine, not because I bought your bullshit. I just meant you shouldn't leave, because of him. Not you *can't*. You can. I won't stop you." He nodded at the door. "You can go anywhere you want."

So can you, Eden thought.

"I really can't." He mopped his face one last time and tossed the washcloth in the direction of the sink, missing by a spectacular five feet. "Not for a while."

He sighed and leaned over to scoop up the washrag and throw it at the sink before it stained the floor.

It missed *again*.

Mick snorted. And unless Eden was already losing it from the quiet of the mountain and was projecting onto Mick, he swore he could see a hint of amusement under all that blankness. Mick's eyes looked glazed and given up from this close: flat gray and devoid of light. His eyebrows were blond and almost colorless, and he raised them when he caught Eden watching him. It made his frown lines disappear, made him look younger.

"How old are you, anyway?" Eden asked.

"A lot old."

Eden gave him a dirty look. "Answer me."

"Thirty-six."

"I said—" Eden started, automatic. His brain caught up. "Thirty-six?" Not as old as he'd expected.

"Yeah, yeah. Rub it in."

"I'm nineteen," he blurted.

Mick's frown lines appeared and creased deep. "That's too young."

Eden felt himself puff up. "Too young for what? You don't know anything about me."

"Jesus," Mick muttered. "You ever give that stubbornness a rest?"

"You ever give yours one?" Eden retorted, doing a poor imitation of Mick's drawling accent.

Mick pressed his tongue to the inside of his cheek. That was definitely a flash of amusement—at his expense or not, Eden couldn't tell. But instead of answering the question, Mick sat back against the kitchen wall and said, "You gonna tell me what happened in Denver? Boris wouldn't. I don't have a TV." He squirmed. It was somehow a totally different admission from before. "Can't run wiring up here, and after a while the radio just..." He shrugged. "Hard to keep up with."

Eden uncurled from where he'd pressed up to the trash can—which *so* needed to be taken out, Mother help him—and sat cross-legged with his back to the kitchen. "What *did* he say?"

Another squirm. "Nothing."

"You're lying."

"You don't wanna know what he said."

"Don't tell me what I do and don't want," Eden said sharply. It wasn't the tone he was used to taking with older adults—snotty and self-righteous, so they'd pass him along as a waste of their time. Just another dumb, overstuffed, militantly politically correct millennial with no future. But he wouldn't let Mick see him that way. "I want to know what he told you."

Mick's jaw tightened, and his eyes—*no, no, don't*—took on that dead look when he gritted out, "He called you a gypsy slut."

Eden felt a terrible calm wash over him. "Of course he did. What else did he say?"

"Eden—"

"I want to know."

Mick scratched the back of his neck and turned his face away. "He said there were rumors someone tipped off the cops in Denver. Said he couldn't think of any other reason you'd run."

"*Any other reason?*" Eden spluttered. "Like not wanting to go to prison for nothing? I know he's a lawyer, but he can't possibly believe that strongly that the law in this country is actually on our side. Because it never is. And I didn't do it," he added, seething. "I wouldn't do that. They might not have been my pack, but I knew them."

Gracie from the women's shelter, who busked by the farmers market on weekends and donated everything she didn't need for food to the shelter's kitchen. Noah, who had survived two abusive relationships and had nearly died rescuing his dog from his second partner. Old Mr. Kahlan, who lived in a hollowed-out stoop on Perch Street, who was blind and told stories about the wars to anyone who brought him scraps of food.

Eden had sequestered himself away from all of them, but eventually. Eventually he would have gotten to know them. Eventually maybe some of them would have been a pack.

They may not have been anything, but they were an "almost." All those people he'd seen in Denver. Hollow-eyed boys and girls traipsing out of the same motel rooms he made his living in. People trying to make the best of what they had for their kids. The tent cities, where wolves formed wary packs.

"Hey. Hey." Mick moved suddenly. His voice was soft. "Hey. I'm sorry. I didn't mean to do that."

"You didn't do anything."

"I know what going off to a bad place is like," Mick disagreed. He hesitated, then reached for the cuff of his left pants leg and hiked it up. Underneath was smooth metal extending down into his boot. Eden caught himself wanting to touch and held back, even when Mick nodded permission. It wouldn't be right to touch him when Eden had told him off so many times for the same thing. "Used to be a boxer," he explained before Eden could open his mouth.

Eden peered at his leg. *Don't touch.* "This... doesn't look like a legal hit."

"It wasn't."

As per what Eden was quickly realizing was usual, Mick didn't go on. Eden untied his hair and combed through it with his fingers to occupy himself while he said, "It was two weeks ago. I was staying in the top half of a parking garage that was closed for construction, so they didn't see me. By the time I got downstairs..." He closed his eyes, remembering the burn of tear gas on the back of his tongue. "They said they'd discovered some kind of underground trading ring. With illegal cryptocurrency and black market goods and drugs. And they said wolves who were immigrating to and emigrating from the city were the ones running it because they were transient. They were..." He swallowed a wave of renewed nausea. "People were screaming. Howling. I ran." Because that was it, really. The most important part. "I ran."

"You shifted?"

Eden nodded and combed his hair back to where it had been and re-tied it with the raven feathers. "I got out, and this was the first town I could find where the border security wasn't increased."

"So you applied to the ad because you needed a cover," Mick said, matter-of-fact. He waved one hand. "Like I said, I don't care. That doesn't bother me. What bothers me is how you ended up in that trap."

"I thought you didn't care?" Eden said, giving him a tiny, lopsided snarl-smile.

Teasing, he realized. He was teasing. And not just as a defense mechanism.

Mick, to his surprise, loosened up and teased right back. "Since I'm the one who had to go out and ruin my favorite gloves burying it, yeah, I care."

"I chickened out," Eden sighed. "I thought you were going to be an old woman who wanted me to take care of her cats or something. Then Boris told me exactly what he'd made me sign."

"Yeah, he's like that. A dick. As for me: old lady? Not so much." Mick stretched his legs out, letting his hand rest heavy on the prosthetic one. "Old man, sure." With absolutely no warning, he added, "So you can shift without the moon."

Nope. No matter what casual rapport they'd skirted the edge of, Eden didn't want to have this conversation. He didn't want to know if Mick would trot out some bigotry that would fester in Eden for the rest of the month. Diversion time. "You can't buy groceries to save your life."

Mick curled a lip at him, eyes glinting. "I don't buy 'em. Your hair's cut funny."

"It's cut *stylishly*." Well, it used to be. "Anyway, who'd take style advice from you? You have terrible taste in interior decor."

"You have terrible taste in clothes. Are those jeans glued on?"

"Not yet." Eden cut him a toothy smile. "Kids these days don't get that done until they wear them for at least four days in a row." The utter confusion on Mick's face—did he actually believe that?—made Eden laugh. He circled a finger, indicating the ceiling. "Plus your house is literally falling down."

"Yeah, well, you smell like rotted rosemary. It's disgusting."

"That's *your* soap I smell like! You're insulting yourself now."

Mick squinted. "There wasn't any soap out there. You used my leather scrub?"

"*Leather scrub?* You let me take a bath knowing there was no soap for me to use?"

An awkward pause. Mick seemed very interested in staring at the varnish—which was spotty and in disrepair—on the floor. "I wasn't in a good mood."

"Yeah, me neither." Eden flicked a crumb on the floor at him. "A bath with real soap would have been nice. That stuff was all rotted."

"You're lucky you got a bath at all." Mick closed his hands on his knees and for a split second, Eden thought he saw him smile. It evaporated too quickly to get a good look. "Well," Mick said, patting his thighs. "We're stuck with each other."

Yes. They were. For thirty whole days.

It would be fine.

Mick picked himself up, apparently taking Eden's silence for the end of their conversation. He paused at the table, scooping up his plate of pancakes, then slouched outside with it after an awkward little look over his shoulder.

Eden could have done way worse, he decided.

He could have been stuck with *Boris*.

CHAPTER FOUR

If Eden was going to live here for a month, he was absolutely not going to continue to allow this place to deteriorate and rot in its own filth. He wasn't cleaning because he was Mick's *wife* or because he wanted a job-well-done pat on the back from Boris. He was cleaning because he didn't want to live in a hovel.

He would just treat their marriage like the job he'd thought he was applying for. They'd be roommates, and Eden would keep the house so it didn't fall apart, and, in all likelihood, would end up cooking too, if he didn't want to eat packaged noodles and Hungry Man meals that expired three years ago.

Mick disappeared from the yard, his plate left on the porch, and Eden went ahead and left it there to make a point. Yes, he was going to keep the house. No, he didn't have to pick up after Mick like he was five years old. Ground rules. That was how he was going to get through this. Ground rules and taking it one day at a time. He could think about his survivor's guilt and he could think about where to go from here once he had the means to make the decision.

After breakfast, he pulled his hair up in a high bun and opened all the curtains, which had the wonderful effect of showing exactly how much dirt was caked on the windows. And on the floor. And the ceiling.

Eden found saddle brushes in the shed with the tub. The half-collapsed shed in front of it had been propped precariously with bowing two-by-fours, but a quick peek revealed that was where the toilet and a leaky showerhead were. He let them be, filled his security bucket with lukewarm water from the brass tub, then scrubbed every inch of the cabin's windows, until there was real light filtering into the place. It made it look a little less like a shithole—*sorry, Mother*—and a little more like it fit into Eden's nature-chic aesthetic.

It still didn't smell any more like pack. Boris's scent had been wicked away by the wind, and the city, with the rest of the MacClair pack, was too far away to carry over the towering pines and the snap of snow that cascaded down from the mountains. All Eden could smell inside was Mick's tea cabinet and, once he pried the windows open with an unwashed fork, the fresh, clean air. And Mick himself, wild and woodsy and thick with depression.

Eden became more and more certain that it was a lasting depression when he cleaned off Mick's bed, piling all the books and jars and, from under Mick's pillow, a ratty neon-green stuffed lizard, into a basket he found in the bottom of the kitchen pantry. Mick's sheets were... not in the best of shape, so Eden stripped those off and took them back to the brass tub. It was kind of gross, really, how soaked into the fabric Mick's scent was. If Eden wasn't a wolf, he was sure he would have found it a lot grosser. But instead he inhaled carefully before he turned the water on, and all he got was a big whiff of chemical fatigue. No sex and barely any emotion.

For lack of any soap, he stole some jasmine from Mick's teas and dumped it into the bathtub, then filled it and left it to soak.

Walking through the pitted yard with all its piles of junk reminded him he had a long way to go, but for the first time, he... he had a *home*. A real home, one he wasn't squatting in, one where he didn't have to stay awake in shifts to make sure no landlords were paying surprise visits to see if the apartments weren't filled past capacity. He had a real home, no matter how bad the circumstances, and he was going to make it livable.

He was completely resolved, right until he stepped back into the cabin and spotted Mick bent over his bed, fingers bitten deep into the lumpy mattress. "Where are my things?" Mick asked without moving. "*Where did you move my things?*"

Shaken, Eden took the basket from the couch and held it out. "Here. I'm washing your sheets."

Mick snatched it from his arms and cradled it to his chest, glaring balefully at Eden over the top. "Don't touch these. I don't touch you, you don't touch my shit." He whirled and started unpacking the basket back onto the bare mattress, removing each thing from the bin with trembling fingers and putting it back exactly where it had been on top of the sheets.

For the first time, Eden actually looked at the stuff. The three books were old, and when Mick smoothed a palm over the worn covers, they smelled like perfume. The jars of herbs... Eden took a deep sniff and found chamomile and peppermint and pomegranate. The other bits Mick took out more slowly: a piece of rough twine knotted in a circle; a scrap of dull, folded leather; and the small stuffed lizard, which he replaced under his pillow.

"Go ahead," he muttered. His voice was the scrape of a shovel in grave dirt. "Tell me I'm too old for that thing."

Eden shrugged a shoulder. "Whatever keeps your nightmares away."

It was a totally wild guess on his part, but Mick paused. "Huh." He shook his head and handed the basket back to Eden. "Dunno where you got that from."

"It's yours."

"Probably not." Mick rubbed a hand back through his short hair. "I bought the place with furniture. Didn't really do much to it."

"Like clean?" Eden couldn't help asking. "Dust? Is your plate still on the porch?"

Mick drew back, nose wrinkling, but under Eden's steady gaze, he slunk out and fetched it. He tried to put it in the basket for Eden to handle, but Eden shot him a withering look, and he took it to the sink instead. Even ran water over it. "Look, I never got into a routine," he said, sloshing the water around. "Why bother?"

"Well, for one, you live here. I've lived in abandoned buildings with better hygiene than this place." Mick was literally just moving the dish around in circles, so Eden went over and waited for him to get the hint and move out of the way. "Do you have dish soap?"

"Uhh..."

"Do you have a piece of paper?" Eden sighed. "And a pen?"

Was it sad that he was getting excited?

Mick scrounged up a legal pad and a pencil and sat at the kitchen table without being prompted. "What am I writing?"

"Shopping list."

"There's a woman who does that for me," Mick said.

"Well, do you give her a list?"

Mick shook his head. "She gets whatever shit she thinks I need."

Eden wanted to ask exactly what it was Mick did need, since all of this clearly wasn't it. "Well, I want to give her a list. Dish soap. Laundry detergent. Air freshener. No, incense. Incense sticks. Sponges. Real towels." He felt sort of lightheaded when Mick wrote everything down without a single word of complaint or questioning. He hadn't seemed like the sort to indulge, but Mother, Eden was glad he was. Still... "Tell me if I'm, um, spending too much."

"It's Boris's money," Mick said. "Pack settlement all went to him, so he pays for—" He snapped his mouth closed with an audible click of bone on bone. It made Eden want to see him shifted, see him bare *those* teeth. What color would he be? Tawny golden brown, like his hair? Would he be tiny and stocky as a wolf, too? More fox-sized? Eden would have more height on him with his leggy wolf form. They'd make a good hunting team: Mick could scare prey out, and Eden could hunt it down and pounce, tear open bellies and throats and present them for Mick to see what they'd done together.

Just like they'd worked together at the trap.

Mick cleared his throat. "You awake over there? What's next?"

"I'm fine." Eden shook his head and moved on to another plate instead of the one he'd been mindlessly scrubbing for who knew how long. "Um. Milk. The fattier the better." Better to leave the prying for another day. "Eggs."

"She won't bring eggs. They break on the way up the mountain."

"I could go get things," Eden said. "I know how to drive."

"Truck doesn't work."

The breakfast plates were as good as they were going to get. Eden set them on a dish towel on the counter to dry.

Sweat dripped down the side of his face. His arm was nearly healed now.

It felt good, sweating the poison out.

"Show me," he said.

~~*

"Where the fuck did you learn to hotwire a car?" Mick asked. He had his arms crossed on top of the truck's open driver's side window, and was watching Eden fiddle with the wires he'd ripped out of the dash, apparently utterly unperturbed by the fact that Eden had in fact taken his entire dashboard apart to do so.

Eden rubbed two wires together, looking for a spark that refused to be coaxed out. "Around."

"I don't even know how to hotwire a car."

"Yeah, because there's lots of cars to steal up here," Eden said blandly.

Mick wrinkled his nose, then reached in to touch the button to pop the hood. "Come look in here if you know this stuff too."

"I'm kind of surprised you don't." Eden extracted himself from the rubble of the dashboard and shook his shirt out, scattering dust everywhere. Mick was giving him a look, so he shrugged. "You know, you seem like a big, burly man's man kind of guy."

The look soured. "So I'm not because I don't know how to fix a truck?"

"Uh. Well, I wouldn't put it like that." He did have a point. Eden of all people should know better than to tell someone what did or didn't make them a man. "I just assumed..." Nah. Better to shut up now, while he was halfway down and not the full six feet. "Never mind. I'm sorry, you're right."

That seemed to take Mick more by surprise than anything else. "Fine." He slipped his fingers under the hood and flipped the catch to lift it. He had blunt fingers, kind of round at the ends, with big fingernails that looked capable, or workmanlike. He looked like the kind of man who could live in a tree and hunt for his food and be just fine, self-contained and independent of any other person. If only he wasn't a wolf. "Here, look."

Eden circled around to stand next to him, peering in at the engine. It was a standard Y-block V8, rusty and used-looking, but Eden would bet it'd work if it had the right kind of doctoring. "How long has it been since you started it?" he asked, leaning in.

Mick hissed and reached to pull him back, only to stall his hand half a foot from Eden's arm. "Don't— I'm holding this up," he said, wiggling the hood. "There's no thing, I don't want to drop it on you."

Eden frowned. "There should be." He picked at the lip along the front, looking for the hood stand, but Mick was right. It was missing.

He glanced up to see Mick giving him a thin smile. "I know *that* much about cars." With a raised eyebrow and a nod at one of the gaskets, he said flatly, "That's the on button."

"... Are you joking?"

Mick squinted one eye. "No."

Eden laughed and leaned back into the truck's guts to give it a critical once-over. "Just keep holding that up for me, then. And seriously, when's the last time you started this?"

The moment of dead silence radiating from beside him was weighty. "Why d'you think I was joking?"

Hands buried in the engine, Eden twisted to prop his chin on his arm. "I think... you joke and don't expect people to get it. Or maybe you don't know you're being funny, I don't know. I used to say stuff all the time and my sister would laugh."

Mick snorted. "Correct me if this's some social nicety I've missed out on, but I think that's called being made fun of."

"I'm not laughing at you," Eden said.

Mick's shoulders fell.

Oh.

"I'm not laughing at you," he repeated. Mother, this man had issues. Eden hadn't felt the need to step this lightly since he'd gone through a rebellious phase when he was nine and he'd had to train himself out of swearing around his parents after he decided saying "shit" would make him more popular with the local high schoolers. "Why don't you try telling a joke

401

and following through?" he suggested, plucking the dipstick out and sniffing it cautiously. Oil was coagulated around the end, and it smelled like rot and curdled batteries. Great. Eden held it out, saving Mick from having to answer him. "This has gone bad, look at it."

"Oh." Mick frowned. "Then put oil on the list, I guess."

Huh. Eden wasn't sure why he'd expected Mick to say *then you're stuck here just like me because I'm not fixing it*, especially after their heart-to-heart on the kitchen floor. It would take time to unweave his expectations of Mick from the reality of him, he supposed. And he wouldn't feel guilty for prejudging if it meant watching his own back in case this went south in one of the million ways it could.

"I—yes," he managed. "Sure. On the list."

They closed up the truck and went inside. Mick took a piece of bread left over from breakfast and disappeared into the woods again. Eden dug Mick's dirty and cracked corded phone out of its inexplicable hiding place in the kitchen cutlery drawer and dialed the number on the fridge. He got ahold of Claire, an old woman with a cigarette-rough voice who sounded both suspicious and relieved to talk to him.

She read the list back to him at the end of the call, and coughed in badly covered astonishment when he asked for her to pick a couple of random "I don't know, something that's selling well" books from a bookstore and bring them along, too.

"For, uh, for you?" she rasped.

"For both of us." Mick seemed to like books, so why not? Anything that kept them both occupied. "Actually, maybe four books? Hardbacks, if you can find them." He made a note on the list and felt a vicious stab of victory at knowing he was spending Boris's money on something he desperately wanted, and Boris couldn't even complain about it.

Claire coughed again. "I didn't know he read."

"He does now," Eden said dryly.

She laughed, a nervous wheeze. "So it's... it's all right, then? Up there?"

"It's fine. He's an interesting room—husband." No, better not call Mick a roommate. He seriously doubted Boris would be happy if Eden went around spreading rumors about the nature of the marriage.

Their marriage.

He wrinkled his nose.

Claire pounced on the stumble. He could practically hear her ears perk. "Room husband?"

"It's a—um, yes, a thing. A trend. The kids are doing it? New thing."

"Ah. Kids," she sighed. "Well, dear, you let me know if there's anything else. Especially around the full moon, you know." She lowered her voice. "He always asks for odd things at the full moon."

"Food?" Eden asked, a little glad. He had weird cravings before the full moon, too.

She paused. "No. But I'm sure he'll tell you. I'll see you tomorrow morning." She sounded deeply uncomfortable, and hung up right away, and for the umpteenth time, Eden was left standing there in the middle of the cabin, with no clue what he was supposed to be doing now.

It was disconcerting, going from being constantly on alert to... this. Used to be around this time, after the lunch rush at various city restaurants, he could start looking for stuff to scrounge. The real picking came after midnight, when shops dumped out what hadn't been eaten that day. Bakeries were good for that. Sandwich shops, too, as long as he got there before the meat started to spoil. If he spotted others he knew in the same area, they would tacitly agree to band together, guard each other's backs, and watch for the police, who'd lurked around every corner hoping to catch an act of public indecency on their fancy chest cameras. Before Denver, whenever Eden couldn't get enough johns, he'd watched his own back, stealing if he had to and paying as often as he could, with dropped change and crumpled dollar bills he fished from the trash piled up around gutters. Half the time he'd wondered if eating scraps and spending nights lying awake thinking he should give up and go panhandling was punishment for leaving his mother and his sister. For selfishly escaping.

It wasn't like he hadn't tried to contact them. But by the time he felt solid and secure enough to find a payphone and call home, their apartment's number had been disconnected. His mom liked to move often, chasing jobs for her green-friendly landscaping business. The fact that they'd left wasn't surprising. But they hadn't left a forwarding mail address, either, and the landlord either didn't know or didn't care where they'd gone. There was nothing.

He'd expected that from his dad. Not from her.

A shadow crossed the front door. Eden jumped, almost dropping the phone, but it was only Mick leaning in the doorway, arms crossed.

"Jesus, kid," he said, inclining his head. "You okay?"

"Yeah." *Not really*. He hung the phone up finally, cutting off the operator's friendly, bored voice, and closed the drawer. "I'm fine. I ordered the groceries."

Mick moved, so Eden assumed he was leaving and turned to pick through the fridge, hoping there was something to eat in case Claire didn't make it out today. Mick coughed a few seconds later. "Can I ask you something?"

Here it was. Eden steeled himself for the inevitability of an invasive question. "What?"

It took a few more seconds for him to spit it out. "Every time I come back, you smell sad. Is it me?"

He turned his face away so Eden couldn't see his expression, but the back of his neck was flushed ruddy red. Eden turned his back and put his hands flat on the kitchen counter so he'd have something to look at. It was easier to talk like this, without having to stare each other in the face. "No. Not really. No," he amended, because it wasn't and there was no point making Mick feel any worse than he obviously already did. On impulse, he added, "What's your family like?"

"You're really asking me that?"

"I mean your family other than Boris."

"Don't have one."

"At all?"

Mick shook his head. "My ma was pack leader. Boris's dad married in when I was twelve."

"That's a long time to put up with him."

"You've got no idea." Mick nodded at the drawer where Eden had put the phone. "When did she say?"

"She didn't."

"Fantastic," Mick grumbled. He tugged at one of his flannel sleeves. "Do you want, uh..." He waved at the newly clean windows and the bucket of suds Eden had—oops—left on the floor. "I can help. Or I can go outside."

Eden raised his eyebrows. "You can go outside and what?"

"I dunno. Chop some wood or something."

"Uh-huh." Tossing a dish towel over his shoulder, Eden crossed his arms and propped a hip on the counter. "So what do you do up here all day? Normally?"

"Find traps, mostly."

"Does that do any good?"

"Probably not. But what else am I gonna do?"

"I don't know. Go downtown?" Eden suggested, sounding more hesitant than he wanted to. But the longer he stared at these four walls, the itchier he got. It wasn't even that he couldn't camp out in a library or at an internet cafe for a few hours to zone out and feel like a normal teenager—it was that he was so totally disconnected from the real world, and from the news. At least he used to be able to keep tabs on his hometown, and could Google his mother's name every once in a while.

Mick grunted. "I don't go downtown. You can go down all you want when you fix the truck, but I don't."

"Why not?"

"I just don't."

Eden wrung the dish towel in both hands. "Fine," he said. "Help me move the couch." Mick seemed surprised his interrogation was over, but Eden ignored it. Together they moved the couch away from the fireplace and found a clean outline of wood that showed just how badly the rest of the flooring had been treated. Eden moved the wooden stool/coffee table too and found a circle of bright cherry wood under that as well. He sighed and got down on his knees, picking at the clean, whole circle, and absently drew a rune in it with his ashy finger: another circle, with dots littering the inside in a spiraling pattern, plus a mark that mimicked the curve of a claw.

"Here." Mick set the bucket down by his other hand. "What's that?"

"Nothing." Eden swiped his hand over it, smudging it away. "Traditionalist junk." He dunked his dish towel in the bucket and scrubbed the circle until the edges blurred and the floor started to come clean. Unfortunately, that meant the whole towel was black by now, so he stood to get another one, only to run right into Mick.

Mick's armful of dish towels tumbled to the floor, and he stumbled in his haste to back out of Eden's space. The heel of his prosthetic's boot caught on the stool, and his eyes went wide, and suddenly all Eden could see was the full-moon circles of his pupils as he went over the drop-off back on the muddy cliffside, where this man the town of Wildwood thought was a monster freed Eden and then let the wolf trap silver tear into his hand so he could save Eden's life a second time.

Eden had touched him then.

He snatched Mick's arm and yanked him upright. Mick was bulkier than he seemed and it brought them chest to chest, Eden's chin level with Mick's forehead, both of them breathing hard again, panting for air in the pouring rain while the mud clung to them and brought them down into the earth. Mick went stiff, staring at Eden's throat, and Eden leaned away because sex was for anyone he wanted, but his throat wasn't. Traditionalist stuff, Mick would sniff.

Mick didn't, though; instead he looked politely down and took a step back. But he didn't take his arm back. Eden prepared himself for the wave of revulsion and *get it off get it off*, but it never came. He looked down at his hand on Mick's flannel sleeve and squeezed a little, experimentally. Mick stayed still.

When was the last time someone had touched *him*? Eden doubted Claire doled out friendly hugs when she came up to visit, and as far as he could tell, she was the only one who ever made the trek out of the town, where Michael MacClair's name was whispered like a curse.

Eden had learned to hate being touched because of the people who touched him.

What if Mick learned to crave it because of all the people who didn't?

They weren't either of them okay. They barely knew each other, and all that they did know of one another was the bad stuff, the raw stuff they couldn't help showing off because of the stress and sickness of the situation. But this...

"This is okay," he heard himself say.

Mick met his eyes. "Yeah?"

Eden turned Mick's hand over and touched the not yet healed pattern of cuts from the silver chain on his palm. He laid their hands flat together and tucked his thumb under the edge of Mick's sleeve. Let their skins rest together. Mick was shaking.

"Yeah," he said.

CHAPTER FIVE

It would have been nice if everything got magically better after that. If Mick became the one exception to Eden's aversion. But as they moved around each other preparing dinner—well, Eden told Mick what to do and Mick generally acted like he had no idea what a spoon was for, much less a whisk or a strainer—Eden found himself sinking into the same familiar habits. Making extra room, keeping his elbows in...

Mick didn't seem to mind. He retreated too, back to the blank-faced, weary silence from the day before.

Eden couldn't believe he'd only been here a day. His time in Wildwood felt like a time loop, or like he was frozen, living one second as ten so time stretched out more and more. Thirty days was getting to be a more and more distant goal every minute.

Claire didn't come that day, so they ate boxed mashed potatoes (expired) and instant gravy (no expiration date, probably expired), plus juice from some freezer-burned cranberry concentrate. Mick vanished afterward, leaving Eden with the dishes, which Eden also left, because, as Mick would've said, screw that.

With Mick gone, Eden poked around the cabin some more. He didn't really *mean* to mess with Mick's stuff—he was on his hands and knees, scrubbing a dish towel as far as he could reach under the bed when he hit something, and ended up unearthing a box of junk from under the bed: a couple stacks of Sudoku books, some playing cards, and a very, very dusty King James Bible wrapped in a silk scarf. Eden scoffed and plucked it out. He didn't know much about Catholicism, but he did know that lots of the humans behind the anti-wolf laws said they were Christians, and that they didn't like people who spit on their body, which was "a gift from God."

Not so different from the traditionalists, huh.

He opened the Bible in his lap and was hit with a whiff of wolf smell and perfume so strong he had to close his eyes to let his body process it. The scent had been preserved in the scarf. Eden inhaled carefully, picking out the threads of the scent. It smelled like Mick, but not. Like pack, but not.

Dead pack.

Dead relative.

Oh.

"You're going through my things again," Mick said from the doorway.

Eden jumped, barely saving himself from slamming the book closed. "This was your mother's," he said.

A crease pinched between Mick's eyebrows as his frown lines deepened. "It's not yours."

"No, I... you're right." Eden lifted the book scarf and all and offered them to Mick. "You're right, I'm sorry."

After a terse pause, Mick came forward to take them and closed the book with gentle reverence, then wrapped the scarf around it and tied it off. He waved to the Sudoku books. "You can have those."

"Thanks." Eden scooped them out. "I asked Claire to bring us something. Fiction."

Mick hovered over him, the bible held to his chest. "Right."

Eden cleared his throat and scooted away. "Sorry. I asked you to not to touch me and you didn't, and I completely ruined my side of the bargain."

"Nah. Forget it." Mick replaced the Bible and pushed the box under the bed. "We're even now." Eden's confusion must have shown on his face, because he added, "For this afternoon."

"Oh. Well, that was..." But no, he shouldn't discount it. That had been significant. "Okay. We're even."

Mick pressed his lips together in what might have been a smile and offered him a hand up. It was the kind of offer Eden could take or leave; Mick's hand was soft and open, his gaze middle-distance instead of boring into Eden.

That was why Eden let him down gently. "I'm not ready for that yet." He grabbed the end of the bed and got up that way, holding the Sudoku books. "Maybe someday." In the interest of honesty, he added, "Maybe never."

"Up to you." Mick dropped his hand. "Want tea?" He wandered off without waiting for an answer, drifting to the tea cabinet.

How did he *do* that? Look aimless and purposeful at the same time? Lost but with direction? It was a mystery to Eden, the same way Mick's easy acceptance of all his weirdness—him being trans, him being an off-moon shifter, his haptephobia—was a mystery. "Sure."

Mick opened the cabinet and gave Eden a sly, knowing little look. "Any allergies?"

Eden rolled his eyes. "Just the silver thing, joke man."

"You got it, boss." Mick picked out two teacups and filled a pot to set on the stove. It boiled quickly, but by the time it whistled, Mick had packed two small cloth tea bags with scoops of herbs and flowers from various jars. Eden sniffed the air, then stuck his tongue out, tasting lavender and honeysuckle and something earthy, like mushroom but sweeter.

As odd as the combination smelled, the first sip was *amazing*. "Mother," Eden breathed, blowing the steam off his cup before taking another, longer drink. "You ought to sell this."

Mick shrugged. Eden ought to start taking a running tally of how many times that happened a day. "It's good, I guess."

"It's great." Eden cupped his hands around his and breathed it in. "My mother would love this."

"You could send her some."

Eden flexed his toes on the cold floor and buried his face in the cup until it was all gone. Mick poured another splash of hot water on the bag without him asking, and the herbs started brewing a second time. "I can't," Eden said. The tea darkened in slow increments. He swirled the bag around, spreading the woodsy color and letting it take the water over. "After I ran, they moved. She didn't leave a forwarding address." *She doesn't want to talk to me.*

Why should she? You left her there. Without even telling her where you were going. You disconnected your phone. How stupid can you be?

Stupid enough to have to get help from all the wrong places before helping himself by doing all the wrong things. Stupid enough to wind up here, no matter how bearable Mick was.

Had he just been fooling himself all today, thinking he had a rapport with Mick? Thinking they'd be okay? Was that confusingly easy acceptance of Mick's just a front?

Apparently oblivious to Eden's rapidly approaching breakdown, Mick finished off his tea and offered, "Maybe your dad wouldn't let her."

Eden licked his lips. "Mom would've done it if she wanted to."

"You don't know that." It sounded like he was trying to be gentle, but it came off like he was gargling a bucket of nails instead, all prickly and raspy with the blunt ends turned the wrong way. "Sometimes shit happens—"

"Please don't say for a reason."

"Hell no. I may've been raised Catholic, but I'm not an idiot."

That was reassuring. He'd lied too many times to johns and fellow street kids alike, telling them his parents had died or that he'd run away from a foster home, and lots of them had told him it was better this way, or that he was always meant to run, if that was what had happened. Like his choice to go had been a privilege of fate, not his own selfishness. "I left my sister," he said quietly. "I left my sister and my mother with him."

Mick set his tea cup down. "Did he ever hurt them?"

"No."

"Just you."

"Don't make me spell it out for you." Eden tried to swallow his anger but it was thick and hot in his throat, throbbing unpleasantly. It wasn't even aimed at Mick. It was aimed at himself. But it was a rush of destructive power, and Mick happened to be the one in his path. "What, do you want me to tell you all my sordid little secrets? All the stuff that happened in my perfect daddy's perfect house? Do you want to know so you can be *better for me*?" He slammed his cup down on the counter and it splintered, shattering porcelain into the sink and all over the floor. "Do you want me to spill it all to you so you have a reason to feel sorry for me instead of thinking I'm a spoiled child who ran away not because he was being hurt— oh no." Mick was shaking his head, so Eden got right up in Mick's face. "No? That's not right? Then tell me exactly what you think of me, why don't you?"

"You're scared," Mick choked out.

What? "Scared of what?"

Mick nodded to the scant distance between them, to Eden's body blocking him in against the sink. "Being trapped."

Eden felt his mouth drop open.

Mick was gripping the counter so hard his knuckles were white. "Don't look so surprised. I know exactly what it's like—you have to know that."

"You can go anywhere you want," Eden said. Parroting what Mick had said to him.

"No, boss." Mick shook his head. He didn't take his hands off the counter. "You don't get it. I can't."

"Because Boris is here?" Because "Monster Michael" was really a better person than him?

"No."

"Then *why*?"

Another shake. "You got your secrets, I got mine."

Eden didn't feel like he had any secrets left. He felt raw and bare and fragile, and he *hated* it. He stepped closer to Mick, purposefully looming over him. Mick didn't shrink from him—of course not. "I know you feel sorry for me."

Mick snorted. "Is that honestly the card you're gonna pull with me? The 'stop pitying me' card? You're really saying that to the guy with one leg who can't even get his own groceries because his family's that fucked up?"

"So it *is* because of Boris."

"Kid," Mick sighed. "Jesus. That's not it. I don't give two good goddamns about Boris or what he does. And listen up: I don't give *four* good goddamns why you left your parents. People leave all the fuckin' time, boss. It's just 'cause you're so young that people think it's tragic."

"I left them." That uncomfortable lump crept back into Eden's throat. Everything he'd held back saying when he was occasionally—very occasionally—asked how he was, everything he'd bottled up to himself and pushed away by focusing on living here and now, trying to scrape by from one day to the next. "I made it hard on myself," he whispered. "All of this—it's all my fault. If I'd just stayed..."

"Hey, what the fuck?" Mick's hands came up finally, but he didn't touch. Just let them stay on either side of Eden's shoulders like he was shaking him. "Are you the same person I pulled out of the mud yesterday or not? Because *that* boy would've bit my fucking face off before he admitted he was wrong." Eden scoffed and Mick held up a hand. "Okay, okay, maybe not a *great* thing, but kinda charming."

"Charming," Eden said flatly. "It's charming that I ran from my family, and that I ran from everyone in Denver—"

"Boss," Mick interrupted. "Look at this." He threw his hands out wide, encapsulating the whole cabin. "Do you see this place? What's it look like?"

"Honestly? A disaster."

Mick widened his eyes. "Do you know that thing they say about humans looking like their dogs?"

"... Yes?"

"Well, it's true. But more than that, people's *houses* look like them. You keep thinking I don't know what's what, but I *do*. You think I don't know how I live?" Mick stared hard at him. "I know exactly how this looks 'cause I know exactly how it *is*. I'm a thirty-five-year-old grown-ass man whose stepbrother has power of attorney. I can't leave here. I don't clean shit 'cause what's the point if it's just me looking at it every day until I die? I hate this—" he shook his left leg, "—and I hate being up here and I hate being bored all the time, but there's no point in changing it." He took a huge, gulping breath, looking stunned by how much he was talking. That made two of them. "The real point is, I'm self-aware enough to know I got a good hook on this self-pity thing, and I'm starting to think it's a good thing I don't ever see anyone, 'cause they'd probably leave after two minutes and avoid me forever."

Eden swallowed around the lump. "I didn't leave."

"Well, yeah," Mick snorted. He rolled his eyes. "Till death do us part. You're stuck with me."

For thirty days, he didn't say, but they both heard it.

It really wasn't funny. Eden laughed anyway. The sound was awful and sounded even more self-pitying than his whole speech. "Isn't that the worst of it, though?" he said softly. He couldn't stand Mick seeing his face, suddenly, so he swayed closer and leaned sideways, hiding it in Mick's flannel lapel. "If I didn't have that stupid contract, I'd've left yesterday and not ever looked back."

"I wouldn't blame you. No, don't get all offended. Hear me out. You keep blaming yourself for all this—"

"I did this," Eden said. "I thought I could make it on my own, I—"

"—and you *did* make it on your own—"

"—ended up here—"

"—and I'll let you go," Mick finished. "Obviously. Like I said, who'd want to look at this shitpile for the rest of their life?"

A little tartness creeping into his tone, Eden said, "You, apparently."

Mick made a face. "I don't count."

"That's your problem. You should count. What are you blaming yourself for?" Mick flinched, but Eden barreled on, on a roll now. "Come on. You're so excellent at calling me out, so try psychoanalyzing yourself for a moment."

"That's my secret," Mick reminded him. Then he paused, looking thoughtful. "Your people—"

"*Excuse* me?"

"Traditionalists." Mick raised his hands between them. "I meant traditionalists. You have a story—"

"Parable."

"—about the moon, right? The one your dad used to screw with you?"

Eden nodded slowly. "The moon abandons you if you commit an unforgivable sin."

"Pretty ironic that a guy who thinks he committed one twice gets to change whenever he wants then, huh?"

"All right, fine. Maybe it is just a story," Eden muttered. *Sorry*, he apologized to the moon, but it was half-assed and he knew it. How could he not think it was just a story? His entire life was an exercise in the parable's disproval. "Why do you even care, hmm? What do you care what I think?"

"I have to live with you for a month. One of us has to be functional."

"Speak for yourself!" Eden snapped, before he saw the humor—real humor—in Mick's face and realized, "Wait, you mean... *me* as the functional one?"

"Why not? You have all that twenty-something vitality about you."

"I'm nineteen," he reminded. "And you just finished lecturing me about how I'm too pathetic and self-pitying to function."

"Gaaaghrgh," Mick groaned, letting his head fall back. It abruptly bared his throat, and Eden had to look away. "You really are a stubborn little shit, aren't you?"

"That could be my title on my business card."

"I'll bet. Look." Mick set his hands back on the counter. "Stay and play Boris's dumbass game for a month. After that, if you want I'll hire you an investigator and you can find your mom."

"I don't want your money," Eden said out of principle, though his chest ached at the idea of coming so close to his mother. "Don't argue with me, please. I've come this far not taking charity, and I don't want to start now."

"Consider it a severance package. They still have those, right?"

"Mick." Eden stepped away and rested a hand lightly, purposefully, on his chest. It wasn't as easy as it had been the last time, since neither of them was falling. "Listen to me. I said no. When I leave, I don't want anything tying me down. But..." He chewed on the inside of his cheek. Wanted to laugh at himself. Wondered if he was letting himself be so open with Mick because in a month they'd never see each other again.

"But I will find her," he promised, more to himself than Mick. "Even if she doesn't want to talk to me, I'll find her."

"What's her name?"

"Isa," Eden said. "Isadora. And my sister's Kezia."

"Pretty."

"Better than 'Boris'."

Mick barked out a laugh. "You got that right. Thank God his daddy didn't name me. I'd've been... I dunno, Alfred or Clive or something."

"Alfred's making a comeback," Eden said, dropping his hand away at last. He'd almost forgotten it was there, resting on Mick's heaving chest.

"Why the hell...?"

"Batman."

"Wonder Woman's better. Or she was in the eighties."

"Have you been up here since the eighties?"

"Nah. Just got too old for comic books."

"That's a blatant lie." Eden tugged his shirt straight, then his sleeves, for extra measure, covering his arms up. He felt as wrung out as their dish towels, which... "Oh, shit!" He clapped a hand over his cursing mouth and spun to see the wet dish towel he'd been using on the floor, water already soaked down into the wood, leaving a fat stain sticking out under the bed. "Oh, no, no, no, it stained."

"Can't that be stylish too?" Mick picked the towel up and threw it into the sink. "We can do a whole row of 'em."

Eden grabbed the bucket—too cold to use by now—and went out to dump it over the front porch railing. "Haven't I already told you that you have a terrible sense for decorating? I've honestly been friends with people who decorated twenty-dollar tents with more care than this place."

"Used to belong to some rich friend of Boris's." Mick padded out, his flesh foot bare and the end of his white prosthetic leg, which Eden hadn't expected to have *toes*, making tiny hollow thumps with each step. He curled over the railing, bracing his elbows. The setting sun cast his face in creamy yellow and pink, softening him. "Guess he wasn't much for decorating either."

"Rich people." Eden sighed and let the bucket drop to the floor. "No offense."

"Can't take any. I only have savings from before. All this comes out of Boris's money. And the only reason the jackass pays for shit is because he has to do a yearly expenses report and if he stopped writing checks for his scary fucker of a stepbrother, the town would wonder. And that might hurt his chances at the precious mayorship."

"Again, no offense, but I'd rather live in a sewer in Queens than live here with him as mayor." Not that he was going to stay anyway, but the idea of Boris running the whole town was abhorrent. "He does realize he can't force everyone to get married to solve all his problems, right?"

"After this time, I hope so. Don't think this is exactly going in his favor."

Definitely not. And less so when Eden marched to his office at the end of the month and asked for divorce papers that Boris wouldn't legally be able to deny him.

Then again, worrying about legality wasn't one of Boris's pastimes. "I don't know if he'll let me leave."

"He will." Mick patted the railing and straightened. "Trust me. I'll take care of it."

"Let me talk to him first."

"Yeah, yeah, boss."

"Why do you call me that?"

Mick stopped halfway in the cabin. "Seemed rude to call you bossy. You wanted to be in charge, so there you go. You're better at it than me anyway."

I wanted to be in charge when I didn't know who you were.

That would be a lie, though. He wanted to be in charge now, too, if only to make sure what seemed like a controlled and safe enough descent stayed free of turbulence. "If I knew it was you I might not have run," he said, desperate for something to say that was appropriately nice in response to Mick's respect. "If I knew it'd be like this I would've just let him bring me up here."

Mick pressed his lips closed. "Ah, kid," he said, and smiled. "No, you wouldn't."

CHAPTER SIX

Claire came by two days later with the full list of groceries, a handful of books—more than Eden had asked for—and a few quarts of synthetic oil. She was a tiny woman with short wiry hair and long skirts and peppermint perfume, and she bustled in and out as quickly as possible, refusing Eden's offer to help carry the packages inside.

Mick had made himself scarce.

"Where is he?" Claire asked when the last package was on the counter. She stopped and sniffed before Eden could answer. "Oh my. This looks much cleaner than usual."

"It's a work in progress," Eden said, trying not to preen. He'd cleaned the whole ceiling this morning, peeling off years and years of tobacco smoke stain and cooking grit, and then he'd swept the kitchen and scrubbed down the stove and the fridge in a silent cosmic plea for Claire to decide today was the day they could have fresh food.

He was practically salivating over the veggies. Real fresh veggies, crisp and ripe from the farmers' market. The things he could *make* now...

He thanked Claire and signed off on the yellow receipt pad she carried. The total wasn't as much as he'd thought it would be, and he made a mental note to bump up the expenses for next time. Maybe he'd hire a dump truck to haul away some of the debris outside. Oh, and he could buy real paint, because the kitchen would be much livelier in yellow...

"Dear?" Claire was holding out his carbon copy of the receipt. "Sir?"

"Sorry! Sorry, I'm a little distracted." He took the receipt and folded it up, sticking it in his shirt pocket. He'd worn a binder today—one of the few precious things he'd paid to lock up at every hostel he'd stayed in, and had hidden under the mattress in every motel and sketchy pay-by-night Craigslist rental room—so when his shirt pulled tight across his chest, it drew no attention.

His lapse in focus, however, did. "What are you thinking about?" Claire asked, almost a whisper. She cast a furtive glance at the front door. "I think it's such charity, what you're doing, you know."

"Charity?"

"Well, you know." She pressed her hand to her chest. "Poor boy. I knew him when he was a pup, you know. He was always so rambunctious. And then the accident. I wish it hadn't changed him so much, you know."

Mick cleared his throat from the door. "I need to talk to you," he said, and Eden knew instantly he was talking to Claire, not him—his voice, though respectful, was toneless, and he held himself like he was just another one of the boards that made up the house.

Claire picked at her scarf. "You know I prefer voicemail. My memory these days..."

"It's not about the order. Please." Eden tilted his head in question; Mick waved him off, ushering Claire outside. He led her all the way back to her rickety Oldsmobile and kept his voice low, but pity for him— Eden's ears were sharp. "I need to ask you for a favor. Whatever you want me to pay, I will. It's for Eden."

Claire let out a surprised "oh!" that spurred Mick on. "Yeah, it's for him. I need you to take him to a hotel. A nice one, not that shi—um, dump down on Chestnut."

"That hotel closed, Michael. Mrs. Leland moved to Falsworth."

"Oh. Well, whatever hotel is nice. It's only for a couple days."

Eden pressed up to the front door, muted with disbelief. After all their revealing conversations, Mick was going to send him away?

Claire sounded flustered. "I'll have to talk to your brother to see what rate he wants to work out..."

"That's fine. If he won't pay it, I will. Do you want me to write down the days for you?"

Brief silence, and then Claire took a sharp breath. "Michael... no."

"Please."

"You know I want to help as much as I can, Michael, I do, but that's... you know I can't do that."

What could he be asking for in addition to a hotel room? Oh, Mother, what if he was trying to convince her to smuggle Eden out of town under the guise of giving him a few days of adjustment? Eden almost burst out of the house right there.

Except Mick said, "It's before and *after* the full moon. Not the day of."

"I realize that, but it's still too close," she argued tremulously. "I'm sorry, Michael. I won't. I just cannot stand for the life of me to be around you like that."

When he was shifted? No, it couldn't be that, because if it were, it would be both of them she'd be worried about, not just Mick.

"It's for his own good."

Claire sniffed, but audibly gathered herself up with a tight little sigh. "I won't. I'm sorry. Even if I was willing, your brother would be very unhappy with me for doing so." Her Oldsmobile's door creaked as she pulled it open, and then the engine started and she trundled down the slope toward the winding mountain path.

Mick stormed past the front door a minute later, and Eden heard the telltale, now-familiar sound of his ax coming loose from the tree stump he always buried it in when he was done angry-chopping enough wood to last them ten winters. Nothing Eden could say right now would get through to him, and most of it was just as angry as Mick sounded, which would only make it all worse.

That didn't mean he was letting this go. He'd put money on the fact that Mick's reason for getting him a hotel room and Claire's reason for not wanting to come to the mountain on the full moon were the same. Whatever the cause, Mick didn't want Eden knowing about it.

Aggression was the most likely culprit, Eden thought. What with Mick and Boris being stepbrothers, there was probably some blood feud there—which would explain why Mick was isolated, and why Boris was so distasteful toward him. On the full moon, it would escalate, since Mick was within Boris's pack borders. Keeping him on the mountain alone was the safest way.

But Eden felt entirely safe around Mick; that was so rare anymore that he couldn't remember the last time it'd happened. Mick's aggression didn't seem uncontrolled, only... pointed. And always pointed right at Boris.

425

He sighed and chanced looking out the window to watch the ruthless ripple of Mick's body as he swung the ax over and over. It was more apparent now than ever that Mick was able-bodied enough to keep the house in order. He just *didn't*.

Maybe that was part of what was wrong, too.

Eden made the executive decision to give Mick a while to calm down, so to pass the time, he put away the groceries and stacked the books neatly on the coffee stool, then examined the synthetic oil. He was almost completely certain it wasn't the right kind for the truck, and when he propped the hood open with a sawed-off two-by-four and wormed himself flat under the engine, it became apparent that the thing needed way more than an oil change to fix it. He managed to get the oil pan gasket loose, only to see it was gunked full of rotting fluid—just like everything else. Even the antifreeze smelled like it had gone off.

So that left him with two problems: one, this thing wasn't moving.

And two, for some reason, Mick wanted *him* to.

~~*

Eden made dinner for them both, then took his plate and one of the new books out to the bathtub along with a brand new bottle of soap. He couldn't get himself to mind that it had oatmeal in it and was supposed to smell like "rosy-fresh hibiscus" and instead smelled like oversweet candy. He dumped some in the tub, climbed in, and put a board across the top of the tub so he could rest his book on it and eat his roasted vegetables at the same time.

Claire had good taste in books. He barely noticed the sun going down, and only stopped when the light fell off his page and he had to scrounge up a rusted oil lamp from the depths of the shack. It coughed to life under the touch of a dubiously lit match, then sizzled and crested up and down like an unreliable motor.

Speaking of...

Mick had been so quiet while Eden made dinner, barely looking up from the book he'd claimed, that Eden had lost his nerve to push the full moon thing. Honestly, he wasn't convinced he'd get a straight answer if he asked outright. If it bothered Mick enough, he might come to Eden with it, and then it would be easier on them both. Mick wouldn't feel like Eden had pried, and Eden wouldn't have to deal with wading through bullshit with the added risk of Mick shutting completely down if Eden asked the wrong question.

He didn't think it would be preferable for Mick to get angry at him the way he got at Boris, but he also hated seeing Mick vanish into his head the way he did. The person Mick was when he laughed with Eden, and when he made tea and tentative jokes, was a complete one-eighty from the person he was around even Claire, who posed no threat to either of them, not like Boris. But to her he'd been the same way: cold, standoffish.

"Pretty ironic that a guy who thinks he committed one twice gets to change whenever he wants, then, huh?"

Yes, well, it was also ironic that for someone who obviously wanted company so badly, Mick put a lot of effort into turning people away.

The comparison was right there, a dangling fresh fruit, ready for Eden to pluck, peel, and splatter in Mick's face, but as the week wore into the weekend and then turned to Monday, he couldn't find the right time to do it. To ruin the easy routine they slipped back into. Mick woke up the morning after Claire's arrival in a much better mood, and he offered to take Eden fishing, so they spent half the day catching fat trout and roasting them with wild tubers in a towering bonfire. Mick ate five fish on his own and kept plowing through them, which was a miracle, because Eden gorged on two and was sure he'd never eat again.

"Where do you *put* all that?" he groaned, hand on his stomach.

"Secret," Mick mumbled around another bite.

Feeling dozy-full and warm, Eden giggled, "Are you storing fat?"

"Winter's not for seven months, boss."

"Mm, I don't know. It's cold up here."

And then Mick shrugged off his goosefeather coat, which he'd painstakingly patched with mismatched scraps of fabric, and plopped it right over Eden. "I'll eat as many fish as I want," he said primly, and stared into the fire, daring Eden to say something about the jacket.

He didn't say one word.

After that he used it whenever he wanted. It hung on the hook by the door, and if Eden was the one who went out to get more firewood, or to take a bath at night, he wore it draped around him. Mick took it out fishing and hunting—he had traps of his own, small, for squirrels and rabbits—and on his weird trips around the yard where he prodded things, then left them exactly where they had been.

Another routine of theirs was tea. Mick made it for himself at all three meals, and as soon as he noticed Eden sniffing with interest at the blends he put together, he made two bags of each one. Eden found out quickly that he loved fruity teas and hated anything with chai or hazelnut. Mick avoided those, but everything else was up for grabs. As soon as Eden thought he'd seen odd with the mint-rhubarb-dandelion-"touch of shallot" tea (very good despite how disgusting it sounded objectively), Mick would offer him something twice as unusual, then pretend not to care when Eden admitted it was good.

In return, Eden cooked anything he could get his hands on. Claire came and went once more, while Mick was out in the forest. This time, Eden had asked for more fruit, plus some seasonings and a full bottle of cooking wine, so he sautéed chicken and mushrooms and made marsala, made tacos with pineapple and sour cream, made mango salsa, tried and failed to make borscht.

Tried and failed not to be completely charmed when Mick forced himself through an entire bowl of it despite the bitterness.

The longer he stayed, the faster the days passed, and the more he wondered at the origin of the suspicious whispers he'd heard in Boris's office. People couldn't know Mick personally; no one came up here. No one *tried* to know him. Sure, he was a grump, was convinced he was about ten years older than he actually was, and he still drifted off beyond Eden's reach on plenty of occasions, but he was neither cruel nor violent, and he definitely wasn't a complete bastard like his stepbrother. And he didn't once step beyond Eden's boundaries. Didn't once try to touch him. Didn't once push about his mother and Kezia, though Eden had a feeling he hadn't heard the last of the offer to hire a P.I.

Other than that, living sequestered in the mountains was... good. Relaxing. Eden had forgotten what it was like to be relaxed all the time. To feel comfortable and safe. To go to bed at night wrapped up in his scent and someone else's, someone he trusted. He didn't even hang the bucket on the door anymore, because he knew they'd both wake up if anyone tried to get into their den.

And between the two of them? They could handle any intruder.

Even Boris.

It was all so painlessly great, he forgot to steel himself against the inevitable.

So when it fell apart, he wasn't ready.

He wasn't ready at all.

CHAPTER SEVEN

"I called you a cab for tomorrow," Mick said, the night before the full moon. It was the first thing he'd said to Eden all day. He'd stayed out of the cabin almost the entire morning, doing who knew what, while Eden baked his grandmother's birdseed bread as an offering, then had zonked out on his bed and slept all the way through the sun-dappled afternoon. Now that he was forcing himself to be conscious in the same room as Eden, he was twitchy and pale, avoiding Eden's eyes. He looked worse than he had half-drowned and yelling at Boris. "It's gonna be here at four."

Eden paused, knife halfway into the newest loaf of bread. "Oooo... kay." He felt bad for the way Mick's shoulders immediately went loose, because he followed it up with: "Did you think about asking my opinion before you did that?"

"It's a free two nights in a nice hotel." Mick limped to his bed and pulled a duffel bag out from underneath, shaking the dust off it... and all over Eden's clean floor. "You can use this for stuff."

"Mick!" He grabbed the bag out of Mick's hand and underhanded it out onto the porch. "I just swept!"

Mick hunched in on himself. "Sorry."

"Apology accepted. You can make it up to me by sweeping." Eden pulled the front door closed in case Mick got the idea to shove him out it and lock the door. Crude but effective—or not, since Eden would

431

just camp out in the tub shed all night. There were worse ways to spend a full moon. "I don't want two nights in a hotel." He didn't want to think about it: how sterile the sheets would be, how the air conditioning would smell fake and wrong, how he'd be sealed off from the moon. He knew he couldn't run, not in the town and definitely not on the mountain, but being stuck—*trapped*—in a hotel room would only make it worse.

Of course, he could've avoided this if he'd pushed the subject with Mick earlier. Truth was, he'd hoped Mick had given up since Claire had refused him. "How did you even get a cab to come up here?"

"Paid 'em a lot." Mick frowned at the front door. "You need to pack."

"Mick. Look at me. I'm not going anywhere. Especially not to a hotel. If you want me to stay out of the cabin tonight, that's fine." That was an obvious, logical solution. So it shouldn't have been as difficult to force out as it was. "I can stay in the shed."

Mick's hands curled into fists. "Boss... Eden. Please. I haven't asked you for anything..." He coughed and tried, "Now, I know you've done a lot around the house. And thanks. But this isn't something I need you to do. Okay? Secrets, boss. I'm allowed to have my secret if you can have yours."

That thick flame of curiosity hadn't died over the past couple weeks. Living day in and day out with Mick had cooled it a little, but not enough that Eden wanted to just let this go. He couldn't forget Boris telling him about Mick that first day.

"He's not... well."

Eden had assumed Boris was talking about Mick's depression and what he'd thought then was self-isolation. But it was more than that—Eden was so sure it was more than that. And he was no closer to finding out what it was. Maybe two weeks ago, he would've played pathetic, or come up with another lie to get Mick to keep him around. Now, though... *damn*, he wanted to know, but he wouldn't hurt Mick to do it. Mick hadn't touched him once, had put extra effort into *not* touching him, and he'd never referred to him by the wrong pronoun or asked any invasive questions. And he acted like he'd as good as forgotten Eden's moonless shifting.

"Fine," Eden said.

Mick's mouth went slack with surprise. "... Fine?"

"Fine, I'll go." Eden retrieved the bag from the front porch and gave it a good shake before he brought it back inside. Mick still looked stunned. "Look," he said, closing the front door and slumping against it to put them on an almost even height. He gestured between them. "This? Hasn't been nearly as bad as it could've been. You..." *are worlds better than I expected. You deserve more than this. Than staying here.* But he couldn't say any of that, because he was going to leave in thirteen days, so he fell back on an old joke. "You could've been like your stepbrother. I asked you to respect my boundaries, and you have. So..." He hugged the duffel bag. "I'll respect yours. I'll go."

There was a second of complete stillness that seemed to center on Mick, like he was a swirling black hole suddenly preserved, frozen in an uneven spin. Then Mick let out a breath and said tonelessly, "Oh."

Was that *disappointment* on his face?

"You *do* want me to go, right?"

He nodded once. "Yeah. I mean... Yeah. That's why I, with the car. The taxi. That's why the taxi. You should pack," he finished, only vaguely firmly. It was the firmest thing about his entire garbled speech. "You should pack. 'C'mon, chop chop, the hotel's on Boris's dime."

Eden let the duffel slip to the floor. *Be a good person be a good person be a good person—* "Are you lying to me?"

"No!" Mick's top lip crept up to show off one of his blunt human canines, which, at moonrise, would lengthen and sharpen into smooth weapons. "I ordered you a cab. D'you think I'd do that if I didn't want to?"

Yes. "That's not what I meant." Eden ducked his head to try to get a look at Mick's face. Mother knew two weeks squashed in the same one-room home hadn't made Mick any more willing to meet his eyes when they were having one of their surprisingly common serious conversations. Honestly, the last person Eden had had so many *talks* with was his mother. "And you know that," he went on. "Listen, if you want me to leave, I'll go. I will. But if you want me to stay and you're sending me away to try to *protect* me or something, then I suggest you rethink your decision, because I didn't spend the last two weeks scrubbing this house up and down just to have you condescend to me because you think things are going to get a little hard."

Mick gaped at him. "That's not it."

"Then what is it? Hmmm?" Closemouthed silence was his only answer—as usual. So Eden followed their usual graceful routine and guessed wildly. "Are you territorial on the moon? Did you invite your stepbrother for a run?" That one earned him a scoff—something that broke through the manufactured blankness—and he surged on, heartened. "Do you... I don't know, do you...?"

"What happened to respecting my boundaries?" Mick grated out, shutting Eden right up. "I said it's a fucking secret and here you are making me talk about it. How is that respect?"

"I," Eden started, but that was a good point. He didn't know what else he was going to say, whether he could fix this or not. And he was selfishly glad he wouldn't have to find out.

Because he knew that sound.

They both swiveled toward the door, tracking the telltale rumble of Boris's Chrysler. Then they looked at each other, and it came across clear as day: no more time for arguing. They were on the same side.

Eden dove outside and grabbed the duffel bag, and Mick held the door for him to come back inside and throw it under the bed. "He never comes up this close," Mick said, shaking his head once, sharply. "Never." He shook his head again, and suddenly Eden was right back to worrying he'd have an aggression problem to deal with.

"Hey." He pushed himself into the doorframe with Mick, stared into his face from a claustrophobic angle. "Look at me. Are you going to be okay?"

Mick's chest heaved, but he nodded, holding Eden's eyes.

"Are you *sure*?"

"I'm sure."

"Stay with me," Eden told him, and, for a brief moment, put his hand over Mick's on the door. Just like that. Mick blinked, but held himself perfectly still.

Eden almost smiled.

Boris's Chrysler crested the hill.

He dropped his hand away.

"Here we fuckin' go," Mick muttered, squaring his shoulders.

He was right. Boris was bright red and spitting mad the second he got out of his car. He slammed his door behind him and stomped to the house, a crumpled sheaf of papers in one hand. "Michael," he said, stopping at the bottom of the steps. "What's this I hear about you getting a hotel room? With *my* money?"

Mick shrugged. "Kid needs a place to go."

"The *kid* has a place. Right here. Like your contract states." That was what he was holding. He held it up, where a section had been viciously circled with red pen. "Do you need me to read it for you? Hmmm? Do you both need a refresher in reading comprehension? Here we go." He smoothed the papers obnoxiously on the railing and read, "*Eden Dalca shall remain on the premises for at least thirty days.*"

"Oh, fuck you," Mick snapped. "That wasn't in the old contract."

Eden started. Mick had read it? He'd assumed it had been left to drown in the mud and rain.

"It doesn't matter what was in the original." Boris leaned toward them. "Do you honestly think anyone in this town will listen to a single legal claim you make? *You*? And you." He flicked a hand at Eden. "You weren't paying any attention to what you signed in the first place."

"That doesn't matter." Eden bared his teeth, parroting Boris's bullshit right back at him. "You breached the contract. Changing it renders it null and void." He saw a glimmer of surprise on Boris's face and felt a mean stab of satisfaction. "So that means Mick and I can do whatever we want."

"You *and* Mick? What kind of fantasy are you living, missy? Mick is in *my* pack."

"He isn't," Eden said, so loudly Mick flinched next to him. "This isn't how you treat a pack. This isn't how you treat your family. He's only in your pack when it's convenient for you. You can't stop us from doing anything—from going anywhere we want. That only means we have to be married."

"And you want to be married and *take* him somewhere?" Boris looked ready to laugh. "What did you do to her, Michael? Do you have some special kind of tea in there I don't know about?"

Mick pounced on him.

They hit the ground to a chorus of cracking twigs and the uncomfortable sound of bone striking earth. Mick recovered first, sweeping himself up onto his hands and his flesh-and-blood leg. "When're you gonna learn to shut your mouth, Boris? Huh? You couldn't do it to save your goddamn life."

Boris snarled. He got up slower, leaving the contract on the ground. "Well," he said, wiping blood from his mouth. "What's gotten into you? Was that because it wasn't true? Or because it was?"

"Fuck no, it's not true. I'm not *you*." Mick paced around him in a half-circle, head lowered, upper lip curled back, so wolf-like that he may as well have been shifted.

"Mick," Eden said, warning him.

"I'm fine, boss," Mick said without looking at him. He brought his elbows in, set them with his fists up, his shoulders loose and relaxed. "Are we gonna have this talk finally, Boris? Are we gonna do this?"

Eden braced himself in the doorway, ready to jump.

But Boris didn't take the bait. "I don't have anything to say to you. You think what I did was terrible? At least I didn't kill anyone. And if you're so unhappy here, as it's become obvious you are, even with a chew toy, then you can go. Yes," he said over Mick's rising growl. "You can go. And take your wife with you."

"Why'd you even bother?" Eden cut in. He couldn't *not* say anything. "Why bother with the ad if you wanted to kick him out all along?"

"I'm a man of honor," Boris said, puffing his chest out. "Whether or not your pack deserves you, as a leader, you have to support them. Your kind—you *drifters*—wouldn't understand."

Mick clicked his teeth together and moved to stand between them. "Watch what you say, Boris. You might not get back off this mountain."

"Oh, please. You won't kill me." Boris took a step back, to Eden's delight. "People know I'm here. Should I disappear, they'll know exactly where to look. And who to blame."

"Who?" Eden said. "Their great *leader*? You talk a lot, but you haven't done one thing to support Mick. You put him up here. You cut him out of your pack."

Boris's eyes narrowed. He opened his mouth, closed it, and opened it again. "Wait... Ohhhh, oh, Mickey. You haven't told her." He grinned up at Eden. "You wouldn't be so eager to take his side if you knew what he did."

"I do know," Eden said. He didn't give Mick or Boris the chance to say anything. "I do know. And it doesn't change a *damn* thing."

The clearing filled with silence. Mick's shoulders were still, like he wasn't breathing at all.

"Fine," Boris said. "Then obviously I've succeeded as a matchmaker." He nudged the toe of his pristine leather shoe under the edge of the contract and flipped it over, pushing it toward Eden, before heading for his car, dismissing Mick entirely. "I want you out of my town," he said, back turned. "Then everyone can hear about how the degenerate dragged my poor brother away from his charmed life. And it was charmed, Michael. You'll find out soon how good you had it."

"Tell them what you want." Eden came down off the porch to pick up the contract. Boris sneered at him one last time, no doubt to give Eden the impression that he was supposed to be *very* worried about the upcoming rumors. Then he climbed in his car, spun it around to go back down the drive, and it was done.

Eden reached for Mick's sleeve.

Mick gave at once to his tugging and let Eden tow him to the cabin. "What the *hell* just happened?"

Eden led him inside. "Something good," he said. "Something good."

CHAPTER EIGHT

Neither of them was in any shape to do much more than fall into bed after that. The moon had risen by the time Eden cleaned up his baking stuff and put together a small dinner, and Mick ate as quietly as he usually did. But when Eden went to make his nest on the couch, Mick cleared his throat and nodded at the bed.

"I was thinking maybe..." And Eden's disappointment and horror and hundred other emotions must have shown on his face—Mick was quick to say, "No, no, I was just wondering if you wanted to move the couch over here for tonight."

That... was unexpected. "Sure," Eden said. He cocked his head. "Why?"

Mick shrugged. "Kinda sucks, getting kicked out your pack."

Your terrible pack, Eden wanted to say. *Your pack that hates you. Your pack run by your manipulative spoiled brat of a brother.* He didn't say it, though. He helped Mick push the couch over so it was wedged next to the bed, with the two walls and the back of the couch forming a den in the corner.

Eden crawled in first, burrowing deep into the worn cushions. The window over Mick's bed opened on the moon, so close to full. Eden stared out at her. She would feel the sorrow of Mick's pack connection being severed, no matter how awful Boris was.

He buried his face in his arms. "I'm sorry."

"Huh?" Mick said from behind him. Something clattered.

"I'm sorry. For what happened with Boris."

"Eh. Don't be." The kitchen light went off, and Mick appeared, easing himself into bed and arranging his body around his collection. He didn't seem inclined to say anything else, but after a while, he rumbled, "Thanks for lying to his face."

Eden smiled. "I wanted to do worse than that."

"Took care of that for you. Shoulda punched him, though." He sighed. "My mama would hate this. The town, the pack. She'd be ashamed of us."

"Of them."

"I didn't help."

"They didn't let you, you mean."

"You don't even know what you're talking about," Mick said. "You don't know anything about me."

"I know you like tea. Enough to buy nice China for it."

Another sigh. "The tea set is my parents', from when they got married."

Eden watched the moon move past the trunk of a swaying pine. "You can start over," he said, barely audible.

Mick turned over—away from the moon and toward him. "You don't know."

It wasn't right for Eden to push, it *wasn't*. "You could tell me."

"You don't want me to," Mick said, and turned back over, and that was that.

~~*

The next morning, Mick's testiness was, if possible, even *worse*.

By dinner, he was pacing in front of the door with his favorite tiny sparrow teacup in hand, snarling wordlessly. At half past seven, it was starting to get to Eden in a bad way, so he snapped, "Will you *sit down*?" To his surprise, Mick dropped right there, then looked just as surprised as Eden. "Better." Eden paced to the front window himself, peering out at the long slope of the drive and the trees beyond. Night came early in the mountains at this time of year, sometimes really early when the sky was bogged down with rain. There wouldn't be rain tonight; tonight would be clear. The air tasted crisp where it breathed in through the cracks in the cabin's wooden logs. He fixed Mick with a look. "We're both stuck here. You can't spend all day worrying about it. I'm not."

"Oh yeah? You've got a lot less to worry about." Mick took a resentful sip of his tea.

"Do I really? I haven't got a pack either."

Mick wrinkled his nose. "Is this your first moon in your life without one?"

Eden winced. "No," he admitted.

"Then don't pretend it's the same."

"Don't take a tone with me."

Mick growled deep in his chest and put his teacup down on the floor. "Don't boss me around."

"I thought that was the reason you called me boss in the first place."

"What, so's you could boss me around? What, so you could be my *alpha*?"

"Oh, come *on*." Eden whirled on him.

"Oh, come on what?" Mick clambered to his feet, his fists clenched. "Like it's not true? You came into my house like Boris's fuckin' contract gave you a right, and you—and you took over all my things, and moved them, and *cleaned*—"

"You had mold growing in the fridge."

"And got your scent everywhere," Mick thundered, his voice reaching terrible levels of fury. The kind of slippery anger that made Eden's hair stand on end. "I don't want you in here for this. I don't want you in here for the moon. You better start walking." He jabbed a finger at the door. "Boris doesn't give a shit anymore, so for tonight, take your shit and get out. Come back tomorrow."

It was more than contrariness that made Eden dig his heels in—literally. "What are you going to do up here by yourself? Hmm? What is it that you do when no one sees you, Mick? What does Boris think is so bad?"

"*Nothing*," Mick said. His voice wasn't very loud at all anymore.

Eden didn't say anything. The only sound in the cabin was their harsh breathing. The tug of the moon was descending already, threading itself into the fibers of their bodies. Calling them home. And for the first time in years, this call didn't make Eden want to run. It made him want to lock the doors and the windows and bed down here, in their den, so he could show Mick that he hadn't only lost a pack—he could trade that one, that damaging one, for a new pack. That Eden was right here. That Eden had been on his own for so long, too, and couldn't they do it together, now? Couldn't they curl here, burrow down on their floor in blankets and drink tea together from Mick's delicate China cups?

This call made him want to stay.

"Stop." He lifted his head. "Stop trying to get me to leave you. If you really wanted to, you would have been trying the whole time I was here. Not just now. Not at the very last moment. You don't want me to go." No, he didn't like how that sounded. "So say nothing and I'll stay. Tell me to go one last time, and I'll do it." He picked up his bag and put it on his shoulder as a sign of his—weak, so weak—resolve. "I'll go down the mountain and hide from your stepbrother and sleep somewhere that doesn't smell like either of us. And the howling and the running I hear will be just them."

"They don't," Mick said, hoarsely. "They don't run."

He hadn't said "go."

Somehow Eden knew this was his last chance. That even if they left Wildwood together tomorrow, there would be something lost if he didn't prove himself as a packmate now. If he didn't take care of Mick at the most crucial moment. "Mick." The bag made a soft cloth thump when he dropped it to the floor. "Tell me what happened to you. Please."

"You know what happened to me." Mick jiggled his prosthetic leg. "Boxing match."

Eden moved in on him. "What happened after that? What does it have to do with the full moon? The real story. I do want to know. I promise. I want to know."

"You just won't leave it alone, will you?" This time Mick didn't sound defeated or resigned. He sounded a little fond. Maybe a little grateful. So Eden held his ground, left the gap between them for Mick to spill all his secrets, because Eden could see he wanted to. He clawed and raged and pretended he didn't, but it was goring him inside, whatever it was. "You better sit."

Eden nodded and turned to hop over the arm of the couch.

"Not there." Mick waved jerkily at the bed. "If you—want."

His nest of memorabilia. Eden approached it carefully, putting his ears back, so to say. Testing it out until Mick levered himself up first to sit with the stuffed lizard in his lap and the rest of the collection clustered around him. Eden sat at the end of the bed, legs crossed, elbows resting on his knees. Mick had tied his hair a touch too tight; he left it to pull at his skin. "Should I not talk?"

"Probably best." Mick turned the lizard over and over in his hands. "This was my brother's," he said without any lead-in. "My little brother. He was nine. Youngest in the pack." He squished it between his hands and a tiny red tongue lolled out from the mouth. Mick stroked it with the pad of one finger. His explanation came choppier: "The boxing accident. It wasn't. An accident. It was Boris."

"Excuse me?" Eden winced and slapped a hand over his mouth. "Sorry."

Mick gave him a flat look. "Boris propositioned a woman from another pack. Only she found out he was taking cases for people who had the cash to make sure they got off innocent. So she said no. He humiliated her. In public. Pictures..." He pressed his lips together, stroking the lizard's soft fur, smoothing it down then spiking it up the wrong way. His fingernails left ragged uneven patches of faux fur sticking up. Without thinking, Eden reached out to fix it, and their fingers brushed. Mick froze—not an angry freeze. A wary one. He thought Eden would be angry.

Eden turned his hand over and spread his fingers apart.

Here, on Mick's bed, of all places, he felt like it was okay to let this man be the one to touch him.

And when Mick did, when their shades of skin were pressed together, he felt the moon's approval resonate like a bell in the back of his mind.

A fine tremor ran through Mick, and he squeezed Eden's hand, but didn't look up. "Pictures of her. Texts. All kinds of shit. Some of it made up. I was boxing. Some of her sisters, they got together and hired a guy. Pretty well-known boxer. Told him to kill me." His free hand drifted to his prosthetic. "Almost did."

How can you even stand to be around him anymore? "So you made it out."

"Sure. *I* did. But packs like ours, old packs. Packs with ties to humans. Someone's always lookin' for a way to switch up leadership. When they think the pack's weak. Me getting my ass beat. That was weak."

Eden felt the blood drain from his face. "Your parents."

"Rival pack from Seattle. My mother. My stepdad. My brother. Some of my cousins. They came to help. I was in the hospital. Didn't heal fast enough. Didn't know it happened till a couple weeks later. Boris didn't tell me. Didn't tell me." Mick bowed his head, breath coming in pained pants. He closed his other hand on his prosthetic so hard Eden heard something crack. Eden put his hand over Mick's, prying his fingers away from the knee and holding both his hands. Mick let him do it, maybe looked grateful for it, but he kept talking, hollowly now, like reading a grocery list. "Went home. Mom was dead. Drake was dead. No one else was blood. Boris took over. No will, he said. No named successor. Not true. Not *true*. Should've been me. Mom wanted it to be me. Always said so. But I can't."

Pain rolled off him in crushing waves. Eden whined in the back of his throat. "Why not?"

Mick scoffed. "Why not?" He shook his leg. "*Why not*? There's a reason."

"What's the other reason?"

"Always asking so many fucking questions." Mick dropped his head again.

This time, Eden nudged in closer and caught him, pressing their foreheads together. "You'd never tell me anything otherwise." He nuzzled Mick's cheek. "I want to know things." Mick twitched toward him, his hands tightening—but he was holding off, Eden could feel it. "It's okay." He unwound one of his hands from Mick's and rested it on his shoulder to guide him. "You're allowed."

Mick leaned against him, pushing his face into the crook of Eden's neck. "You'd find out anyway," he said, muffled. "Haven't wanted to talk this much in years. Not to anyone but you." He moved his hand to Eden's knee. Eden touched his in return, pressing his fingertips around the edges of the prosthetic, learning it by feel.

He wasn't sure how much time passed before Mick raised his head and twisted around to see out the window. It wasn't yet night; the moon though was visible over the trees, pale, barely a fraction as bright as she would be when given all the light for herself. "Now you'll find out." He faced the kitchen and took both Eden's hands.

They sat in silence for a while longer. Mick swept his thumbs occasionally up the sides of Eden's palms, never so rough with Eden as he was with himself, but otherwise they didn't move. Tension curled itself in Mick's body, starting at his knees and shoulders and working itself up through his spine and his neck, until he sat so stiffly, glassy-eyed, that Eden worried he was having some kind of fit and was too stubborn to tell Eden about it.

Then the moon washed over them.

Eden welcomed her touch like he never would anyone else's, not even Mick's. "Come on," he invited, and stood, pulling Mick's hands. "Come on. Let's go outside."

Mick stayed sitting. "You want to run."

"No. I want to look."

"All right." He let Eden lead him out onto the front lawn, the cool damp grass sticking to their bare feet.

The darkness was patchy, not velvety and embracing the way it would be later. This was enough for Eden, and the shade of the towering pines hid them away from Wildwood and everyone else. All the people who'd touched him, all the people who'd tried to take who he was. And all the people who'd hurt Mick for something he didn't do, and then left him to suffer the consequences for the rest of a life he barely wanted anymore.

"Come on," Eden said again, and shed his clothes. Mick didn't look, but Eden would have been fine if he wanted to, if he wanted to see Eden's body, female as it was. Maybe someday he'd be fine if Mick wanted to touch him, too, in all those places, but not yet, and they had a while to wait, both of them, until Eden would try it.

Now he welcomed the sense of slippage that came with his transformation. His expanded lungs blew his chest out wide, to wolf-size, and he collapsed and rose as he was meant to be.

He wanted to see how Mick was meant to be.

Mick hadn't changed.

Eden jigged on his feet. *"Come on."*

Mick gave him a strange smile. His eyes were wide in his pale face. "I can't."

Eden wished he understood immediately. He wished some well of realization would crash down on him, so he could *get it* and wick that awful expression away. *"We don't have to run."*

"Listen to me." Mick dropped to one knee—slowly, laboriously. He held his hands up like a cradle, and Eden obliged him, slotting his muzzle into them. Mick stroked the sides of his face and drew him closer. "Listen. Eden. I can't. I. *Can't. Change.*" While that worked itself into Eden's numb brain, Mick went on. "Ever since the match. Since my leg. I can't. No matter what I do. I *feel*—I want. I feel..." He raised a hand.

"You feel her."

Mick nodded. "But she don't feel me."

"You don't know that. She didn't abandon you." Eden pushed into Mick's hands, keeping them at eye level. *"What have you tried?"*

"Everything. It just don't work anymore, boss." Mick rocked back and stood, leaning heavily on his flesh leg. "All those things you traditionals say about the moon?" He spread his hands. "Here you go. Case study one."

"I'm case study one." Eden stumbled toward him, desperate not to let him duck out of this conversation. How strange was it, how coincidental—that a wolf who couldn't shift and a wolf who shifted too much would be brought together, both packless, both wandering?

Not coincidental at all.

"What do you think traditionalists—most of them—have to say about me? About my body? What do you think my father told me, Mick? What do you think he said, when I told him I didn't want the gift Mother Moon gave me?"

"It's not the same."

"I didn't say it was the same. I'll never understand what you went through—and you'll never understand what I did, either. But we understand something mutually, don't we? How many other wolves get to shift like we do? This isn't a sin. It's not a curse. You're not cursed."

Ah. There was the wave of realization.

This was why no one in Wildwood wanted to be around Mick. This was why he wasn't part of the pack anymore.

This was why Boris wanted him taken care of. Why he was happy to leave Mick by himself up in the woods, so lonesome and cut off he didn't smell properly like wolf anymore.

"You didn't even do anything."

"I lost," Mick gritted out. "I lost the fight. I made our pack look weak."

"That's ridiculous." Eden pawed at his good leg. *"You did what you could."*

"It wasn't enough."

"It doesn't matter!" Eden leapt up, planting his paws on Mick's chest and putting their faces close. *"It happened years ago. Don't you think you've gone over this enough? You live here, you don't get yourself anything you need—you don't even have a pack. But you could. You could have a real house and a real yard and a real truck. You just don't want anything nice for yourself."*

Mick had the good grace not to shove him. "You don't know jack shit enough about me to say what I do and don't want, *boss*."

"Then let me figure it out." Eden flexed his claws against Mick's shirt. Debated what he wanted to say. Debated whether or not it was more running to say, *"Let's go as far away from here as we can get."*

"Do you think that's gonna fix all our problems?"

"Fix them? No. But I want to go. Boris wants us gone. You don't have to stay here. I don't want you to stay here."

Mick closed his hands over Eden's paws. "It's a bad idea. Don't you wanna go find your mom? You should do that. Don't mess with me any more than you have to. Get the divorce finalized and leave, and I'll go my own way."

"No. We should go," Eden repeated, his conviction only strengthening. Mick's breath shuddered out of him. Out and in. His heart beat strong on Eden's paw pads. *"You have money. I know some people. We can go places. Like a honeymoon."*

He let his mouth open, let his tongue loll out so Mick could take it as a joke if he wanted to. *"Then we'll be gone and he can do whatever he wants."*

"He'll get elected no matter what he does," Mick muttered.

"This town deserves him."

Mick glanced up and laughed, startled. "Yeah," he said. "Yeah, I guess it does."

"And you don't." He licked his lips. *"Maybe you can deserve me instead."*

Mick's voice was soft. "Dangerous words there, boss."

"Pack up your tea," Eden retorted, feeling brave and reckless. The kind of reckless he hadn't let himself be in a long time. Not fearful reckless, or desperate reckless, but happily reckless. Reckless because he wanted something that would be good for him and had a feeling it might work out. *"We can just do the honeymoon. For real. Go somewhere nice. If you don't like it, we'll split up."*

"Uh-huh. That's your plan."

Eden left him with a friendly lick to his jaw. While he was still sputtering, Eden dropped to all four paws and collected his clothes in a bundle. *"Thank you,"* he remembered to say. *"For telling me."*

"Yeah, well, you're welcome. Hope it was a magical moment for you. And, uh, thanks for reacting to all this like a total fuckin' weirdo, I guess."

"You honestly expected me—me—to react badly? Who's the bigger weirdo here?"

Mick shrugged. "You never know how people will react to anything."

True, Eden thought. You never knew who you could put your faith in. If your reaching hand would be met with kindness or chains. You never knew. It was a risk every time. Eden would never stop minding his skin. He'd probably have good days and bad ones, and one day, if he wanted to let Mick touch him deep, he'd have trouble reminding himself that it was all right. But any doubt he'd had about the moon watching over him and disapproving of what he'd done to stay fed and sheltered was gone, vaporized by her light.

She wouldn't have brought them together if he hadn't done something right.

He knew that for certain.

"So," Mick said. He put his hands on his hips. "Honeymoon, huh?"

EPILOGUE

They decided on Montana. Eden packed up the few things he had, and Mick painstakingly packed his tea and his parents' tea cups, and his brother's lizard, and his books. They called a taxi and actually got one this time, and on top of that got a good deal at the lone used car place in Wildwood. "He probably told everyone to get us out of here as fast as possible," Mick muttered as he was counting out hundreds to pay for the beat-up 1998 Corolla they'd decided on. Eden had brought food, but they stopped for greasy McDonald's cheeseburgers, which Mick practically whimpered over and said he hadn't had for years. And then they were out of there.

And they were still married.

Eden supposed it should've been weird. But they didn't talk about it. For Eden, it was comfortable. The way he figured it, one day they'd get tired of each other, or need to part ways, and they'd dissolve it.

Or they wouldn't, and they wouldn't.

What had been in that contract didn't matter anyway. And—not that he'd expected it to go otherwise—Mick didn't even seem to consider taking "honeymoon" to mean Eden was ready to speed up what they had going. He kept his hands to himself and bought them two-bed motel rooms without Eden telling him to... although Eden had to tell him plenty about everything else. His gaps in knowledge of the world hadn't seemed so drastic on the mountain, but out here, Eden was constantly fielding his distaste for credit-card chip readers and Siri, and his questions about why the hell people wore scarves in summer and skinny jeans at all, plus his fascination with Starbucks Frappuccinos.

They took turns driving. Eden spent most of his passenger seat time dozing, but Mick was always alert while Eden drove, watching road signs and curling his lip at bad drivers. He engaged with the world in a way Eden hadn't expected; instead of withdrawing further into himself, being on the road brought him out, made him take up more of his own body. Occasionally he talked with that same rolling ease in his voice he'd had on their first night together, when Eden wasn't capable of being anything but trapped and terrified.

Eden wondered if that was how he always used to talk.

On their sixth night out of Wildwood, Mick pulled them over at a decent hotel instead of a random roadside Super 8. "This okay?"

"Mmm, yeah," Eden mumbled, stirring. He swiped a hand over his eyes to clear the sleep-blur and blinked up at the hotel's green neon sign. Raising an eyebrow, he asked, "What's the occasion?"

Mick cleared his throat and pointed at the front doors, where a large sign said Fully Equipped Business Center! "Thought we ought to figure out where we're going."

"Right." Eden hopped out and dragged his fingers through his hair to push the long half where it belonged. The short half was getting there too. *Need a cut*. He grabbed his pack and fell into step with Mick, who got them a room and immediately asked for the local takeout menus, as had become his habit.

Eden couldn't blame him for being enamored of ready-made hot food.

They decided on Chinese, and Eden was still in the shower when he heard the knock on the door. "Stay in there, I got it," Mick said, footsteps passing the bathroom. Eden finished up and wrung out his hair. Only when he was dressing did he realize he'd grabbed one of Mick's shirts instead of his own. He sniffed it, considering the implications of wearing it when it was so soaked with Mick's scent.

Then he decided he might like those implications.

Mick had the various food containers spread out on his double bed when Eden emerged, and was poking around in one. "Think they got it wrong. Did you say no chestnuts or no cashews?"

"No cashews." Eden perched on the edge of his own bed, curling his hands in his lap self-consciously. He was aware of the T-shirt's fabric clinging to his body, was aware of how loose it was over his chest and arms, and how it was an inch or two too short at his belly.

"Oh. Good." Mick handed a container over, and finally looked at Eden. His gaze stayed on Eden's, and Eden was treated to seeing his pupils slowly fatten.

Eden rolled his shoulder where the shirt had slipped down and reached to take the food, letting his fingertips graze the back of Mick's hand. "Thanks."

Mick nodded once and busied himself with his own food. Eden hid a grin in his moo goo gai pan. By the time he reached the bottom of his white box, he'd migrated to Mick's bed so they could watch *Whose Line Is It Anyway?* reruns.

"Hey, boss," Mick said, as they were enduring a Slap-Chop commercial.

"Hmm?"

"This is good."

"You want a Slap-Chop?"

Mick rolled his eyes. "No. I mean you and me." He waved a hand in the couple feet of space between them. "This is good."

Eden knew he meant it. Knew that if this was the closest they ever got, Mick would be okay with it. Which was why he was okay shuffling over and laying his cheek on Mick's shoulder. "Yeah," he said, closing his eyes. "Yeah, it is."

The crick in his neck the next morning was worth the good night's sleep. Mick nudged him out of bed early, talking about beating the crowd to breakfast. Once they'd packed in enough waffles and scrambled eggs to sustain them, they found the Fully Equipped Business Center! and Googled around on two of the computers until Mick stopped scrolling, coughed, and said, "This looks okay."

So he shelled out three thousand dollars for the two-week honeymoon package at a wolf-friendly dude ranch. The price made Eden want to die a little, but Mick treated it with the same blitheness he treated everything that didn't interest him, and Eden tentatively got over it. He tried not to dwell on how he used to survive on less than one hundred dollars a month.

His and Mick's cabin was one of eight clustered in a semicircle around the main farmhouse. At the first night's dinner, the ranch owner Leanne introduced them to the others: three more couples, all of them human. They pried more than Eden was comfortable with. Every one of them wanted to swap engagement stories and be regaled with each other's tales of their wedding day jitters.

Inevitably, the attention turned to him and Mick. "You two," said Tracy, the thirty-something accountant on her honeymoon with a former client of hers. She shot them a smile over the lip of her wine glass. "What's the story?"

Eden opened his mouth, and just... he just didn't have it in him to make something up. "It was, uh," he started.

"Oops," Mick said, a second before his glass crashed to the ground. Eden jumped, and one of the husbands across the table flailed, almost knocking his glass over too. "Shit, I'm sorry, let me clean that up."

"No, no, I've got it." Leanne stood and bustled to the kitchen.

Mick put a hand to his forehead, looking at Eden out of the corner of his eye. Eden took the hint and reached to feel for himself. "You're warm," he said. "Are you not feeling okay?"

"Just a little dizzy. Must've been all the driving today."

"You folks go on to bed," Leanne said, coming to mop up Mick's spilled water. "I'll send over breakfast in the morning, how's that?"

"Fantastic, thanks," Eden said with feeling. He hurried outside with Mick in tow and sucked in a deep breath of night air outside, under the crescent moon. "Nice going."

"Thought you were gonna pass out from stress or something." Mick moseyed past, hands in his pockets. The horses roaming the pasture closest to the house whickered at him. "Yeah, yeah," he called back.

Eden panted in a few more breaths and followed, the exhaustion of the day kicking in. "We're going to have to say something eventually." Maybe not today, or tomorrow, or to these people, but eventually, to someone.

Mick nodded. "I'll figure it out, how's that?"

"Worrisome. What are you going to tell them? You found me in the middle of the woods? People are going to think I'm a forest spirit."

"No such thing."

"There is so such a thing."

"Well, what's so bad about people thinking you are one? People're gonna think all sorts of shit about us. You know that way better than me."

"Maybe I don't want to add another thing to the list," Eden said, kicking a stray rock out of his path.

"Then you come up with something, boss," Mick said mildly. "And I'll tell 'em whatever you want."

"Deal." Eden had a feeling it would end up being a watered-down version of the truth. *I answered an ad. We met through his family. Our wedding was small.* He'd have to tell his mother the real truth someday, so he may as well get practice in.

The cabin thankfully had two bedrooms—despite the previous night, Eden wasn't ready to start sleeping together on a regular basis—and Eden's room faced the paddocks and the moon. He curled in the middle of his bed, expecting to be awake for a while, but he fell asleep fast.

Breakfast was delivered to their door the next morning, but lunch was with the rest of the honeymooners. They seemed to have collectively decided not to ask any more questions, and instead the bunch of them relaxed into friendly, empty chatter, the kind of talk people shared in line at the grocery or on the bus.

With that hurdle cleared, Eden could relax too. Mick was as at ease with horses as he was, and the two of them spent plenty of time away from the others, exploring the ranch's couple thousand acres.

On the tenth morning, Mick was quieter than usual getting ready, and was the first out the door closest to the paddock, where, hilariously, the horses would gather every single morning so they could whicker at him on his way to the main house for breakfast.

"They love you," Eden cooed, not for the first time.

Mick didn't try to muster up complaints about wanting his damn breakfast anymore—he let himself be stopped and distracted, offering his hands to the three horses' soft noses. He and Eden stood there together in the cool gray light of dawn until a cabin door creaked open and Tracy's cheerful voice called, "Good morning!"

"Morning, Tracy," Eden greeted her.

Tracy crunched her way through the gravel to lean on the fence next to them. "Chilly out here in the morning, isn't it?"

Not for wolves, but, "Mmhmm," Eden agreed. Tracy moved to pet one of the horses, getting a little too in his space for his comfort, and before he could do anything about it, Mick shifted over so Eden was in front of him, his arms loosely bracketing Eden in against the fence. Eden pressed his lips together, pleasantly embarrassed by how okay it was.

Tracy hummed, scratching her fingers through a polite bay gelding's mane. "You two make a good couple, you know. I mean, of course you know. But sometimes, you can really *tell*, you know?"

"Uh," Mick said.

"Thanks," Eden said.

The cabin door banged behind them. Tracy waved to her wife, giving Eden and Mick one last smile. "See you at breakfast!"

Eden lasted all of ten seconds after they'd gone to the main house before he laughed.

"What!" Mick muttered.

"You've got to come up with something better than 'uh' and 'um'. What happened to 'I'll figure it out'?"

"Making up that kinda bullshit is different. I could say we met scuba-diving or falling off a cliff and no one would know up from down. But I don't know what to say to *that*." Mick leaned around his shoulder to greet another of the horses. His cheeks and the tips of his ears were flushed red.

"You could just say thanks."

Mick grumbled at him, let him go, and pressed up to the fence. Eden kept catching himself watching Mick sideways out here, amid the prairie grasses and wildflowers and trees and mountains neither of them had seen before, let alone been stuck on. He kept catching himself and thinking the person he was seeing unfurl was who Mick used to be, when he was Eden's age, a wild young boxer hell-bent on doing his pack proud.

If Eden thought for a second Mick would listen to him, he'd tell him that he was making his new pack pretty proud, too.

That would take a while for them to get to. Mick had soft spots too, places he didn't want people poking their fingers. Soft spots and scrapes and silver scars on his hand that matched the ones on Eden's forearm, where the trap had bound them together.

"Question," Eden said, easing up to sit on top of the fence. One of the horses shoved her head into his lap, sniffing his pockets for treats. He rubbed her ears in his hands.

"Yeah, I *am* gonna laugh at you if she knocks you on your ass."

"Don't get cocky. You'll end up on yours next."

"Oh yeah? You gonna put me there?" Mick growled, subsonic and playful.

Eden growled right back. "Maybe I will."

Mick laughed and knocked his shoulder lightly against Eden's hip. "What's the question?"

"Say I'm working on not being as opposed to the idea of spending your money anymore, now that I know it came out of Boris's pocket."

"You wanna find your ma?"

Eden rubbed the mare's cheek as she scraped her face on his thigh, itching her jaw. "I was thinking we could continue our road trip. See if we can follow where the investigator thinks she might be." Go toward home, instead of away from it. Go toward the old pack he missed, and bring his new pack with him.

Mick was silent for a long time. Then, "No," he said.

Eden's stomach sank.

"No, I think we need something better to drive before we go off road-tripping." A tiny, sly smile curled Mick's mouth. "Now, I've never done one of those self-searching trips like you college kids do now, so I'm no expert, but I'm pretty sure our piece of shit won't make it."

"I'm no expert either, what time do you think I had to go road-tripping?" Eden shoved him. "Also, you're a fucking jerk."

"Look at you swearing."

"Have to wash my mouth out with soap," Eden muttered. "And yours too."

"Traditionalist."

"Brat."

Mick blinked. A little fission of... *something* ran down through his body like a live current; Eden saw goosebumps flare on his arms. He shoved Eden back. "You sure you want me to tag along with you?"

"Who's going to help me if I get stuck in another trap?"

"Jesus Christ. I don't know how you're already joking about that shit." Mick offered his arm for Eden to brace on and jump off the fence.

Eden hopped down and dusted his hands off. "Years of practice."

"Oh, whatever. You've got that traditionalist guilt going."

"That's nothing compared to Catholic guilt." Eden let their shoulders rest together.

"Hey," Mick said.

"Hmm?"

"Should I just say thanks?" His hand lit tentatively at the small of Eden's back.

Eden forced his own hesitance away and rubbed his face on the side of Mick's neck, like he'd done on the full moon. "You should just say thanks."

Mick touched the back of his neck, hugging Eden briefly before they broke apart to follow Tracy to the main house, where the lights were already on and a warm meal with fifteen people who didn't know a thing about either of them beckoned.

"I've been thinking about changing my name," Mick said suddenly.

"Mmm?"

He rolled a shoulder. "Seems like it'd be better. Plus I got a legally bound second last name it'd be real easy to switch to."

Eden eyeballed him. "And harder to switch back from should you decide you're done with this. You're only married to me. I'm not asking you to marry into my mother's pack without having met her."

"Can't be worse than mine, even if you are traditionalists. Just, you know, something to think about."

Which meant he'd already been thinking about it for a while, and had only now worked up the social willpower to bring it up.

"You can have it," Eden said. "I'm just warning you, for your own good."

"What a sweetheart."

"Ugh, no."

Mick's eyes sparked with mischief. "A dollface?"

He looked so much better out here.

For him, leaving home wasn't running. It was an exercise in repairing himself.

Maybe it had been for Eden, too.

"You might be on to something," he said.

"Dollface?"

"*No*. Traditionalist guilt."

"Oh. Well, yeah. Moon still likes you just fine after all, doesn't she?"

"Yeah," Eden said. "She does." He shook himself and kicked his boots against the board at the front of the main house, getting dirt and dust off them. "And don't even think about using dollface. I've got a perfectly good name. You should use it. C'mon. I know you can."

"Yeah, yeah." Mick pulled the front door open. "Eden Dalca," he said, "do you wanna give me the honor of letting me eat my breakfast now?"

"Yes I do," Eden said loftily, and went in with him.

Fin

About the Editor

AMANDA JEAN is an editor (and writer) of queer romance, and when not wrangling manuscripts, she can be found watching space documentaries, looking at pictures of shoes, and attempting to read for pleasure. She has worked with Less Than Three Press, Torquere Press, NineStar Press, Siren-BookStrand, Athgo International, The Typewriter, and the Seattle-based literary magazine *POPLORISH*. Amanda also serves as the LGBT Director for Alternating Current's *The Spark* and handles publicity for a roster of Alternating Current authors. Before she became an editor, she paid her dues writing dreary freelance content.

Find her on twitter (@amandahjean) and at her website: amandahjean.weebly.com

About the Authors

ELEANOR KOS

Eleanor Kos is a writer and storyteller. Peculiar obsessions include archery, grammar, and the tying of knots. Most likely demise: buried under an avalanche caused by insufficient storage space for 12 million sorts of tea.

Website: https://eleanorkos.wordpress.com/

AUSTIN CHANT

Austin Chant is a bitter millennial, avid gamer, and Social Justice Cleric. He has a lot of feelings about robots. His interests include cooking everything, petting friendly dogs and cats, and writing about all kinds of rad queer people. He lives in Seattle with his partner in crime, a pleasant collection of game consoles, and an abundance of tea. In the regrettably large amount of time he spends not writing romance novels, he works in interactive media as a game designer and does his best to stay awake through college. He'd love to exchange words with you on Twitter (@austinchanted).

Website: http://austinchanted.weebly.com

Helena Maeve

Helena Maeve has always been globe trotter with a fondness for adventure, but only recently has she started putting to paper the many stories she's collected in her excursions. When she isn't writing romance novels, she can usually be found in an airport or on a plane, furiously penning in her trusty little notebook.

Website: helenamaeve.wordpress.com

C.C. Bridges

C.C. Bridges is a mild-mannered librarian by day, but by night she writes about worlds of adventure and romance. A fan of science fiction and comics since the ripe old age of twelve, she incorporates her love of genre into her work. She writes surrounded by books, spare computing equipment, a fluffy dog, baby toys, and a long-suffering husband all in the tiny state of New Jersey. In 2011, she won a Rainbow Award for best gay sci-fi/futuristic novel.

Website: http://www.ccbridges.net
Facebook:
https://www.facebook.com/ccbridgeswriter
Twitter: https://twitter.com/ccbridgeswriter
Blog: http://ccbridges.dreamwidth.org

ERICA BARNES

Erica likes pretending to live in a variety of worlds, whether by writing, reading, or watching movies and television shows. She's had work published in NEAT magazine before, and also enjoys writing fanfiction when the time allows. She currently lives with her family in West Virginia.

Twitter: @EricaSBarnes

SAM SCHOOLER

Sam Schooler is an Ohioan university student studying journalism with a minor in American Sign Language and a specialization in African American studies. She is both queer and genderqueer, and she has found a home in writing trope-themed New Adult stories about people of all genders and orientations. She has a wicked and extremely noticeable soft spot for werewolves. After graduation, she intends to flee to Canada to join her fiancée Alex and escape the customs regulations that keep her separated from her truest love: Kinder Eggs. Jeremy Renner played her in a movie once.

Sam's latest news and backlist are available at samschooler.weebly.com. Her personal (and largely fannish) blog is meetcute-s.tumblr.com. If you're feeling daring, follow her on Twitter as @samschoolering to get the full immersive experience.